ENTRESKA NEVERCARE

THE ULTHERIAN ETHIC

ROBIN JOHNSON

Jurasketu Academy Press
Contact Information: *jura.publish@gmail.com*

This is a work of fiction. Names, characters, businesses, places, events and incidents are either the products of the author's imagination or used in a fictitious manner. Any resemblance to actual persons, living or dead, or actual events is purely coincidental. Anything resembling practical advice or information in this work is not guaranteed by the author to be correct or useful and should not be relied upon to make decisions of any kind.

ISBN 978-0-9862973-4-2 (Trade Paperback)

First Edition (Revised)

The Dream of Evermore

Entreska regarded dreams as the fuel that drove all serious endeavors. She believed that the free mind was built of nothing more than dreams. Without dreams, the present merely floated like flotsam on the ocean of time. By dreams, she only meant waking, mindful dreams. Sleeping dreams, she felt merited little attention. She considered them nothing more than the random gurglings of her mind from the stew of the imagined past, present and future.

With her fingers, she forced back her long, sun-bleached hair sending rivulets of sweat unpleasantly down her back. She rubbed mucus and burning salt from her translucent green eyes that were perpetually tinged with red from poor sleep and desert dust. Shaking, she stripped off her clothes and used a cloth to dry off. She stood in the darkness and rubbed her limbs and torso to quell the quivers racking her body. She prided herself on being fit and trim, but now she was feeling only worn and weak. She imagined that her clean and even features were haggard and ugly. She rummaged around for fresh trousers and a blouse in the travel chest. She donned her sandals and ventured from the tent.

Summer nights on the Raffin Plateau were warm and virtually silent. The few insects and small animals that could survive the brutal conditions stayed quiet to avoid becoming dinner for the sand lizards. The late night sky shone bright with great streams of stars that turned the gray landscape luminescent white. No moons showed their somber faces that night. She strolled some distance from her tent and reflected upon where recurring nightmares fit into her theory of dreams. She kicked the dust and sighed...

Dust.

Gray dust.

Gray volcanic dust.

Clouds of gray volcanic dust blowing across the landscape.

Gritty, irritating gray dust that ended up every where in every thing.

Entreska Nevercare didn't really mind dust most of the time. She was a Professor of History and Antiquities, and she lived constantly with dusty books, dusty trails and dusty places. Dust was a natural hazard of her profession, and she couldn't seriously complain without getting howls of laughter from her friends and family.

Her scarf generally saved her nose and lungs from the worst. Somehow, her eyes just got used to the constant irritation. Her clothing and hair were invariably encrusted with gray. That was just the way things were. But she would never get used to her meals being laced with that subtle undertone of grit.

The Raffin had not always been that way.

From where she stood, a sterile wasteland of sand, rock and wind known as the High Raffin stretched before her all the way to the White Mountains several weeks travel to the north. To her back, the rocky gullies of the Lower Raffin fell away to the south and east. Water could be found on the Lower Raffin, but most of the known oases were kept secret by the knowing parties. The lone remaining river that flowed in the whole of the Raffin was the Wrything River, anciently known as the Serpent, which had carved out the canyons known as the Maw of Hell. The modern Wrything River simply dribbled along the bottom of the Maw, a mere shadow of its once mighty self.

For a moment, she dreamed she could see the huge glaciers that once covered the White Mountains. The ice melt had fed the three main rivers of the ancient Raffin: the snaking Serpent, the wicked Scorpion with its dangerous cataracts, and the wide, deep Hammer. The glaciers were long gone, and only a slight dusting of snow covered the White Mountains. The pitiful snowmelt was quickly devoured by the sands of the High Raffin, and the mountains were not so white anymore – just gray and brown.

Entreska dreamed she saw the majestic ancient Black Firs that had once dominated the northern third of the Raffin. The wood of the Black Firs was strong, workable and almost impervious to rot and so every ship in the Jurasketu Navy and merchant fleets were built from Black Fir. However, the wealthy shipbuilders of Endurance and Rook would need to find a replacement since their supplies of Black Fir salvaged from the High Raffin would soon be exhausted. Entreska had often visited the last stand of Black Firs in the world, growing in the pure snows of White Tower. Efforts to grow them elsewhere over the centuries had all ended in failure.

Entreska turned her dream gaze upon the fertile Lower Raffin with its wooded glens, pastures, and fields of wheat and barley. Quaint little villages of hard-working farmers, herders and foragers dotted the landscape. Expertly built roads of stone connected the villages with each other and the cities. Roadside inns hosted cheery merchants, travelers and couriers. The villages and inns were no more. The roads were merely rubble.

Entreska's dream carried her to Duravon, the ancient capital of the Enduring Realm. Entreska imagined thousands of people thronging the stone paved streets of Duravon flanked by endless blocks of four and five story apartment buildings painted blue, red and black emblazoned with emblems of every sort. The city center was dominated by the ancient, elegant Calendria Plaza where the main government ministries and the Chambers of Debate had reigned over a vast civilization spread across parts of three continents. Nothing remained but a field of gray sand.

Eight hundred years ago, a cataclysmic volcanic eruption had entombed Duravon and laid waste to the Raffin Plateau. The calamity had either precipitated or accelerated a change to the climate and the Raffin had never recovered. Two thousand and six hundred years of civilization had been effectively destroyed. Five hundred years later, the province of Jurasketu on the Eastern shore had managed to recreate a central government that could claim lineage to ancient Duravon. They had even audaciously built a new capital, Endurance, and had lined its streets with Calendria trees and their distinctive purple leaves in honor of the destroyed plaza of Duravon. Their dream of reestablishing the glory and power of Duravon, however, had proven less than successful.

Five hundred students and workers had followed her deep into the desert looking for that very city. They understood that their task was a sacred quest to find the lost soul of their civilization.

A survivor of the calamity, an otherwise obscure ministerial aide named Theron Avery, had saved and included a city map with his record of the event - the only eyewitness account extant. That extraordinary discovery amongst some crates of donated material at the Jurasketu Academy combined with the serendipitous discovery the previous year of the Gates of Duravon had brought her to this place.

The Gates of Duravon were a natural rock formation that had overlooked the city from a nearby hill that though deeply buried by volcanic ash eventually had been exposed by the relentless scouring winds. Entreska had thought that finding the remains of the city walls nearby the Gates and matching that to her map would have been relatively easy. From that point, interesting finds should have been theirs for the taking. This expedition was just to confirm the location of the city. Many more summers would be required to excavate the site properly.

Unfortunately, locating the city walls had proven to be difficult. She snorted in derision at her previous optimism. She was extremely worried that she was running out of time. They had been searching in vain for many weeks, and her volunteers' enthusiasm for the difficult work was ebbing. If the expedition failed to find the city, obtaining funding and volunteers for further expeditions would be unlikely.

"Entreska?"

Her instinct to panic and run was stilled at the last moment by the familiarity of the voice and the plain fact that the owner of the voice had recognized her in the dark. She turned around trying to find that owner, Valentine Jones, in the darkness.

Colonel Jones commanded the Black Scorpions, one of the nine elite cavalry regiments of the Jurasketu Army that spearheaded campaigns, conducted raids deep into enemy territory and provided troops for secret missions of all kinds. Elements of the Black Scorpions were always positioned on the High Raffin during the summer to patrol the central Raffin against incursions of Pachinko Puck or his Cumar allies. Normally, they had nothing on the Raffin proper to protect except themselves - but this season they had the additional responsibility to protect and support Entreska's expedition. Normally, Jones deployed a reinforced squadron of about 900 troopers. This year he had brought 1300 troopers, the additional troopers being mostly support specialists.

Having recovered from her fright, she ventured, "Uncle Val?"

She always called him Uncle Val even though he was not. He and her father had been friends since before she was born.

He changed to that drillmaster tone he inflected when angry, "What are you doing wandering about in the dark?"

Barely visible in the darkness, she imagined his impressive, towering visage. His hands would be resting firmly on his hips. His close-cropped gray hair and cold blue eyes were framed by his square, handsome face that was marred only by a slight scar near his left ear. Everyone always commented that Jones had grown more attractive with age. Despite being above average height, she always felt like a little girl near Jones and his athletic bulk.

She replied, "My question of you would be the same."

"I am performing my duty. You are trying to make that duty more difficult to perform."

"Sorry. That was not my intention."

In a softened tone, he asked, "Are you all right, Tresh?"

Are you all right, Tresh? She remembered those words being spoken in the darkness many years ago. Eight years old... An ill-advised journey into the wilderness alone... A massive kirolskan bear looking for trouble...

"Are you all right, Tresh? Entreska?"

"I'm sorry Uncle Val. I was just remembering the time you saved my life."

"Which time?"

"The kirolskan."

"Ah, yes. The kirolskan."

"Do you remember?"

Jones said grimly, "That one I won't ever forget. I'm reminded every morning." Jones always wore a loose, long sleeved shirt under his desert cloak, even on the hottest days, but she had seen the scars that covered his left arm and shoulder. When anyone asked, he always claimed they were battle scars like the rest that crisscrossed his body.

"Uncle Val. How badly were you hurt that night?"

Jones laughed, "The kirolskan got me pretty good. I thought I might lose the arm at first."

"Great Blast. That was your blood! You told me it belonged to the kirolskan. When you disappeared after the rescue, I was told you had left on an important assignment. You must have gone away to heal so I wouldn't find out. Why didn't anyone tell me?"

"Are you kidding? Do you think I wanted that guilt to be laid on a young girl?"

"Oh... Well, I'm not a young girl anymore. I'm twenty-eight."

"Yes. I'm sorry, but until recently, I still thought the story would unnecessarily burden you. And I didn't want you to know I would lie to you. I want your trust."

"Why now?"

He shrugged. "I've seen you suffer greater burdens the last few years, so this one seems minor. But mostly, you mentioned the incident, so the opportunity came to mind."

Shaking her head, she said, "You're a silly old man." They stood watching the stars. "But admittedly I feel pretty guilty about the kirolskan - so you were probably right."

"I was careless. I let the kirolskan get too close. I should have been able to lead it away. Instead, I was forced to kill it and nearly got killed in the process. I don't like violence when there is another way."

Not intending to hurt his feelings, she said evenly, "I believe you, but that's a funny thing for a soldier to say, wouldn't you agree?"

Jones laughed softly. "I have my duty. When my duty requires that I protect, I protect. Often that involves bloodshed. It is the way of a dutiful soldier."

She stated flatly, "Yes, I know. That is not my way."

Jones grunted, "I know. I know. The Ultherian Ethic. You are duty bound not to use violence in any form to achieve your ends."

"Yes. My only protections are prudence and reason."

Jones added tersely, "And soldiers."

Instead of being defensive, Entreska laughed, "Well, by strictly adhering to the Ultherian Ethic we are simply trying to show there are always better ways to resolve disputes. And the soldiers are not my choice. My father always insists on the soldiers."

Jones laughed in return, "Yes. I know. You are as funny as I am. What brought you out here anyway? Couldn't sleep?"

After a pause, she asked, "Do you ever have recurring nightmares?"

Jones grunted, "On occasion. I have always considered them a hazard of command and a disciplined military life. You?"

Entreska sighed, "I'm having a very vivid dream that has grown more complex each and every night. It haunts my thoughts even in the daylight."

Jones grunted again and said, "Goodness. Can you describe the dream to me?"

Entreska licked her lips and related her dream, "*Wolves... vast landscapes... hundreds of soldiers locked in mortal combat... smiling faces... the murals cover the walls and domed ceiling completely... no spot left bare... even the floor is tiled with an intricate map of the Raffin Plateau... the round hall is empty except for a small stone pedestal located in the center... and me... sunlight blazes through the circular hole in the roof... upon the pedestal lies a small, finely carved wooden box... I advance... the hall becomes dark... then brightly lit once again... I advance... sweat pours, stinging my eyes, soaking my clothes... bright sunlight... dimness... darkness... light and dark cycle with each step... my breathing is rasping and labored... I stop in darkness for a moment... waiting... no change... then I step forward into brightening light... forward... dark... further... light... another step... dark... onward... light... I reach the pedestal in brilliant light... I look back... the few meters seemed like hundreds... I squat down and examine the box... it is beautiful... a fine-grained reddish hardwood I do not recognize... beautifully polished with a glossy wax... flexing my fingers and breathing deeply I reach down and open the box... it is the size of a large fist... translucent blue... cut and shaped asymmetrically, bizarrely... I pick the gem up and hold it high into the light... a rainbow of colors splash about the walls and reflect off the tile... a voice whispers 'evermore'... a flash... then nothing..."*

She told him how the first version of the dream had occurred just after they had arrived at the Ruins of Duravon and had consisted of just the box and gem. In the nine weeks since, the dream had gained various details each night. Worse, for no reason she could determine, she always awoke in terror after the flash that followed the whispered 'evermore'. Jones had listened patiently asking no questions.

He grunted. "Evermore? Odd."

"I'm becoming scared, Uncle Val. I tried ignoring it, but denial has not diminished the dream at all. Instead, it has grown stronger and threatens to envelop the entirety of my sleep. Maybe the dream is telling me that I should just pack up and go home."

Jones said softly, "Quitting doesn't seem like you. That worries me. The High Raffin can play tricks on the mind. The heat and desolation are not merely abstractions. Could the dream be wizardry?"

Entreska gave Jones a funny look that he couldn't see. "I thought you didn't believe in wizardry."

"I don't. Even though belief can change what will be, belief cannot change what was or what is."

Entreska smiled invisibly and said, "I don't know. Even if it was, what would be the purpose?"

Jones chuckled, "You're the expert on wizardry, not me."

Entreska grunted a hollow laugh, "If only that were true. It doesn't matter. I need to try and rest."

She kicked the dust in dismay and trudged back to her tent.

Early the next morning the gloom that had intruded her thoughts lifted when one of her best digging teams hit what turned out to be a portion of the city defense wall. After a couple hours of passionate digging, they were able to determine that it was facing the south. This was the opportunity Entreska had been needing. She ordered all available teams to start excavating along the wall to better identify the section. Meanwhile, she returned to her outpost positioned on a small knoll that overlooked the site. Normally, she swung a pick and shovel alongside everyone else, but today she needed to concentrate on the difficult task of matching Theron Avery's map to the newly found wall section and some of the other structures her teams had found over the previous weeks.

Unexpectedly, not long after the teams had stopped digging to avoid the midday heat, Colonel Jones and a man dressed in strange clothing flanked by two soldiers approached Entreska. Her tent sheltered her from the sun. The sides had been pulled up slightly to allow the mild breeze clear passage. Entreska vaguely wondered why Jones was bothering her. She had given instructions to be left alone until her calculations were complete.

Jones said, "Tresh." She looked up but said nothing. "This man came up to one of our northern patrols begging for help. He said he was lost and thirsty. He's unarmed. We've already given him some water. My first thought is simply to detain him until the expedition returns home. He would be well treated, of course, and we would release him when we return to Endurance. But I know you would object without evidence of malfeasance, so I respectfully defer to your opinion."

Entreska looked askance at Jones before turning to examine the man more closely. She ignored the strange clothing for a moment and studied the strange face. His skin was a very dark brown. Entreska checked her own fairly dark tan, but this man's skin was nearly black. His features were unusual, yet pleasing.

She scrutinized the strange, baggy clothes. Hat to boots, everything he wore was encrusted with gray Raffin dust and had numerous rips and scuffs. The trousers and jacket were an unfamiliar design that she couldn't place and sported a seemingly random pattern of small gray, tan and green blocks peeking out from beneath the dust. Both the jacket and even the trousers were nearly covered with pockets.

The boots were made of normal looking light gray leather, but they reached just above the ankles with corded laces. They were too tall for shoes, too short for real boots. The hat was a wide floppy, rather limp thing.

"Thank you, Colonel."

Entreska noted that the black man remained curiously impassive during this exchange.

She asked in standard Jurasketu, "Do you have a name?"

His voice was deep but soft and mellow, "I am Mallory Owens."

She motioned for him to sit down. He readily complied. She stared until he became uncomfortable.

"My name is Entreska Nevercare. I am the Professor of Artifacts and History at the Jurasketu Academy of Learning."

"Artifacts?"

"Yes. I search for evidence and artifacts of ancient civilizations."

"Ah." Mallory seemed puzzled by something. "What ancient civilization are you looking for here?"

"What would you think we would be looking for on the High Raffin?"

Mallory furrowed his brow and looked up as if trying to recall something buried deep in his memory and finally blurted out, "Duravon, right?"

Entreska frowned. His accent was difficult to place making it possible he had come from an isolated area, but only a woefully uneducated or stupid person would not be completely familiar with the story of the destruction of Duravon and the Scattering. She smiled kindly and said, "Of course."

Mallory peered over at her maps, "Any luck so far?"

Entreska set the maps aside and covered them, "Yes. Quite."

"What do you hope to find exactly?"

Entreska chuckled. Even her own mother always seemed to think she was only looking for buried treasure. Of course, as a young girl, much to her mother's annoyance, she did bury 'treasures' in the gardens and then dig them up claiming she had made great 'finds'. No doubt, she loved finding things. Sure, she wanted to find proof that the legends of ancient wizards weren't just stories. While finding finely wrought gold and silver was fun, she had just as much fun digging in the library as digging in the earth. In the end, she mainly had a deep desire to connect with the lives of people long dead. So, diaries, records, contracts, personal goods were often the most valuable finds to her.

Entreska sighed, "Most would think I want to find ancient gold, jewels and silver. But all I want right now is proof that we have found Duravon. That way, we can come back next year."

Mallory smiled, "And then you can look for the gold, silver and jewels?"

Entreska laughed and sighed, "Even if we find any. It would all belong to the Academy and the People of Jurasketu. Neither I nor anyone else doing the digging would profit from it."

Mallory frowned in mock disappointment. Then his face brightened, "Won't you write a book about it?"

Entreska scowled, "No one ever seems to understand."

Mallory rubbed his face, "A well-known hazard of living."

Entreska raised an eyebrow and smiled. She nodded at Jones who merely shrugged. Any stranger could be dangerous, but this man had the abused look of a lost traveler far from home so she doubted he would be dangerous at least until fed and rested. She called for water and lunch.

Mallory gratefully downed a half-liter of water. Then, he sniffed at the food. He shrugged and ate cautiously, then greedily, as he appeared to gain confidence in the taste. He downed another half-liter of water. Then he removed his hat. His hair matched his beard: short, very curly black hair with flecks of gray. He filled the hat partway with water. He splashed some on his face, then poured the rest over his head and replaced the hat with a satisfied sigh of relief. For a Raffin summer day, it was only scorching hot rather than boiling hot. Jones grunted at the stranger's lack of water etiquette, but she waved him to silence. They had plenty of water.

Entreska was a master of languages, both ancient and modern. She was fluent in most languages and passably conversant in the others. She was intimately familiar with every dialect of Jurasketu. She tested out several languages on him. Strangely, he professed ignorance of every language except Jurasketu. She tried to place his origin before coming right out and asking. His accent didn't jibe with any region of Jurasketu, any group of Mountaineers or any of the enclaves of Exiles that she knew. Worse, anyone from the enclaves would almost certainly have known one of the languages she had tested on him.

Finally, she asked, "Where are you from?"

He waved a hand. "I am a wanderer and a prospector. I live mostly off the land and whatever precious stones I can find. I lost my gear in a climbing accident."

"Are you from the White Mountains?"

"Uh. No. Or rather I don't know. My adopted parents never said. We traveled around a lot. When I was fourteen, they were killed by ruffians. I escaped, and I have wandered here and there ever since."

She wondered aloud, "What direction were you traveling?"

"I have recently crossed the Bay of Lydaron. I worked my way across the coastal plain, then passed through the mountains and decided to head out into the desert...."

Mallory trailed off and looked suddenly unsure. She guessed her gaping mouth and wide eyes stopped him. She looked at Jones who caught her eye and twitched his mouth in a decidedly surprised tone.

She asked, "You were in the Blades? Where?"

Mallory shrugged, "Towards the south."

Entreska said evenly, "Pachinko Puck and the Immortals rule there. That is not a normal place to be traveling through. It is unlikely that you would be allowed to pass through unquestioned."

"Yes. That is true. But the area is quite remote and sparsely settled. Most of the area seems to have very limited patrol activity that I was easily able to avoid. Wandering prospectors tend to be good at such things."

Entreska scowled, "But why? There are safer areas to prospect I would think."

Mallory looked at Jones and back to Entreska, "The safer areas are either fully exploited or the competition is fierce and often very dangerous for a non-local. I make my niche in the less safe areas. I figured that the area around the Maw of Hell was probably under exploited. If I get really lucky one day, I suppose I could retire from prospecting and open a tavern or something."

Entreska nodded thinking that made a certain kind of sense.

"Unfortunately, things kind of went awry for me. My situation is kind of dire, so I took a chance on your expedition. I would think my digging skills would be of use actually. I would happily trade them for food, water and shelter."

"Can we trust you?"

Mallory looked puzzled for a moment, "I'm an experienced and careful digger. I'm pretty sure I can be trusted to not damage anything or anyone."

Entreska chuckled, "That is not what I meant. You seem loyal to no one other than yourself."

Mallory looked slightly hurt, "I am a not a thief or a murderer. And I never sell secrets. I keep them instead. And I certainly have no love for the enemies of Jurasketu."

Entreska simply nodded.

Jones suddenly stepped nearby, tugged her shoulder and said in Jurasketu, "Shouldn't we leave you to finish your calculations? I will show our guest a place where he can get cleaned up and find some rest."

Then in a whispered Zattan he said, "I know I deferred to you. And while it is likely he is what he claims to be, his story is very unusual. I think we should be cautious. He might really be a security risk."

She replied in Zattan, "Everything is a security risk to you."

"I have authority in such matters."

She replied reluctantly in Jurasketu, "Exactly. But you are probably right in this case."

Mallory seemed to guess the conversation and held his arms out to the side, palms open and up, "Can I have a chance to prove my skill? Would that convince you I am truthful and possibly trustworthy?"

Entreska laughed, "Very well. We can talk about that tomorrow evening over dinner. My crews sleep during the afternoon. I'll have you work with my best digger, Jack Garth, tomorrow."

Jack Garth was a grizzled Mountaineer. Entreska regarded him as her best digger and close friend. Garth was suspicious, careful and extremely tough. He would keep a close eye on Mallory.

Jones eased close again to Entreska.

He spoke in whispered Zattan again. "That is likely fine. But until I'm convinced he can be trusted, I want him under watch at all times." He glanced back at Mallory. "He looks bigger and stronger than me."

Entreska nodded, "I noticed that myself." They both looked back at Mallory.

She turned to Mallory, "Please don't take offense. But as yet, we cannot be certain of your true intentions or character. So until we decide otherwise, you'll be under close watch by two or more soldiers."

Mallory smiled, "Prudence dictates no less than that."

"Let Colonel Jones show you where you can clean up. We clean and repair our tools in the evening and then get up very early in the morning. I suggest you take the opportunity to get some sleep."

Colonel Jones, Mallory Owens and the two soldiers marched down the hill and toward the encampment.

Entreska returned her focus to the calculations. The critical calculations consumed two pencils, a pile of paper, and the rest of the day. The sun bled across the western horizon. A fitful northern breeze scattered dust over the camp.

The next day, after the morning digging had ceased, she summoned Jack Garth to share lunch. Jack was a short but stout, barrel-shaped man with a squat head, and his huge shoulders simply merged into the base of his skull giving him the appearance of having no neck at all. His weathered, pockmarked face, dirty gray beard and flyaway hair belied his still relatively young thirty-two years. They ate the white cheese and crumbly black bread quickly and quietly. Then she asked what he thought of Mallory.

Garth stared intently at his left hand. He flexed and turned the hand slowly. Entreska smiled and didn't ask if anything was wrong, Garth was lovably eccentric in all things.

"Strong. Tough. Good. Clearly experienced." He flexed the other hand and looked around the tent, at what, she didn't know.

"Experienced?"

Garth grumbled, "Definitely. And much better than those student volunteers you foist upon me."

"I brought them to be your students. You are their teacher."

Garth looked around sheepishly, "Yes. I teach."

Entreska waited.

Garth continued, "Knows some interesting songs that I've never heard before. Don't worry. I made him teach me the words. Friendly. He might be trustworthy."

Garth never let anything interfere with his priorities: digging, singing and drinking, usually in that order. He also rarely offered such an effusive, glowing endorsement. His assessments usually consisted of one word: 'worthless' or 'useful'.

Usually Entreska ate dinner alone, but tonight, she invited Mallory and Jones to dine with her and Mallory's current set of guardians. The meal arrived as they did, and without further comment, Entreska bade them to eat. The meal consisted of pulled pork and Zattan spiced rice, Entreska's favorite when not infused with desert grit.

Mallory started to say something, but she silenced him with a raised hand. Nothing further was said until the meal was finished. Afterward, she explained that she liked to follow the Zattan tradition of no serious conversation during a meal. Mallory laughed.

Jones laughed, "Entreska loves her quaint Zattan traditions. Makes her feel connected to her father I think."

Entreska snarled, "I think it is perfectly sensible to eat peacefully and save arguments for afterward when everyone is feeling in a good mood."

Mallory smiled and nodded in apparent agreement with Entreska. In a more serious tone, she said, "Garth says he thinks you're an experienced digger. So that appears to be truthful. I'm still puzzled how you ended up here."

Mallory bobbled his head and said, "The Raffin seemed to be under exploited due to the long war between Jurasketu and Puck. I stumbled upon your operation purely by chance. I suffered an accident at the northern end of the Maw of Hell."

Jones interjected, "It may be beautiful. But the name comes from how dangerous it is."

Mallory paused then said, "Indeed. Proved to be my undoing anyway. I've lost all my gear. Then just when I thought I would probably perish, I saw your dig. I presumed you were prospecting. And not only was I saved from death, I also thought I might offer my services. Obviously, as you say, there is merely glory and no treasure to divide. Still given my current situation, I'm more than willing to work for just food, shelter and transportation to Jurasketu at the expedition end."

She sighed, "Most of our helpers are volunteers from the Academy. We employ just a few professional diggers. And I would hate to take undo advantage of you."

Mallory frowned, "I see."

She continued, "I can easily provide food, shelter and transportation. I will do that even if you didn't agree to work for us. But I could offer you some of our equipment at the end of the summer in exchange for your sweat and skill."

Mallory smiled, "Oh. I think that is more than fair."

Entreska laughed, "And hopefully at least a minor share of glory."

Mallory laughed.

She looked at Jones to get his reaction. He gave her a disapproving stare, but then nodded assent. She smiled briefly.

She said, "Then we have a deal?"

"Yes. I believe you'll find my work to be of high quality."

"That I don't doubt."

She waved everyone away and closed down her tent for the night. She made notes by lantern light and studied maps for tomorrow's work. She staved off drowsiness as long as possible. She dreaded sleep...

By noon the next day, Entreska finally completed her calculations, and they showed that the new place to dig was over five kilometers from the current base camp. This meant a massive relocation of the camp and an argument. Jones was sure to argue that security would be compromised at the new site. Entreska hated to argue with Jones about anything involving military matters. He argued every point vociferously, and then he would seem unhappy about whatever plan was made, even if the plan was his own, maybe especially then. He didn't like being right, a perfectly understandable attitude considering his grim outlook on most situations.

Entreska took small consolation from the fact that Jones didn't like arguing with her either about military tactics. Entreska routinely perused her father's favorite book on military science, *The Web of Thought*, which not so coincidentally he had written himself, and so she was actually well versed on the finer points of terrain and positioning. So, while lacking in practical experience, she couldn't be easily bluffed or fooled in an argument such as this one. She organized her supervisors to ready the 500 workers and student volunteers for the move. Then she went to face Jones.

Two hours of bickering later, Jones gave in after Entreska offered two hundred of her workers to help prepare defensive fortifications.

Entreska thanked him and started to leave when Jones asked, "How many times have you read that book anyway?"

Entreska smiled and shrugged, "Four or five times completely. But I often reread certain chapters when I feel need for a refresher. I always keep a copy with me."

Jones laughed, "Just like old Glenmorgan, himself."

Entreska laughed and left the command tent. Striding purposely across the brittle, powdery tuvana, she recalled the time when she was twelve and had found her father reading that very book and asked him why he would read a book he had written himself.

He had replied, "Never trust your current vision of the world. Influences beyond your control could be affecting you. A book like this is handy to restore proper perspective. It was written over time with deep study, great resources and revised many times for accuracy, logic and consistency. Such a book provides unexpected insight from a recognizable perspective, my own. Often just by reading my own thoughts, I am able to achieve insight and clarity into current circumstances that seem murky and incomprehensible. The Web of Thought vibrates and mutates in unexpected ways. A partial record of that process can provide useful information that otherwise would be lost in the constant transformation of the Web."

The answer had surprised Entreska for two reasons. First, she had expected a sarcastic response, not philosophy. Second, her father admitted to uncertainty in his thinking, a possibility she had never considered until then. The aura of confidence he exuded affected everyone around him such that he seemed incapable of not having the right answer every time. It wasn't that he didn't make mistakes, he did. But they were always understandable, and he always had mitigation contingencies ready.

The move required two days because Jones insisted that the new fortifications reach completion before the move could actually begin. Entreska used the extra time to thoroughly survey the new dig site. She marked the positions where exploratory trenches would be started. She had calculated the location of the Archives Complex to within a few hectares. The nearly twenty exploratory trenches should narrow the search further in a few days. She just hoped she would be able to actually identify anything they uncovered beneath the volcanic sand.

A Cunning Plan

Rolf pushed several handfuls of sand into a pile before flattening and smoothing the top. Next, a little ways away he worked a ridge up, cupping the sand with his hands. To provide stiffness, he sprinkled water from a bowl that rested on a tall stool near the sand table. He used the back of his hand to feather the ridge sand just so. Upon completing the work, he smiled and wiped his hands together to remove the remaining sand grains.

The Grand Marshal of the Jurasketu Army, Glenmorgan Nevercare, said, "Very nice, son. So what is the plan?"

Rolf Nevercare smiled mischievously. "What would happen if Puck made a late season attack?"

"As you well know, we would withdraw, defend the mountains and let him suffer the winter storms. And so does Puck and his generals. That's why there are no late season attacks across the High Raffin. But now you're about to tell me there's something wrong with that theory, aren't you?"

Cheerfully, Rolf pointed at a burlap mat on the sand table that stood in for the southern salt marshes and said, "If his army stayed to the south and then pushed out of the Raffin to the coast here just above the Wastes, they would mostly avoid the brutal storms. There are no mountains to slow them down, and we have only token troops in the region hunting bandits. From there, they could advance up the coast and seriously threaten Southern Jurasketu."

Glen snorted in disgust, "The eastern end of the Lower Raffin has no mountains all right but it's almost impassable with all the gullies and canyons. Maintaining an adequate supply train through the region would be impossible."

Rolf conceded, "Quite right. But there are ample resources along the coast and a few neutral merchantmen could deliver difficult to obtain supplies in advance before our ships could drive them off and effect blockade. A forty-thousand-man army could make the trek and operate without a supply train for two seasons at least I would think. A smaller force could operate for considerably longer although it would be vulnerable to earlier destruction."

Glen spent a few moments pondering and observing his son. Rolf outweighed him by twenty kilos and towered over him. Yet, despite Glen's advancing age, he still advantaged Rolf in agility and speed, a fact Rolf never seemed to care much about. Rolf was only about agility and speed of mind. Rolf refused to fight anywhere but the sand table or after dinner. To Glen's eternal irritation, Rolf refused to take another field command preferring to remain an instructor at the Academy. Three years before, Glen, already the Grand Marshal for 14 years, tried to force the issue by ordering Rolf transferred to a field command, Rolf simply resigned from the Army without a word. In anger and humiliation, Glen almost retired from the Army himself when three weeks later the Grand Debater used her authority to appoint Rolf the High Chairman of the Academy. Instead, Glen admitted he had made a mistake and even apologized for the way he had tried to handle the situation and from then on kept his irritation to himself.

Rolf always wore clean, pressed tan trousers and a tan collared shirt made of thick linen. He customarily wore the light blue Academy Instructor's Beret, but sometimes he would trade the beret for a simple wide-brim felt hat. For this session, he had brought the beret that currently hung on a hook designed for the purpose near the tent's entrance, next to Glen's own black beret. He mussed his short spiky orange hair with his left hand. His face and hair favored his mother. His build favored Glen's father. He smiled in apparent delight that he had discovered a way their enemy could make them suffer grievously.

Finally, Glen said, "But what's the end game?"

"Our wealthiest and most fertile counties lie in Southern Jurasketu. And we'll be forced to wage an expensive campaign to eliminate the threat. Worse, we'll be forced to permanently improve our southern garrisons and defenses. We can barely afford our current level of national resources committed to war and defense, so the only way we could manage the improvements long term would be to significantly reduce our deployments in the north.

"That would sharply curtail our current practice of aggressively raiding across the foothills of the White Mountains into Puck territory. That's bad because it would discredit our diplomatic justification for keeping bases and large forces deployed near the boundary with the province of Tangur. The Zattan Imperium would complain that our forces are only there to threaten Tangur which is not proper behavior for a sworn ally - never mind that they would be correct."

Glen had to agree, "Yes indeed. Some Royals constantly complain in the Imperium Council meetings that we pay no tribute. The Councilors always advise, of course, that the commerce provisions of the Dotek Treaty bring significant revenue to the Royal coffers without any cost. Jurasketu won't pay tribute if demanded and so there would be war, which naturally the Royals relish because they believe, and rightly so, that war has brought them great riches. Shouldn't more war do the same? They argue.

"The Councilors always win the argument by saying the Imperium cannot fight the long and expensive war necessary to conquer Jurasketu and simultaneously expand into the chaotic but wealthy countries of the Wokometu. Besides the Jurasketu distract Puck and patrol the Eastern Ocean against Valruk incursions at no cost to the Imperium."

Rolf replied evenly, "Yes. But those arguments would be nullified if we defied a formal demand to withdraw. And if there was war, I think they would win - we just have too many enemies and the Zattan Imperium has sufficient resources to slowly grind us to dust. Or... they might insist that you formally seize power and make Jurasketu an Imperium Province."

Rolf cocked his head in thought for a moment.

"Would you? If you had no alternative?"

Glen, who had been pacing back and forth, stopped and stared darkly into Rolf's cold stare. Glen couldn't immediately decide whether Rolf was probing for a pragmatic solution or testing Glen's principles. Rolf could be very indirect at times, dangerously so.

Glen smiled slightly, "Have you forgotten your lessons? The Web of Thought always has alternate configurations."

Rolf smiled in return, scratched his neck and said, "Forget I asked. Anyway, we wouldn't want to withdraw those forces. Even with you still alive, the Governor of Tangur would be tempted to attack with the secret urging and backing of the Royals. And unless we instantly destroyed the Tangur invasion, the Imperium Council might be powerless to stop a full-scale war. Realistically though, I strongly doubt they would make any demands or attack until you are dead - because they are afraid you might very well orchestrate their destruction in the field or outmaneuver them on the Council. And so I think that means they would step up the attempts on your life. Your passing obviously creates a moment of opportunity for our enemies. Your successor on the Council needs to have time to cultivate the relationships necessary to ensure Jurasketu's survival during times of real weakness. Of course, you know that."

Glen pondered for a few moments. Then he said, "Yes. Indeed. Still, though. Whatever the scenario, the deterioration of the strategic situation and eventual defeat would occur much later, after the troops Puck had committed were lost. I cannot see any scenario where his troops escape alive. One of Puck's secrets of success in attracting and maintaining the loyalty of both his Immortals and Cumar mercenaries is that he never needlessly risks their lives. While he personally hates us enough to sacrifice forces to our defeat, his generals aren't nearly so eager to increase the power of their real strategic enemy, the Zattan Imperium, at considerable cost to themselves. I don't think the chances of sufficient forces actually reaching the coast to carry out the threat as described are nearly as good as you present. It's a very risky and unlikely move in all respects."

Rolf smiled, "Indeed. But what if the Governor of Tangur and Puck conspired against us?"

"What are you saying?"

"Suppose that Puck and the Governor of Tangur make battle plans together. If Tangur were to attack in coordination with Puck's late season attack, then there would be seemingly plenty of opportunity for Puck's troops to avoid destruction and even make a big score of slaves and treasure. It would also certainly make the subjugation of Jurasketu by the Imperium very likely. Puck would love that."

Glen expanded his web of thought to include the possibilities. "The Governor of Tangur would not make such a deal with Puck. If proved, the Imperium Council would have the Governor executed for treason. Worse, the Governor would suspect a setup and could not take Puck at his word. If Puck reneged, the Governor knows that should he attack without Puck drawing away our reserves we would likely massacre his army before they could do any harm to Jurasketu. The Imperium Council would definitely execute him for making that kind of mistake. He fears our skill in battle."

"Doesn't matter what the Governor of Tangur does. Puck doesn't have to actually make any deal - he just has to tell his folks that he has."

Glen barked, "Ah. That way when they get slaughtered because there was no attack from the north - it was Imperium treachery to blame. But we're still stuck with the degraded strategic situation."

Rolf grinned, "Exactly. Cunning, eh?"

"Heinous even. Still, he would have to lose a sizable force."

"Bah. Latest reports are that he has around 120,000 Immortals and 160,000 Cumar Mercenaries. Puck deploys some 20,000 Immortals and 40,000 Cumar in defending the Blades against our raids and the possibility of a surprise, coordinated attack by us with the Zattan. If we were forced to become more passive and defensive, he would need less than half that number to protect that approach. As you know, our raids are designed to make Puck maintain more troops in the field that he would like or can afford long term. We expect him to have trouble finding enough slaves and booty to keep all his Immortals and Cumar happy. So, really, Puck would love to reduce his army by thirty to forty thousand men. He could use the savings to make sure the troubled Wokometu states don't fall to the Zattan and if war develops between us and the Zattan - the pressure on Wokometu and his own lands are greatly reduced for decades to come."

Glen rubbed his chin and sat down to think in his ancient and rickety folding field chair. "But really son, do you really think Puck will come up with such a clever plan all by himself? Make no mistake, Puck is terribly smart and diabolical, but such a plan is not exactly obvious."

Rolf pursed his lips and spread his hands in disconcern. "Yes. But what if he didn't have to come up with the plan on his own?"

Glen raised an eyebrow. "Now what would make you say something like that?"

Rolf smiled and walked to the other side of the tent to grab a large pretzel and pick up his draft of Tarfun Stone Brew. He gnawed at the pretzel, slurped some of the ale, and kept looking between the sand table and Glen who had become engrossed with the workmanship of his chair.

While getting up out of the chair, Glen said, "Well, are you going to answer me?" Then he turned his back on Rolf to examine the canvas seat.

Rolf ignored the question and asked, "Is something wrong with your chair?"

"Yes. It's not *my* Chair. I specifically requested that Marshal Juragi have the darned thing cleaned and instead I obviously got the wrong chair back unless...."

"Unless what?"

"Unless Juragi deliberately replaced it!"

Glen flung the chair across the tent where it landed in a heap. "Dammit. Juragi!"

Almost instantly, a very proper young officer appeared in the entranceway of the tent and said, "Grand Marshal, Marshal Juragi has not yet returned from inspecting the kitchens. Do you want me to go fetch him?"

"Lieutenant Eneko, do you know anything about my Chair?"

Looking extremely nervous, the officer replied, "Grand Marshal?"

Glen said pointing at the crumpled chair, "Don't pretend with me. What did Marshal Juragi do with my Chair?"

"Well, isn't that it over there, Grand Marshal?"

"Lieutenant, is it my practice to ask trick questions of my officers?"

"No Grand Marshal. Your reputation for asking direct questions is well established."

"So, Lieutenant, if that piece of trash was my chair, would I be asking you where it was?"

"Doubtless not, Grand Marshal."

"Very good. So do you know where my chair is?"

"Um... Well... Marshal Juragi said it was unsafe and needed to be replaced, so we located a similar, but sturdier old chair we thought you would like."

"So, you admit to conspiring with Marshal Juragi to violate my direct order?"

The Lieutenant started to splutter but Glen motioned for him to be silent. The Lieutenant simply stood at attention as his formerly slicked back blond hair started to rise and go astray. Fear showed in his pale blue eyes.

Glen rubbed his chin and smiled. "Eneko."

"Yes, Grand Marshal?"

"What did you do with my old chair?"

"Nothing, Grand Marshal. Marshal Juragi said he would take care of it."

"I see." Glen paused. "You may now go fetch Marshal Juragi. Do not tell him why."

Running out of the tent, Eneko said, "Yes, Grand Marshal, right away."

Glen walked over to the pretzel table and picked up a pretzel and a draft of Tarfun Stone Brew to match his son. He said nothing while he crunched the pretzel between swallows of beer.

Rolf spoke softly and carefully, "Don't you think you overreacted a little? I thought that lieutenant was going to faint in sheer terror."

"Pah. It's not the chair. Juragi just goes overboard looking out for my personal welfare and I don't like it. Eneko is a lieutenant, so of course he's going to be afraid of the Wrath of the Grand Marshal. I mean after all, I *am* the Grand Marshal. About the only person in the whole damn Jurasketu Army who isn't afraid of me *is* Marshal Juragi. That's one of the reasons why he's my Chief of Staff. And don't worry, I'm not going to punish either of them. Anyway, you still haven't answered my question."

Rolf nodded and slurped some more beer. "Yes. Before I answer that, let's consider how we would counter such an incursion to prevent lasting harm to our strategic situation."

Glen shrugged, thought about Rolf's question and said, "Okay. If we knew soon enough, we could move a moderate blocking force into position on the eastern edge of the Raffin below the mountains. Then, we could swing a large force into the attacker's rear to destroy them. If we could avoid the storms ourselves, that is."

Rolf replied, "Indeed. Your picket squadrons could give early warning, but I don't think we would have sufficient time to mobilize."

"If they mounted a fighting withdrawal rather than the currently prescribed fast retreat, we would."

Rolf chuckled, "You anticipate me. If they delayed Puck's advance by several days rather than using our current policy of saving lives and rapidly retreating to let the storms do our work, we could dash across the Central Raffin with most of our mounted forces and turn in behind the army advancing east. We should be able to catch his army still in the gullies of the Lower Raffin and really make a hash of his army no matter the size. We could achieve a very decisive victory."

Rolf guzzled the remainder of his beer and pointed to a large rut in the sand table. "Even better, after defeating Puck's army we could immediately launch a counterattack with our most elite forces around either end of the Maw of Hell up into the Blades. With any luck at all, we could arrive before word of his army's defeat even reached the Centaur Citadel itself. We could overrun surprised local garrisons and inflict grievous harm to a large swath of Puck's empire. Using freed slaves as militia forces we could keep Puck's army busy for years."

Glen muttered, "Wouldn't our troops have the same problems we discussed for Puck's army? That is not a fertile area - mostly sheep herding. They'll withdraw all the animals north and that region is essentially barren of wild life and food plants, so our forces won't be able to stay long at all never mind the lack of military supplies. The coastal region is very inhospitable and since the operation by necessity would be an impromptu counterattack we couldn't plan to have naval forces in the right area assuming they can beat back any enemy ships in the area - not necessarily a given."

Rolf said, "Very true."

Rolf then raised his hand, dramatically pointed to the Maw of Hell and said, "But what if we had 25 to 40 weeks of supplies hidden in the Maw of Hell? It would make a fine base of operations. Plus, should Puck manage to cobble together sufficient forces to threaten the viability of our forces, we could withdraw the way we came using the Maw to protect our flank. Puck could not prevent our escape."

Glen pursed his lips dismissively. "How would you get those supplies there and prevent their discovery?"

Rolf laughed heartily, "About 30 years ago, a young captain discovered the entrance to a massive dry cavern exposed by a landslide near the mouth of the Maw. The captain had the foresight to briefly explore and then have his squadron hide the entrance with several tons of boulders. Reading the report, I imagine many tons of supplies could be hidden within without chance of accidental discovery."

Glen sighed, "I forgot that the High Chairman of the Academy has access to all action reports from the Army Archives. Still, wouldn't you need to get the supplies there?"

"Well, in the summer, the southern picket pushes to the mouth of the Maw already. We just use their screen to bring up the supplies. The dry cellar conditions in the cave would keep foodstuffs several years if the report is accurate."

Glen gave a half-smile, "Are you questioning the accuracy of my report?"

Rolf said in mock mortification, "Of course not. That's just what I always say when relying on a report. The only reason the report caught my eye was because you wrote it."

Glen nodded. "Well, that's a nice interpretation. But apparently, you haven't been keeping up with the current reports. I've had the southern picket stocking that cave for the last 10 years. I've got over

250 supply and water wagons stashed there, tons of equipment, armor, ammunition, tools, lumber, metal stock, dry goods... Enough to supply a 25,000-man army for two full years of campaigning. All we need to add is skilled soldiers and horses."

Rolf just stood with his mouth open for several long pauses before finally blurting out, "I don't see how I could have missed any such reports."

"Well, it's easy since they haven't been filed just yet. I'm still reviewing them you might say. You know how Marshal Juragi posits that Puck, the Imperium and the Valruk have spies in high positions in the Army. Of course, I'm Zattan and he's Valruk - so maybe he's just hearing rumors turned on those facts."

Rolf said, "Ah. I should have guessed when I saw nothing about the cavern in later reports and the fact that the southern picket seemed to be stationed needlessly far forward. Why didn't you remove the original report?"

Glen shrugged and while gnawing on his pretzel muttered, "Its existence is known to a number of senior people. Should it turn up missing, the wrong people might get suspicious."

"Hmm... You're as paranoid as Juragi."

"More so. Anyway, I've considered the situation and I like your strategic analysis. Is it complete?"

Rolf said, "Yes. I think the harm we would inflict on Puck would allow us to become more aggressive with our northern raids and strengthen our position in that area and hence keep the Imperium at bay for many years to come."

Glen leaned on the sand table. "Yes. That's why I've been secretly building up and freshening those supplies in case the opportunity should arise. You have outlined an intriguing way for that to happen. Now, you should answer my question."

Rolf said, "Hmm... Well, I think you're correct about Puck. He won't likely come up with a plan to cause himself so much harm all by his lonesome. So, we need to help."

"How exactly?"

"Treachery."

Glen muttered, "Ah, Treachery..." as the tall, lean and muscular Juragi sauntered into the tent with his usual expression of bemused indifference astride his sharp, age-lined features.

Brushing the dark hair from his equally dark eyes, Juragi said, "Treachery? Has Chairman Rolf discovered a plot or are we just speculating again?"

Pointing a crooked finger at the wrecked chair, Glen said, "Rolf and I ever speculate. But I, myself, have discovered a plot most foul - look there."

"Ah. The chair..."

The Legend of Pachinko Puck

Mallory Owens leaned back in the ancient oak tavern chair and rubbed his face in thought. He loved missions, especially difficult ones. His commanding officer, General Lang, knew that and reserved as many as she could for him.

Naturally, the difficult missions tended to have impossible legal and practical limitations. Mallory, not the least deterred, would devise a highly creative, complex, detailed mission plan that purported to navigate through those difficulties. General Lang would usually approve the plan with only minimal review. Then Mallory would spend considerable effort practicing and preparing to execute the plan with confidence and precision. Of course, his plans rarely survived the legal and practical limitations inherent in difficult missions. Naturally, he would have to improvise and this usually meant property destruction, chaos and loss of life that tended to be significantly higher than predicted in the plan.

Afterwards, Mallory would make a verbal report to General Lang, who howling with laughter at his sheepish explanations of why he deviated from the original plan, would tell him to compose an official report of the successful mission that explained how everything occurred without a single illegal action on his part. This usually would leave his reports at odds with the laws of physics, but fortunately, no physicists read the reports, only military bureaucrats.

But now Mallory was lost somewhere in the far reaches of the galaxy and a long way from General Lang and her missions. He listened with hidden desperation to the drunken man talking through the singing and clanking of tankards.

He said, "Yes. He's four hundred years old at least." The man, jaw thrust forward, stared at Mallory with his one good eye, the left one, daring Mallory to call him a liar.

Mallory kept his round, soft face placid but not quite believing what he was hearing. The man, who called himself Craig Henderson, had been an interesting find. The locals labeled him a lunatic who would tell his crazy stories to anyone willing to buy him a few rounds of his favorite brew. Mallory resolved to do nothing to antagonize the man on the theory that if he was not crazy he would provide useful information. If he was just crazy, then the classic rule of never provoking crazy people applied.

While drawing his relatively small hands across his clean-shaven pate pausing to rub his smallish ears, Mallory asked, "Where did you learn this?"

The man relaxed, pushed back his fluffy brown, gray-streaked hair and adjusted his green-eye patch. Then he leaned forward again and whispered, "I commanded The Immortals of the Sunrise."

Mallory whispered back, "Who are they?"

Mallory hunched forward, tucking his legs under as though trying to conceal his tall and muscular frame that dwarfed the man sitting across the small table from him. The man twitched with obvious dismay at the question.

"It is the oldest and most famous regiment in Puck's Army. Your ignorance of affairs on the Raffin is surprising."

"Why?"

"I have never met anyone who speaks Jurasketu so well while knowing so little about Raffin."

Mallory had a natural talent for accents and languages that had served him well in his occupation. He had quickly acquired the rhythms and intonations of the local English dialect that had the interesting distinction of being known only as Jurasketu and not English. He was still trying to pick up several highly divergent versions of Español that were also common, but virtually everyone seemed to speak Jurasketu as the language of business and trade. Since he had only been on the planet for two weeks, his ignorance of affairs on the Raffin was actually perfectly understandable.

Mallory grunted and said, "I'm actually quite new to this area. My ignorance is exactly what I'm hoping you can rectify."

The man shrugged.

Still incredulous at the alleged age of Puck, Mallory asked the next fateful question, "How long ago was Duravon founded?"

"What? The Jurath Calendar fixes its starting year as the year of Duravon's legendary founding by Jura the Wise, and we are currently in year 3429. You've never heard this story?"

"No. We don't use the Jurath Calendar." Mallory slumped back into his chair utterly confounded. He was lost not only in space but deep in time, epically so. Mallory knew the twenty-four Primitive Worlds by heart that had existed at the time of the Accident. He had scouted all of them from orbit and set foot on seven. There were another 300-odd modern colonies and bases on Old Earth-like planets. Simple geography established that this planet was not any one of those planets. He had initially surmised this was an ultra-secret Primitive World that even had been kept hidden from someone who worked for an ultra-secret government agency charged with monitoring such planets. But that was almost certainly wrong.

Somehow, the Accident had dropped him four or more millennia into a mysterious future on a planet that either had been developed as a Primitive World after his Accident or had degenerated into its current state after some local or possibly galactic catastrophe. He stared skyward wondering at the current status of human civilization and whether that should infect his plans and actions in some fashion.

Henderson's gnarled hands played with his empty tankard while waiting for Mallory to say something else.

Eventually Henderson asked with mild concern, "Are you okay?"

Mallory banished his puzzlement and said, "Yes. I simply need another drink." He ordered more Tarfun Stone Brew for Henderson and himself.

Before the order arrived, Mallory asked, "Is Puck human?"

Henderson scratched his unshaven cheek indifferently. "Some say he is a Demon. I believe him to be human despite his unusual appearance."

"So, you've seen him yourself?"

Henderson shrugged, "Naturally. Regimental commanders routinely met publicly and privately with Puck."

"What does he look like? He's unusual you just said."

"Yes. Despite his age, he appears to be no more than fifteen or so. His skin is a most peculiar shade of purple. His green eyes burn with mischief. His hair is bright orange. He loves fine clothes, but he will wear a soiled, ragged nightshirt to otherwise formal meetings with ambassadors. He is stranger than the Night of the Hungry Moon."

Mallory learned later that every 114 years, the largest moon appeared to consume the other four in one those strange quirks of astronomical systems. The drinks arrived, and they both immediately took a sample.

Wiping his mouth, Mallory asked, 'When did you see him last?"

He said sadly, "Ah. That day I remember well. I received my punishment on the Autumnal Equinox of 3402."

"Punishment?"

"Yes. My regiment was defeated and slaughtered in the White Mountains by a Jurasketu force. I managed to survive, losing this," he tapped his eye patch, "and returned to face Puck. I had been one of his favorites, so I was spared execution and instead was sent to Slave School."

"School?"

"It's a joke. It's the part of the Centaur Citadel where new slaves are collared, abused, taught proper slave behavior, and then abused some more. Fortunately, my friends managed my escape before my enemies could devise a special pit fight to their joy and my pain. Amusingly, Puck used the escape as a pretext to execute one of my enemies, the Citadel Commander, whom he had begun to dislike."

Mallory sneered, "So. Puck runs a slave state?"

Henderson said, "Formally or informally, most people are slaves to someone."

Mallory said, "Not where I come from."

"Whatever you say."

Brushing aside the issue, Mallory said, "Yes... Did you say that Puck's skin is purple in color?"

While pointing to a cloth hanging from a wall that had a deep purple field with an orange star in the center, Henderson said, "Purple as that banner over there. Strange, hun? I mean, there are millions of people on the Earth with skin colors ranging from pale to ruddy to various shades of brown. And so someone is the palest, someone is the ruddiest, and someone is the brownest. Being nearly black as you are, I would wager that you are easily the brownest. Yet, that doesn't seem impossible given the range of browns. But I've never heard of anyone who even claimed to have heard of someone with purple skin of any shade other than Puck."

"Maybe it's not his natural color. A dye perhaps?"

He said with a shrug, "As you say." He picked up and began gnawing a stale bread roll.

After ordering another round, Mallory asked, "How do you know he's four-hundred years old?"

"I don't actually. It has been written and spoken that a man named Pachinko Puck fitting his physical description has ruled the Western Zetu for four hundred years. Puck said it was true. He certainly seemed to have the experience, skills and wisdom of someone who had lived a long time despite his youthful appearance. Many of my friends in Puck's Army often said privately that they thought he was a Demon or a Wizard out of legend with the gifts of seeing and manipulation. I don't know with certainty.

"Whatever his secret, the living legend of Pachinko Puck has built a modest empire that covers most of both shores of the Bay of Lydaron. The Jurasketu who claim the legacy of the Raffin and even the powerful Zattan fear his armies and power. The weak minor states of the Wokometu that he doesn't yet control, like this one where we quench our thirst, tremble in constant terror and try to appease him with gold and slaves. Puck always said he didn't want to be bothered with administering an overly vast empire, so the current situation suits him fine. Except for the Jurasketu. He hates them and constantly plots their doom."

"Not too successfully I surmise."

Henderson laughed, "No. The military leadership in Jurasketu has proven competent and resourceful for many decades. There is also the High Raffin Plain flanked by rugged mountains on the north and salt marshes to the south. They use the terrain and their alliances to full advantage."

Mallory nodded picturing the Bay of Lydaron in his head flanked to the west by Wokometu and to the east by Zetu with its forbidding terrain.

"Why does he hate the Jurasketu so much?"

Henderson shrugged. "I don't know. He doesn't say publicly and privately I only heard curses for the Jurasketu. No reasons. The Jurasketu have always despised and mocked him. Maybe that's all."

"Do you hate the Jurasketu as well?"

"Nah. I don't hate anyone. Hate does not profit one's purse or soul."

Mallory sniffed in derision.

"Laugh as you wish. I only became a soldier for the adventure. To me, at the time, life was but a game of chance. Puck's Army offered the chance for a lot of action and material reward. Then, I did not even understand what good character meant, never mind care."

"What about now?"

"Now I know the measure of good character. Cost me an eye and most of my life. But at least I know, even if I don't always care. I'm not a philosopher, so don't ask me to explain good character. If you don't know, I'm not going to be able to explain it to you. You'll just have to learn for yourself."

Mallory nodded politely. He wasn't concerned with philosophy at that moment, but he decided right then that his destiny lay with Puck. "Tell me more about Puck and the Raffin..."

For ten straight days, Mallory used a significant fraction of his meager monetary resources to keep Henderson supplied with drink while he told Mallory many things about Puck, the Raffin, and other aspects of planet history. Mallory had questioned Henderson very carefully about the Centaur Citadel and Puck's habits. Henderson seemed to have supplemented his personal knowledge with more recent information from contacts he still had in the Immortals. Once Mallory learned enough from Henderson, he paid for passage in an uncomfortable and not very safe looking river coach to Port Deliverance to explore the mission he had just invented for himself.

Port Deliverance lay astride several islands at the mouth of the Tarfun River and according to Craig Henderson controlled a significant portion of the shipping trade on the Bay of Lydaron. The wealthy, teeming city of more than a hundred thousand persons supposedly was an independent city-state ruled by an oligarchy of merchant families. Henderson claimed, however, that those families all owed secret allegiance to Puck. This allowed Puck's Empire to obtain goods and conduct profitable trade that would otherwise be difficult due to the antipathy of the Jurasketu, the Tarfun Defense League, the Zattan Imperium and the several smaller Wokometu states that continued to oppose him.

Port Deliverance's strong naval forces and natural defensive barriers made it practically invulnerable to attack. According to Henderson, Puck had subverted the most powerful merchant families over the course of the last two centuries while building upon the city's reputation for neutrality and lack of territorial ambitions.

This made Port Deliverance perfect for Mallory.

Normally, money would not be a problem for Mallory. For missions on more civilized planets, he would be provided with the usual untraceable credit accounts. For missions on a Primitive planet like this one, a large supply of suitable local coinage, bullion, precious stones or other barter would have been provisioned along with everything else. But Mallory was not on an official mission, and so he had nothing obviously usable as even barter. Essentially, except for his hunting knife, everything he possessed was priceless. He had already sold the knife for 200 republicans, which was a nice sum for just a knife, but it was hardly enough since marginally adequate food and lodging required 3 to 5 republicans a day, and to maintain a decent lifestyle he would need 10 to 15 republicans a day.

The trouble was he wanted to hire a sailing ship that not only was willing to secretly place him on the Eastern shores of Puck's Empire but also pick him up later. Not only would that require a fast ship with a competent captain and crew - but one willing to take serious risks just for money. Such a captain and crew would necessarily be smugglers and unlikely to be entirely trustworthy considering the risks and the money involved, so an expensive and elaborate regime of safeguards would be wise to avoid a fatal betrayal. Such money could by no means be obtained through regular jobs should he deign to get one. With effort and months or years, he could legally wrangle his considerable skills into a small fortune, but that would expose him to scrutiny that might be uncomfortable or even dangerous to bear.

That meant he would need to raise the capital by extralegal means. If he had the right local contacts, he could probably raise enough capital to stage an elaborate confidence game. With his surveillance gear, he was confident of making a high payoff with no one being able to trace the crime to himself. But making the right local contacts might take months or years followed by months of planning, hiring and organizing to stage the game which itself might take weeks. He might as well start a legitimate business.

The other option was robbery, an epic robbery. He certainly had the equipment and skill to rob anyone or anything. Should things go wrong, he could certainly shoot his way out of trouble since the locals seemed to possess nothing beyond 17th century technology and no firearms while he had several modern firearms plus body armor, not to mention explosives. Since Henderson alleged that all the big merchant families were secretly loyal to Puck, they should be his targets. In fact, even if he had the money already, he might have robbed them anyway to finance his expedition. Mallory loved irony. And nothing could be more ironic than making Puck's own allies fund his demise.

For starters, Mallory decided to get a menial job on the docks. That would give him some time to learn enough information to determine the right target. It would supplement his meager monetary resources without having to immediately risk criminal activity, allow him to learn which ships and crews he should approach, and learn other important bits of information from the locals without directly arousing suspicion. So far, his mere appearance hadn't seemed to cause any overt reaction by the local authorities. Not that he was particularly afraid of them. It would just be very inconvenient. Many people would die, and worse, it would totally ruin his current plans.

In a few days, Mallory quickly earned the respect of his workmates and the supervisors with his uncomplaining attitude and almost supernatural strength and endurance. Mallory was half impressed with himself for not losing his cool whenever he was being treated as the dumb menial worker he was pretending to be. He had to grunt a lot when given instructions to avoid saying anything impertinent.

General Lang had always laughed during plan reviews whenever Mallory was going to disguise himself as a menial worker. She howled with delight as she regaled the number of times Mallory had turned a mission into a blazing firefight because someone powerful had insulted his intelligence. Mallory always snarled that she was exaggerating and he had been perfectly capable of keeping his cool - the situations had simply progressed to the point of violence anyway and the drama of a supposed nobody turning on the high and mighty always appealed to his romantic if unwise self. General Lang had simply laughed harder at the denials.

His second week on the job, he was invited to the weekly dice game with his unmarried workmates. Apparently, the idea was to gamble until one of them had most of their collective wages. The big winner would be obligated to select and pay for their food and lodging for that week in a bizarre method of pooling their resources and choosing a leader - especially considering the game allowed almost no skill whatsoever. Mallory would have declined, but he was anxious to make some friends.

To Mallory's dismay, he quickly lost 80% of his week's wages. The eventual winner, a small, wiry man named Walter cackled with glee and said, "My sister promised me that we could stay at the Passion Cove for four weeks for free if we cleaned out the cellar."

The faces of the other six men brightened considerably. Three at once said, "For free?"

"Yup."

Two at once said, "What about meals?"

"Provided, of course."

The youngest asked in a quavering voice, "Um... What about...

Er... Um..."

Walter shook his head, "No discounts. But using all our money plus a little I had saved up, I've paid for us to have two girls for the whole week break. And with food and bed covered for four weeks, you'll have three weeks of money to do as you like."

Everyone whooped except Mallory who asked, "What exactly is in this cellar?"

Walter looked puzzled, "Hun. I didn't ask her. She just said the last owner never threw anything away and until now she hadn't needed more storage space. Now she does. So she wants it cleaned. Seemed easy enough and a good deal for all."

Mallory shrugged, nodded agreement and everyone else went back to being excited. Mallory had been an operative almost his entire adult life. He had never wanted to be an absent or dead husband or father and so had deliberately not entered into any conventional relationships and had taken the usual steps not to father any children until he retired from active service. On the other hand, while he was not a monk or particularly prudish, paranoia and caution limited his activity, especially on Primitive Worlds. And so the prospect of spending four weeks in a brothel wasn't nearly as exciting for him. Worse, cleaning nasty, vermin infested cellars wasn't exactly on his list of healthful activities.

To Mallory's surprise, the Passion Cove catered to the merchants and craftsmen of Deliverance rather than laborers and sailors as he had expected. Located on a peninsula about two kilometers from the docks, the Passion Cove was actually a nicely renovated old estate with a large manor house, an opulent private bath house crowned by a sixty foot tall windmill that powered a well-water pump, an enormous carriage house, a well-outfitted boat house and three sets of spacious servants quarters. Walter's sister, Annette, a matronly middle-aged woman, greeted them coolly and showed them their sleeping quarters that turned out to be the attic of the boathouse. Not the best, but the beds were clean and vermin free.

Although Port Deliverance has the smell and feel of a dirty port city, most residents including his workmates were very well groomed, regularly cleaned their garments and with few exceptions bathed daily at either private or public baths. The city proper has sewers and even regular refuse pickup. Deep wells and cisterns supply fresh water for cooking and bathing. Brightly painted windmills dot the landscape outside the city. The area experiences warm and humid weather all year round.

A hulking, dark haired younger man brought their dinner of vegetable soup, white bread and Tarfun Stone Brew. Mallory had to turn away to hide his bemusement at the obvious dismay of the men who obviously had expected a fairer member of the Passion Cove to serve dinner. Walter had to expend a bit of energy calming the grumbling.

Cleaning the cellars proved to be major undertaking. Located under the servants' quarters, they had been used as refuse dumps for years apparently. Scary-looking and often venomous vermin of all sorts now called the cellars home.

Most colonists routinely and ruthlessly slaughter all dangerous beasts larger than a house cat in all civilized regions. Moreover, the overly aggressive or lethal smaller beasts were methodically killed or driven away from dwellings and farms. The remainder were tolerated to the extent that food supplies or dwellings were not greatly threatened. Naturally, though, the names of vermin were usually recycled from Old Earth: rat-things were rats; bat-things were bats; bug-things were bugs; lizard-things were lizards; spider-things were spiders and so on. Sometimes the collection of vermin on a given Primitive World was only troublesome because of overpopulation due to predator extermination or farming practices. On other worlds, the vermin could be downright nightmarish. This World tilted slightly toward the nightmarish side because of the high number of venomous creatures.

Mallory convinced Annette and Walter that they needed to smoke the vermin out first. They sealed the cellars up and they built a relatively clean burning fire and used a wood frame covered in fabric to direct the smoke into the cellars. Within a few hours, most everything had been asphyxiated or poisoned with toxic fumes. Then it was shovels and wheelbarrows for a day and a half. They were very weary the next day at their paying job and found themselves being berated for poor efforts in loading a particularly large shipment of Tarfun Stone Brew.

Communal sleeping arrangements were a little inconvenient for Mallory in that he wanted to continue secretly using his ultra-modern equipment. His large, olive green duffel bag, made of a nigh-indestructible composite fabric, bristled with security features and woe would come to they who laid an unwanted hand on it. Within he kept his folding rifle, several hundred rounds of standard, armor piercing and guided explosive ammunition for the rifle and the 5mm automatic, small demolition charges, surveillance gear, medical kit, microfilament climbing gear and spare clothes.

The duffel bag, officially designated as a Secret Utility Mission Pack or SUMP, was also a marvelous computer with a folding fabric touchscreen disguised as a small leather-bound logbook tucked into a side pocket. A special implant just behind his left ear provided a direct mind controlled interface to the computer. The implant was connected to his speech and auditory brain centers. Mallory had needed to spend several weeks learning how to issue silent commands and listen to the output to his auditory system. Should the implant malfunction, he could use direct voice control or the touchscreen for silent control.

Typically, Mallory used his Darkglasses for the visual interface rather than the touchscreen. The display on the Darkglasses could be controlled with mental commands via the implant. In addition to providing a visual display, the Darkglasses, as the name implies, allowed incredibly clear computer enhanced vision in total darkness and even thick smoke. The Darkglasses naturally had numerous options ranging from the practical to the completely silly like transparent overlays, zooming, split screens, display windows, and automatic on/off based on where the wearer was looking.

The implant, glasses, touchscreen all could maintain communication with the bag up to 500 meters distant. The bag supposedly drew power from ambient heat, but Mallory never quite believed the explanation of how that worked exactly and held a deep suspicion that the bag's builders didn't want to admit they were using some highly toxic substance to provide power in violation of regulations. The bag could easily be converted into a backpack configuration for extended foot travel.

To avoid raising suspicion, Mallory pretended to be very modest and so always changed clothes and arranged his equipment in the boathouse store room. In addition, he took his daily baths after everyone else, very late by lamplight. Bathing alone allowed him to safely hide his 5mm automatic plus his Darkglasses under his towel within easy reach. Mallory felt extremely naked without his weapons.

The first week at the brothel passed uneventfully and the promised week break celebration went as planned. Annette supplied two women, both reasonably pretty, but more importantly, well schooled in the art of appearing eager to have intimate relations with men whom a woman otherwise wouldn't have given a second glance.

Mallory feigned an illness and retreated to the bath. The two large moons, the dark red Lantern and the bright white Child, were out in the early evening and provided ample illumination, so Mallory didn't bother with a lamp and simply left the window unshuttered. After soaking for a little while, he decided to amuse himself by reading. He donned his Darkglasses and with a simply mental command, he summoned his place in the current book he was reading, *The Three Musketeers.*

He had only read about six pages when he heard a muttered curse outside. Mallory mentally ordered the Darkglasses to close the book.

Annette's voice just outside the bath barked, "Dammit. I told them to always close the damn shutters after dark."

Mallory vaguely remembered that instruction but had considered that to be only necessary when he wasn't actually in the bath. Of course, showing no lights, Annette obviously assumed that no one was. A moment later, the shutters were banged shut from the outside leaving Mallory in total darkness. This didn't bother Mallory since the Darkglasses gave him excellent vision, so Mallory remained quiet and intended to simply continue enjoying the bath.

The bathhouse actually had three separate baths each with its own lounge and entrance. A common storage and plumbing control room served as a junction of the bath's three wings. The one Mallory occupied was the servant's bath, while quality built was nothing special. The other two baths, however, sported gold fixtures, intricately carved marble, and elaborate fountains. Mallory heard several people enter the larger of the two baths. They kept their voices low. In the last week, Mallory had observed no one else visiting the baths this late, and so he was intrigued. Quietly, he slid out of the water, patted himself dry, pulled on a silk bathrobe, grabbed his 5mm automatic and silently stole into the storage room to listen at the door under which lantern light seeped.

Annette's voice tinged with concern said, "You can't keep doing this. You're going to get caught one day."

The reply was a barely audible, "Hmmph."

Annette continued, "I should be able to get these six into a respectable life in a couple of months. But I can't take any more until then."

A soft but distinctly male voice replied, "I know. I can ask nothing more."

Mallory heard clothes landing on the marble floor and the splash of water.

There was an audible gasp of aggravation, and Annette said, "They have Citadel Tattoos. Did you take them from an Immortals unit?"

The soft deep voice replied with a note of amusement, "We liberated them from an Immortals outpost, yes. The specific regiment was the Immortals of the Black Flame."

"And didn't the Immortals pursue?"

With a soft laugh, the deep voice said, "Well, we liberated the Immortals from their earthly burdens first. We didn't want them to suffer the terrible shame of having misplaced their slaves."

A long pause was followed by a sigh, and Annette spoke again, "I wish you wouldn't talk so glibly about killing. Even if they deserved much worse."

A contrite deep voice softly said, "Sorry. I forget sometimes that it pains you for me to talk that way, but you know that it is my manner of speaking. In some ways, my humor lessens the burden of conscience the killing of even such bastards as those brings."

Annette sighed heavily, "You are right. Ignore my admonition."

Then she said, "Why do you do it?"

"Why do you take them in?"

Annette laughed, "You know I cannot refuse you. Your mother rescued my mother and me in the same way. Why?"

"I don't know. I know it's pointless really. Not for those few that I rescue obviously, but in the grand play of things it is nothing. I just fantasize that our raids bring aggravation and distraction onto Puck."

"My dear Buck, I don't think he cares. If he even knows, he probably assumes you are nothing more than bold pirates who want the slaves for their market value - not for freedom."

For a long while, Mallory could hear only the sounds of bathing and quiet whispers. Mallory leaned closer to the door.

Annette said, "Why don't you have a bath yourself? You've got time. Even pirate captains need a decent bath every once and again."

Soft laughter, "I'm not a pirate. Well, mostly not. But a bath would be nice. It has actually been a week."

"Very good..."

Without warning, the storage door opened catching Mallory completely by surprise and clipping him on the side of the head. He staggered back with a deep shaking groan of pain. Then he snatched off his Darkglasses and stuffed them into a pocket. He kept the automatic hidden, but ready inside the other pocket.

Annette, who had just opened the door, stood agape. The sea captain stepped back. His gray-streaked black hair hung lankly on his square, unshaven, wind burnt face. He was not tall, but lean and sinewy. He wore a purple suede jacket over a gray blouse and gray leather pants. He shifted on his purple knee-high moccasins, stared at Mallory with cool green eyes, and held out a long, bejeweled dagger that only moments before had been in a fine leather scabbard hanging from his belt.

Mallory knew Annette recognized him so he didn't flee. Thinking quickly, feigning total innocence he grunted, "Sorry. I needed another towel and tried to find one in the dark..."

Annette stepped back still gaping and managed, "Come out here."

Mallory hesitated but stepped into the flickering lantern light. The six freed slaves made no move to cover themselves and stared out from the large bath in wonder.

"Are you all right?"

The question surprised Mallory somewhat as he tried to shake the fog out of his head, "I think so."

"Why didn't you say anything when I closed the shutters?"

Mallory frowned and shrugged, "I dunno. I guess I didn't mind."

Annette looked at the sea captain who only shrugged and continued to point the dagger in Mallory's direction. She looked back at Mallory and stared piercingly.

Instead of launching into a denial, Mallory stated flatly, "Yes. I heard some of what you said. And you have my admiration and respect."

Annette twitched an eyebrow, "That's nice. I'm glad. Are you sure you were just looking for another towel?"

Mallory frowned and rubbed his throbbing temple, "Really I was. But then I heard voices. I couldn't help but listen for a moment. I am human after all."

Annette chuckled. "Indeed. But the good Captain here values his secrecy. And so do I."

"And?"

"We don't want someone to go talking about any captain or freed slaves or anything."

Mallory appeared shocked, "Who would I tell? Besides, I have a very poor memory for such things."

Annette thought some more and then said, "Why are you here and not there?" She pointed in the direction of the boathouse where his workmates were enjoying themselves.

Mallory could see how that looked really suspicious.

"Er... I wasn't feeling well - and thought a nice hot bath would help."

Annette raised an eyebrow, obviously unconvinced that any man would consciously have foregone being entertained by one of her employees. She folded her arms across her chest, clearly dismayed. The sea captain remained placid but the dagger stayed ready.

Annette leaned back and said, "And did the bath help? Before the knock on the head, that is."

Mallory brightened slightly, "Well I think it did. But I wouldn't say I was fully recovered just yet. Even without the sudden headache."

Annette looked at the sea captain who nodded ever so slightly and lowered the dagger. Then she said, "Very well. I'm sorry about the headache. Don't let us keep you from your bath."

Mallory turned to go with a feeling Annette probably was not yet finished with him. He didn't think she or the pirate captain would try to murder him or anything. Anyone who would rescue slaves would not kill an apparent innocent. He would have to be on his guard, of course, in case they weren't just anyone. Then on a sudden inspiration, he turned back.

"Captain?"

Annette looked cross, but the Captain inclined his head in answer.

Mallory started to speak and nodded at the women still bathing all too seductively, and said, "Could I... er... speak to you and Annette privately?"

The Captain replied, "I don't see why not? Shall we?" He returned his dagger to its scabbard and pointed at the lounge behind him. Mallory went first followed by a seething Annette and the still placid Captain. Annette turned up the two lanterns that occupied a low marble table in the middle of the room.

Mallory whispered, "Let me be straight as I can. You have no love for Puck. Neither do I. And you undertake dangerous actions simply to annoy Puck and free a handful of his slaves. Perhaps you would be willing to undertake a somewhat lesser risk that may lead to his downfall?"

The Captain's face went from placid to that of mild surprise.

Annette gaped and in a not so quiet whisper said, "What? Are you saying you are not really a dockworker?"

Mallory looked annoyed, "Well, I wouldn't consider it my main profession, no."

Annette narrowed her eyes, "Then what is your main profession?"

The Captain glanced briefly at Annette but then his expression returned to placidity. Meanwhile, though, his hand moved back to the hilt of his dagger.

Mallory responded quickly with a truthful but very misleading answer, "I am most often paid as a soldier."

Annette sneered, "You don't even have so much as a knife. But you would have us believe you want to take on Puck? How could we think of you as anything but mad?"

Annette's reaction, while not entirely surprising, did give Mallory sudden pause. Her use of "we" seemed to imply she was in alliance with the Captain in other matters than just smuggling freed slaves. Mallory couldn't be sure, but he had the feeling that Annette was a spy. Was she just a trader in secrets or loyal to something more than money? Certainly, a high-class brothel provided a perfect cover for access to highly placed individuals. Clearly, people could arrive by boat, apparently with the expectation of privacy, if not secrecy, as evidenced by the other man in the room. The Captain was also evidence she consorted with pirates and smugglers.

It seemed terribly implausible that she worked for Puck. Could she be working for the rulers of Port Deliverance not knowing their true master? For that matter, could the pirate Captain be working for Puck - and only pretending to free slaves? Yet his need was great, so Mallory decided to play them both as suitable partners while trusting to firepower to rescue him from their treachery should they prove false or foolish.

"Failure is madness. Success is genius."

The Captain stifled a laugh but Annette only twitched slightly and most definitely failed to smile or laugh as Mallory had intended. Instead, coldly she asked, "Who is your master then?"

Mallory pressed his lips tightly together and said honestly, "Currently, I am my own master."

Then she said, "So... Would it be too much to ask why a mercenary would take on such a difficult task as bringing about the downfall of Puck all by his lonesome?"

Mallory was nonplussed, "I never said I was a mercenary. And

I'm not. Nor have I ever been."

Annette frowned in consternation, "Okay. Of all the myriad goals open to an unemployed soldier with no master who is not a mercenary, why choose the downfall of Puck?"

Mallory grinned in response, rubbed his pate and said, "I decided Puck needed to go just minutes into a long conversation with an exiled Immortal. I have been diligently working toward that end ever since. It seems that others, like the good Captain, here, share my goal. So I would hardly consider my desire madness. And hopefully I won't have to do it entirely by my lonesome."

Annette said, "It is one thing to want. It is another to fulfill. How exactly does working on the docks bring you closer to that goal?"

"Only indirectly. I need money to live on. And much can be learned by an attentive man on the docks. Especially since I need ship transport to effect the next stage of my plan."

Annette raised an eyebrow, "So, you have a plan?"

"A broad one. I need to do some reconnoitering first before I make final plans."

Then, the Captain broke in, "And so I'm guessing the action of lesser risk you want is simply to be dropped on the Zetu coast with some supplies? Alone?"

Mallory smiled, "Indeed. Although I would ask that you would pick me up later as well. We could work out a selection of projected dates, signals and places for my return covering a variety of possible scenarios."

The Captain nodded, "Naturally. And so as you said, it would only be for reconnoitering purposes?"

"Precisely. Originally, I had planned to hire a suitable ship - but I'm hoping that maybe you would do it for a promise of an undetermined reward should I manage to return."

"Consider the proposal under consideration."

"Thank you."

Annette goggled at the Captain and then said, "How exactly were you going to afford to hire a ship since you just admitted that you need to work to just pay your living expenses? I daresay it would require about 5 years of gross dockworker pay to hire a pirate willing to brave the Zetu coast. I also find it highly unlikely they would bother to return for you."

"Well, I was working on raising the necessary funds. Yes. And I was planning to escrow the lion's share of the fee pending my safe return. Yes. None of that is simple. Yes. Which is exactly why I've made this plea to the good Captain in the first place. Otherwise, I would have kept my silence."

Annette eyed Mallory with a withering gaze for some time. Mallory never flinched and simply maintained a warm smile.

She sighed heavily, "How can we be sure you're not trying to set the Captain and his crew up for an ambush?"

Mallory thoughtfully considered that for a few moments, "Well, it seems highly unlikely that this meeting is anything other than a total coincidence. It wasn't my idea for your brother to choose this place for our weekly lodging - and extending our stay to four weeks. I believe he said it was your idea. Was the good Captain's arrival here planned for today? And did anyone other than you know that plan that could tell me? And those are just the things known to you. If you knew my full circumstances, you would likely conclude that our meeting is an astounding coincidence. Although I think it may turn out to be a happy one if the good Captain does consent to help me."

Annette looked at the Captain.

The Captain shrugged, "He's right Annette. No one, not even you, knew I was coming until yesterday when I sent advance word. And I haven't been in the Bay of Lydaron for nearly six months. So it seems terribly unlikely this... er... man... was sent here to gain my trust to trick me into an ambush that wouldn't be all that likely of success. By the way, do you have a name?"

Annette said, "He said he name is Terry. Is that really your name?"

Mallory smiled, "No. It is Mallory Owens. In return may I have the good Captain's name?"

The Captain laughed softly, "That is no secret. I am Buck Jules. I am Captain of the *Inky Darkness*."

Mallory nodded and placed his right hand flat on his chest in the manner of formal greeting he had observed as customary in Port Deliverance. Jules did the same in return.

Captain Jules said, "Do you have a particular date in mind?"

Mallory took the question as a very receptive response to his proposal. So, he considered carefully. The locals used a strange monthless calendar. They did use seven-day weeks, working five or six days and then resting one or two depending on the profession. The local solar day was 25.17 Standard Hours and the local solar year 350 local days that worked out to be 367.06 Standard Days. Days were tracked based on the days since the last equinox or solstice.

Each season had 12 weeks comprising 84 days followed by a holiday festival of three to four days right before each equinox and solstice.

"I was hoping to be in and out before Autumn 60. I figure about 20 weeks would give me enough time to trek in country, scout thoroughly and return. Its Spring 21 right now, so any time before the Summer Solstice would allow that."

Captain Jules smiled, "We, that is, my ship, will depart for Rook by way of Port Styphlee in two days' time. The winds are favorable for diversion to the eastern shore of the Lydaron. Would a little ways north of the Wrything River suit your purposes?"

Mallory pursed his lips in thought. He had studied the geography of Puck's Empire in great detail using several local sources validated against the detailed photomaps he had taken before his fateful crash landing. He nodded, "It would. Quite nicely."

"Excellent. We berth tomorrow morning at the South Docks. You can meet us then. Do you mind helping load?"

Mallory grinned, "Not at all."

"Very good. We can work out a list of pickup places and dates for your return after we are underway. On the morrow, then?"

Mallory replied, "On the morrow."

He turned to leave looking at Annette for approval. Annette appeared not entirely pleased by the turn of events, but indicated Mallory should exit the room as he intended. Mallory returned to his bath and decided to spend another hour soaking.

In the morning before anyone woke, he silently gathered his things. Amid the stagnant smells of the cool morning air, he trooped past the North Docks. He crossed the impressive, wide stone bridge that connected the city with the islet known as the South Docks to find the *Inky Darkness* hoping that his newfound good fortune would last.

A giant windmill powered clock tower dominated the skyline of the South Docks. Standing 40 meters high, the tower was garishly painted in bright blue, with a yellow clock face, red hands and green windmill blades. Mallory had discovered that the local timekeeping was as odd as the calendar. The day was divided into twenty 40-minute hours. Each minute was comprised of 80 seconds. The local second was approximately 1.4 Standard Seconds. Therefore, each minute was really 113 Standard Seconds and the local hour 75 Standard Minutes. The really strange bit was that each day began at the local summer solstice sunrise - so local time varied not only by longitude but by latitude as well. From there, the hours were counted off starting with First Hour, Second Hour, and so forth up to 20 into the predawn with no distinction for before or after noon.

Mallory had surmised this made timekeeping for travelers, ships and military units a nightmare. But he had discovered he was wrong. Apparently ship navigators, troops and most travelers carried a table of moon and sun positions plus either a transit or sextant and reasonably accurate clocks. So, if anything, exact position could be found with a sun reading, a couple of moon readings and the tables to find position and even time of day to the minute with three moon readings when available.

Mallory's silent musings on time were interrupted by the appearance of the City Militia. While he watched the double file of well-disciplined soldiers bedecked in blue and gold march past, his thoughts drifted to that of the big merchant families and how they owed the continued possession of their fortunes and power to his good fortune. Mallory frowned at that disappointment, but then he smiled. He would be in need of a mission once the current undoing of Puck was completed. Mallory never lacked in confidence.

The Chasm

Entreska was summoned to see something Garth's team had uncovered. After descending into the trench, Entreska found Mallory leaning on a pick and not looking very happy.

She said, "Tired?"

He pointed to his left knee and chuckled, "Rookie mistake. I twisted my knee throwing too big a shovelful."

Entreska cringed, "Ouch. Are you going to be okay?"

"Probably. But I didn't want to miss the excitement. I've had worse."

Entreska laughed and looked to Garth, "You wanted me?"

Garth explained that their trench had dropped all the way to the ancient street level. Then they had located the curb and the building. He pointed at the wall where a bronze plaque read "DURAVON ARCHIVES - MAIN GALLERY." Garth shrugged and said finding the main steps was easy from there.

Entreska almost swooned from excitement or the oppressive heat - she wasn't sure which. She staggered back a little, caught her breath and said, "Wow. Great job Jack. Even if you did get a little carried away there."

Garth shrugged meekly, "Time is short."

The street level fell 17 meters below the surface. Garth's team had taken three days to reach the street. After reaching the street, they had removed three times as much material in just seven hours. Entreska was somewhat shocked at the speed they had excavated. Garth was her lead digger precisely because his teams took their time and did things properly. Of course, time was short.

Garth's team had carefully brushed away the remaining tuvana from the stairs and landing that led up to the three-meter high, one-meter wide, bronze double doors. The facade, stairs, doors and landing looked to be in perfect condition, preserved in the bone-dry tuvana. The doors imitated an intricate geometric pattern commonly used on raised panel wooden doors in ancient Jurasketu.

Entreska waited several seconds for something else and when nothing was forthcoming she said, "Will the doors open do you think?"

Garth grunted and said, "Well. As you can see, they open out. We cleaned around the edges and oiled the top and bottom pins. But they hardly budge. Mallory and I think the doors are barred from the inside. We checked the opening, and amazingly, it seems to be perfectly level and square. So we don't think the doors are jammed or anything. Normally, of course, we would have found the roof collapsed, so this would be of no matter, but incredibly, the roof survived intact. Mallory and I suppose the ash from the eruption was relatively cool and so the clay tiles and wooden beams supporting them remained in good working order. As I recall, Professor, you said the Gallery building has no other windows or doors."

Entreska sighed. Finding the building in near perfect condition was a dream come true, but now she would have to damage it to get inside.

Mallory nodded, "We could probably remove some roof tiles, lower someone down inside, open the doors, then repair the roof."

Garth and Entreska nodded in agreement.

Entreska said, "Good idea. But why don't we wait until tomorrow? It's pretty hot. Everyone looks beat and Mallory should rest his injury."

After a quiet lunch, Entreska took out Theron Avery's account and studied it once more for details that might be relevant now that they were almost inside the Archives. The map and other descriptions indicated that the Archives Complex covered nearly two hectares including lawn and courtyard. Reputedly, all the buildings in the Old City had been built to resist siege craft, so she hoped that some of the other buildings would be discovered relatively intact like the Gallery building. The Archives Complex contained more than the enormously valuable yet mundane government records. In his account, Theron Avery indicated that other valuable instruments and artifacts of Jurasketu civilization were stored in underground vaults below the Archives Complex.

Potentially, the vaults could have survived the disaster without too much damage. Theron had been an assistant working in the Library that was housed in the Archives. When the ash began to fall, he had been ordered by the Chief Librarian to flee the city through the underground tunnels that lead from the building. When Theron had asked why the Chief and the other archivists weren't coming, the Chief had replied that their duty lie in preserving the records which they would now seal into the vaults for recovery when the city would be restored. There would not be sufficient time for them to escape. Theron's duty was to let others know what happened and where and how the archive materials could be found.

Interestingly, Theron Avery's account had been lost until Entreska found it two years ago. While doing the dreaded inventory sifting, she had happened upon his account. Apparently, a donation of stuff including the manuscript had been given to the Academy by an unidentified citizen. The box had been set aside unrecorded and unregistered. There was quite a large collection of such stuff stored in various rooms of the Academy. She had been assigned the task of sorting and cataloging these materials upon receiving her position at the Academy. Usually, she conned two or three students into doing most of the work. Anything they couldn't easily identify, she examined herself. Avery's manuscript and maps were such items. After checking against some other descriptive materials, she became convinced that Avery's story was not a fabrication.

Entreska ate dinner alone and continued to study until wakefulness left her to her dreams. In the twenty days of dreams since she had told Jones about the dream, the room had gained a door and a short unremarkable hallway.

She stood in the street... The purple sky roiled... Thunder... Spikes of lightning careened this and that way... The great bronze doors swung closed with a boom... a peal of thunder rumbled and punctuated the moment... She walked around the right corner of the building... An opening near the center... She approached... a short hallway... dark... a dead end... the stone suddenly rolled away... longer hallway... musty, damp... something skittered... something else crunched underfoot... iron door... opens easily... tunnel carved from the rock... dark... lantern in cubby hole... light... down the tunnel... back... around... left... fork... right... curving left... warm dry breeze... It should be cold... left... left... right... narrow... wider... tile floor... tile walls... color and pattern... a bronze door... intricate geometric design... open the door... the round hall...

The next morning, Entreska had Garth's team work around the right hand corner from the Main Entrance. She stayed to watch and occasionally help and they were rewarded after about 10 hours of digging.

Garth gave a bellow, "Well. How about that? There is an opening. And a hallway. Lantern!"

Garth examined the opening very carefully while waiting for the lantern. "I'll wager this was some kind of escape hole. Clever... Look at this."

Entreska stepped closer and she could see that a large bronze plate covered a section of recessed floor. The wall on the left side of the plate was recessed two meters. This oddity was quickly explained by an even deeper recess on the right side that held a huge, upright wheel of stone that had obviously been blocking the hallway off from the street.

Garth grunted, "The recessed floor slopes to the right. Probably had an easily removable wedge holding the stone wheel in place. Remove the wedge and the wheel rolls to the side allowing escape."

Entreska nodded in agreement.

Mallory brought Garth a lantern, lighting it first.

Garth edged forward cautiously into the hallway. "An iron door! Um... Oh... No lock... A tunnel!"

Mallory said, "Shall we follow?"

"Naturally."

Mallory went into the tunnel. Entreska came along behind with three more workers carrying water, lanterns and equipment. They followed the tunnel for at least an hour through numerous twists and turns. Garth kept up his running commentary. She would have said it was exactly like her dream, but, of course, it wasn't. Several times Garth would stop and shush them to silence. He would listen for several long seconds. Entreska listened too, but she had no idea for what she was listening.

Mallory muttered, "Damn humidity. Outside too dry. Inside too wet."

The mist hung thick in the tunnel. Wetness from the walls and air compelled by gravity congregated on the tunnel floor making it very slick. All six of them had suffered at least one slip and several bruises. If the temperature had been only slightly higher, the tunnel would have made an excellent wet sauna.

Garth groaned and sighed, "I'm certain I can hear rushing water."

Alarmed, Entreska blurted, "Are we in danger?"

Garth shook his head, "No. But this could mean that our progress may be impeded by flooding or active water. It may be difficult to reach your round room."

Entreska had told them that Avery's account indicated that the round room could be found at the end of this tunnel. It did not. Her father believed in giving the impression that he had visions that guided his decisions. She normally did not. He said that soldiers liked to believe that their commander could see things they couldn't. Her father said he could, but it was based upon intuition that he defined as the combined knowledge, logic, study and experience expressed through the Web of Thought.

They had traveled 1500 paces through the tunnel before resting. Entreska congratulated herself on instructing one of the workers to count his paces. Minor details sometimes make the difference between good and bad luck. They each snacked on a small portion of dried meat and bread taken from a gargantuan sandwich Garth had brought with him and consented to share (not without some major badgering). Normally quite good despite desert grit, the mist made the bread soggy and the slight sulfur smell spoiled the flavor of the meat. The sound of rushing water provided a constant background din.

Soon thereafter, they came to the source of din. Ten paces of straight tunnel led to a chasm roaring with the underground water. The chasm ran perpendicular to the tunnel and extended fifty meters or more to the right and left of the tunnel. Although it was hard to say for certain in the dim light through the mist, the arched cave roof reached fifteen or twenty meters above their heads. The water made a grand roaring entrance high on the left end of the chasm and then fell at least fifty meters to the bottom. Steam hid the bottom and ultimate exit to the right from view. The chasm was over twenty meters wide. The continuation of the tunnel could barely be seen across the misty chamber. They held their lanterns high attempting to light the whole extent of the chasm.

They just stared in awe and wonder for a minute before settling into a gloom of disappointment.

Entreska sighed, "Damn."

Mallory muttered, "Damn indeed."

Jack Garth nodded and looked at Entreska, "What now?"

Entreska shrugged, "We retreat and devise a plan to cross the chasm."

Entreska fumed almost all day. The chasm was preventing resolution of her destiny or at least her dreams anyway. The military engineers had ruled out bridging or scaling the chasm. Jack Garth suggested filling the chasm with rocks. He estimated that it would only take three weeks but with a set of caveats deeper than the Maw of Hell.

She didn't have three weeks. They had already stayed two weeks longer than planned. Colonel Jones had given her a strict ten-day deadline for wrapping things up - soon the Raffin Winter storms would begin. Ironically, she had achieved her original goal almost beyond expectations. She had found the Archives. She had proved Avery's account and map genuine. She would easily be able to raise support and funding for a repeat expedition next summer with more specialists and likely several of her more esteemed colleagues. In many ways, it was a triumph of her very young career. She should be having a celebration. Instead, she fumed.

A little before dinner, Mallory turned up with Jack Garth at his elbow.

"May I speak with you?"

Entreska shrugged, "Of course. Please sit."

"I have an idea for bridging the chasm."

Entreska sneered, "So you know more about bridging than the renowned engineers of the Black Scorpions?"

Mallory rubbed the top of his forehead and seemed to carefully consider his reply, "Well. I know it seems a little implausible. In my own lands, I'm not considered an expert by any means, but I do know how to build a bridge that can span the chasm. And we can build it in a single day."

Entreska stared trying to decide if Mallory was joking. He was clearly unusual. Most everything about him seemed inconsistent with her expectations. That he would claim and possibly actually know how to build such an amazing bridge seemed perfectly consistent with that. She looked to Jack Garth who simply smiled in return.

Finally, she said sardonically, "Really?"

Mallory smiled, "Yes. Really. We can build a lightweight truss frame bridge from the materials at hand. And come to think of it, we can run guy ropes through eyebolts anchored high into the tunnel walls."

Entreska stared at Mallory, "What exactly is a 'trust frame' bridge?"

"Truss. Truss frame. Um... It's a very common technique where I come from. I've already done the calculations and worked up a precise design and even a scale model made from paper. It should bear the weight of many men and span 25 meters, which should be more than sufficient. Jack and I revisited the chasm this afternoon and carefully estimated the distance at 18 to 20 meters. We can cut all the materials up here. Probably take a couple hours at the most with a full team of carpenters. At the same time, another group could install the eyebolts for the guy ropes. Then we take the cut lumber down to the tunnel and assemble. Done."

Dead silence.

Mallory raised a finger and retreated from the tent to return a few minutes later bearing the aforementioned drawing and a scale model. Mallory then launched into an explanation of how the bridge worked by compression and tension of the framing members. Entreska was well schooled in mathematics, physics and building techniques and so was completely fascinated by Mallory's explanations.

Eventually, filled with wonder Entreska smiled and said, "Will this really work?"

Mallory smiled back, "Certainly. We've used it for centuries in both wood and steel."

Entreska blinked and turned to Garth who had simply nodded approvingly for the entirety of the conversation, "Jack? What do you think?"

Garth shrugged, "What have we got to lose? He seems to know what he's talking about."

Garth was right. What did she have to lose? She waved a hand, "My engineers and workers are at your command, Engineer Owens."

Mallory nodded with a slight hint of trepidation, "Hopefully, I will fairly earn the title."

Mallory and Garth turned and left.

Entreska informed Jones early the next morning.

Entreska stated flatly, "Owens has designed a special bridge to cross the chasm. He said it will only take a day to build. I gave him permission to proceed."

Jones hesitated, looked away and then stared sidelong at Entreska until she became uncomfortable.

Finally, she asked, "Yes?"

Jones spoke quietly, "If, and I say this with some skepticism, Owens succeeds in this bridge. I would have to mark him an extraordinary talent despite or maybe because of his rather odd behaviors – in that such genius often arrives with strange absurdities."

Entreska laughed. "Often enough to be noticeable."

Jones continued, "I might also suggest that we do whatever is necessary to make sure he gets and stays on our side."

"Yes. I agree."

She had a momentary thought that Uncle Val was intimating something suggestive, but she ignored it. Then, they went to observe Mallory and the work being performed in a row of five large shade tents.

In the first and second tents, ten burly men wielding finish saws worked furiously cutting 8cm thick planks into lengths of 1 to 2 meters with angles on both ends and some longer planks with simple square ends. Twenty students labored to bring lumber to the carpenters, hold the lumber in place, and collect the cut pieces to bring them to Mallory in the third tent for inspection. Rejects were discarded or returned for recutting. Mallory labeled each acceptable piece with ink, marked off the piece from his cutting list and added it to the neatly stacked pile.

Entreska did not see Garth. So she shouted over the sawing, "Mallory. Where is Jack?"

He smiled and pointed towards the Duravon Archives site. Then he shouted back, "He's down at the chasm supervising the eyebolt placement."

Entreska nodded. She and Jones moved to the fourth tent and watched four, shirtless, sweat and ash streaked Black Scorpion blacksmiths busily fashion thin copper plates 8cm wide and 20cm long. The stack of finished plates numbered over a hundred. She was told the plans called for 400 plates.

In the fifth tent, four students, while constantly wiping sweat away, took turns carefully stirring horrible-smelling concoctions that gurgled away in two huge cauldrons. Entreska edged closer willing herself not to vomit from the odor. One cauldron contained a black tarry substance. The other contained a milky white tarry substance.

Entreska, with eyes watering, sniffed and asked, "What is this stuff?"

All four students shrugged and said in unison, "A two-part polymer epoxy."

"What?"

One student, wiping the sweat from her face, said, "Two-part polymer epoxy. It's a special glue. After it cools, you mix a bit of each together and then you have a couple minutes before it sets up. Apparently."

Jones blurted out, "What for?"

"To securely fasten the gang plates to the truss members. Or so Engineer Owens said."

Pretending comprehension, Entreska and Jones nodded, looked at each other and quickly returned to Engineer Owens.

Entreska shouted over the constant din of the saws, "How is it going?"

Mallory shrugged, put down his checklist, secured it with a rock and motioned for them to move away from the tents. Entreska and Jones followed him away from the din of sawing wood and hammering metal where normal voices could be used.

Mallory nodded in the direction of the work, "Pretty good, the metalwork is taking longer than I thought, though. No knock on the blacksmiths mind you - who seem to be really competent - not that I would really know. I just totally underestimated the work involved in making what I needed. Plus, the heat is a real killer. They promised to work this evening and get all the plates made. So we can still start assembly tomorrow. The cycles of sun and moons make no difference in the tunnels. I did have a bit of a scare when I realized we didn't have the right type of nails to secure the gang plates. But then I remembered I had some epoxy yeast..."

Mallory suddenly trailed off and placed his hand to his jaw.

Entreska said, "What's the matter?"

Mallory shrugged. "Nothing. As I was saying, I remembered that I knew how to cook up some epoxy."

Jones gruffed, "Didn't you just say epoxy yeast?"

Entreska nodded, "Yes. You said epoxy yeast. What did you mean by that? How does this epoxy stuff work anyway?"

Mallory frowned and studied both Jones and Entreska for a moment. Then he smiled and said, "It's a two part polymer epoxy. It's really cool stuff. One gel is called the resin. The other the hardener. On their own, they are just smelly, slightly caustic gels. And as long as they are kept separate, the gels will last for months or years in storage. But mix them together, in just a couple of minutes the hardener turns the resin into a rock hard substance that permanently bonds a wide variety of materials together. You can do metal to metal. Wood to wood. Metal to wood. Cloth to wood. Cloth to metal. Damn near anything. It's really amazing stuff..."

Mallory kept describing the incredible uses and advantages of two part polymer epoxies for at least ten minutes. Finally, Jones and

Entreska excused themselves and returned to the Command Tent to discuss the logistics of closing down the encampment and returning to Jurasketu. Only much later would Entreska realize that Mallory had avoided explaining what he meant by epoxy yeast. And that explanation would prove far more interesting that she could have ever imagined.

Just after lunch as the expedition took its afternoon rest to hide from the heat, Mallory stopped by the Command Tent where Entreska was still discussing logistics with Jones. He said he was on his way to check on Garth and the eyebolts, but that everything was on schedule. They should be able to get everything ready for assembly tomorrow. Entreska thanked him and hoped this crazy bridge would really work and she would have an answer to her dreams.

Entreska slept heavily through the sapping heat of the Raffin afternoon. She awoke to an unusually brisk wind that was dusting the camp with a pinch of the Raffin plateau. Within the hour, the sun dragged itself across the horizon smearing the sky with orange and brown. She ate dinner quietly. Then she dispatched a sentry to inform Colonel Jones she was going to observe the bridge building at the chasm.

Entreska could hear the clatter of wood and metal on stone from a considerable distance as she approached the straight section of tunnel adjacent to the chasm. She extinguished her oil lamp and left it with a row of other unlit lamps. The air was slightly smoky, but breathable and brightly lit by a dozen lamps like the one she had brought. About 20 students, six Black Scorpions, Garth and Mallory labored to assemble the bridge under extremely crowded conditions.

A full five meters of bridge was already assembled but no more bridge members could be added in the tunnel. The bridge resembled a huge sled with one-meter tall skids and a bed spanning two thirds of a meter. While Entreska watched, Mallory attached two ropes to the nose of the bridge. The ropes ran up to two sets of pulleys hung from the eyebolts attached to the walls near the tunnel mouth. The other ends of the ropes were being held by two groups of four students each standing further back in the tunnel behind Entreska. Mallory and Garth then retreated to the rear of the partially completed bridge and instructed the students to hold the ropes taut. Mallory and Garth pushed against the bridge and slowly it edged into the chasm until only one meter remained in the tunnel.

Mallory reached up, locked the lower pulleys and then signaled to the students to relax. The students, whom Entreska recognized as being amongst the strongest in the expedition, relaxed but did not let go of the ropes. Then the Scorpions and Garth started assembling more bridge under Mallory's direction. The two-part polymer epoxy was mixed up and applied to the metal gang plates which were placed on either side of the truss joints. In seconds, the epoxy gripped and after a minute Mallory would nod and the next set of truss members were brought forward and joined to the existing ones. In another ninety minutes, they carefully assembled the full 25 meters of bridge by repeating the same process while increasing the number of students on the rope with each four-meter addition. One final push and the chasm would be spanned.

Entreska suddenly felt a presence beside her and started when she saw that it wasn't a student. A moment later, she recognized Colonel Jones who had assumed his command survey pose, fully erect with hands clasped behind his back.

"Uncle Val. Decided to see for yourself?"

He merely nodded.

Entreska thought that Mallory was breathing a bit rapidly, which she surmised was due to nervousness. Then Mallory asked her to stand near the front and watch the nose of the bridge to let them know where it was in relation to the continuation of the tunnel on the other side of the chasm. Mallory, Garth and all six Scorpions began slowly pushing the bridge further out.

Closer... Closer...

Clunk.

Mallory bellowed, his voice barely audible over the crashing roar of the chasm, "Damn. What's happened?"

Entreska shouted back, "It's just a skosh too low."

Garth and Mallory started screaming at each other until Mallory reached up and locked the ropes down. The ropes creaked under the strain.

Mallory looked around nervously, "Damn. The torque moment is scaring me. Garth! Go back and tell the students on my signal to lean back on the ropes."

Garth nodded and scooted back down the tunnel to the students who were edging this way and that trying to see what was going on.

Mallory released the locks again and waved back to Garth and the students who leaned back as directed. The nose of the bridge eased upward ever so slightly.

Entreska turned back, nodded and shouted, "It's clear!"

Mallory and the Scorpions immediately pushed a full meter of bridge into the other tunnel nearly downing the students holding the ropes. About two meters remained in the tunnel on their side. Elated, Entreska watched as Mallory raised his arms in triumph and shouted with glee. Garth made a movement that the students interpreted as a command to let go and they did. The bridge sighed as it settled into position, the ropes slack. Everyone cheered.

Garth and Colonel Jones joined Mallory and Entreska as they peered across the bridge. Garth said, "So... who goes first?"

Jones said firmly, "Mallory designed it. I believe the honor is his."

Mallory frowned and said, "So failure kills the designer. Hard to argue against that."

Entreska laughed nervously, "Are you afraid?"

Mallory smirked, "Nah. But I will take precautions."

Mallory put on a climbing belt and attached a rope, carefully tying a type of knot Entreska had never seen. He smiled at her and nodded to Garth. Garth helped Mallory run the rope through the pulley system. He strapped an unlighted oil lamp to his waist. With Garth belaying the rope, Mallory pranced out onto the bridge and bounded across. The bridge didn't even creak. On the other side, he raised his arms in victory and danced about.

Mallory lit the lamp and returned across the bridge stooping to inspect the members. After a few minutes he finished, all smiles.

"Looks good. The epoxy appears unaffected by the heat and steam so far..."

"So far?"

"Well. It's supposed to impervious to high temperatures and immersion - but who knows - maybe we made a bad batch or something. Anyway, shall we cross?"

Entreska hated remarks like that. They made her worry that failure is imminent, but simultaneously leaving her with the feeling that her worry might be needless. She hated that especially, needless worry.

Mallory and Garth looked expectantly at her...

Entreska hesitated to answer. She could soon be facing her dreams. She hoped that her sanity would survive.

"Across. Yes."

Garth went first. Mallory insisted, without dissent from anyone, that only one person should be on the bridge at one time. Entreska followed Garth across, then Mallory, and then Jones. All of them brought lamps across. They admired the chasm for a while. Light from two sides gave a different cast to the falling water.

Entreska let Garth lead the way. He gave a running description. After only a few meters, the tunnel became more like a carefully constructed stone hallway with smooth perpendicular walls and ceiling that was wet and slimy from the mist. The stone walls yielded to dark green tile forty or fifty meters further on.

The distinctive odor of alkaline saturated steam was replaced by a clear, crisp smell. Entreska thought that very strange.

Garth announced with some surprise, "A bronze door!"

Entreska trembled in fear and anticipation. She moved forward holding her lamp high and behind her left ear. She asked Garth, Jones and Mallory to move back - their lights blocked her view. They obliged. It was the exact bronze door from her dream. Taking a deep breath, she reached for the handle and pushed. The door swung open easily.

Entreska stepped into the circular hall and walked into her dream...

Entreska frowned. The dreamlike light provided by the lamps failed to match the bright sunlight of the dream. Disappointed, she surveyed the hall carefully looking for details from the dream. Alone, the map of the Raffin Plateau on tile floor represented a priceless find. The scenes in the murals were unmistakable. Many of the details exceeded her memory and expectations. Her fear ebbed in the marvel of the hall.

But something was missing...

The pedestal!

Virtually on cue, Jones exclaimed, "There's no pedestal and box."

Entreska advanced to the center of the hall and spun about. She put the lamp on the floor and stared at the ceiling hole that wasn't there. No box. No gem. No hole.

She heard Jones swear softly. He alone besides her knew that her dreams somehow represented reality, except not exactly it seemed. Then she heard a soft and distinctly female voice. Entreska froze.

"I said. Can you understand me?"

Entreska said nothing.

"Can you understand?"

She looked back over her shoulder. Mallory, Jones and Garth all stood somewhat open mouthed in wonder and pointing at the tile map and murals. They appeared to hear nothing.

Sorcery?

"Something like that. You do understand."

Garth, Jones and Mallory remained oblivious.

Entreska started to speak.

The kindly, voice said, "No. Don't speak out loud. Your friends might think you're mad."

Entreska thought/said/imagined, *"They probably think that already."* And then on sudden inspiration, *"Are you the source of the dream?"*

"Yes and no."

"What does that mean?"

Entreska searched around the hall in a desperate hope that she might find the source of the voice that plagued her head. *Voices. Crazy people hear voices. Voices that tell them to do terrible things.*

"We are responsible for the dream. You are not crazy, and we would never tell you to do anything terrible."

"Can you understand my every thought?"

"No. Only strongly held and focused thoughts. We can also sense emotion. We sense fear in you. Please do not be afraid. There are many reasons and things to fear. But we only want to help."

"We?"

"There are eleven of us."

"Who are you?"

"My name is Jasmine Moonstalker. I am the Voice of the High Wizard Council. The others are the last surviving members of the High Wizard Council."

The Voice of the High Wizard Council?

Entreska took long deep breath. She had to be hallucinating.

"You are not."

Entreska thought, *"I think that's difficult to prove. Any proof you offer can be dismissed as further hallucination."*

Entreska imagined she felt an ethereal frown of dismay.

Mallory asked, "Are you okay?"

Entreska snapped around finding that Mallory had stepped close to her. "What...? Yeah. Sure."

Mallory frowned. Jones stepped forward to join Mallory. Mallory glanced at Jones and said, "What pedestal and box was the Colonel talking about?"

Entreska glanced helplessly at Jones, and to buy time, she feigned confusion, "What?"

Mallory briefly smiled, changed back to a concerned look and said, "Pedestal and box. The Colonel implied you were expecting a pedestal and box."

An excellent lie arrived to the front of Entreska's head and she said, "It was in Theron Avery's notes. There was a box that contained some unspecified priceless artifact. It was supposed to be in this room which otherwise matches his description."

Jones nodded in agreement.

Mallory shrugged, "Disappointing. Could they be hidden somehow?"

Everyone shrugged in response.

Mallory began examining the murals. Garth knelt and examined the tile floor. Jones peered up at the ceiling.

"If you made the dream, where is the pedestal and box?"

There was no answer, but moments later, a blinding light filled the room. Then nearby, Entreska heard the sound of grinding stone. She stepped back. Darkness replaced the light. Some seconds passed before her eyes could readjust to the poor lamp light.

In the center of the room, there now stood the small stone pedestal and hardwood box from the dream.

The Voice said, "There. Now are you happy?"

"Yes and no."

She felt an ethereal smile.

Entreska smiled, *"Okay. You win. Any hallucination this real might as well be taken for reality."*

"Belief does not change facts."

"Other way around."

The Voice did not reply.

"Where are you exactly then?"

"The boundaries of our existence are unlimited yet firmly fixed."

Entreska sighed. Not only was she plagued by dreams and voices in her head, but also the voices uttered evasive nonsense. It was like having an incomprehensible mystic trapped inside one's head.

Mallory, Garth and Jones crowded up beside Entreska.

Jones pointed and said with a hint of trepidation, "Are you going to open it?"

Entreska looked around at the incredulous faces of Mallory and Garth. She stepped back. "I don't know."

"What is the significance of the jewel in the box?"

"It is our boundary that is firmly fixed. Open the box. And behold

Evermore."

Entreska hesitated no longer. The box had no lock or clasp. Just a simple hinged lid. She stepped forward and carefully swung the lid up. She drew forth the translucent blue gem and held it out before her. The gem reflected muddy lamp light. While dreamlike, it was nothing like the dream.

Mallory exclaimed, "Wow."

Jones and Garth moved closer with obvious interest.

"Evermore is a gem?"

"It manifests that way, yes."

Manifests? Entreska relaxed, hunched over a little and peered deeply into the gem. Jones, Mallory and Garth did the same to the point of making her nervous. She still did not understand the purpose of the dream or the importance of the gem.

Garth said, "Professor. Is it too late to change the purpose of this expedition from learning to prospecting?"

Entreska stared aghast at him for a moment and then burst out laughing realizing he was just joking. Mallory and Jones continued to stare in amazement at the gem apparently missing or ignoring the joke.

"It is more valuable than it appears."

"More than priceless?"

An ethereal chuckle shuddered around the edges of her mind.

"Indeed. Even more than that. To us, it is our very existence."

Entreska said aloud, "What?"

Mallory said, "We didn't say anything. Are you hearing things?"

"Why do you say that?"

Mallory said carefully, "Normally, when someone says 'What?', they are implying they didn't understand something someone said."

Entreska said, "Yes. You are right."

"Are you hearing things?"

She said, "No."

"Then what?"

"I was just thinking aloud. I often argue with myself to force clarity in my thinking. Sometimes thoughts leak out."

Mallory considered this for a long moment and then jogged his head in apparent understanding. Then Garth and Mallory moved over to examine the box and pedestal. Jones mostly looked up at the ceiling.

"So how long have you been the Voice of the High Wizard Council

anyway?"

"I have been the Voice ever since the Transformation nearly two-thousand four-hundred seventeen years ago."

"The Transformation?"

"Yes. We were all once flesh and blood."

Entreska waited for more explanation, but she was disappointed as none seemed to be forthcoming.

"What are you now then? Spirits?"

A distinct feeling of indecision roiled through Entreska's mind. She waited patiently though for a response to her question.

"We are not exactly spirits. Circumstances created in the gem by our efforts allow us to exist here. A proper response requires a fairly elaborate explanation. I'm afraid your friends would become impatient and your provisions scarce should I attempt to explain now."

Entreska lowered the gem and sat on the floor. Garth and Mallory ignored her and examined the pedestal closely. Their movements and comments indicated they were trying to understand the pedestal's mechanical operation. Jones noted that she had sat down, but made no comment and continued to observe the room in obvious apprehension.

"Why the dream? What do you want?"

"We have been trapped ever since the Great Burning Blast. We wanted out."

"Out of the gem?"

"No. That we cannot do. Out of this place, this room. To where we could do some good."

"But why me?"

"You were not the target. We were not even aware that you were affected until we saw the dream in your mind when you entered the hallway outside the room."

Entreska snarled. She couldn't believe this. Her sleep and sanity had been compromised by errant magically induced dreams? Had Colonel Jones somehow guessed right that she was a victim of sorcery? It was either that or she had gone crazy. She put her head in her hands.

"We told you. You are not crazy."

"If I wasn't the target, then who was?"

"We cannot say."

"Why not?"

"It's rather complicated. But essentially we don't know."

"What if I said I'm not sure I can trust you? Ignoring the possibility that I'm simply hallucinating and so I should not be trusted instead."

A hint of amusement suffused her mind.

"I would say you are paranoid and wise. Our intentions are worthy and ethics strong. But those are just our statements. You have no actions by which to judge us. We understand. Irony undoes us. We kept our existence a closely guarded secret known only to a select few trusted individuals in the Archives. We trusted almost no one. We can hardly complain should you choose not to trust us. But consider where and what you have found."

"Let us suppose I bring you to the surface, then what?"

"That is more complicated. We can provide powerful assistance to Jurasketu. We prefer that our existence remain hidden to but a necessary few."

"Well, I am well-connected to the Jurasketu Army."

"How so?"

"My father is the Grand Marshal of the Army. And my oldest brother Rolf is the High Chairman of the Academy - the Army War College."

"Really? Hmm.... Our effectiveness in military contexts is actually fairly limited. We are much more valuable in political and diplomatic situations."

Entreska pretended to study the gem closely and frowned.

"I have connections there as well."

"Excellent. The storms approach soon. I suggest you return to the coast. I can explain things on the way."

Entreska was hesitant. She was missing something.

"What about the dreams?"

"They will stop. I apologize for any discomfort they may have caused."

Entreska snorted in disgust. Discomfort indeed.

She noticed that Mallory and Jones were staring at her with concern. She glanced around innocently and then stated firmly, "Let's go. I want to examine the gem in the comfort of my tent. And... This must be kept completely secret. The existence of the gem must remain unknown until I say otherwise."

Jones stared hard at her. Mallory cocked his head and smiled very faintly. Garth seemed very disappointed.

Jones said, "Very well. Seems wise. Who knows? We may very well have a spy or two in our camp. With two thousand folks, it is hard to tell for certain. I will give the order to leave tomorrow."

Entreska nodded ignoring the potential swipe at Mallory being a spy. She was exhausted. She reached out and gripped the back of Mallory's hand. "Thank you, Bridge Builder Owens. Your bridge is a marvel - in some ways more than this room. Do you still wish to accompany us to Jurasketu proper and Endurance?"

Mallory smiled broadly, "Of course. I have no other plans at this point. I have never been there. Will you show me around?"

She replied most innocently, "Certainly."

Entreska concealed the gem in her tool bag she wore for expeditions that usually contained a brush, a small notebook, a miniature pick and a gouge. They exited the room disappointing both Mallory and Garth who wanted to look around some more. Entreska overruled them saying they looked exhausted and needed some rest. After a moment's consideration, they had nodded agreement on both points and the four of them trudged back to the chasm and across the bridge.

Entreska thanked the students and Scorpions waiting anxiously in the hallway and told them they had discovered a room of great beauty, historical value and even mysteries. Unfortunately, she added, the storms drew near and so the mysteries and room would have to wait until next year. The students cheered, but Entreska wondered whether that was because the expedition was a success or just that they were going home. Probably both she decided. She gave a similar speech to the crowd of students and Scorpions who awaited them in bright moonlight at the tunnel entrance. Their response was similar.

The four of them made their way back to the Command Tent where Jones without explanation ordered the lieutenant on duty to double the guard at Entreska's tent. Jones also instructed the lieutenant to summon Major Vest and the other senior officers to discuss last minute military matters related to the departure of the expedition tomorrow. Garth and Mallory quickly departed showing obvious signs of fatigue.

Jones shooed Entreska on to her tent and some sleep when she tried to show interest in the staff meeting. Six Scorpions escorted her back to her tent where they remained thereby satisfying the order to double her guard. Inside her tent, elated, she took the gem from her tool bag and wrapped it in a scarf. Then she collapsed onto her sleeping blanket, the wrapped gem tucked to her bosom. She slept fast and soundly. Entreska awoke the next morning - late. She was sweating profusely from the early afternoon heat. She sat up and brushed the sweat away - but otherwise felt very refreshed. The dreams had stopped. She sighed with relief. She pulled back a corner of the scarf to reveal the gem or Evermore as the Voice had called it. She sighed again, this time with apprehension. What in the Great Burning Blast was this thing really?

Entreska spoke softly, "Why should I trust you again?"

Echoes of a softly building chuckle filled her head. "You probably shouldn't. Know this. We trust you. We can see into your thoughts. You should take that as a compliment. We do not give our trust lightly. We certainly wouldn't have spoken to you or revealed the gem had we not."

"You were desperate to escape your entombment. You said so yourself."

"Ah. But once the way was opened. Someone else would or could be made to come to the room. We may have been desperate - but we are ancient and very patient. Another would have come. Eventually."

Entreska nodded to herself in casual agreement.

"Can you see into anyone's mind? And communicate like with me?"

"No. You are exceptional. In most humans, we can only perceive primitive emotions. We can sometimes read partial thoughts from one in ten minds. We can read complete thoughts from only one in a hundred minds. Full conversational exchange, like with you now, is apparently possible with only one in twenty-thousand. The strength of the wizard can slightly affect these ratios, but not significantly. Each mind also has its own distinctive cast, so if we've touched a mind before, we can find it again, even at great distances."

"So is my mind weak or strong?"

"An interesting question. Both. You are more susceptible to influence and attack. What that really means is that you are highly attuned to wizardry. In times past, you would have been a likely selection for training in the science of wizardry. The fact that you picked up our summoning in your dreams shows your potential."

Instead of being pleased with that statement, Entreska thought it only gave credence to her hallucination theory.

"Can you see into the mind of Mallory or Colonel Jones?"

"We can only sense their emotions. We sense worry in both."

"Too bad. It would be nice to know Mallory's true character."

"I suggest you rely on yourself for that."

Entreska frowned.

A feeling of puzzlement spread across her mind.

The Voice asked tentatively, "How many troops does the Jurasketu Army have on the High Raffin?"

Although the exact locations were somewhat indeterminate, it was no secret that elements of the Black Scorpions and Dawn Spiders patrolled the upper and lower ends of the Maw of Hell respectively. The High Raffin and White Mountains were strongly held by several regiments of regular and reserve Mountaineers.

Entreska chuckled at the impossibility of concealing anything from the Voice. How could she lie to the Voice? The truth would always form in her mind - no matter what lie she would nominally wish to tell. And there it was - no more than three thousand. A frown washed across her mind and ended in pursed lips.

"Why do ask?"

A feeling of grave hesitation engulfed her.

"So not forty thousand?"

"What? Forty thousand. No."

"Uh-oh."

"Uh-oh?"

"Uh-oh. Rhenda has detected a large army of about forty thousand that lies just to the northeast of the Maw of Hell. Some are moving directly this way. The rest towards the Lower Raffin."

Entreska blurted out loud, "Who? How?"

"Rhenda is a member of the High Wizard Council and resident with me in Evermore. We take turns doing long range reconnaissance, it is her turn."

At that moment, a deep male voice outside her tent said, "Professor Nevercare? Colonel Jones wants to see you right away. There is a problem."

Entreska bellowed, "Damn." Then she added, "I'll be right out."

She and her escort found Jones outside his Command Tent staring west. He stood, feet apart, hands on hips and staring at the horizon.

Entreska walked nervously to his side. He briefly glanced in her direction. Entreska croaked, "What is the problem?"

"Puck's Army comes."

"What? How many? What quality?"

Jones turned to answer but stopped with an open mouth as he saw Garth and Mallory approaching. Then he scowled and nodded to a group of soldiers standing near the Command Tent. They instantly brandished their long fighting knives and rushed over to Mallory and Garth who immediately threw up their hands in surprise.

"Arrest Owens. Leave Garth be."

Entreska started in surprise, "What? Why?"

Jones glanced at Entreska, "Suspicion of spying."

Suddenly, a gust of wind showered them with dust.

Spitting dust and anger Garth pushed past the soldiers and strode up to Jones. Once there, Garth bellowed indignantly, "Spying? Have you gone mad? He's done nothing except dig trenches and build bridges that your boys couldn't hope to manage!"

Jones snarled, "Puck's Army comes."

Garth's expression went from anger to horror. "No!"

"Yes. At least five banners of Cumar and six regiments of Immortals headed this way. No more than three days march to the west."

Garth whispered, "Great Burning Blast."

Jones snorted.

Entreska sank to her knees...

Gurf Nadon

Twelve large desert wagons, their detail hidden by a coat of gray desert dust, were cluttered in a jagged line with their draft animals no where to be seen. Human corpses also encrusted with dust could have been mistaken for the droppings of some enormous desert beast. Glenmorgan breathed heavily and wondered grimly who they had been.

Glen was there because his favorite Scout Captain and only slightly coincidentally his youngest son, Zemfrekis, had begged him to inspect the scene personally. Discounting for aging skin and graying hair, Zemfrekis resembled his father physically in every way, lean, strong, wavy brown hair, soft, kindly features and green eyes that twinkled. But the sweaty, dust-encrusted man who greeted Glen at the outskirts of the scene had a grim countenance.

"What is wrong son?"

"I must show you. This way."

Suppressing irritation, he and his small entourage including Marshal Juragi and Lt Eneko walked with Zemfrekis towards the wagons. The other five members of the investigation team joined them as they neared the wagons: three men and two women. Their tan boots, pants, hooded desert jackets, faces and hair were streaked with sweat dampened gray dust. They all bore the lightning bolt insignia of the Northern Command Regiment on the right shoulder of their tan Scout uniforms - as did Glen, Juragi, Zemfrekis and the rest of his entourage. Of the five, Glen only recognized two: a grizzled old Surgeon named Henry Morrison and a sunburned, veteran Scout Master named Lisa Trukale. The other three were young, junior Scouts and barely distinguishable from one another despite two being male and one female. All five wore uniformly sullen expressions.

Glen noticed at once that the wagons were Cumar built. He paused to peer inside what was likely the rear wagon in the train. Two men encrusted with dusty, black dried blood from fatal head wounds lay dead in very unnatural poses in and amongst the unmarked boxes and sacks in the wagon interior.

Glen muttered to himself, "Great Burning Blast." Then more audibly to his son, "Zeke, have you determined what happened?"

"Sort of. That's not important."

Glen stopped and looked closely at a corpse lying near the wagon - also a victim of a fatal head wound. "What? Sure it is. These are Cumar warriors. Dead at least a day–"

Still walking, Zemfrekis said, "More like seven actually."

"Our vanguard only reached here yesterday afternoon. So it wasn't us. The Scorpions?"

Zemfrekis stopped and turned back. "No."

Glen was losing his patience with his son's odd behavior. His son's usual ultra-professional demeanor was completely missing.

"Scout Captain. Deliver your report."

Zemfrekis sighed heavily and said, "Yes Grand Marshal. If you insist."

"The wagons are of Cumar manufacture as you can see from the wheel assembly. No one else makes them like that. The tools, clothing, jewelry, tattoos and anatomy show fairly convincingly that the majority of the victims are male Cumar warriors, seventy-two, in fact. The remaining six are Cumar women, apparently Guardians of the Valperium from their special tattoos, body paint and clothing.

"The Cumar were taken by total surprise, most never even drew their swords. None strung their bows. These two factors indicate a night attack. No body is more than a few meters from any of the wagons. There is nothing to show that they had mounted an organized defense or even tried to flee.

"The nature of the fatal injuries is very surprising and mysterious. No injuries from blades of any kind. Thirty-four of the victims suffered brutal, cranium shattering blows to the head. The rest suffered similarly brutal impacts to the chest or throat that ruptured organs, pulverized flesh and shattered bones. Only two victims received more than one wound and all seemed to have been killed or incapacitated instantly. Neither the bodies nor the wagons show any obvious signs of ransacking before our scouts found them.

"From experience, although it's hard to tell in the dry desert air, we conclude that somewhere between 3 to 10 days has passed since the slaughter. We also firmly agree that the draft animals dispersed unattended and unburdened to the west. The wagons came from the southeast. No other tracks are evident. The theory is that the attackers must have followed the wagons for some distance since our scouts found no evidence of intercepting tracks for at least 15 kilometers back down the trail. Then, since the wagon trail clearly showed only tracks coming to the site of the ambush, the attackers must have departed from the wagons to the west covering their escape with the dispersal of the draft animals. The attackers left no direct evidence to their identity or existence except for the slaughter itself."

Zemfrekis turned and nodded towards Morrison who took the cue and stepped forward.

"Grand Marshal. Captain Henry Morrison."

Glen nodded in recognition.

"The injuries are like those from a war hammer swung full force. I can't imagine another weapon that would consistently produce injuries like that. But war hammers aren't exactly precision instruments or particularly stealthy. It also seems unlikely that the only injuries were all fatal ones. I saw no limb injuries at all. None. I don't see how one could be used inside the wagons effectively either."

Stroking his chin, Juragi said, "Maybe they were killed somewhere else and then moved here?"

Morrison replied, "I don't think so. The body placement, blood and gore are very convincing they died right where they lie. It's possible I suppose, but why would anyone do that?"

Juragi said, "To confuse someone like us?"

Trukale said, "I'm confused alright. Plenty of easily transportable valuables were left untouched, so we can safely rule out bandits. Rival Cumar or Immortals would never forsake quality war booty. Who does that leave?"

Juragi added, "The only other folks known to have regulars anywhere near the High Raffin are us, our Mountaineer allies and the Zattan. But I can't see units from any of those groups abandoning the animals or failing to search the wagons for potential information."

Trukale raised an eyebrow, "Must be someone we don't know."

Morrison asked, "How could that be? Who would be on the High Plain of Raffin that we wouldn't know?"

Glen thundered, "Precisely. Who?"

Eneko suggested, "Maybe they were looking for something in particular. And found it quickly leaving everything else for the dead."

Everyone nodded that was possible.

Smoothing back her sweat-laden, blond hair, Trukale began,

"Maybe..." She paused, and then seemed to have a sudden realization. "It would seem that the attackers appeared from nowhere. But maybe they were there all along."

Juragi asked incredulously, "What do you mean? Hiding in the sand?"

"No. Nothing like that. I mean treachery. Suppose the attackers were spies or traitors. In the darkness and confusion, the Cumar would not have understood what was happening. Four to six experienced warriors supposedly standing watch could have killed everyone within two or three minutes. They would have killed the best warriors first before anyone even had an inkling that anything was wrong and quickly moved on from there. The few that roused themselves from slumber to resist would have been expecting an external foe and would have fallen victim to the familiar voices and faces. Such a small group would have no time for looting or might have gathered more than they could carry without making a mess. This wasn't an ambush. It was treachery. There is no other reasonable explanation."

Morrison scoffed, "Yes. But the Cumar all favor their short heavy swords."

Juragi replied, "Maybe they wanted to throw off an investigation."

"I suppose – but I would think a good ransacking would have helped confuse things..." The scouts became engaged in an animated argument over whether or not ransacking would have confused their investigation. All except Zemfrekis who remained silent and sullen which Glen noticed belatedly.

After allowing the argument to go on for a while, Glen turned to his son and asked, "What do you think Zeke?"

Zemfrekis shrugged. "Who can say? I still need to show you..."

Glen sighed in apprehension and nodded. He motioned for his entourage including Juragi to stay there.

When they reached what had been the wagon belonging to the Guardians of the Valperium, Zemfrekis stopped and pointed to a body that lay face up in the sand. She was clothed in a red silk, sleeved tunic trimmed in gold, a gold leather belt clasped about her midriff, red sandals laced to mid-calf. Her unnaturally red hair was braided severely. Her face was painted gold. Her arms were decorated with swirling tattoos. From her attire and tattoos on her now gray arms, she had been a Guardian of the Valperium - before her throat had been destroyed.

Glen bent closer, silently praising the lack of strong odor, not sure what he was supposed to see, and so several seconds went by before he spotted the item that Zemfrekis must have intended to show him.

"No."

He groaned, knelt and touched the silver locket that lay near the woman's ear. He yanked on the simple silver chain that remained wrapped around the ruins of her throat. The chain snapped a link, recoiling to slap his chin. He stood back up and examined the locket carefully as the chain slid away to the sand.

The engraved silver locket had been a present from Glen's grandfather to his grandmother. He read the Zattan script letters, *Fentuk Vorath Riska*, which roughly translated into Jurasketu means *Love of my Life, Riska* and began to cry. He had given the locket as a gift to Entreska on her seventeenth New Year in observance of the Zattan tradition of Gurf Nadon.

Gurf Nadon. The Quality of a Belonging Long Possessed. Zattan believe that certain special items, when possessed by someone with an extraordinary quality for a sufficiently long enough period become imbued with the capacity to confer that quality upon others. Naturally, this would only work if the item were given freely by the possessor or their rightful heirs. Glen's grandmother, Riska, had always been extremely lucky avoiding accident and ill events with complete disdain for skill or plan. She always left things to chance, and chance never failed her.

Gurf Nadon. Glen had never believed in Gurf Nadon. He thought it was a stupid tradition. He had just wanted Entreska to have the locket, and he had used the opportunity. Entreska liked quaint Zattan traditions, as she called them, and so he had thought she would appreciate the gift, which she did. Or rather, she had....

In a halfhearted try at hopefulness, Zemfrekis offered, "Maybe it was lost or stolen? Her body is not among any here. She might have been taken prisoner somehow..."

Glen ignored him and stalked away from the wagons and over a wide dune. He stared into the desert and beyond. Puck's soldiery didn't take prisoners except as slaves. Jurasketu consider slavery a living death, an abomination. It is freedom or death.

He thought the Incomprehensible, his beautiful darling Entreska dead. He imagined her cold, twisted and dead like the thousands of bodies he had seen in his campaigns. He fell to his knees and pounded the sand with his hands. Sand lizards hiding below the disturbed surface scattered and burrowed in all directions before his onslaught. He stopped after a while and breathed heavily in the hot, dry Raffin air.

Disaster. Complete disaster. Darkness in the blazing sun. His mind went black...

The purple-hued Demon broke the chains and rampaged through his mind laying waste to the misty vales and green hills. Trees burned and houses exploded into rubble. Unchecked, the Demon ruthlessly destroyed everything in its path. Glen bellowed in agony at the destruction. Glen issued a stream of obscenities that offended even himself. The Demon laughed hysterically at his anguish. Everywhere lay bloody and broken bodies that rapidly turned to rotting, bloated corpses that became bleached and scattered bones that washed away into dust. The Demon demanded sacrifice. Glen shouted his submission. The Cumar? Yes. The Immortals? Yes. Puck? Yes. Yes. The Demon danced and pranced in celebration, twisting and circling ever tighter and faster. Blood. It wanted blood.

He slumped onto the hot sand...

"Glen?"

He opened his eyes. The sun had not moved.

"Are you alright?"

Quietly he said, "No."

"He's okay."

Juragi waved the others away. All withdrew back over the dune except for Zemfrekis who came closer in a deepening gloom.

Glen sat up.

With dark eyebrows knitted tightly together and placing a weathered hand on Glen's shoulder, Juragi asked quietly, "Are you okay?"

"What do you think I meant by 'no'?" He sighed and rubbed his temples. "I've been extremely lucky that I've never lost a child. But I have feared Entreska's death countless times – she is so reckless. But now I have killed her. Worse, I have also killed hundreds of innocents, my best friend, the Scorpions. And more will die yet." Glen groaned as if in pain.

Zeke spluttered, "What are talking about? You've killed no one. Not this time anyway."

Glen moaned, "No. I knew it was too dangerous. I should not have allowed it."

Juragi turned away from Glen and spoke in a quiet but firm voice to Zemfrekis, "Zeke. Let me have a few minutes alone with your father... please."

Zemfrekis hesitated but then nodded and retreated as Glen and Juragi watched.

Glen put his hands on his face, muttered and lolled his head side to side.

Juragi sighed a deep, deep sigh. He pulled Glen's hands from his face and stared deeply into Glen's eyes. "The Demon has returned. Has it not?"

Glen tilted his head to the side and said, "Yes. It's back."

Juragi grimaced and looked out into the desert.

Glen sat miserably thinking not only how he had failed her. He had failed his oldest and most trusted friend, Valentine Jones. He had failed the Black Scorpions. He wondered what he was going to say to Meredith. He had told her not to worry.

Juragi said quietly, "Come. We'll deal with the Demon later. Your army still has important work to do."

Glen nodded wanly, took Juragi's hand and rose to his feet.

As they trudged back to their horses, Glen spoke at length with Zemfrekis and asked him to return at once with all speed to White Tower to tell Meredith what he had found and their belief as to Entreska's fate. It was inevitable that rumors of the demise of Entreska's expedition would soon reach Jurasketu proper. He wanted Meredith to hear from family first even if the news was bad and to let her know they would have the full story soon enough. Zemfrekis protested he was needed by the Army, but Glen insisted.

Later the next day, Glen stood on the southernmost rim of the Arattaque Rise and marveled at the rawness of the High Raffin in the late afternoon sun. Clouds of gray desert dust billowed across the rocky waste two hundred meters below and tens of kilometers in every direction. The Maw of Hell lay 50 kilometers to the southwest. He never could understand the name. The enormous canyon was beautiful from within and without. The evening or morning sun melds with the many hues of rock and shadow to produce a slowly turning carousel of color. Midday light produces a splash of reflected color from the frothy Wrything River that winds down the canyon base from a series of violent hot springs near the northeastern edge. In younger days, he had reconned the canyon many times as a scout with the Black Scorpions. Those were exciting, easier times.

For the High Raffin, the Arattaque Rise has a bounty of potable water provided by a sprinkling of a few dozen springs. By this virtue and its position, the Rise can be used as a base for operations across the entirety of the Central Raffin. From there, an army can strike in any direction quickly and with full force.

Normally, a squadron of the Black Scorpions was stationed on the Rise during the Raffin summer for training and sentry duty, but Glen had diverted them to the suspected ruins of Duravon at Entreska's request. Only a small detachment had stood watch. They had been picked up several kilometers to the east where they had withdrawn before the advance of a second-line banner of Cumar cavalry.

Glen pondered the strategic situation. Twenty-three days ago, his spies and scouts had reported unusual, large and potentially dangerous eastward movements by Puck's forces towards the High Raffin. If the reports were relatively accurate, Puck had sent his best commander, General Saffron, ten Cumar banners and at least six banners of Immortals - nearly 50,000 troops - into the Raffin. Taking no chances, Glen had immediately dispatched orders to Colonel Jones to make an orderly withdrawal of Entreska's Expedition and most of the Black Scorpions. He also sent his active reserve of three light regular regiments directly into the High Raffin to cover the Black Scorpions retreat.

The ruins of Duravon were a thousand kilometers from White Tower and so the relay of the orders to Jones and the return of his receipt confirmation should have taken only five days. Instead of the expected acknowledgment, to Glen's horror, in only four days, he received word that both relay post lines had been disrupted by likely enemy action and neither copy of his orders could be confirmed as delivered.

Only three scenarios seemed plausible to explain the large troop movements and disruption of his relay posts: a fully executed feint, an attack designed to destroy the Duravon Expedition or Rolf's postulated late season attack. Nothing else in the Web of Thought seemed remotely possible given Puck's usually very conservative military strategy. And so, if Puck was even contemplating the last scenario, he would likely feint first to confirm that the Jurasketu Army would adhere to expected doctrine. It had been over ten years since Puck had seriously tested the Jurasketu defenses with anything beyond a probing force and more than seventy since he had attempted a serious attack or feint across the Raffin.

Glen didn't really think an attempt on Entreska's Expedition seemed the likely strategic aim. In the first place, no one but himself, his wife, Juragi, Rolf, Entreska, Zemfrekis and Colonel Jones had known that Entreska's expedition was actually headed for Duravon's Doom. The Expedition had been recruited under a banner of exploring an interesting site in the Lower Raffin - something that had been done a few times before. In the second place, the expedition had planned to be wrapped up 30 days ago, but had extended their stay at the last possible moment. And secrecy had been nominally maintained throughout. If any of the knowing folks had leaked the true destination deliberately or accidentally, Puck would have tried such an attack earlier in the summer to ensure that the Expedition would actually still be there to be attacked. Of course, the other two scenarios likely had the same effect as attacking the Expedition - but that was a side effect rather than an aim it would seem.

So, Glen had been faced with a dilemma. The far most likely scenario was that the attack was a feint, and so he should do as always - withdraw to the Kirolskan Mountains and let the storms do their work. Otherwise, Puck would learn the revised Jurasketu strategic response and ruin Rolf's cunning plan. Additionally, if Saffron didn't know that Entreska's Expedition was out there, a strong response from Glen might alert Saffron that *Something Important to Glen* was and Saffron might maneuver differently to the ruin of all. Naturally, if the attack was real, he needed to make a strong response. And he was also afraid that in any case only a strong response could effect rescue of the Black Scorpions, Jones, the Expedition and, of course, Entreska.

In the end, Glen opted to risk sacrifice of Rolf's cunning plan and make the fastest possible strong response to give the greatest chance to rescue Entreska's Expedition. He had scrambled all available forces from White Tower. Fortunately, a late summer exercise had been in progress, so in just three days he was able to send 8 light regular regiments, 2 heavy regular regiments, the Northern Command Regiment and most of the Swamp Rats after the three lights already dispatched. Two days later, five heavy regiments, half the Dawn Spiders and four regular lights followed. All the regiments were making more than 60 kilometers a day. In addition, two reserve lights had raced south from the White Mountains after being notified by semaphore.

Glen once again reviewed the relative merits of his troops. He had commanded and trained troops in both the Zattan and Jurasketu armies. Both armies outfitted and trained all their regiments as cavalry. Soldiers from both armies could operate from horseback in almost any terrain or weather condition with almost any weapon. Both armies employed heavy and light cavalry. The lights were usually armed with bows, lances, and sabers and wore only light leather armor while riding on fast, unarmored horses. The lights carried many arrows and primarily operated as missile and scout troops. The heavies were usually armed with bows, lances, and axes and wore heavy but flexible steel scale armor while riding stout horses clad in steel reinforced leather armor. The heavies often dismounted to fight foot troops armed with polearms that would resist a cavalry charge. The lights would dismount and operate as skirmishers in difficult terrain.

The Jurasketu "specials" like the Black Scorpions were better armed and equipped elite light cavalry that could conduct specialized military and spying missions of all sorts in addition to being highly capable and feared fighters. The Zattan had their elite units as well, but they weren't particularly distinguishable from their regular units in equipment, organization or training.

The Zattan had better horses and were considered to be slightly better horsemen and just generally tougher. The Jurasketu, on the other hand, fought with greater discipline and skill on foot, and by virtue of better equipment and talent were better military engineers. Both armies were unrivaled in their deadly archery skills.

The Cumar provided the light cavalry for Puck's army. The Cumar were excellent horsemen, but they don't fare that well matched up against Zattan or Jurasketu light cavalry. Mainly, they were used as scouts, flankers and marauders.

The Immortals regiments, on the other hand, although they were highly mobile using horses and wagons for transport, only fought on foot. Every Immortal regiment was divided equally into three types of troops that fought in concert. Heavily armored pikemen formed the basic maneuver unit of Immortal regiments. The pikemen were nearly proof against heavy cavalry charges and could charge enemy formations with deadly shock value. They were somewhat vulnerable to archers. The second group was dangerous longbowmen, moderately armored and carrying back up shield and sword so they could act as medium duty infantry when need arose. The last group was heavily armored melee troops armed with shields, light crossbows and a motley collection of swords, axes and maces.

The Immortals deployed the pikemen in front with the bowmen

behind. The armored melee troops were deployed on the flanks and interspersed with the pikemen. Immortals were extremely well disciplined and motivated troops, but their heavy armor often limited their endurance and mobility on the battlefield. Glen always tried to avoid directly engaging the Immortals, preferring to pepper them with arrows and force them to move around as much as possible to tire them and disrupt their lines.

Glen's request for a declaration of an Emergency by the Grand Debater had been quickly granted so that reserve units could be assembled to take up the posts vacated by the regulars - and provide reinforcements should that be necessary. In an amusing twist of military bureaucracy, the Eastern Command was responsible for Southwestern Jurasketu, so Glen had ordered them to patrol aggressively into the Lower Raffin and prepare defensive positions against a possible Puck raiding force. The Jurasketu naval forces were also pressed into action.

All told, the Jurasketu force that had galloped across the Raffin in near record time consisted of seven regular heavy regiments, fifteen regular light regiments, half the Dawn Spiders, most of the Swamp Rats, two reserve lights sprinting down from the White Mountains plus a command regiment. His main force of regulars was about 60,000 soldiers. The reserve lights, specials and the command regiment represented another 10,000 effectives.

Five days out, a full banner of Cumar had arrived from the south in front of the main advance apparently to act as a strategic blocking force against probing and reconnaissance forces. Unfortunately for the Cumar, and fortunately for the Jurasketu, Glen's covering force of three light regiments had already passed by. The Cumar had simply slipped themselves straight into a deathtrap. The Jurasketu Army pushed the outnumbered Cumar warriors who never surrender against the vanguard and annihilated them.

Years of training, preparation and doctrine had worked almost to perfection. In sixteen days, the army had covered nearly 950 kilometers. The previous day, while Glen had been at the scene of the Cumar wagon train ambush (or treachery), the lead elements of the Jurasketu Army had quickly surrounded and annihilated the Cumar warriors guarding the Rise where Glen stood. General Saffron, while obviously understanding the strategic importance of the position, had sent only a few hundred second-rate Cumar to keep and hold the Rise. This meant to Glen that Saffron had not anticipated this fast counter stroke and probably still did not understand the size of the force headed his way. Under other circumstances, Glen could not have been more proud of his army and their extraordinary accomplishment. As it was, it was all for naught. *All for naught.*

To the southeast, through the distant haze, he could make out the decapitated summit of Duravon's Doom. *The Demon waved to him from the high rim before dropping into a butt slide down and over the low rim culminating into a slowly arching swan dive. A huge puff of desert dust marked the conclusion of the Demon's descent. The Demon screamed with delight as it tossed the broken blocks of the Old City into the Maw of Hell. The Demon insisted he render assistance. Glen bled tears and promised there would be no further delay.*

Glen heard someone running up behind him. He quelled his emotions and calmly turned to look. The scout picked her way across the rocky ground. Messengers always ran in the Jurasketu Army. She presented herself in the usual way, stock still, feet together, right fist placed in the center of her chest. Glen nodded and smiled. She reminded him of Entreska, same age and build. Her eyes were blue, not green, but her mouth and hair were not dissimilar.

After catching her breath, she barked, "Grand Marshal. Marshal Juragi wishes to give you a report."

"He does? Well, tell him I'll receive the report here."

She hesitated, obviously unsure. Glen speculated that was probably because Juragi had told her to fetch him off the rim no matter what he said. Juragi probably thought Glen might be thinking about Entreska and clearly wanted to annoy him with a report as a distraction. He would be right and wrong. Juragi was right about Entreska, wrong about Glen coming back from the brink.

Glen, not quite using an imperative, cajoled, "Go on. Tell him."

The young scout could not resist the second issuance of an order from the Grand Marshal even if it only sounded like a suggestion. She trotted away.

Glen thought about Entreska. When she was twelve years old she had announced her career plans but with typical Entreska misdirection...

"Glen? Why aren't there more women in the Army?"

"More? There are more women in the Jurasketu Army than any other army in the whole world. Nearly two in ten of our soldiers are women, although most of them are in the Scout Corps or Light Cavalry regiments."

"Is it because women don't like to kill people?"

Glen replied sternly, "Entreska. No one in the Army likes to kill people."

"How come everyone says you do?"

Glen clenched his fists tightly, "Who says?"

"Everyone."

Glen snarled internally, but he couldn't answer her right away. He certainly didn't like to kill people, but he made no secret of enjoying victory. In other words, he loved warfare a bit too much and a bit too openly. His soldiers loved him for that attitude, but now his daughter despised him. He recovered his composure after a few long seconds.

"Well, you shouldn't take everything everyone says seriously. They confuse my celebration of survival and victory with enjoyment of killing. There is a difference."

"Yes, Glen."

She paused for a while thinking. Glen waited quietly.

Then she announced in that matter-of-fact way only a child could, "I don't want to be a soldier."

Glen nodded in surprise that she felt the need to make the announcement. Neither he nor Meredith had encouraged her to choose a profession. Neither of them had expected Entreska to join the Army that was certain.

"That's okay. Your mother and I will always be proud of you if you choose an honest profession. We will always love you, regardless."

With mock-disbelief, she asked, "You're not disappointed?"

Glen had the distinct impression that the conversation was headed in yet another direction. Glen replied firmly and quickly, "Of course not."

"I want to be a professor of history."

"If that's your choice, I'm sure you can make that so."

"Yes, Glen. I want to discover and understand what was."

"I'm sure you will."

"I will what?"

Glen turned to see Juragi wearing a puzzled expression of raised eyebrows, wide eyes and out-thrust lower lip. His ragged desert cloak fluttered in the hot wind. As always, he failed to use the cloak's hood, so his hair had collected a fine matte of gray dust.

Glen muttered, "Nothing."

Juragi shrugged and gave him a tactical update while Glen listened patiently.

"The capture of the Rise will not escape Saffron's notice beyond next morning at best. Six Immortal banners are now confirmed 60 kilometers west drawn up near the top of the Maw - which protects their right flank and provides an ample supply of fresh water. Three Cumar banners - all front line - have already been surprised in turn and badly mauled by the eight regular light regiments we sent southward along the northern edge of the Lower Raffin. Two front line Cumar banners are concentrated near Duravon's Doom. The remnants of the banners we mauled yesterday plus two more identified this morning are withdrawing towards the mouth of the Maw. We are making a flanking pursuit.

"The Swamp Rats have already penetrated into Saffron's left - undetected we think. As you directed, the two lights supporting the Swamp Rats are trying to stay back undetected about 70 kilometers to the northwest of us. The three second-line Cumar banners guarding the Immortals left flank will be engaged by the two reserve light regiments moving down from the White Mountains in coordination with the Rats tomorrow morning. They have been instructed to simply prevent the Cumar from moving south and not to pursue if they withdraw west or north.

"Here at the Rise, we have five of our seven heavy regiments, three light regiments plus the Dawn Spiders. Two lights and two heavy regiments are advancing against light resistance towards Duravon's Doom. We have definitely achieved complete strategic surprise and tactical surprise at some points. Saffron's response is sluggish indeed. I doubt he yet understands his peril and how much force we can bring against him."

Glen nodded approvingly.

"One more thing, Grand Marshal. An important dispatch from the Grand Debater arrived just a little while ago." Juragi handed the unopened letter to Glen.

"How do you know it is important?"

"When would an express dispatch from the Grand Debater be anything other than important?"

Glen said, "True," and then unsealed the letter and read the brief message. Without comment or emotion, he handed the letter back to Juragi for him to read. Juragi's eyes widened in disbelief.

"Great Burning Blast, Glen. I thought you said we should not worry about your cousin. Didn't you say he couldn't get the votes on the Imperium Council to become the Governor of Tangur?"

Glen frowned. "We were betrayed it would seem."

Juragi spat in disgust, "As you know, some of Murok's best regiments are already deployed in Tangur. We should withdraw as soon as we can to prevent Murok from taking advantage of our current force misalignment. I think continuing the attack would be very risky, Glen. We can collect our dead next summer as best we can. Nothing we can do for them now."

"Very good advice, Juragi."

Juragi nodded and turned to leave.

Glen barked, "Wait."

Juragi stopped in mid-turn and looked back at Glen over his shoulder. "Yes, Grand Marshal?"

"I didn't say I wanted to change my orders."

With a deep frown, Juragi pivoted his body back to face Glen.

"Oh. But..."

"Murok will not attack. The Imperium Council will not approve a war resolution just now. And if he launched his own war, he has to achieve victory in weeks or face execution for treason. You know very well that he cannot despite our current force disposition. He has a more complicated plan I'm sure. But time is on his side not ours - so amusingly we actually have a little time for ourselves."

Glen paused for effect.

Then he said in a quiet voice, "That means it is time for bold action to achieve our deliverance."

Juragi sighed in resignation.

Glen smiled reflectively. Juragi hated bold action.

The Inky Darkness

Mallory occupied his time by observing the crew of the *Inky Darkness* go about their morning chores in what appeared to be a leisurely if disciplined fashion. Mallory had volunteered to help but had been laughed off as being too inexperienced to even swab the deck. The moderate southwesterly breeze and calm seas had the ship running fast and smooth almost due east and on course for a rendezvous with the far shore and his new found scouting mission. Cirrus clouds diffused the midday sun, but it was still reasonably warm. He wondered if General Lang would find this mission amusing. He wondered if she was even still alive.

Mallory watched languidly as the ship's lean and craggy First Officer, Karl Jones, picked his way around the cleaning detail and came up to where Mallory was leaning against the port railing. Mallory raised an eyebrow in acknowledgment.

Jones asked in a gravelly voice, "Mister Owens?"

"Yes?"

"The Captain respectively asks you to join him for lunch in his cabin."

"Excellent. I'm famished."

The First Officer flashed a jagged smile and beckoned Mallory to follow him. Mallory staggered along the deck trying to keep his balance against the almost imperceptible pitch and roll.

Captain Buck Jules greeted Mallory warmly and bade him to sit down at the small but fancy eating table laid out with finely turned wooden bowls filled with nuts, fresh fruit, fresh brown bread, spiced oil, and dried meats. Two elaborately carved wooden mugs containing Tarfun Stone Brew completed the tableau. Mallory gladly took the starboard chair. Jules took the remaining chair. The table was situated to give both of them a view out the stern windows. A dour old man with wispy white hair and wearing fine blue linen stood unobtrusively off to the side - apparently Buck's valet.

Even with his limited knowledge of wooden sailing ships on any planet, Mallory could tell the sleek *Inky Darkness* had been built for maximum speed and strength. Unsurprisingly, given the implication of piracy, a few hours of observation had convinced Mallory that every member of the crew was an experienced warrior with many showing more than a few battle scars. He estimated the crew to be almost 150, which seemed to be far more than the size of crews he had observed while unloading other merchant vessels. Curiously, although it clearly had been designed as a working merchant vessel, the ship had been appointed more like a luxury yacht in every aspect.

Mallory could not help but comment, "The pirate life is a good one apparently."

Buck smiled, "Most of the time. Eat. The spiced oil is the finest available. Just swirl the bread in it like so."

Mallory complied and instantly became addicted to the bread and oil. While he ate, he looked around the luxurious cabin. Everything seemed to be made of the finest materials suitable for use on a sailing vessel. Captain Jules had a collection of fancy daggers, swords and axes secured on one wall. A secured glass cabinet contained three shelves of leather bound books held in place by removable wooden slats. An exquisitely done oil painting of a beautiful woman wearing sea captain garb was fixed on the opposite wall. A large opulent four-poster bed and a compact, gorgeously finished writing desk completed the furniture. Two other wooden cabinets almost certainly contained clothes and other goods. Everything was clean and polished to a beautiful shine.

Mallory stopped and stared at the portrait.

Buck smiled, "That is my mother."

"She is a sea captain?"

Buck nodded, "Was. She died five years ago."

"Sorry."

Buck shrugged, "No need. She lived a long, eventful and profitable life. I miss her terribly, but nothing is eternal. I suspect not even the Earth and Sky."

Mallory nodded with a slight knowing smile, "Indeed. You may be right about the Earth and Sky. What about your father?"

Buck looked away, "I haven't seen him in years. He may yet live. I heard rumors he is working the northern coasts."

"Sorry."

Buck smiled showing crow's feet beside his green eyes and

grabbed some nuts, "No need. My mother raised me alone. I learned everything I know about sailing from her. She was widely regarded as one of the best ever. Try the cashews - they are especially good."

Mallory followed eating orders again. While eating some particularly delicious salted cashews, his implant signaled that a sailor was attempting to examine his duffel bag. Mallory smiled briefly to himself having expected nothing less. He assumed the sailor had been instructed to make a close but covert examination. Of course, the sailor wouldn't be able to open the bag even with extreme force. In addition, Mallory had secretly anchored the bag to the cabin floor. There was really nothing the sailor could do to damage or remove it. Mallory ordered the bag to do nothing except to stiffen if struck.

He had assumed that a long distraction like lunch would be arranged so that someone could peruse his belongings without fear of discovery. Before that, since his cabin door opened onto the main deck and Mallory had spent the morning with nothing more to do than be observant, anyone entering the cabin would have risked being seen. He would have been shocked if no one had tried to open the duffel bag and examine its contents. He had even deliberately raised suspicion by insisting on carrying it to his quarters himself. He had not been disappointed, but the sailor and Buck definitely would be.

Mallory returned to the conversation at hand and asked, "Did you inherit the *Inky Darkness* from her?"

"Indeed."

"Was she a pirate too?"

Mallory noticed a smile from the old man.

Buck laughed, "She was not a pirate. And neither am I. Anna just calls me that to annoy me."

"I'm slightly confused then. Your crew seems a bit large for a mere merchant ship."

Buck's green eyes twinkled, "The *Inky Darkness* is not a mere merchant ship. We specialize in the extremely lucrative practice of expeditiously and safely transporting high value perishable merchandise, other valuables, messages and the occasional important passenger. And confidentiality is always assured."

Mallory nodded with immediate understanding.

"I'm curious then. Was the ship designed as a pleasure yacht and converted by your mother for that purpose?"

Buck smiled, "No. My mother designed and commissioned the

Inky Darkness expressly for that purpose."

"Really? It does seem like a nice way to cap a successful merchant career."

Buck laughed, "Actually, the *Inky Darkness* was her only command."

Mallory closed an eye and leaned his head over. Then he straightened up, drew a large sip from his beer and said, "Now my curiosity is fully stoked. Can you give me the full story?"

Buck looked askance, "What version of the tale have you heard?"

Mallory shrugged, "Assume I know nothing. Which would be entirely and completely accurate. I am a stranger to these lands and the first I heard of the *Inky Darkness* was last night."

Buck bobbled his head and took a mouthful of cashews. Then he sipped some beer, leaned back and looked deep in thought. Mallory waited patiently.

Buck leaned forward, "I find it highly improbable that you have never heard of the *Inky Darkness*, but I'll play along. Precious Jules, my mother, was the bastard daughter of Admiral Harry Jules and Priscilla Williams – daughter of Tafford Williams who served as the Grand Debater for a number of years."

"Oh? That must have been embarrassing."

Buck laughed, "I'll say. Admiral Jules was Commander of the Fleet with grown children and a devoted wife. Priscilla was only seventeen."

Mallory shuddered. "Ick."

"Indeed. Worse, he fled with Priscilla to parts unknown."

With widened eyes, Mallory said, "Willingly?"

Buck frowned, "Yes. She was a free spirit as they say. And was known to be anything other than naive. So it was said anyway – according to my mother."

Mallory paused a moment and considered the potentially delicate politics, "So is the *Inky Darkness* an outlaw with respect to Jurasketu?"

Buck laughed again, "No. My grandfather had considerable wealth some of which he had managed to smuggle out when he went into exile. It is still not known where they went or even what ultimately became of them other than they had one known child – Precious Jules. Twenty-five years after their disappearance, she appeared one day in Gilfary and commissioned the building of the *Inky Darkness*. She claimed to be their daughter."

Mallory nodded, "No offense, but I suspect that her claim was openly questioned. It wouldn't be the first time someone has tried to trade on another's celebrity."

Buck smiled, "None taken. She was able to prove her claim. It was said she strongly resembled both her putative parents in looks, bearing and voice. She had Harry's family ring and a necklace that belonged to Priscilla. She paid for the building of the ship with gold. Her skills as a Sea Captain were to prove legendary. None doubted that she was who she claimed to be. Although she refused steadfastly to say anything else about her parents even to me."

Mallory nodded, "Interesting."

Buck continued sardonically, "The Williamses were most outraged by her appearance and demanded action by the government to press Gilfary to arrest her and seize her assets. But they were to be disappointed. Their faction had fallen from favor in the years preceding the appearance of my mother. She says they were arrogant and despised by many for a number of transgressions that sapped their influence. Folks almost reveled in their shame it would seem. Interestingly, the Admiral's other children remained withdrawn and silent on the whole matter. His wife had died heartbroken a year after his exile and his children had slipped quietly away to live on the remote shores of Saven."

"Where is that?"

Buck looked puzzled, rolled his eyes, got up, went to the glass cabinet, pulled out a heavy chart book and opened it on the writing desk. He beckoned Mallory to come look.

Buck muttered and pointed, "Saven is a large, and one would have to say, idyllic island 400 kilometers south of Endurance. Here. The Jurasketu Southern Fleet is based there to take advantage of its fine, deep sheltered harbor. It has very favorable winds year round and plentiful fresh water, fruit and nuts. The local sea creatures provide very high quality oils and unique hides. There are unique and desirable spices grown on the island that have provided enormous wealth to the local non-military population and occasional income to enterprising sea captains."

Buck paused to smile and raise an eyebrow.

Mallory smiled in return, "I see."

Buck continued, "Over the years, wealthy Jurasketu families have established residences on its tropical shores for escaping the cold rains of winter and societal pressures in Endurance when occasion merited. This is Gilfary, an ally and trading partner of Jurasketu, several hundred kilometers almost due south of Saven on the Southern continent. Anyway, my mother spared almost no expense in the building of the *Inky Darkness* including importing Black Fir from Rook. This was before it was recognized that the supplies of Black Fir have been nearly exhausted. An export ban was established not long after the building of the *Inky Darkness* – some say because of it. My mother assembled a crew and began a splendid and profitable career in the perishables trade. The *Inky Darkness* is one the fastest ships ever built and she possessed excellent charts and navigational skills to complement them."

Mallory laughed, "I don't suppose that the old Admiral took his personal charts with him eh?"

"My mother had to deny that was the case being the charts were property of the Jurasketu Navy – but everyone knows she had them. And her father had spent many years plying the Bay of Lydaron scouting, raiding and spying on Puck and the other states scattered around the bay."

Mallory nodded in admiration, "And you have them now, of course?"

"Naturally. I keep them updated. I've even been known to sell copies to deserving folks. And not for a paltry sum either. Some of them are literally priceless at this point."

"I can imagine..."

Mallory drifted off into thought and his jaw dropped. He currently possessed the most accurate topographical map of the entire planet including more than 100 meters below the surface of the waters. He simply had to turn his computer images into paper charts, maps and atlases, and he could raise a considerable amount of money honestly and secretly if done judiciously. Captain Jules would be a perfect intermediary. He should have thought of that before. He sighed.

"Is something wrong?"

Mallory snapped back to the moment, "Sorry. I'm fine. Your story reminded me of something. Nothing important."

Buck shrugged, closed the book and returned it to the shelf.

Mallory watching this was struck by a book on the higher shelf amongst what appeared to be a collection of histories, stories and poetry collections. He pointed at the thick book whose title and author in gold script on the stem was *Wizards: Legend or Fact* by a Professor Entreska Nevercare. He asked, "Wizards?"

Buck nodded, "On the whole, a very entertaining book actually.

She takes great care to present a seemingly objective case that wizards once existed. She even claims Pachinko Puck is one. But personally, I'm not buying. I'm too much of a cynic. A hazard of my trade I suppose."

"May I?"

Buck shrugged, "Be my guest."

Mallory took the book back to his chair, wiped his fingers on a napkin and opened it.

"Henderson, the exiled Immortal I told you about, claimed Puck was a Wizard and over 400 years old. What do you think of that?"

Buck pursed his lips, "The Immortals senior commanders are a clever bunch. In fact, I've long thought that Puck is merely a puppet. The unnatural and outrageous skin coloration, complex tattoos, ridiculously eccentric behavior and reclusive nature are the perfect cover for a puppet that gets replaced every dozen years or so. Using some secret potion or whatever to dye the puppet's skin was a stroke of genius. When the existing Puck starts to look old, they find a look-alike, apply dye and tattoos, replace the personal imperial servants, dispose of the old Puck and call the replacement - Puck. The tattoos and skin color are so distinctively dominant that only someone with regular personal contact would likely notice the difference at all. The senior commanders would limit access to Puck for entirely valid security reasons and Puck's alleged eccentricity. As long as the senior commanders accepted him as the Pachinko Puck, no one would question it. And if anyone did dare to question, they would be moved along the circle of life with alacrity."

Mallory shrugged, "Why would the new Puck go along? Wouldn't the replacement realize their puppet reign would be brief?"

Buck laughed, "Puck gets unlimited access to fine food, strong drink and concubines. No actual work involved other than appearing eccentric and signing decisions made by the senior commanders. And then a promise of an equally happy retirement to some secret village in the tropics somewhere. For all we know, there may very well be such a retirement village."

Mallory snorted, "Murder seems like the easier and safer course. But I'll have to say I'm a bit skeptical, Henderson said he met routinely with Puck."

Buck shrugged, "People naturally always try to make themselves more important than they are. He could easily have exaggerated that part of the story."

Mallory nodded, "Possibly. Then again. I suppose it is certainly more plausible than a four hundred year old wizard."

Buck laughed, "Indeed."

Mallory thumbed through the book. "May I borrow this for the afternoon? It would give me something productive to do."

Buck waved a hand. "Of course. You may keep for your journey if you like."

Mallory nodded his head and weighed the book in his hand, "Thank you. I'm not sure I want the extra weight - but thanks for the offer."

Mallory considered for a moment. Henderson had given him considerable information about the Jurasketu Army. "Nevercare is an unusual name."

Jules nodded, "Zattan choose their own surname when they become an adult. Jurasketu do not. And guessing your question, the answer is yes. Professor Nevercare is related to the Grand Marshal. She is his daughter."

Mallory nodded, "Interesting. Trading on his fame?"

Buck shrugged, "A little I suppose. Really though. It is a good book."

Mallory smiled in response. The mention of the Grand Marshal reminded Mallory that he would be tromping in the wilderness. He was planning to simply steal or buy any supplies he needed from locals. But it was always good to have some knowledge of local dangers and water sources.

"Captain. Is there someone amongst your crew that is familiar with the water sources and dangers in the Western Zetu?"

Buck leaned back, "That would be my First Officer, Karl Jones. He was born and raised in the Blades. You can't have him."

Mallory chuckled, "No worries. I work alone. I just wanted ask him for some local intelligence."

Buck laughed, "Fair enough. He's off duty at Eighth Hour. He can be talkative once you get him started. But again, do not even hint that he could join you. No one has greater cause or desire to get revenge on Puck and his cohorts than him. I've been very worried that he'll ask to join you, and I really can't refuse him if he were to ask."

"Understood. Not to worry. I need to work alone anyway despite the value he would likely provide. Hopefully, he'll be satisfied with providing me with local survival tips and general intelligence."

Buck nodded.

"What do you hope to accomplish?"

Mallory shrugged, "I want to confirm some things Henderson told me and see some things with my own eyes so that I can get a better measure of what challenges I might face. And hopefully formulate a reasonable plan."

Buck rolled his shoulders in apprehension.

"The Immortals are extremely competent warriors in all respects. You should be wary. The Immortals rely on the Cumar to conduct scouting missions and patrols. The Cumar are less competent warriors, but they are excellent horsemen and trackers. Avoid them and cover your tracks."

Buck signaled to the old man, "James. Coffee for me. Mallory?"

"Please."

The now identified James went to fetch coffee. A minute after the valet left, Mallory received word from his bag that the sailor had given up. Mallory wondered if Buck had sent James for coffee simply to check on the sailor's progress.

Buck smiled, "James was one of my mother's first crewmen and sailed with her for forty years if you can believe it. He's been my valet for the last ten."

Mallory nodded admiringly.

Buck gave him a look and asked, "What about you? Do you have family?"

Mallory shook his head, "Zero wives. Zero children. Two disappointed, if understanding, grandparents-would-be."

"You still have time."

Mallory chuckled, "If I survive this enterprise, maybe I'll explore that. Probably more rewarding."

"I don't know. Children can be pretty disappointing sometimes."

Mallory laughed, "Indeed we can. What about you?"

Buck sighed, "I gravely disappointed my mother in that. I was actually born and raised on this ship. It's the only home I've known. But I didn't want that for my children. I wanted..."

Buck looked out to the sea for a long moment before continuing, "As a boy, I asked every crewman what their childhood had been like so I could compare to my own. Many reported such terrible childhoods that I really hope they were exaggerating or just making things up entirely just to see the look on my face. Others would tell tales of fantastic childhood adventures that were not to be believed. But the stories were good enough that I didn't care if they were made up. Just a few took the time to give me a real idea of growing up on land in a pleasant place with loving and caring parents. I think they were exaggerating as well. And yet, I longed for that."

He sipped his ale for a moment. Mallory remained silent.

Buck continued, "I wanted that for my children. But I didn't want to be an absent father. I couldn't be both a sailor and have the life I wanted for my children. So I never seriously pursued marriage. And no children. Kind of sad really. I like to think I would have been a good father."

Mallory simply nodded and they sipped ale in silence.

Finally, Buck sighed, "Let us consider something else."

Mallory gave him a quizzical look.

Buck pointed to his weapons wall, "No offense but for a soldier, you seem inadequately armed. I kind of expected you to ask for a loaner sword. Or spear. Or bow. Or something."

Mallory shrugged, "Well. I had to sell my hunting knife not long ago. But I have a solid secondary utility knife that I was expecting to handle my cutting chores."

"I mean to say, I'm willing to loan you a quality sword or a bow and quiver or both if you wanted them."

"Oh. That is very kind of you. But I don't want them. I'm not particularly skilled with either to be honest."

Buck frowned, "Well. What are you skilled with? I have a large collection of mundane and exotic weapons."

Mallory suddenly realized he had blundered stupidly into a discussion of his martial skills. That was not a discussion he wanted to have. "My best skills encompass scouting, survival and intelligence gathering. My weapon skills are mostly found with knives, staves and grappling..." *Not to mention rifles, pistols, explosives, missile launchers, grenades and most heavy weapon systems.*

Buck gave a puzzled look.

"I'm a scout. I plan to be very unobtrusive and not be seen. I would not likely win a sword fight against a unit of trained warriors. It's not like I plan to attack a detachment of these Cumar or anything."

Buck waved a hand, "It's your mission."

Mallory nodded, "But thank you for the kind offer."

Buck shrugged and rubbed his forehead, "Let us suppose you find a weakness in Puck's defenses. What then? If you are merely a scout, how will you exploit that?"

Mallory pondered how to answer safely. The answer turned out to be easy. "I plan to put together a team that can." *That team being himself.*

"Similar to the fashion in which you secured this passage?"

Mallory laughed, "I am a patient man. And fortune smiles on those ready to seize the moment when an opportunity presents itself. In a sense, you have done the same."

Buck nodded and smiled. "Can I ask that you allow me some role in forming the plan or on your team?"

Mallory smiled, "Sure. Although remember, this whole enterprise may indeed be madness. I wouldn't want you to come to harm trying to help me."

"Life is dangerous. I am not shy about taking such risks. And besides sanity is limited while insanity knows no bounds."

Mallory bellowed in laughter.

"Anyway, I'll retire to my quarters to read and then talk to your First Officer at Eighth Hour later in the afternoon.

"Why don't you stay here and read instead? The view is better and James will see to your comfort."

Mallory demurred, "I wouldn't want to bother you."

"Nonsense. I'm spending the afternoon doing inspections. So please. And feel free to look at my map books for your research."

Mallory nodded and made a mock salute, "You're the Captain."

Buck laughed, "I am that."

James returned with the coffee and they continued to discuss the geopolitical situation for another hour. Buck shared information he thought interesting about Puck's empire. Finally, Buck announced that he had neglected his duties long enough, and he should be about them. With that, Mallory left the book on the chair, nodded a thanks to the valet indicating he would indeed return in a few minutes to read the book, and then left the cabin with the Captain saying he needed to get something from his bag.

Mallory entered his sleeping cabin and looked around. The cabin had two windows that looked out to the starboard side allowing ample light from the afternoon sun. Tucked into the back of the cabin, a set of cabinet drawers with brass handles arranged in two rows of three supported a spacious two-person bed laden with pillows and blankets. Expensive sets of heavy and sheer curtains framed the bed. A hinged writing desk was bolted to the interior wall. Two heavy, plain chairs flanked the desk. An elaborate carving covered the upper portion of the interior wall. A highly polished wax finish accented the fine, light grain of the Black Fir, which Mallory was told had been named for its bark rather than its wood. The duffel bag was parked under the writing desk. Mallory couldn't tell that it had even been disturbed, so whoever had attempted to look inside had been instructed to be careful.

Amused, Mallory looked around trying to decide if there were peepholes or other means being used to observe him. Smiling, he mentally issued the unlock command to the duffel bag, then casually reached down, flipped open a side flap, and pulled out his leather logbook. He closed the flap and retreated to the bed. He took off his custom fitted short leather hiking-style combat boots and sat down cross-legged in the bed. He rubbed his feet for a minute in case anyone was watching and because it felt quite good. He oriented himself such that his arms, head, body and sleeping curtains blocked visual line of sight into his lap where he carefully opened the logbook. He mentally called up the surveillance video on the logbook display.

For fifteen minutes, a small wiry sailor, whom Mallory did not recognize and so probably worked below decks or had night duties, fiddled with the various flaps that should have opened but naturally did not for the sailor. Remarkably, the sailor never seemed perturbed by his lack of progress. Eventually he tried to move the bag and discovered that it was somehow stuck to the floor. The sailor actually smiled at that. He pulled out a thin wooden rod and twisted himself various ways around the desk while he poked and prodded the entirety of the bag looking for mechanisms or means to convince the bag to reveal its secrets. Eventually, he gave up and with a long look of admiration left the cabin. Mallory imagined he would enjoy listening to the report given to Captain Jules.

Mallory also wondered about what the good Captain would think about that. Mallory suddenly became worried he had been having too much fun. An unopenable bag seemed to belong in the realm of the supernatural, but maybe Buck would just believe it was mere trickery. Mallory resolved to be more careful in the future with exposing his bag to even nominal scrutiny. He sighed reminding himself that such resolutions often fell prey to the exigencies of reality. Mallory returned the logbook to its slot and locked the bag.

As Buck had suggested, Mallory returned to the Captain's suite. Under James' watchful eye, Mallory began reading Professor Nevercare's book on Wizards. He wouldn't have time to read it carefully and completely between now and tomorrow night when he was expecting to be put ashore, so he decided to skim read the book and concentrate on certain areas if they merited closer reading. It turned out to be fascinating if not quite believable. Nevercare seemed to take great care in putting together evidence. Mallory was impressed by her research if not her conclusions.

Captain Jules returned around Ninth Hour and reminded Mallory that his First Officer had gone off duty at the Eighth Hour. Mallory cursed, saved his place in the book with a ribbon and rushed off to find Karl Jones.

The First Officer proved to be an enthusiastic fount of wisdom and valuable information concerning the Blades and Puck's governance. Karl alleged that Puck had personally murdered several members of Karl's family. That would explain his desire for revenge and eagerness to help. The information provided by Karl complemented everything he had learned from Henderson and helped explain some of what Mallory knew from his space reconnaissance. Karl hinted several times that he would be a perfect guide, but Mallory politely demurred saying that he only worked alone. Around Eleventh Hour, dinner arrived in the form of warm sausages, fresh baked flat bread and ale. Six hours and several mugs of Tarfun Stone Brew later, Karl had to admit he needed sleep. And so did Mallory.

The next day, Buck allowed Mallory to continue reading and studying in the Captain's suite. After morning inspections, the Captain and the First Mate joined Mallory to discuss a landing spot. James provided a pot of coffee and a plate of dried fruit. While Mallory mostly listened, Karl and Buck discussed all the possible suitable landings. Eventually they narrowed the list down to an area just north of the Wrything River Delta called the Melted Hills.

Buck pulled out the appropriate chart and pointed, "Here. There is a sheltered cove with a large ring of rocks impassable to anything bigger than a skiff. Under cover of darkness, we sail up to the rocks and drop the dinghy with a crew of seven plus Mallory. They row ashore, pull the boat into the woods and hide. Meanwhile, the ship pulls back out to sea. Tomorrow night, the crew rows back out and we pick them up. Mallory can proceed into the wilderness and begin scouting."

Mallory nodded, "What are the dangers?"

Karl shrugged, "The rocks. And there is an off chance that fishermen acting as spies for Puck spot the dinghy rowing ashore. And I suppose, a very unlikely chance that a random Immortal or

Cumar patrol stumbles upon the crew hiding in the woods. Of course, an undiscovered sea monster living in the cove could unexpectedly overturn the dinghy."

Buck snorted, "In other words, no real danger at all. The Immortals and Cumar don't patrol this area. The fishermen avoid that area because of the rocks and lack of usable catch. And while there are plenty of sea monsters to go around, few seem to inhabit that area."

Mallory looked hesitant, "Sea monsters? And what about the rocks?"

Buck shrugged, "My charts are excellent. The dinghy is stout. The crewmen are masters at their crafts. And Karl is joking about the sea monsters."

"I am not."

"Stifle the nonsense."

Mallory smiled at their bravado hoping it was born of real experience and not just bravado. And he hoped Karl was just joking.

Karl twitched a frown, "The Captain is likely correct. He usually is. I think the real problem is recovery. Mallory needs to be able to signal us without attracting attention and with us knowing that it is really him. And we probably need an alternative should the primary location become compromised."

Mallory and Buck waited patiently while Karl reviewed the charts.

Karl scowled, "I recommend the Blue Salt Cove south of the river. It requires crossing the river and a further hike of 200 kilometers, but it will almost certainly be deserted. Mallory? Here."

Mallory frowned, "How will you know the primary is compromised?"

Buck laughed, "When you don't show up."

"Oh."

Buck tilted a smile, "Do we have to have a signal? We could just go ashore on the appointed days. If Mallory is there, we meet him at the hiding spot and return to the ship the next night. Done. Simple."

Karl groaned.

Buck scowled, "Okay. Signal... The best would be a fire. Easily seen. There is a cave. Here." He pointed at a location on the headland. "Place the fire back in the entrance a little and it can only be seen from the sea."

"How will you know it is me?"

Karl shrugged, "Use a coded sequence?"

Buck flicked his hand, "Nah. There are numerous far better places to shelter away from the damp and cold shore. We'll just take our chances. We see the fire. We send the dinghy ashore that night. No fire. We assume Mallory isn't there and we'll proceed to the secondary at the Blue Salt Cove. Fortunately, the Blue Salt Cove requires no signal. We can just sail into the cove. If you see us, wave and we'll send a boat ashore. Agreed?"

Mallory nodded.

The Terror

Entreska and her volunteers' dubious approximation of a double file column stretched for over a kilometer along the trail. Choking dust served to isolate each little section from the whole of the snaking body. Entreska could barely see her comrades. The dust even obscured the Raffin Sun (but not its heat). The pungent sweat of her mare overwhelmed all other smells and served to reinforce the sense of isolation that she felt.

The lack of roads or even regular trails on the High Raffin meant they made whatever trail they liked or rather could create. Without a regular trail, untrained, inexperienced riders in a dust-obscuring wasteland, not unexpectedly, can easily become lost. The requirement for speed exacerbated this potential problem. Within just a few kilometers of breaking camp, the last third of the column missed a directional change. Retrieving the lost portion required nearly two hours. They were forced to reassign a number of the Scorpions from scout duty to column maintenance. Despite the diligence of the Scorpions, Entreska and other experienced riders, they had continued to suffer problems throughout the day.

Although the Scorpions on scout duty could easily spot their pursuers, no one in the column proper could see anything at a distance, but their pursuers could see them from many kilometers distant. Entreska focused her thoughts on a section in her father's book: *Maneuver and Movement*. All movement should be concealed unless a demonstration of force would serve to deceive the enemy. This includes all forms of strategic movement, scouting, tactical maneuvers, supply trains, and even moving about camp. Her father and the Jurasketu Army that he commands follow these admonitions meticulously and passionately. After a fast initial flight, they would soon have to switch their strategy.

Late in the afternoon, Major Vest approached Entreska. Vest showed no signs of fatigue. He never did. Vest was Jones' most senior

Troop leader. He was slender of body and face, well groomed, with dark hair and eyes. He smartly brought his horse up beside hers and smiled at her with his unusually white teeth.

"We should stop now and make bivouac."

It was time for the strategy change. She asked, "So early?"

"Yes. I think a short rest now will allow us to make good time after dark. We need as much distance as possible as soon as possible. Certainly the cooler night air is preferable to the Raffin heat."

"Hmm. What about the problem we're having with stragglers? The night travel will only compound the situation."

"We'll just have to go little slower and work harder."

She nodded with fatalism.

Vest turned and rode to the front of the column to give the halt order.

She choked down her dinner alone: hard bread and dried meat with mustard. With a few minutes to think, she started to cry. Jones and his troops planned to sacrifice themselves trying to hold up Puck's Army. She almost couldn't bear it. It would be her fault that they died. Worse, Garth had insisted on staying so he could hide the Duravon Archives and then help with the defenses. She should have been the one that stayed - but Jones had insisted it was her duty to lead her Expedition to safety.

She felt terrible about Mallory. She had argued vigorously against his arrest - but Jones wasn't about to give in. She had to save her students and workers. There simply wasn't time to convince Jones otherwise. He, too, would die because of her.

The Voice said flatly, "Puck's troops haven't reached the City yet."

"Mallory?"

"Don't know."

"Why not?"

"Our powers do not encompass everything."

"I thought you said you were not limited by time and space."

"An exaggeration. Our abilities to directly affect the world are still restricted by proximity and physics. Wizardry must obey physical laws like everything else."

She always thought of wizardry as being in defiance of physics.

"Ignorance has its limitations."

That wasn't very nice, but just the kind of thing she would have said to a student who expressed an unsophisticated view in one of her classes at the Academy.

"Sorry. We don't mean to be patronizing."

"No apologies required. What about Puck's cavalry? Are any of his units near?"

"Puck's cavalry is scattered across the Lower Raffin. We can detect nothing near, but we can easily be overlooking small detachments and individual scouts."

"So we could be in danger?"

"You are definitely in danger."

"Why can individuals and small groups escape your attention?"

"There are many factors. As I've told you, we are incapable of reading anything other than primitive emotions from the majority of humans. For those from whom we can obtain more specific thoughts that can tell us friend from foe, time is required to focus and make the identification. There are thousands of humans currently swarming the Lower Raffin. Admittedly, the Raffin is easy compared to scanning a city of hundreds of thousands, but the difficulty remains. Often, no proper identification can be made in a reasonable time because a readable mind is preoccupied with the hardships of the Raffin, numbed by the same or simply asleep. To be honest, I've never tried to be the eyes of a mobile army before."

"We are not a fighting force."

"Regrettably, you are right."

Entreska considered the explanation and found it wanting. *"Why don't the others help?"*

"The others are all greatly fatigued. It will be some time before they recover their strength. They generated the conditions that ruined your sleep these past weeks. I did not help with the summoning, so that I could scan for any results."

"Really? Where does your strength come from? Being that you are only spirits in a large crystal."

"That is needless to say, an oversimplification. But the truth is we don't wish to tell you."

"Why not?"

"We consider that knowledge extremely dangerous. That knowledge is an integral secret of wizardry. And so we worked to suppress that knowledge."

"Apparently Puck has that knowledge."

"Apparently so. How? We don't wish to speculate."

"But you have an idea."

"Yes. We simply do not wish to share this information with anyone."

She certainly didn't feel as though she knew or understood much of anything.

"Some of us agree with you. Some of us don't agree."

"That I'm lost in a storm of ignorance?"

"That is not our intention. The problem lies with our basic policy and purposeful existence. We firmly believe that knowledge of wizardry is inherently uncontrollable and unmanageable. The resources that are required to gain great power are readily available to any individual with the knowledge and skill. A wizard can easily manipulate the requisite numbers of followers to wreak havoc on any culture or political system. They are many roads that can lead to the destruction of civil society. Some are broad and based upon raw power. Those are the easiest to identify and contain. Others involve subtle uses of influence and manipulation that are very difficult to identify and even harder to contain.

"In short, unrestricted access to wizardry leads to disastrous circumstances, and worse any access to wizardry leads to unrestricted access quickly. Even now, hundreds of years later, here we are influencing you, my dear Entreska, to take us into your confidence to work our will. Although you were not the one we sought, you came and fulfilled our desire nonetheless. We deserve your contempt and condemnation."

"Yeah. Yeah. Yeah... Puck uses wizardry to make us and others suffer. Can you stop him?"

"No. Not directly. We can neutralize many of his abilities. Mostly we can provide knowledge and protect people from Puck's direct influences."

"That could be all that is required."

"You could be correct, but we do not all agree."

She considered that for a moment.

"Does that mean you could do more to aid us?"

"No. Our rules prevent us from certain direct activities. Puck, however, has no such restrictions."

"You mean yes you could, but no you won't."

Silence.

"If we do as Puck, we are as Puck. We would be obligated to destroy ourselves."

"You and Uncle Val."

A feeling of bemusement passed across her mind.

"Anyway, you had best give me a picture of whatever troop positions you can..."

Late, the next afternoon, the Voice woke her from slumber. Her tent provided relief only from the burning sun, not the brutal heat and humidity. Sweating profusely, she was delirious with the heat and didn't understand what they were saying.

She shouted in alarm, "I'm late for class."

The Voice said, "What? No. You are still on the Raffin. You need coherence."

A damn fool statement. Anyone who lacks coherence couldn't understand such an admonition in the first place.

"What?" Then more calmly, she said, *"I was trying to rest."*

"The enemy comes."

"Oh no. Where and when?"

"From the north, coming fast, the lead elements will be here in less than four hours."

Forgetting her sandals, she leapt to bare feet and ran to Major Vest's tent. She roused Vest, who before she gave him the news, muttered, "Our enemy comes?"

"Yes."

He said with a half-smile, "Colonel Jones warned me that you would know."

"He did?"

Vest replied, "Yes. He told me what he had seen in the hall, and some of what had been said. He also swore me not to reveal his oath-breaking."

"So to make up for the Colonel's transgression, you do the same?"

"The Colonel simply wished for me to trust your visions. I simply want you to know that I will try as he wished."

She nodded and gave Vest the sketchy details the Voice had supplied her. She borrowed a pair of his sandals to return to her tent. She had burned her feet on the sand. She quickly made ready for travel.

Vest decided to divide them into four groups. One group, about one hundred good riders including fifty Scorpions, led by Vest, would ride north then east to provide a diversion. The other three groups of about 150 each would strike off in southeasterly directions towards the Lower Raffin. Each of these groups would be led by fifty Scorpions. Vest gave strict orders that stragglers would be left to their fate, death was close upon them and the situation was desperate. They had absolutely no chance in combat against veteran cavalry, even say only a third their number. Their only course was to flee. Vest wished to increase somebody's chances by scattering in the hope that their enemy had insufficient numbers or desire to pursue them all. Entreska didn't like his plan, but she had no credible strategy of her own to offer. So, they did as Vest ordered.

They didn't bother to collect their tents or a majority of their supplies. They just mounted up and took off. They rode as hard as possible to achieve as much separation as possible. Increased distance would elevate their chances of escape, assuming, of course, that they weren't riding directly into the path of more cavalry. Colonel Jones had estimated the Cumar cavalry strength to be over ten full banners. She didn't believe all of that cavalry had been deployed to this region, but two or three banners could easily seal their fate.

The Lower Raffin was very flat with a number of dry, shallow riverbeds and rain washes. The ground was very fine sand mixed with gray, gritty clay. Enough moisture seeped from the depths to allow the baking summer heat to turn the mixture into brittle, little plates, the size of tea saucers. The horses' hooves shattered them into powder with every step. The searing heat easily lofted the disturbed, airborne powder toward the sky marking their position for kilometers. At least, they would see the Cumar approach by their dust plume. Nor could their enemies lay in ambush, there wasn't any place to hide. They continued to ride as hard and fast as possible.

The gray clay dust tenaciously clung to sweat soaked clothes and moist skin. Then the sun's heat dried and baked the dust creating a gray crust cloaking everyone in the column. The longhaired desert ponies probably thought it was funny. The ponies' coats ranged from gray to white to mottled. Now, the riders resembled the ponies in color. They looked like ghost riders on ghost ponies. Entreska feared that is exactly what they would become.

They pushed their ponies as far as they dared, then just after dark they dismounted and walked, letting the ponies gain a measure of walking rest. A military force faced with the need to penetrate an enemy cordon of superior might and number has two choices. One: mass and strike like lightning to produce a breakthrough. Two: scatter like small animals and pass through the enemy lines by stealth and guile. They couldn't attack; they weren't soldiers. They couldn't scatter; they weren't skulkers. They just had to hope for an incomplete cordon and a heaping helping of luck.

The exertion used up a lot of their water. They were carrying as much water as possible, but they couldn't continue to flee across the Raffin for long without acquiring some more. The Scorpions worked them to one of secret oases they knew. They spent as much time as they dared replenishing the water skins.

Only a few hours after the northern contact, the wizards in the Crystal broke their silence again. "East and south. Two, possibly three large groups of fast moving troops. Most likely cavalry."

The two large moons beamed cold reddish tinged light across the Raffin.

"All Cumar?"

"All Cumar."

Entreska chuckled, "Oh well. I guess we die then."

A female student walking beside Entreska asked, "What?"

Entreska, fighting back tears, said, "Nothing."

The student asked, "What's wrong?"

Entreska whispered, "Puck's cavalry comes."

Entreska ran forward to the young Troop Leader named Park Jones. She spoke quietly, "Puck's cavalry is now moving east and south of us. We are cut off."

Jones nodded and then turned to stare at the horizon for a short while. She thought he was imitating Colonel Jones for a moment, but then he said, "I see no dust plumes. We have some time to plan. Come, let's confer."

Jones summoned his second officer, a rough-hewn Mountaineer, named Jeremy Fisk. Jones wiped sweat from his face, using a soiled rag that left him ashen in appearance.

Fisk spoke, "We have few choices. I do not suggest east or south. We will not escape detection."

Jones snarled, "What? Go back?"

Entreska muttered, "We're dead. Let's just face up to it. We have nothing to lose. We can try anything."

Jones nodded, "Yes. Hmm... Well, how about this plan. We send most of our ponies off to the southwest in the morning. Their dust trail and tracks will draw plenty of attention. Then, we go back north retracing our own tracks."

Entreska said, "What good will that do?"

Jones continued, "At a point further north. We step off the trail and cover our tracks. The northern elements of Puck's cavalry will likely be pursuing Vest and his men. By the time anyone finds our trail, the signs will be poor and they won't suspect we doubled back. At least, not right away."

"Then what?"

"There is an oasis in a hidden canyon less than a few hours march from our trail. We can hide there."

"What we will do then?"

Jones said, "We can rest and plan our next move."

Fisk said, "What with no ponies? Suicide?"

Entreska nodded, "Perhaps not. The Cumar might believe we have escaped. Or we might be able to slip to the north and around. Puck's troops will be looking east and south. Our warnings should have been communicated some time ago. Troops from the northern pickets or even a fast cavalry regiment moving up from White Tower might be probing their way south to investigate. We might make contact and find safety with this plan."

Fisk shrugged, "But don't we still need the ponies?"

Jones spoke, "We must have the diversion. Most of the students don't ride sufficiently well enough to make the ponies necessary, at this point. We simply walk. We really have little choice."

Entreska forcibly brushed back her grimy, sweat-streaked hair and wished they could just surrender. Entreska felt a distinct sadness permeate her whole person. The emotion was not hers, however. She only felt regret that they would die.

She asked the Voice, *"Why are you so sad?"*

"I know the joys of a long life. I cannot feel anything but sadness for those who are so young and faced with the terror of death."

"I suppose us youngsters don't really understand, do we?"

"Your courage only increases my sadness. But do not despair, as long as you live, there is hope."

"Do you mean that we should surrender?"

"Possibly. That time is not yet at hand."

"Even so. Cumar only take prisoners to be slaves or sacrifices. Jurasketu consider slavery a living death, an abomination. And so it's freedom or death. That is our way."

Silence.

They continued to rest until the Eastern sky began to glow with another impending sunrise. Entreska rested but slept little. Before her long weeks of nightmares, she would have not done well by resting without actually sleeping. She would have been seriously distressed.

But after the nightmares, she was a veteran non-sleeper, so she was hardly discomfited.

To her surprise, Jeremy Fisk announced that he would take the ponies to the southwest. Fisk brushed off her questions. Park Jones confirmed the action.

"The ponies will find themselves abandoned and attempt to return. If led, they will go some distance providing a more substantial diversion."

"But what about the Mountaineer?"

Jones smiled, "Fisk? He's more likely to survive on his own than with us. In fact, I've told him to forget the diversion if discovered and escape back to Jurasketu. He's lived through much, much worse predicaments than this. He doesn't want to leave us. I had to give him a direct order."

Fisk went southwest. The rest went north. They had about 250 ponies. They kept seventy-five and sent 175 with Fisk. Entreska walked in the lead. Jones and his troop trailed behind. They worked back and forth to confuse their tracks. They needed to make their double-back tactic non-obvious. With the passage of several hours, wind and dust will degrade the tracks to such a degree that direction of the tracks will be difficult to determine. Or that was the idea.

The desert wind was quiet, and they walked their ponies. The combination reduced their dust plume to a mere wisp by comparison to the ponies racing to a waterless death in the Lower Raffin. They marched the entire day, but taking frequent breaks. The heat sapped their energy. Seven students collapsed and died from the heat. Each time, they quickly covered the body with sand and marched on after taking the dead's remaining water.

They covered nearly forty kilometers in the day's march. They had walked in their own footsteps for the first twenty-five. Park Jones already had a suitable place in mind when he had proposed the double-back plan. They had crossed a rocky flat. The flat extended some distance perpendicular to their original tracks, so it provided a perfect departure point for their double back scheme. When they had first crossed the flat, they had traveled some distance along its major axis in an attempt to break the trail and lose pursuers. The Scouts checked the northern tracks and found no signs of pursuit. That, at least, was promising they thought.

They left a few items to help a pursuer find the original trail. They didn't want anyone searching the length of the rocky flat and accidentally discovering the new tracks before finding and following the old ones. Finally, they escaped to the east. Park Jones led them to the hidden canyon and oasis near the eastern end of the flat.

They marched a little faster along the rocks, letting the weakest ride the ponies. The rocky flat was covered in just a thin layer of coarse sand that remained earthbound when disturbed. Using ponies pulling light drags, they obscured their tracks sufficiently for the wind to cover them completely within a few hours. Two hours after reaching the rocky flats, they slipped into the hidden canyon. To their relief, it had not been visited recently. Jones believed that he and his patrol, that had discovered it four years ago, had been the last visitors.

The oasis lay astride a very slight rise that extended for several kilometers along a crooked but mostly north-south axis. No other terrain features existed close enough to provide the vantage necessary to see the hole in the Lower Raffin from anywhere other than the very rim itself. The location hid the canyon because almost nobody ever happened to walk through the two-hectare area comprising Park's Canyon, which is what everyone started calling it soon after they had made camp. No humans other than military patrols would ever have reason to enter the area in the first place. In fact, the only known visitors in recent memory were Park Jones and other Jurasketu cavalry, and they had been there exactly once before.

Hopefully, anyone diligent enough to search this area would focus on the very visible trail they had left and follow the tracks to the south and never look their way. Entreska felt, as did the others, that they would avoid the current pursuit. Exiting the Raffin would be another matter. Entreska wished they could just hide and wait the Cumar out, but she actually feared the storms more than the Cumar. With the Cumar, there was at least a chance of escaping their notice. The storms allowed no escape.

The column just barely squeezed into the canyon. Seventy-five ponies and two hundred-odd people don't exactly fit well into a small hole in the ground, considering one-third of the available canyon floor was covered in water. The steep sides dropped some 20 meters to the canyon floor except for the southeast corner, which sloped at a lower, negotiable angle accessible to humans and sure-footed ponies. A heavy volume of water trickled from cracks in the north wall creating a crystal clear pool. The north and west edges of the pool merged into the sheer rock walls. Near the walls, the water turned out to be over three meters deep. The pool became increasingly shallow to the southeast until it simply faded into wet mucky ground where a thick bramble of whiteberry bushes mixed with grasses grew. A roomy, dry cave reached back behind the east wall near the northeast corner.

Brambles did not prevent the ponies and most of the able bodied from splashing directly into the water quickly turning it murky brown. Jones and Entreska reluctantly quelled the enthusiasm and enforced a curfew on noise. They organized the distribution of clean water (from the trickle on the wall), dried fruit, and meat.

They already knew from Park Jones that the water was sweet, with a heavy mineral flavor - but otherwise pure and drinkable. Entreska heard someone speculate that the water would have brought high prices in the Jurasketu Medicinals Trade. Irony poured from the limestone walls. Entreska figured they drank enough to purchase a fine Lenvecha in the Jurasketu countryside.

The fifty who were worst off were carried into the cave. Water and food was then brought up to them. Heavy shadows filled the cave as dusk approached. The ponies were herded into the southwest corner after they had allowed them to drink their fill. The ponies carefully nosed around the prickly, poisonous brambles to get at the edible grasses. Entreska hoped they wouldn't have to resort to eating the ponies.

Jones posted guards in shifts of ten. The guards would lay in a low sand covered tent watching the landscape through a slit and pretending to be a small mound of dirt. Anyone more than twenty meters away would never spot the deception. They could watch for approaching enemy (or friends) for as far as they could see, which was a fair distance, perched on the rise, as they were.

Exhausted, Entreska sat on a flat rock near the north wall and dangled her bare feet in the cool, soothing water. She wondered about the others. She hoped that the other groups had escaped, but she knew their chances were slim. Colonel Jones, Garth and the Black Scorpions were doomed. So far, they had only barely avoided the Cumar cavalry. Only Park Jones' skill, knowledge and luck had kept them from disaster, and yet, they were no closer to real safety, and worse they had sacrificed most of their hoofed transport. The other two groups needed as much luck and skill to elude what seemed to be a fairly substantial force of Cumar cavalry deployed to prevent escape. Vest and his group probably had the best chance, given their greater skill and speed, but Entreska felt Vest and his troops would do everything to draw extra attention to themselves without regard to their own safety. The Black Scorpions were definitely the heroic types. Their heroism and devotion to duty would probably get them killed.

"I have news"

"Don't tell me if it's not good news."

Silence.

Entreska didn't ask for another ten minutes, more from perversion than aversion.

"Tell me."

"Vest's group still lives. The ruined city is besieged. Both sides are engaging in great efforts, but the battle is not formerly joined."

"That's not so bad, I guess. What about the other groups?"

"One group encountered a large Cumar detachment yesterday. I believe they were all killed or captured."

Entreska softly, but audibly blurted out, "Blast." She also kicked up water in frustration. Several people looked her way, but she ignored them and they said nothing.

"The other group?"

"They have avoided a direct encounter, but they are suffering greatly from the heat and exhaustion of evading pursuit. The group will not likely remain intact through tomorrow. I'm sorry."

"Ironic isn't it?"

"What is?"

"Although I try to focus on normal daily life in my studies, a major portion of my work has been devoted to studying what happens to people in tragic circumstances. I have often wondered what it would be like. I often imagined myself in their place."

"Yes, that is ironic."

"No. That is not ironic. I always imagined myself as the innocent. Termination of existence is something everyone must face."

"I cannot agree, giving myself as counterexample."

"Now, that is ironic. But you know what I mean. Wizards who live in crystals don't really count. Nor do I wish to tread into the metaphysics of the afterlife."

"You are right. Please continue."

"Misfortune, poor judgment and time all render their verdicts on living things, and the verdict is always death. Many rail against this as unfair in some way. I think that is silly and foolish. People say life is unfair. They are right, and they are wrong. In that, life is not fair, it is fair. I don't mean that as sophistry. Fairness comes from expectations. Life is not expected to be

fair, hence it is."

"Life is fairly not fair, I agree. Is this your irony?"

"No. My actions have brought unfairness to the Black Scorpions and the workers who followed my quest into the High Raffin. They suffer because of my actions. That is the irony. I never imagined myself as bringing ruin and death on so many. I did not imagine myself as the agent of tragedy. I don't see how people like my father and Uncle Val handle the terror."

"The terror?"

"The terror of leading people who trusted you into pain and death."

"Ah. That I understand. I've known that terror myself. But all is not yet lost."

"Even if we survive, the tragedy remains. I am not sure I wish to survive."

"As you say, life is not fair. You acted in belief no harm would come. Malfeasance was not your aim. Puck and his troops are responsible. They are the unlawful. And I think you give too little credit to your students and the soldiers. Did you deliberately deceive them to the risks? They certainly knew that danger awaited them. They took the risk onto themselves. Many relish the prospect of danger."

"Malfeasance? No. Deception? I deceived myself. Negligence? Arrogance? Disregarding the obvious risks for glory? Yes. I must hold myself accountable."

She felt another wave of sadness that was not her own.

"I must seem pathetic to you."

"Nonsense. You are not pathetic. We caused suffering far beyond this in years past through negligence and towering arrogance. We are even probably responsible for Puck in some indirect way. It is most likely, some action we did or did not take allowed Puck to gain his power. Unfortunately, I think that is the way of all things. Holding yourself accountable to life's inherent unfairness is also silly and foolish. You are a good leader. The survival of those who remain might depend on your skills as a leader. So, it would be irresponsible of you to give up because you have experienced difficulty."

Of course, Entreska could only agree. She would not be able to escape her responsibility.

She continued to sit with her feet dangling in the cool water for some time after dusk. Two small half-moons and a full phase of the Child eventually rose into the restricted view of the sky offered by Park's Canyon. The white light of the large moon masked all but the brightest stars. Entreska thought wistful nothings as she studied the moon's mottled face.

Often people say things about rotten places to die or ways to die. They'll say "Wouldn't that be a *painful* way to die" or "Boy, *that* would be a terrible way to die" or "I can't imagine dying *there*". Entreska couldn't see the sense in any of their speculations. The terrible thing about dying wasn't the where and how; it was the when and why. Pain was irrelevant. Save the "quick and painless death" talk for the cowards. If you live, the pain becomes an interesting memory to relate over hot tea after dinner. *Where* only matters to the survivors, and only while they live. Graves and markers are there to remind the living that they are mortal and provide fixtures upon which to hang their grief.

Well, just damn all that.

An anonymous death made no difference to the dead. In a few thousand years, it would matter to no one but the archaeologists. She amused herself with thoughts of some future digger finding their remains and pitiful belongings in layers of sediment while investigating this hole. What would such a digger think? Sorrow for the dead? Would the digger even have an inkling of why the bones lay here in the first place? She muffled a laugh and withdrew her legs from the water. She reclined on the rocks and stared at the sky, knees bent, hands locked behind her head. Soon she rolled to her side and tried to sleep fast.

The Winds of Chaos

Glen quietly slurped Tarfun Stone Brew from a mug as he formed his battle plan over a light dinner of mild cheese and soda crackers. In the morning, the two heavy and two light regiments pushing toward Duravon would wheel and advance directly on Saffron's troops instead. Four of the lights pursuing the fleeing Cumar would turn and attack the Cumar at Duravon from the south and west. A light regiment from the Attaraque would race down and press the Cumar at Duravon from the north so they could not threaten the forces moving against Saffron. The Swamp Rats and the two reserve lights would engage the three Cumar regiments on the Immortal far left.

The two heavy and two light regiments commanded by General Urkiza would attack and fall back attempting to entice Saffron to press them against his two Cumar regiments at Duravon (not realizing they would be under a crushing attack). Two heavy regiments and a light under General Welkin would then fall on Saffron's left flank. Saffron would likely be expecting the flanking attack since a feigned frontal attack and disorderly withdrawal enticing the enemy to pursue into a trap was a classic Jurasketu tactic. He would either turn his flank to meet the attempted envelopment (most likely) or force-march to the north in an attempt to outflank the expected flankers. In any event, nearly all of Saffron's forces would be engaged enabling the real flanking force the time and space required to make a decisive attack.

A force of two heavy regiments, the remaining light and the Dawn Spiders under Marshal Tang would advance quickly, just south of the Swamp Rats holding off Saffron's flank guard, and drive almost assuredly and unexpectedly onto Saffron's rear. The one remaining heavy regiment would remain in reserve - with the expectation that the five lights would make quick work of the two Cumar banners at Duravon and provide strategic reserve by the next day.

If Saffron got impetuous, his entire force would be destroyed - otherwise they would be badly mauled and forced to withdraw down the western side of the Maw. Glen summoned his command staff who quickly drew up the required detailed orders for immediate distribution to the regimental commanders. Once satisfied that his orders were complete and in transit, he retired to his sleeping tent for his evening brandy. He also requested the most melancholy flute player available. He would not likely need to make another decision until tomorrow afternoon when battle and scouting reports arrived so he had resolved to indulge his sorrows before engaging in remorseless revenge.

Glen eased himself down into his ancient folding chair and sipped his brandy. Lieutenant Eneko announced the arrival of Rath the Flutist who appeared wearing the insignia of the Dawn Spiders. Rath saluted, smartly banging his fist off his broad chest, and his rounded features showed no fear or nervousness usually seen in those appearing before the Grand Marshal for the first time. Glen waved a sloppy return salute. Glen hated the practice of saluting but had never been able to muster the necessary courage to face the traditionalist uproar and accusations of madness that would accompany any attempt to do away with it.

Impressed by the lack of fear, hoping it wasn't actually a sign of languid stupidity, he asked, "What is your normal duty, Trooper?"

Rath barked, "Grand Marshal. Flight Leader, 4th Flight, 3rd Troop, Knife Squadron, Dawn Spiders."

Glen raised an eyebrow, "The Dawn Spiders' Knife Squadron is - or rather was - on picket duty at the southern Maw. How did you come to be here?"

"Grand Marshal. I had been on leave. Colonel Fuller gave me Command liaison duty when we rode from White Tower."

Glen nodded.

Rath cleared his throat, his military perfection softening suddenly, "Er... Grand Marshal... Uh... Have there been any reports?"

Glen frowned, "No. I'm afraid not. They seem to have vanished for the moment. Their fate will be known soon enough I'm sure. And there is no need to invoke my title at every utterance, please."

Rath sighed, "Yes, Grand Marshal. Thank you."

Glen suppressed an involuntary grin and then asked, "Do you know *The Lament of Yangulor*?"

"Yes, Grand Marshal... I mean... I have a most satisfactory interpretation. It often brings tears."

"Indeed. I am in need of tears. Please make yourself comfortable."

Glen waved at the collection of pillows and chairs situated on a large rug that occupied most of his rather opulent field tent.

"Thank you."

Glen drank too much brandy and did indeed cry on the third rendition. He wanted to worry about the coming battle, but he could not. His troops and officers were excellent, well-trained warriors. It was extremely unlikely that Saffron would even realize he needed to make an unexpected and necessarily brilliant move to escape defeat - much less make such a move. Glen's army had superior forces, position and information. Saffron was doomed.

This only deepened Glen's gloom. His darling Entreska and his best friend would still be dead. Why hadn't he anticipated this scenario? From all the evidence, Saffron had been after the Expedition. Nothing else could explain Cumar blundering all over the Raffin chasing defenseless students. Saffron had allowed his Cumar cavalry to be unbelievably scattered to the point where they had become themselves nearly defenseless against the counterattack that the Jurasketu had mounted. How could Puck have known?

Timing argued against treachery. Unless... Unless... Maybe the spy or traitor didn't know the Expedition plan, destination or schedule at all - just had followed the Expedition and then relayed information to Puck. That would explain the delay in gathering forces to attack and the fact that the attack seemed to occur 'too late'. Glen cursed the Raffin. Still, the size of the attack force seemed out of kilter with the target. By marshaling a large force, Saffron had given the Jurasketu ample time to muster a countering force.

Admittedly, a reinforced squadron of the Black Scorpions ensconced behind field defenses with unknown reserves cannot be regarded as an easy target and so possibly Saffron had believed he needed enough force to overwhelm the defenders to accomplish his goals in a timely fashion. The fact that forces had been deployed to disrupt communications and even attempt to block a relieving force indicated that Saffron had feared a swift counter stroke. Glen frowned... That didn't make sense entirely - Saffron had destroyed the Scorpions and the Expedition, but he was still holding his position despite evidence that a substantial counterattack was in progress. Somehow, his goal was incomplete. *But what?* "What?"

Rath dropped the flute from his lips and asked with concern, "Grand Marshal?"

Glen looked around. He rubbed his face and waved a hand,

"Sorry. Just thinking aloud. Keep playing please."

Rath shrugged and changed tunes to a haunting rendition of *The Wreck of the Golden Boar*. For making the change without permission, Glen almost reprimanded Rath who appeared to be watching carefully for Glen's reaction. Instead, Glen nodded his head in approval and Rath relaxed.

Late the next morning, Glen awoke exhausted and drained, but unrepentant. He splashed some water on his face and staggered over to the Command Tent. He never ate a real breakfast, but Eneko had his usual field concoction of molasses and coffee spiked with a dollop of brandy ready for him. When not in the field, he preferred fresh cream instead of the molasses - and more brandy. He sipped his coffee and surveyed the strategy map. The Command Staff was arguing over the purported position of two Cumar Banners south of Duravon. The map showed that his troops were on the move, but unless something unusual happened, there would be no battle reports until later in the afternoon. When those reports arrived, everything would likely need to be packed up and moved west to follow the battle.

Juragi arrived after lunch having been off solving some logistical problem with water. He discreetly asked to speak to Glen privately. Glen consented and they stepped outside into one of a handful of mild weather days seen on the Raffin.

Juragi, with a wry tone, said, "Good weather blesses our battle plans."

Glen muttered, "Blessed be our plans."

Juragi chuckled halfheartedly and then, in a casual tone that Glen from long association knew was anything but casual, asked, "Did you happen to address some of the troops without my knowing?"

"Can't I do so without your permission?"

Juragi sighed, "You are the Grand Marshal, not I. I was merely trying to ascertain whether or not you had addressed the troops."

Glen frowned, "No. I did not. Why do you ask?"

Juragi shrugged, "The troops seem to be talking about getting revenge. Almost too eagerly. The talk amongst the officers is we're going to take the fight all the way to the Centaur Citadel. I was just curious if you had said something that implied we might."

Glen raised his eyebrows in surprise, "Nothing of the sort. I've been my usual circumspect self."

"And you didn't order Colonel Humble to study how Saffron might retreat to the Citadel?"

Glen shrugged, "I did order that. The two Mountaineer regiments and the Swamp Rats might be able to partially disengage and send a squadron or two to temporarily block Saffron's retreat. They could easily delay his retreat for a day or two without loss to themselves yet leave Saffron suffering in the cold without adequate supplies causing additional casualties."

Juragi narrowed his eyes, but nodded in understanding and converted his gaze to look across the gently blowing sands.

Glen gave him a sidelong glance and wondered if Juragi knew Glen's mind better than he did.

Juragi harrumphed suddenly and said, "You can't bring her back. And you risk the safety of Jurasketu. And your continuance in command."

Glen remained impassive at what was essentially a grave insult.

"I am risking nothing."

Juragi tucked his chin against his chest, folded his arms and threw a furtive glance at Glen. Then he looked up and away into the desert and sighed.

Glen chuckled, "You disagree?"

Juragi turned to face him and said, "You and I might agree. But will the Demon?"

Glen cocked his eye and shrugged.

The Demon marched closer with exaggerated arm swings and foot stomps that flung sand in all directions at each pounding step. At Juragi's words, the Demon stopped and smiled. Its left arm reached across, grabbed its right elbow and with a horrible crunching sound and with a great gout of black blood snapped the arm off. Still smiling, the Demon flipped the arm up and then snatched it out of the air.

The Demon waved the still twitching arm above its hairless, grotesquely wrinkled head and then began to rhythmically slap itself across the face with the self-dismembered arm. Left, right, left, right. With each slap, a blood mist spewed from the opposite ear like steam from a boiling kettle. Glen observed impassively as the Demon increased the speed and violence of the slaps. The head began to snap back and forth with each blow. But yet the Demon smiled...

Glen carefully considered what he had to say next. Juragi had to be convinced of his sincerity and truthfulness. Glen breathed deeply and willed himself to believe the lie he was about to tell. In truth, he had been forming this lie for some time. Since he kept and maintained many secrets as both the Grand Marshal and a member of the Imperium Council, it should be easy enough to field a reasonable sounding, pretend secret as perfectly real and deceive soldiers trained and eager to respond to commands especially when they believed so much in his leadership as they did.

This was not some harmless lie. Thousands of Jurasketu soldiers would die, be crippled and suffer if things went well. If things went poorly, the whole army could be lost and Jurasketu would likely fall to Imperium machinations in a decade or more should that happen.

Juragi would not be privy to the lie and not allowed to consciously choose his path. He would act as though it were true and thus totally failing in the duty entrusted to him by the Jurasketu Army, which was to ensure that lawful orders of the Grand Marshal were carried out. But these would not be lawful orders, seemingly so, but unlawful nonetheless. Even if Puck were overthrown, Juragi would not escape court martial and at least complete disgrace.

Military commanders routinely have to make decisions that result in pain, injury and death to their own troops. His soldiers understood that was going to happen. It was their noble and solemn duty as members of the Jurasketu Army. Glen knew that most of his army was willing to risk that sacrifice in pursuit of revenge for what Puck and the Cumar had done or would do. Such sacrifice was willing and honorable. Sacrificing Juragi's honor without his consent was distinctly different.

Nearly twenty years ago, Glen, at considerable risk to his own life, has rescued Juragi from horrific torture and certain death. Juragi had been a teenage, idealistic Valruk nobleman intent on changing Valruk for the better and in the course of events had sought help from Jurasketu. Glen, then serving a term as a marine officer, had become his secret contact. Unfortunately, a Valruk spy in the Jurasketu Army betrayed them and Glen had led the landing party in the famous *Raid on Throok* to rescue Juragi after his arrest. Their lives had been bound together ever since. While Valentine Jones had been his best friend, Juragi was the younger brother he had never had. Jones was dead. And now Glen planned the ruin of Juragi. The consequences of the path he chose would be sorrowful indeed and not least to himself. But it must be done. The Demon demanded action.

Glen spoke in a low whisper, "Recently, I secured secret orders and authority from the National Council of War and the Grand Debater. Should Puck attempt an attack across the Raffin, I can order a counterattack and pursue to the Centaur Citadel and attempt to dethrone Puck if good opportunity should arise."

Juragi stared darkly and then brightened slightly. "Is that why Chairman Rolf went with the Dawn Spiders down to the Maw? To visit your secret supply cavern?"

Glen frowned to cover his utter surprise and worse dismay. Rolf hadn't mentioned he was going to visit the Dawn Spiders. Well, that wasn't entirely true. They had discussed it but nothing had been finalized. But Juragi knew. Juragi also knew about the supply cavern. Had he told Juragi about that and forgotten?

"How did you know Rolf was going with the Dawn Spiders?"

Juragi looked puzzled for a moment. "I ran into Rolf as he was preparing to depart with the Spiders whilst you were up inspecting the Tangur border. He told me he was going to inspect your secret supply cavern. I didn't know what that was, but Rolf seemed to think I should have known - so I acted as if I did. What is the secret supply cavern anyway?"

Glen sighed, "It is the thing that seemingly has deprived me of my son in addition to my daughter."

Juragi almost pleadingly said, "You can't be sure of that. I know we haven't heard from the Spiders - but they probably scattered and withdrew after they realized the size of the forces... The Spiders are a resourceful bunch and their circumstances were different from that of the Scorpions..." Juragi trailed off unconvinced by his own statement.

Glen nodded in real agreement, "You are right. Rolf is ever resourceful and the Spiders didn't have to protect a bunch of students." Glen clenched his fists. He had cried himself out the night before. Today, he only had room for revenge. Glen surmised but sounded certain, "And yes, Rolf had gone down there to ensure the secret supply cavern was well stocked and ready for use as a forward base as I had planned for this moment. Soon, the winter storms will come and cut our supply lines. Even if we seize a coastal town, we cannot be certain our fleet will be able to best Puck's fleet and the winter weather in the Bay of Lydaron can be testy at its mildest. Therefore, the cavern is necessary. It should have enough food, fodder, wagons and material to supply 20 regiments for a year, 10 regiments for two."

Juragi's jaw dropped, "Great Burning Blast. You do intend to force the Centaur Citadel."

Glen shrugged, "That remains to be seen. We must defeat Saffron utterly to effect any such plan. And hope the Cumar that attacked south of the Maw have not despoiled the cave."

They returned to the Command Tent after Juragi noticed a messenger arriving there. A messenger had come from the Swamp Rats making the Second Hour Report, "...the Cumar pickets in the area have been swept clean. The three Cumar banners have been engaged by the 45th and 63rd Reserve Lights that force marched from the White Mountains and straight into battle without rest. The 1st and 4th Heavies, the 14th Lights and the Dawn Spiders have already passed them to the west apparently undetected."

This was regarded as excellent news.

Soon, around the Eighth Hour, the Fourth Hour report from the Feinting Force arrived. "General Urkiza wishes to report that his forces have engaged four Immortal banners and withdrew in feigned poor order. Low casualties. But Immortal pursuit very restrained and minimal."

This was viewed as disappointing but not unexpected.

Additionally, "...the 3rd Heavies and 26th Lights were being organized for another feint or holding attack as circumstances warranted. The 15th Heavies and the 32nd Lights were swinging back around to attack the Immortal right flank near the Maw of Hell to seal off an unlikely escape in that direction and prevent Cumar fleeing the Lower Raffin from rallying there as well."

That was not in the plan, but was seen as good thinking by General Urkiza.

Two hours later, the Third Hour report from the Duravon Force arrived. "The 42nd Lights moving south engaged two Cumar banners a bit further north than expected. Will act as holding force until 2nd, 5th and 6th Lights can attack later in the afternoon."

The argument about positioning of Cumar banners near Duravon broke out anew with some anxiety over the 42nd Lights' ability to withstand a determined attack from the Cumar banners. The strategic reserve, the 11th Heavies, was ordered to move in that direction in case Cumar banners came rampaging towards the headquarters.

Another hour passed and the Noon or Sixth Hour report from the Flanking Force arrived. "General Welkin wishes to report that his forces have made a strong attack on the Immortal flank. The 7th and 8th Heavies repulsed with moderate losses. The 19th Lights are tracking Immortal movements which seemed to be a bit chaotic in response to the attack."

This was also viewed as disappointing, but not unexpected. There was some concern about the chaotic enemy movements. Since the Immortals should have and seem to have foreseen the Jurasketu flanking attack, Saffron's forces should be moving with conviction. Possibly, Saffron had become concerned with a lack of information flowing from his far left flank. The Swamp Rats and the Real Flanking Force had completely cut communications in that direction. If Saffron was paying attention in the midst of the excitement, he would realize that something terribly wrong was happening in that direction. Hence, he might act in a conflicted way in response to the initial flanking attack. That is, chaotic movement of forces might ensue. Either that or the 19th Lights had things confused. They would just have to await the next reports.

As dark approached in the Twelfth Hour, Glen and his ravenously hungry staff were stuffing themselves with sliced sausages and doughy bread when several important reports arrived simultaneously. Amidst much spluttering and choking, the messengers were brought forward.

The Eighth Hour report from the Duravon Force proclaimed, "Two Cumar banners annihilated after being trapped between 42nd Lights and the other three lights. The 5th Lights Fork Squadron suffered over 200 hundred killed and more than 300 seriously injured leading the assault. The 42nd Lights suffered nearly 100 killed when the two banners desperately attempted to escape the trap. Otherwise, minimal casualties."

The Seventh Hour report from the Flanking Force reported, "General Welkin wishes to report that Saffron is retreating in confusion. The 7th and 8th Heavies are making a flanking pursuit, sweeping south to the Maw while the 19th Lights are moving directly west trying to establish contact with either the Swamp Rats or the Real Flanking force."

The Ninth Hour report from the Feinting Force backed up the Flanking Force report. "General Urkiza wishes to report that the 15th Heavies and 32nd Lights crashed into a Cumar banner trying to retreat past the Maw. They are still battling the remnants. The 3rd Heavies and 26th Lights made contact with 7th Heavies and have swung into pursuit between the 19th Lights and the 8th Heavies."

The staff began muttering about the inadequacies of the 7th and 8th Heavies, but Glen told them to quit bemoaning the point, as those problems were known before the battle had been joined. Glen felt the battle was going moderately well - total victory would depend on how fast Saffron could retreat and how quickly Marshal Tang and the Real Flanking Force was moving to cut him off. Glen desired to be closer to the action.

Despite the approaching darkness, Glen ordered the Command Regiment on the move. Glen, Juragi, Eneko and the Command Regiment First Troop, immediately departed on horseback to make contact with the Swamp Rats or 19th Lights. The rest of the Command Regiment would follow at best speed. Colonel Humble was ordered to ride ahead using messenger relays to personally lead the two Reserve Lights and Swamp Rats to the blocking positions he had picked out in the Blades. The 11th Heavies, 2nd Lights and 6th Lights were ordered to replace the Swamp Rats and the two Reserve Lights and destroy or drive off the Cumar.

Aided by strong moonlight, they rode almost all night finally stopping at the Eighteenth Hour when they ran into the 8th Heavies Kitchen Squadron. Glen rousted the squadron commander, Captain Ben Williams, from his command tent and demanded to know the local situation. A sleepy Williams explained that he was caring for 350 wounded troops and exhausted horses from the Flanking Force. Otherwise, he knew nothing that Glen didn't already know from reports. Glen ordered rest for himself and his command troops. They awoke at the Second Hour, the morning sun already beaming across the blustery landscape.

A report from the Command Regiment said they had packed up and left at the Fourteenth Hour. They would likely arrive there at the Seventh Hour. Glen dismissed the messenger with his thanks and decided he would not wait. He wanted to catch the Real Flanking Force.

After a quick breakfast, they rode off to the northeast. Fortunately, the relays had been given notice and estimates of his moving position, so the reports kept arriving in relatively good order to him despite having become a rapidly moving target.

The Eighteenth Hour report from the now reinforced Flanking Force brought mostly disappointing news, "General Urkiza wishes to report that he has assumed command of the pursuing forces. The 7th Heavies have halted from exhaustion and casualties. The 8th Heavies have lost contact with the enemy. The 3rd Heavies and 26th Lights are engaged in night fighting with the Immortal rear guard of unknown size and are unlikely to be able to press the pursuit until noon."

They caught up with the 19th Lights at noon. While in conference with the 19th Lights commander, almost simultaneously, two reports finally arrived from the Real Flanking Force. One report, the Tenth Hour Report from the previous day, said, "Marshal Tang wishes to report that the 14th Lights and Dawn Spiders have seized enemy supply wagons and disrupted all supply trains coming from the Yellow and High Passes. The 1st Heavies and 4th Heavies are driving southeast toward the Maw." The second report, from just the Second Hour that morning, said, "Saffron moving at top speed. At least four Immortal regiments moving rapidly southwest along the edge of the Maw. The 1st Heavies and 4th Heavies forced to rest before resuming pursuit. The Dawn Spiders racing south to scout for potential Immortal reinforcements moving north and further disrupt Saffron's communications. The 14th Lights are keeping the Yellow and High Passes blocked awaiting Colonel Humble. Colonel Fuller gives opinion that Saffron is making for the Needle's Eye. He has sent two Troops to scout the Eye. He requests permission to take and hold the western point of the Eye and then pursuit could bottle up the Immortals in the narrow valley where there would be no escape."

This was disappointing news at best. Although Fuller was likely correct, diversion of the Dawn Spiders to the Eye would leave Saffron relatively unmolested and he might guess the Eye blocked and would instead continue south along the Maw and head for the coast. Saffron apparently had decided he was not going to compound his strategic error of failing to retreat earlier, so Glen needed to press the issue. Glen searched the Web of Thought for a solution...

He granted Fuller's request. The Dawn Spiders would block the Eye. The 14th Lights were ordered to abandon the Yellow and High Passes on the theory that Saffron could not use them, and no reinforcements were coming that way and if they were Colonel Humble and the Swamp Rats would arrive soon enough to prevent such reinforcements from doing harm. Next, the 14th Lights would make a determined attack on the fleeing Immortals. The 14th Lights would hopefully delay and disorganize the Immortals enough for the rest of the army to catch up and effect the total defeat.

He also sent a change of orders to Colonel Humble instructing him to force the Yellow Pass and drive rapidly northwest and seize the village of Deer Creek that guarded the southern approaches to the Citadel. They should get there in about three days. If the fleeing Immortals were not totally destroyed, Humble would have to withdraw as the retreating Immortals pressed against them and the campaign would end in a lost opportunity and likely courts martial.

Against Juragi's advice and some reason, they rode ahead into the chaos of the pursuit, in an attempt to meet the 14th Lights moving to attack. Reports were a little slow to reach them despite the closing proximity to the front. It was near the Tenth Hour before anything caught up.

The Fourth Hour Report from the 15th Heavies was encouraging, "Outflanked and destroyed Saffron's rear guard comprised of almost the entire Immortals of the Thunder and a partial Cumar Banner. Resuming pursuit with the 3rd Heavies, 8th Heavies and 26th Lights. The 32nd Lights remain at the top of the Maw to protect against the appearance of unaccounted for Cumar Banners."

The Sixth Hour Report from the Real Flanking Force was intriguing, "Marshal Tang wishes to report that the 1st Heavies and 4th Heavies have resumed pursuit. No contact with enemy made yet. But the Dawn Spiders report that Saffron has slowed. The 14th Lights still await the arrival of Colonel Humble." Glen chuckled, not anymore. He would likely get the next report from the 14th Lights in person from the commander.

The foothills of the Blades slowed their precipitous ride, but they finally stumbled upon the leftmost troop of the 14th Lights as the sun bled its death throes across the sharp outlines of the Blades. The harried troop commander, a certain Lieutenant Morkstern, assigned them a surprisingly grumpy guide to help locate the regimental command.

After an hour of blundering around in near darkness and listening to a constant, rather annoying stream of obscenities from the guide, they located the regimental command post taking temporary shelter near a pitiful stream flanked by equally pitiful trees and brush. The 14th Lights commanding officer, Colonel Joseph Brown, his right arm in a sling from an arrow wound, just nodded and kept peering at a lantern lit map when his aide announced the arrival of the Grand Marshal. Then he jerked his head in astonishment when Glen stepped up and peered at the map.

Colonel Brown's mouth hung open a moment, and then he recovered his composure, "Grand Marshal. We weren't expecting you."

Glen smiled briefly, "No. I would imagine not."

Colonel Brown deepened his already permanently furrowed brow and said, "Is there a change of orders from the attack ordered at Sixth Hour yesterday?"

Glen shrugged, "No. Not unless you have information that would indicate a change?"

Brown pursed his lips and nodded, "No. Grand Marshal. The Knife Squadron should reach The Eye by Third Hour and the Laundry by Fifth Hour. The Fork is making a deliberately feeble attack on the Immortals vanguard. It will take time for them to decide whether a major force has reached the Eye first or just a scouting force. If Saffron presses immediately, the Fork will resist strongly to encourage the first interpretation. Otherwise, they will just pester until the other squadrons arrive. The uncertainty will certainly help sow chaos when the other squadrons attack the Immortals right flank. If we're lucky, Saffron will respond strongly and pursue."

Glen nodded approvingly, "Good plan. We need just a few hours delay."

A messenger arrived a few minutes later causing a burst of cursing from Brown before the messenger had said a word. "Saffron is withdrawing further down the Maw."

Brown dispatched a change of orders for his regiment sending the Fork and Knife scrambling across the rugged foothills to try and get ahead of Saffron. Glen didn't think they would. The Laundry and Kitchen would pursue directly hoping to slow Saffron with harassment.

Glen sent instructions to Fuller instructing him to continue blocking the Eye in case unexpected enemy reinforcements moved down from the Citadel. Glen felt his opportunity was slipping away.

In the early morning hours, Juragi accosted him as the 14th Lights Command Troop began to decamp. "Glen. If we have not caught Saffron by this evening, we will need to retreat. We've had two mild storms already. A strong one could do grave harm."

Glen shut his eyes and rubbed his hands across his ears to avoid seeing or hearing the Demon who was trying to get his attention. Glen focused as hard as he could. Juragi was right. The Army must withdraw by evening unless a miracle halted Saffron. Glen nodded and opened his eyes to see a great relief wash over Juragi who had been suffering deeply under the stress.

A commotion several meters away drew their attention. A grimy, blood streaked messenger gesticulated wildly while speaking to several staff officers. Raised, yet unintelligible, voices carried to where Juragi and Glen stood. Juragi was clearly annoyed by this overt lack of discipline. Glen, however, trotted over to the disturbance with

Juragi belatedly in pursuit.

Without announcing himself, Glen barked at the grimy messenger, "Who are you?"

In a wave of fear and recognition, the staff officers, soldiers and grimy messenger turned towards Glen, fell silent, froze and then stiffened to attention. Glen normally would have smiled and made a joke about Grand Marshal's not biting - but instead repeated his question with more urgency.

The grimy messenger, recovered his presence and shouted, "Grand Marshal. I am Scout Master Robert Clawfoot, Dawn Spiders, Knife Squadron–"

"What? Knife Squadron? How?"

Breathlessly, the Scout continued, "Yes. Grand Marshal. Chairman Rolf wishes to report that the Dawn Spiders made contact with Immortals Force at Fifth Hour, yesterday. Immortals halted, but expected to resume movement soon. Dawn Spiders have since withdrawn from contact and will skirmish with the Immortals to slow their movement down the skirt of the Maw. Please advise."

Glen blinked once and then barked out a laugh. Then not realizing that Juragi had followed him, he turned back and bellowed, "Juragi!"

Juragi cringed slightly but said nothing. Glen clapped him on the shoulder and said, "Tell Marshal Tang to rush things along! Colonel Brown! Where's Brown?"

Juragi sprinted off to find a suitable messenger. A few seconds of shouting brought a disheveled Colonel Brown running up to Glen. "Grand Marshal?"

"Chairman Rolf has conjured a miracle and blocked Saffron's retreat. We must press immediately to battle."

Uncharacteristically Glen thought, Colonel Brown showed no sign of astonishment and instead turned on his staff officers, "You heard the Grand Marshal! I want all squadrons on the move immediately! Battle dress and water only! The Second Troop under Lieutenant Graves will collect remaining equipment and catch up this evening!"

Glen turned to the grimy messenger, "Scout Master Clawfoot. Tell Chairman Rolf that light troops will engage before Sixth Hour. Heavy troops will attack Saffron tomorrow no later than evening. Continue to skirmish as long as possible."

The messenger saluted and departed in haste on a fresh horse.

Showing proper senior command nonchalance in the face of battle, Glen waited until Juragi returned to issue further orders,

"Order General Urkiza to release his regiments except for the 15th Heavies to General Welkin who will bring them under Marshal Tang at best possible speed. General Urkiza with the remaining lights at Duravon and the 15th Heavies should proceed to the village of Deer Creek and join with Colonel Humble. He should secure the area, scout for Puck's forces and press the attack where he will."

Juragi breathed deeply, smiled and said, "I told you Rolf was likely still alive."

Glen laughed and then grimly replied, "Yes. Yes he is. Hopefully, he will still be once this battle is concluded."

Juragi nodded and said, "And the weather around the Centaur Citadel will not be kind. The winds will be howling."

Glen shrugged, "Our troops can handle it. We will not be short on food. If anything, the winds will impede the defenders more than us. So, I think that The Winds of Chaos will roar over the Citadel."

Juragi grunted, then turned and ran off to find a messenger.

Glen reflected on his plans. Saffron was finished. Two weeks of war had totally destroyed Puck's forces bordering the Raffin. While Glen knew that as many as five Immortals regiments would likely winter around the Centaur Citadel, the remainder of Pucks' forces were largely elsewhere. Most were arrayed against raids through the White Mountains and defending the northern river plains against attacks by the Zattan Imperium. The rest were raiding Wokometu or maintaining order in the rich potato and rice fields of the coastal plains.

Most if not all of Saffron's messengers have been intercepted, and so Puck may actually be ignorant of the true military picture for several days. Glen planned to rectify that ignorance in a most dramatic fashion, by knocking on Puck's front door with forty thousand troops. He flexed his wrists and pantomimed knocking on a door drawing a few sidelong glances from soldiers hurrying past.

The Escape Artist

One of the most important physical qualities for being an escape artist is a suitable ratio of hand to wrist size. Small wrists and big hands are a really bad combination. Fortunately, Mallory had massive, powerful wrists and relatively small hands for his size. He also had the most important mental quality - a very high tolerance for pain.

They had put him in a covered wagon designed as a brig. An iron cage filled the wagon interior. A chamber pot, held in place by an iron hoop, occupied a front corner. The other front corner had a heap of old, surprisingly clean blankets. The iron door had a heavy lock. A large, lidded bucket of spring water held station near the door. He was the only prisoner.

His wrists and ankles had been manacled. They had been tightened using heavy bolts. Mallory had done the usual trick of expanding and angling his wrists just enough to prevent the manacles from being tightened properly. He was certain he could pull his hands free in seconds. That left the door lock and the ankle manacles, which were attached by a chain to the cage. Both required tools. The other problem was the two guards stationed at the front of the wagon. They had taken his eating knife and money purse containing his few silver and gold coins. Surprisingly, they hadn't taken his clothing or shoes. That made things a lot easier.

Mallory wondered for a while if Entreska or Garth might help him escape. Of course, they were trying to organize the entire Expedition's escape so maybe they wouldn't have time or inclination. Or now they had their doubts about him, too. Not that he could blame them. The arrival of Puck's Army was terribly disconcerting. It added one more item to his litany of misfortunes.

Mallory sat, sweated and watched what he could see of the withdrawal. The long weeks of working together in the heat had honed the teamwork of the Expedition. Even though the planned orderly withdrawal with all equipment turned into an abandon everything but transport, food and water - all the students and workers were gone by noon. All that remained was a rear guard of Black Scorpions who busied themselves preparing defenses and destroying equipment. They didn't look like they were going to be leaving. No one seemed to be making any preparation towards attaching horses or mules to his prison wagon. He looked like he was going to stay with the rear guard and die or be captured by Puck's forces if he didn't escape. Mallory chuckled to himself. It was evident that his quota for unfortunate events was not yet filled. But he wasn't dead yet. He would wait until darkness. He napped the rest of the afternoon away in a heavy sweat.

Towards dusk, a soldier lightly rapped on the bars. Mallory woke with a weak smile. The grim-faced soldier smiled weakly back, "Dinner." Mallory greedily took the wooden plate heaped with unexpectedly good fare consisting of fried bacon, dried apples, pickled olives and fresh bread. Mallory ate clumsily being sure to cover his hands with as much grease from the bacon as possible.

The soldier watched as Mallory ate, so Mallory said, "Do we have long?"

The soldier hesitated in thought as if deciding whether or not to converse with Mallory. After a time, shrugged his shoulders and said, "Who can say? At least a day. Maybe three if the Immortals are sufficiently cautious."

Mallory smiled, "Well then. I guess my prison term will be quite brief."

The soldier laughed, "One could say the same for my enlistment."

The soldier left. Mallory feigned indifference as the soldier disappeared into the approaching darkness. Not long after that, the constant guard presence was exchanged for periodic visits from a walking sentry every 20 minutes or so. Mallory was not surprised since he felt all along that the guards had been there to secure him against someone trying to free him rather than escaping on his own which should have been impossible to manage ever much less in a short space of time. Anyway, a slightly happier Mallory was left to consider his escape plans alone while the last rays of sunlight slithered away into the shadows.

He would need to travel northeast to retrieve his equipment and weapons that lay hastily buried 30 kilometers distant. That would potentially require moving through Puck's army, as it most assuredly would be encircling the ruins of Duravon. A horse would impede that part of his journey to safety and might be risky to obtain, but he should be able to run that distance in about 4 hours comfortably. Once he had regained his equipment, with the chaos of war swirling, he should be able to secure a desert pony and flee eastward toward Jurasketu. He concentrated on remembering the relevant terrain and thinking over various alternatives but none seemed better than the one he had already chosen.

His thoughts drifted to Entreska. He wondered if he should try to find her. That seemed a trifle difficult since he would be viewed by the Black Scorpions accompanying her as an escaped prisoner. At best, he could do nothing but surveil her and do what? Once he recovered his equipment, he had just enough ammunition to slaughter an entire regiment. If he had a good defensive position, he might be able to manage doing exactly that. But he didn't have his body armor - and mobile cavalry wouldn't feel obliged to assault him on his terms or reliably panic if he made an attack. He would just have to hope she and her students would reach safety on their own.

When the small red moon rose a couple hours later, Mallory set to work. He drank some water. Then he laid down in the blankets pretending to sleep in case someone was watching that he couldn't see. He took a few deep breaths and steeled his mind for pain and then aided by the bacon grease yanked first his right, then his left through the manacles. He pulled and massaged his thumbs afterward to make sure they weren't misaligned from the trauma.

While still laying down, he undid the velcro holding his right epaulet in place and fidgeted with the detached epaulet until it came apart into two cloth tabs. The tabs were connected by an 80cm long piece of Diamond Thread, a nearly unbreakable carbon filament wire studded with what would be best described as diamond dust. Mallory slipped the thread around the bolt holding his right ankle manacle in place, and using the cloth tabs as handles, he began sawing. Mallory didn't want to make too much noise or tire himself out, so he slowly pulled back and forth applying light pressure allowing the thread to do all the work. In only five minutes, however, he cut through the bolt. The left ankle manacle only took five minutes more. He carefully and slowly removed the manacles to make sure that any observer, despite the dim moonlight, would only see the expected movements of a restless sleeper. He pulled a blanket over himself to hide his liberated feet and hands, threw another blanket over the empty manacles, and waited a few minutes for the sentry to pass.

After the sentry dutifully shuffled past, Mallory turned to the cage door lock. Mallory rolled over facing the door as if tossing in his sleep. A few minutes later, he carefully snaked the Diamond Thread over the heavy bar lock. Next, he wrapped a blanket corner around the door to hold it shut once the bar was cut. The bar was thick and the sawing took nearly fifteen minutes to cut all the way through. He reassembled the epaulet and returned it to his shoulder. Then he covered up for the next sentry pass that came right on schedule.

Mallory lay still afterward and rested planning his next move. After the next sentry pass, he would slip out the door and skulk his way out of the camp. He would probably try exiting to the south and then head around to the northeast. It would be simple enough. However, if he was spotted either leaving the wagon or later on - he decided that his tactic would be to run like a madman screaming that Puck's Army had infiltrated the camp - hoping that would provide enough distraction for him to disappear into the night.

While thinking his next moves through, four soldiers approached nearly invisible in the dim moonlight. In a panic, fearing he would be 'waked', Mallory hastily sat up against the cage near the door and rearranged the blankets over himself and the manacles. Two soldiers held back while two others approached the cage directly. Mallory watched carefully trying to appear bored.

This failed when he recognized one of the soldiers to be Colonel Jones. Instead, he tried not to appear shocked and said, "Colonel. I continue to most emphatically deny being a spy for Puck or any enemy of Jurasketu or even having bad intentions towards any Jurasketu citizen."

Jones uncharacteristically smiled, ignored the pleading and said, "Quite frankly, I'm surprised you're still here. I would have expected you to have escaped by now."

Mallory couldn't decide whether or not Jones was taunting him or goading him or something else. He made no reply.

Jones frowned, "Where's your sense of gallows humor?"

Mallory decided he was being taunted. "Probably where you left your trust of bedraggled strangers."

Jones laughed heartily. "That's better."

Mallory smiled weakly remaining impassive and still. He dared not move and reveal his lack of restraint or accidentally jostle the door open. The young lieutenant to the right of Jones shifted his body ever so slightly indicating his discomfort with the situation. Mallory waited for more, but when nothing was forthcoming, "Did you want to ask me something? Or did you just come by to taunt me?"

Jones smiled again, "Neither. I came to release you. I'm convinced you are not the spy."

Jones waved to the men behind him. A soldier bearing a heavy wrench and several keys hustled up and stepped in front of Jones as he moved aside. He fumbled with the keys and finally picked one out. He inserted it into the lock and then his jaw went slack. Without turning the key, he reached out and tugged on the bars of the door. With a slight scrape, the door swung out and the severed end of the bar fell, clattered against the wagon and bounced to the ground. Everyone including Mallory stared at the piece of metal for a long moment. Then all the soldiers stared at Mallory who tried to look surprised. Then they all turned to look at Jones.

Jones frowned, looked sternly at the soldiers and then looked back to Mallory. He held Mallory's gaze for a moment and then burst out into deep but quiet laughter. The other soldiers looked around in mild terror at their apparently deranged leader.

Jones, still laughing, pointed at Mallory and said, "Take off that blanket."

Mallory shrugged and pulled the blanket down to reveal that the manacles were no longer attached to him. Jones laughed harder. Mallory maintained a simple look of mild disappointment and remained where he sat.

Jones stopped laughing after a time and held out his hand to assist Mallory from the cage. Mallory stepped out and brushed himself off knocking metal dust from his sleeves.

Mallory started to ask a question, but Jones silenced him with a gesture and led him back to the Command Tent where he gave him a tumbler of whiskey, which Mallory gladly took and sipped.

Mallory asked, "And, why exactly, are you convinced I'm not a spy."

"Not *The Spy*. You may very well be *a* spy."

"Ah. I may indeed. Then who is *The Spy*?"

"A carpenter named Carl Wurtz. We caught him sneaking towards the west after the departure of everyone else. In his despair at getting caught, he taunted and threatened us."

Mallory recalled the man and thought him unlikely. He was a burly, seemingly happy man. Then Mallory brightened, "So, the evacuation was a ruse to capture the spy?"

Jones frowned, "Ruse? No. Puck's Army comes indeed. But we suspected there was a spy because yesterday morning we found, quite by accident, a small cache of food, water, gear and weapons buried a ways from our encampment."

Mallory froze in slight terror for a moment before he recalled that Jones said Wurtz had been sneaking west, and Mallory had cached no water - not having any left by that time.

Mallory recovered and asked, "And so Wurtz told you I wasn't the spy?"

Jones laughed bitterly, "No. And we certainly wouldn't take his word for it if he had. But we knew there had to be someone who had given away our position to Puck. And the most likely candidate seemed to be you. It would have been irresponsible to not arrest you. However, now since the only reason I arrested you has been seemingly removed, it would be irresponsible to continue holding you prisoner."

Mallory merely nodded.

Jones became sullen and stared into the distance.

Mallory asked, "What now?"

Jones appeared puzzled for a moment then nodded, "Ah. Yes. No reason for you to stay here. Given your skills and obvious intelligence, it would be a crime for you to die with us."

Mallory sighed having sensed for some time that Jones was planning on attempting to hold Puck's army at Duravon. Mallory spoke with obvious desperate concern, "Why aren't you planning a fighting withdrawal and try to screen the fleeing students?"

Jones became stone faced.

Mallory sighed. "Sorry. I couldn't help but ask."

Jones smiled, "We will give you water, food and two horses. If my guess about your skills is correct, operating alone, you should be able to make Jurasketu with a little luck. Here is a letter giving you my protection. If you follow the top edge of the Lower Raffin, there are several guarded and unguarded oases where you can find water. Just watch for the bats. You can traverse several hundred kilometers of desert, can you not?"

Mallory nodded grimly, "I have. I can." He paused and then asked, "Do you think the students and workers will make it?"

Jones looked around and waved a hand, "Probably not. No. If we'd had another day of warning it would have been different..."

Mallory nodded even more grimly.

Jones smiled slightly, "Would you do me a favor?"

"Anything."

"Can you get my favorite horse to safety? My youngest son, Henry, is a well-known merchant that lives in Endurance. I have a letter giving my last thoughts of this day. Please bring the horse and letter to him. And show him the courtesy of at least a brief stay."

Mallory managed to show no hesitation, "Certainly. It's the least I can do." Mallory hesitated a moment and then said, "Why me? Why would you trust me with your horse and letter?"

Jones laughed, "They are only important to me and maybe my family. I cannot waste Army resources on such personal matters at this time. And besides, if I have any wisdom at all, I'm certain that you are important to Jurasketu's future and my horse is strong indeed. May he allow you to reach safety. I only ask that you consider Jurasketu worthy of your help."

Mallory could say nothing more than, "I do. Thank you."

Within twenty minutes, Mallory found himself fully outfitted for travel and riding Colonel Jones' favorite horse, a massive dark brown stallion of obvious excellent quality and disposition, amusingly called Dandelion. He was traveling east away from the death trap that Duravon had become. That was the good news. The bad news was that Jones had decided to send two messengers to report what recently had transpired in Duravon. That was bad news because they were intended to travel together. Now, he would have to escape them.

They traveled a hard 60km that night and fortunately saw no signs of Cumar. They stopped around mid-morning to rest the horses, eat and catch a little sleep themselves while the to-be-avoided mid-day sun boiled away.

While Mallory rested, he curled his lip in aggravation. The messengers were not to be taken lightly. Attempting to subdue them was probably too risky given his lack of proper weapons and their training. He could probably overpower both if he was willing to kill them or disable them - but that wouldn't do. Despite his arrest, the Jurasketu had been decent and kind. He couldn't count them as an enemy in any fashion and the two messengers didn't threaten his life. Or did they? Had Jones been lying? Was he being escorted rather than accompanied back to Jurasketu? Mallory pondered hard. Such a plan seemed too subtle and problematic. Jones was likely sincere. But what if he refused to follow their course or dawdle in order to be left behind? Had Jones given them orders to arrest or kill him in such circumstance? It was possible. Jones seemed ever cautious.

They continued moving east more slowly in the late afternoon and evening. Near dusk, Mallory got the opportunity he wanted. The wind picked up suddenly. Dust began moving. The two worried messengers conferred and decided to head for an outcrop a few hundred meters ahead to take shelter from the coming storm. They urged their horses ahead at a gallop. Their packhorses snorted in irritation at being pulled along at a brisk pace.

Mallory shouted, "Dammit. You stupid horse. Not again. Not now."

Twice already that afternoon during rests, Mallory had taken the occasion to make it seem that his pack horse had gotten its lead rope snagged on his rear saddlebags trapping the packhorse too close to Dandelion. He had made it happen again whilst the messengers had been conferring.

The two pulled up, but Mallory dismounted and shouted, "Go ahead. Go ahead. I'll get him free in a minute."

They eyed the billowing storm, shrugged and resumed their race to the supposed shelter.

Mallory busily, but not very efficiently, spent time unsnagging the lead. While keeping an eye on the messengers to make sure they weren't watching too closely, he shifted as much fodder and water as he could from the pack horse to Dandelion who didn't complain about the additional load. He remounted as the storm gathered force and urged the horses forward. He was still 300 meters from the outcropping when the dust began to sting and cut down on visibility. Mallory halted and threw a blind over Dandelion's eyes. He pulled out his knife and rubbed on the lead until it frayed and broke. Mallory jerked the packhorse end of the lead and sent the packhorse in the direction of the barely visible outcropping. Then he turned Dandelion into the wind, slit his eyes against the driving dust and drove the unperturbed horse forward as hard as he could go. Mallory had never ridden such an amazing beast in his life.

An hour later, the wind slackened and the dust fell along with the darkness of night. Mallory halted, removed the blind and dismounted. He rubbed the gray dust from his face, nose and ears and used a few drops of precious water to clear the dust from his burning eyes. He gave Dandelion a long drink of water and took a little for himself. After resting for a few minutes, he remounted and urged the horse to resume their journey back to Duravon - or rather a point northeast of Duravon.

The two white moons turned the Raffin grays to stark whites and his horse and clothing to black in contrast. He wanted to ride hard, but he didn't want to tire Dandelion too much after the brutality of the dust storm, and so stayed with a walking pace. He also needed to move cautiously from here forward with Cumar horsemen prowling the Raffin.

Two nights of travel later, he had reacquired his stashed equipment only having to avoid a single detachment of Cumar. Then he made his next plan. First, he changed into his spare set of clothing. His fatigues were in terrible shape, so he had to risk ruining his special Adaptive Camouflage suit. Next, he would ride east to Jurasketu proper, bring Dandelion to the Army headquarters as promised and hopefully find Entreska at the Jurasketu Academy. What he would do after that, he would figure out during the ten or twelve days he had to ride ahead of him. Although daytime temperatures were rapidly becoming more tolerable, he would only travel by night until he had left the Cumar behind.

Mallory avoided a large group of Cumar moving south the next day by literally hiding himself and Dandelion in a sand dune. Unlike regular horses, the agile desert horses were accustomed to lying on the ground and so he had used his tent to cover them both - while keeping his rifle ready.

The following day, while hiding in a gully only partly filled with sand, by one of those tricks of the desert, he heard wagons moving off to the southeast. He climbed out, slithered up to the edge of a dune and used his detached rifle scope to scout the wagon train that was moving north nearly 500 meters away.

A dozen desert wagons pulled by eight horse teams rumbled across a rocky flat that was flanked by small dunes. A few Cumar horsemen ran guard duty alongside the wagon train. Four horsemen herded two dozen spare draft horses at the rear. Interestingly, two of the wagons sported red and gold fringe decoration and were both driven by women wearing elaborate red and gold clothes and face paint. The other wagons were driven by Cumar men, and Mallory noted, bore an insignia on their chests consisting of a gold flame on a keystone shaped red field. Mallory safely concluded that the wagon train must be some kind of religious auxiliary rather than a fighting unit.

Mallory thought it strange that they should be moving north. Then the wagons suddenly halted. The occupants of several wagons spilled out to water and feed the horses. Obviously, the horses needed a rest. Several horses were exchanged for the spare ones from the rear. Mallory noted that these Cumar knew how to manage their beasts properly. Then his throat tightened as two more of the women dressed in red and gold, most assuredly Valperium priestesses as Entreska had described them to him, pulled a hooded and bound woman from a wagon and let her writhe on the hot sand whilst they appeared to rearrange the contents of the wagon for reasons unavailable to Mallory. Was the captive Cumar or Jurasketu?

Mallory increased the magnification and peered intently at the poor woman. He cringed upon seeing that her only clothing was the hooded desert cloak. She flailed desperately trying to place the windblown cloak between her and the hot sand. Her captors ignored her gyrations. Mallory puzzled at a weird prismatic optical effect that seemed to give her exposed skin the appearance of a shattered rainbow. Mallory lowered and carefully cleaned the scope lens. The weird optical effect remained, but only when he looked at the suffering captive and only her skin seemed to be affected. Mallory increased the magnification and decided that the captive's skin must have been painted or smeared with colored pastes. If it wasn't weird science, it must be weird religion instead.

Could the captive be one of the students from the Expedition? Did the other wagons contain more captives? Or was she just some hapless Cumar bound for sacrifice to the Valperium? Mallory would need to find out by having a closer look that evening.

Mallory rode Dandelion north staying parallel and slightly behind the wagons in case they turned west - which seemed likely to Mallory. As the evening winds rose up spraying the miserable dust and sand into all that anyone possessed, the Cumar made to encamp. Surprisingly to Mallory, they did not circle the wagons or otherwise establish a strong defensive perimeter, although they did post sentries. This made Mallory suddenly very nervous. Either these Cumar were extremely careless or they knew themselves protected by larger, competent military formations patrolling nearby.

Worse, they cooked and ate dinner to cheerful music and songs. They got louder as the evening went on. Mallory was convinced they were engaging in celebratory behavior, which gave Mallory a bad feeling about Jones, the Black Scorpions and the Expedition. During the celebration, Mallory carefully studied the wagons for signs of life, using the passive infrared setting on the rifle scope modulated by his Darkglasses, to determine how many prisoners were in the wagons. To his dismay, only the one he had seen earlier appeared in the wagons. To his relief, there were no children amongst the nearly 70 Cumar. Eventually, the celebrants retired to the wagons for sleep. Six sentries maintained watch.

While he hadn't determined for certain whether or not the prisoner was Jurasketu, Mallory decided he should risk rescuing her anyway. He readied his weapons and waited an hour to let the Cumar fall into sleep. Then, he left his nonessentials with Dandelion and slunk across the desert in the moonless darkness using his Darkglasses to full advantage. It took forty careful minutes for him to loop around to the other side of the wagons to ensure no battalions lay waiting over the next dune. Then he carefully approached the wagon with the prisoner. His plan was simple. He would kill the two priestesses that occupied the wagon with the prisoner. Then with the prisoner's safety secure, he would quickly kill the sentries and the rest of Cumar whatever their reaction - to hide, flee or fight.

In most high adventure stories, when effecting a rescue, the hero would survive numerous close calls with death or injury and would be saved by luck and impossible physical feats. Mallory despised stories like that. Yes, random chance could have easily ended his life or career numerous times and, of course, his official reports always exaggerated the odds of failure by a wide margin. In reality, he always had tremendous advantages over his enemies, which was why he lived and they did not. His weaponry, equipment and martial skills far exceeded the skills and equipment of his targets. Most of the time, they never even knew he was their enemy. Worse, he knew and could plan for them, while they usually knew nothing of him until it was over and done.

In other words, in the darkness, he silently reached the back of the wagon containing the prisoner. Two quick shots killed the priestesses. Then six longer shots downed the sentries. The rifle cracks woke up the rest of the Cumar who began trying to gather themselves to see what was happening. Most grabbed their weapons but it didn't matter. Using passive infrared enhanced vision, Mallory ran back down the wagon line and snap shot all the drowsy and mostly drunk Cumar in the wagons in about thirty seconds. Only two bewildered Cumar had emerged from their wagons to challenge the unexpected night attack.

Mallory stopped at the last wagon, changed magazines, then turned and sprinted back the other way, swinging twenty-five meters out to improve his firing angle until he was parallel with the prisoner wagon. Several Cumar had jumped out of the lead wagons, but stayed near the wagons trying to spot the enemy. Mallory simply held his position and rattled off forty more shots killing all but four Cumar who had taken up refuge under the two lead wagons. Mallory moved through the wagon line, swung wide and then ran up to the wagons and finished them off. It was all over in about three minutes. No Cumar had so much as made a threatening gesture in his direction.

Mallory quickly checked up and down the line to ensure that he had not made any mistakes or failed to kill any of the Cumar. He even took a moment to quiet the horses and then scan the horizon for signs of activity. There was none. Then he went to collect his newly rescued prisoner.

He slung his rifle over his back and clambered into the blood splattered wagon. The bound and gagged captive lay motionless trying to hide under a slain priestess and a carpet. Mallory spoke in a soothing voice as he clambered into the blood-splattered wagon. "It's alright. I'm not going to hurt you. Are you Jurasketu?"

The woman perked up and began nodding her head vigorously.

Mallory gingerly pulled the body that was still oozing blood aside and pulled the carpet away. He pulled out his utility scissors and carefully cut the cloth gag and pulled it away. The captive tried to talk but her sore jaw and dry throat allowed her only a croaking cough. Mallory said, "Wait. Don't talk. Let me cut the bonds and I'll give you some water."

The captive sat bolt upright, mouth slack. She turned allowing Mallory to cut the ropes binding her raw wrists and ankles. Mallory handed her his canteen. After only a couple sips, she whispered, "Mallory?"

Mallory froze. Sudden recognition passed across his mind. It was Entreska! "Tresh! Are you all right?"

The whispered reply was, "No. Not really."

"Where are you hurt?" Mallory wanted to hug her but held back not wanting to aggravate any injuries.

She muttered, "I'm just a little sore. The handling I'll survive. It's the other stuff that has rent my soul."

"Did the bastards rape you?"

Entreska shook her head and gave a halting laugh, "No. Apparently, sacrifices to the Valperium are meant to be unspoilt."

Mallory was puzzled but then realized she meant that her companions were dead, "Oh. Yes. I'm sorry. I wasn't expecting to find you."

Entreska rubbed her jaw. "What are you doing here anyway? What happened to the Cumar?"

"Colonel Jones released me. I was trying to flee east. The Cumar I killed."

"What? How? By yourself? I heard loud noises but no fighting."

"I am alone. I killed them at a distance."

"How can you see? It's pitch black."

"I have better weapons and equipment than they. I'll have to explain later. We need to get out of here. More Cumar may arrive tomorrow. We want to be far away. What did they do with your clothes?"

"No idea."

Mallory frowned and decided a light wouldn't matter. He looked for a lantern. After a brief search, he found one and after fumbling about a bit managed to light it. He handed it to Entreska and said, "Okay. See what you can find to wear especially for your feet. Er... my goodness... why did they paint your skin and hair that way?"

"It's not paint. And they didn't."

"Uh... Then who did?"

"We can trade explanations later."

Mallory frowned, "Um... Right. Anyway, you find suitable clothing. I need to go get my horse. I'll be back in about ten minutes."

Entreska looked nervous about being left. Mallory smiled, took her hand, and said, "Nothing to worry about. I scouted them for several hours before I attacked and made sure they are all dead."

Entreska sighed heavily and nodded. Mallory jumped down and jogged out to Dandelion. He returned in good time. Meanwhile, Entreska had found an unsoiled tan shift, a leather belt, laced sandals and a fresh cloak. The largest moon, the Child, had risen providing them better light. Mallory located a fine looking desert pony for her to ride. He also selected two sturdy looking draft horses to carry food and water.

"Mallory?"

"Yes?"

"Do you plan to continue east?"

"Well. From everything I've been told, the High Raffin is to be avoided. No water and the winter dust storms are worst there. So we need to maneuver through the Lower Raffin and trust to my stealth skills, superior equipment and luck."

She frowned, "I think that's a bad plan. The Cumar are all over the Lower Raffin and at least two banners are positioned in the High Raffin."

"How do you know that?"

She smiled faintly, "That explanation can wait. But I know that to be true. I have a better plan. We should go west instead, just a little north of the Arattaque Rise and then skirt the Blades northward to Mountaineer territory. They will give us shelter and shuffle us east to White Tower - Northern Command headquarters. Our chances to avoid the Cumar and the storms will be almost certain. And we should be able to find water and fodder along that way."

Mallory considered the plan. The Cumar certainly wouldn't expect that. They would be significantly behind enemy lines, which meant fewer quality troops on the lookout. He could even slaughter small patrols if need be with small chance of immediate discovery. She was right. Their chances of survival would be better.

"Okay. Let's do that. You should lay in some additional warm clothing though. And blankets. I suspect the approaching autumn is not especially warm in the mountains."

"No. It's quite cool. What about you?"

Mallory said, "I'll be fine."

Entreska shook her head and proceeded to look for additional blankets and winter clothing. She managed to find a heavy fur-lined hooded cloak, additional tunics and a nice pair of fur-lined moccasins. Once the additional warm clothing was acquired, Mallory released the remaining horses driving them westward. Entreska and Mallory followed in their wake.

Towards dawn, they found a suitable gully and camped for the day. Ignoring Entreska's questions, Mallory set up monitoring equipment to alert him to approaching humans or wildlife. He set an alarm on his watch to wake him at dusk.

Mallory woke with the sun low but still dangling in the western sky. Entreska sat cross-legged staring at him. He smiled. She smiled in return. He canceled the alarm, doled out cheese, crackers and dried mutton for them to eat. Afterwards, they fed and watered the horses. With the light of day fading, Mallory motioned for Entreska to sit.

Mallory smiled and said, "Okay. Now we trade explanations. I'll go first if you don't mind."

"As you wish. I'm sure yours will be more believable than mine."

Mallory shrugged, "If that is so, yours will be wild indeed since I think you will find nothing I am about to say remotely believable."

From carefully planned idle conversation during his time with the Expedition, Mallory had learned that the Jurasketu knew their planet, which they called simply Earth, to be a large sphere that orbited the sun at a great distance. They knew the five moons orbited the planet. The fixed stars they did not yet understand. So, he had a reasonable starting point.

Mallory spoke slowly allowing time for each statement to be absorbed, "I have come from beyond the sky. Beyond the moons. Beyond the sun. Wait... I am human - just like everyone here on Earth. I come from another planet that we also call Earth. Though many call it Old Earth. Wait... Many years ago, humans learned how to travel in things called spaceships between the planets and then the stars despite the enormous distances."

"Spaceships? What do you mean - like a sailing ship?"

"Well, empty space, which we call the stuff that separates the planets, moons and stars, is totally hostile to human or any known life. There is no air to breathe. It is both impossibly cold but can be incredibly hot. And the distances are vast. The spaceship must hold and even renew breathable air without the slightest leak. Instead of wind, water, men or horses to provide power, the spaceship is powered by fire contained or controlled by things called engines using not wood or oil but variously interesting and exotic fuels. But in many ways, spaceships are very similar to their ocean going kin in that they must carry everything they need including food, water, air and fuel. And if they break down in the Deep - the outlook is very grim.

"Anyway, those early intrepid explorers found a small smattering of planets among the stars that could support human life. Like this one. And so more humans traveled in spaceships to live there bringing many things from Old Earth."

"But how come there are no other humans here that know this?"

Mallory shrugged, "We don't know that actually. There may be some that do. But, normally, the answer would be that the people who settled this planet wanted that to be so. They wanted to escape from the hell that modern life can be for many. We call them Primitives.

In fact, one of my jobs is to check on such places and keep them safe from those who might use superior knowledge and equipment to make themselves as Angels, Wizards, Lords or Demons as befit their idiom and use the locals as their playthings and worse."

"So Earth is one of these places?"

Mallory sighed, "Perhaps. I'm not sure. Everything is wrong. My spaceship crashed on Wokometu after it was damaged in an accident. The history of human civilization on this planet extends over 3000 years does it not?"

"We're reasonably sure it's closer to four thousand actually."

Mallory gestured, "See. That's the problem. Humans have been colonizing other planets for only 300 years."

"How can that be then?"

Mallory waved a hand, "It can't, of course. It must be either someone other than humans brought humans here or somehow my accident has brought me forward in time - both of which are theoretically possible. Although now, that I think about it, I should be able to make some sophisticated tests to show how long ago the humans of this Earth diverge from the humans of Old Earth and what populations. But the forward in time scenario has the most credence simply because English is well spoken here and dates back at least 3500 years. Modern English was only about 900 years old when I was born."

"English?"

"Jurasketu. It is called English on Old Earth. If I conduct a cursory study of Jurasketu vocabulary and literature, I suspect I'll find a number of words and idioms that derive from technology that doesn't exist here."

Entreska frowned. "What do you mean?"

"I mean that it is likely Jurasketu has preserved words that ought not to exist unless they originated in my world."

Entreska looked at the ground in deep thought. Mallory wondered how much she grasped if any. Then she asked, "But why were you on the Raffin?"

Mallory rubbed his face, "Well. You see. I was thinking Puck was one of those people who would pretend to be a Wizard. And so I was scouting his lands. I ran into some problems and ended up being chased into the desert thinking that Puck might have equipment capable of at least mitigating my advanced weaponry and equipment. That's when I ran across your expedition. I was intrigued. I cached my weapons and equipment. I set my horse loose..."

"...and showed up looking lost."

Mallory muttered, "And very lost indeed."

Entreska sneered, "And you are a spy, just as Uncle Val suspected."

"Indeed. But as Puck's enemy."

Entreska countenance became grim and she sighed, "I don't understand how you killed the Cumar like that."

Mallory shrugged, "I am highly trained in military matters in addition to my other considerable skills. My rifle, as it's called, when it was made represented the developmental apex of a centuries old weapon technology. It fires small metal or ceramic slugs called bullets at very high speed that enable the shooter to reliably hit and kill targets wearing even heavy armor at distances over a thousand meters."

"Great Burning Blast."

He held up the Darkglasses, "And with these, I can see in the dark and see things otherwise not visible. Here try them out..."

Entreska reached tentatively for the glasses and tried them on. Her jaw dropped in total amazement. She handed them back. Then she said, "Very impressive. But with all this fancy equipment couldn't you have rescued me without killing all the Cumar?"

Mallory was taken aback by the question, "Um... I don't know. I didn't consider it actually. The safest and simplest plan was to kill them. Even with my fancy equipment, I am not invulnerable. And they would likely pursue. Besides, this is war and they weren't exactly innocent bystanders."

Entreska nodded in a sad way that Mallory did not like.

"Do you enjoy killing?"

Mallory spluttered, "No. Of course not. It's not something to celebrate. But I can't say I felt too emotional about dispatching those Cumar considering what they had done to your Expedition and I imagine were going to do with you."

Entreska just nodded in that sad way again.

His limbs jostled in irritation. Entreska hadn't even thanked him directly and now she had questioned his ethics. Of course, she was right - he had enjoyed killing the Cumar. General Lang had long accused him of taking a little too much delight in his missions of violence.

Mallory tried to cover his irritation with a little levity and said, "Well. Do you still think my explanations are more believable than yours?"

She snorted, "Not even close. Yours actually make sense given what I've seen of you, and explain many things both large and small."

Mallory frowned and said, "Well. I have many more things to explain, none very believable if you ask me, but I do want to know how you came to be a living rainbow so they can wait."

Entreska laughed softly, "Fair enough. Let's see. I was having these dreams..."

The Essence of Evermore

The Jurasketu Academy Library contained thousands of musty volumes arranged carefully in expensive bookcases decorated with mythical creatures, faces of great minds of the past and citizenry at work and play. Marble topped, large wooden reading tables were arranged symmetrically with plenty of floor space in between. In contrast, the armless, stark wooden chairs were scattered haphazardly around the tables. Entreska scowled and wondered how the librarians and custodians could have left things in such a state. Then she returned to reading her volume on ancient agriculture techniques.

A quiet voice whispered, "Wake up, someone is coming."

"What? Who? What do you mean?"

The Voice proclaimed, "We said nothing. You need to wake. Lieutenant Park is talking to you."

Entreska couldn't speak or move. She panicked a few moments before she felt the dream state protective paralysis subside, which naturally allowed her to realize she had been woken from a dream.

Entreska picked the dried mucus from her eyes and stared into darkness. The large moon had set, but two small ones gleamed low over the Southern horizon.

Park whispered, "A small band of riders approach from the southwest. We are going to ambush them if they get too close."

She nodded and then realizing Park couldn't see her clearly, she croaked a low, "Yes. Do I need to do anything?"

"You could make sure everyone stays quiet."

"I can do that."

Park thanked her and departed.

"Can you see them?"

The Voice replied, "We can feel them. There are not many. Maybe four or five."

"Really? Scouts? No. That doesn't make sense. No one scouts unknown terrain in the dark."

"There are always exceptions to every general principle."

"You know, not everyone would agree with that principle. Nature brooks few exceptions."

"Simply apply the principle to itself and the problem vanishes on its own accord."

Entreska chuckled in bemusement. Mentally, that is, outwardly only an invisible smile showed through. She hoped the scouts avoided their little canyon so that Park and his men would not need to kill them. It was against her Ethic to wish death upon anyone, including her enemies. In a way, battlefields are indeed terrible places to die. Only the strong and brave die on battlefields. Her father always laughed at her concerns, "Yes. Better a few brave men and women rather than untold thousands of men, women and children." He was right, of course, but her argument that their goal should not be violence but conversion to more peaceful ways brought only sneers. She hated that sneer.

Entreska passed on instructions that everyone would remain quiet and went back to her rock to wait for Park to spring his ambush or report the riders had bypassed their hideaway. She did not have to wait long.

She heard a sharp cry. Then the air was filled with cursing, but strangely all the cursing was in Jurasketu. Even stranger, she heard no more arrows or sounds of fighting. The cursing and shouting continued. Intrigued, she decided to go investigate.

Entreska tried and failed to locate her sandals in the dark, so she proceeded barefoot across the canyon floor and up the southeast slope. She stepped on whiteberry brambles a few times, but didn't discover that her feet were bleeding until much later at which time she resolved to keep better track of her footwear. The cursing continued for the two or three minutes she took to negotiate the canyon floor and climb up the slope.

Entreska met Park coming back down. He nearly ran into her, which would have been a bruising experience for Entreska since he was large and stout.

He huffed, "What are you doing?"

"That would be my question, exactly."

"Yes. They're soldiers from the Dawn Spiders and we've wounded one like a bunch of idiots."

Entreska sighed in partial relief. The Dawn Spiders provided the southern anchor to the Jurasketu Army's patrol line across the Raffin.

They patrolled the area just north of the virtually impassable Southern Wastes all the way to the Ruined City and the Black Scorpions' patrol area. More specifically, they were not the enemy. Before she could ask what they doing here, Park answered the question.

He said, "The Dawn Spiders appear to have been scattered. Apparently, Cumar forces surprised and encircled the Spiders four days ago on the morning of Autumn 7. These seven only escaped because they had been manning one of the messenger post stations between the Spiders and Scorpions. Without warning, Cumar appeared from the south. So, the seven were forced to flee. They first went north towards the Scorpions, but ran into more Cumar and so went east instead. They are led by Beck Martinez who was with me when we discovered the canyon. They needed water, so they planned to stop here and rest."

Park continued, "Our spotter realized they were friendly and mistakenly shouted 'Hold Fire' instead of the proper order 'Stand Down'. Three guys heard only the 'Fire' part and loosed their arrows. We downed two ponies and hit a rider in the thigh. So, we killed two of our own ponies and broke the leg of one of our own soldiers."

"We're lucky no one was killed."

Park snarled, "Lucky? We totally screwed up. We're the Black Scorpions, not some rookie outfit."

Entreska could only grunt in assent and stared into the sky. Flickering lights covered the southern and eastern quadrants of the sky. The northern and western quadrants contained but a few speckles of mostly red and blue. She liked stars.

The shouting had brought others carrying weapons up the slope. Excited questions and explanations about the fate of the Dawn Spiders were traded about. Park and Entreska grew quickly nervous about everyone talking and standing up on the ridge, so they ordered everyone back into the canyon and under curfew once more. The wounded man was brought down on a makeshift stretcher. They also brought the two dead ponies down to be hidden off to the side. Park detailed four Scorpions to cover the blood and erase the Spiders' tracks several hundred meters distant.

The incident was disturbing. The Dawn Spiders destroyed in an encirclement battle. Never had such a disaster befallen the Jurasketu Army since John Celeste betrayed a Jurasketu force in the White Mountains nearly a hundred years ago when over two thousand soldiers were slaughtered by Takirun raiders. Entreska went to question Beck Martinez and the fellow survivors. She did not like what they had to tell...

Entreska and Park explained what had happened to them. Martinez listened quietly, nodding knowingly several times. Martinez, when cleaned and wearing something other than a torn uniform, would most definitely be called handsome with a perfect nose and brown eyes, a regular chin and mouth, smooth skin and a pleasant smile.

Suddenly, he asked Entreska, taking her by surprise, "Excuse my ignorance, but who are you?"

"I am Entreska Nevercare."

"Ah, old Glenmorgan's daughter."

She hated that. People always treated her with extra respect the moment they discovered she was *his child*. She couldn't blame her father for that, but she didn't like it anyway. She wanted to be treated respectfully simply because she was a Jurasketu citizen. She always tried to accord others respect regardless of their pedigree or rank.

Ironically, she was reminded of what Valentine Jones would often say to her, "It is easy to treat everyone equally when you know very well they cannot demand greater privilege or ignore you. Everyone fears or loves your father, rightly or wrongly, and this influences their behavior towards you. You speak plainly and demand attention, and they must give it. So don't complain, few are as lucky and deserving as you."

She wasn't feeling so lucky.

"What exactly happened?"

Martinez replied, "We don't know. We had been manning the eastern messenger station and picket. So everything I'm about to say is just from verbal courtesy reports made to us by Scouts conveying the official reports to White Tower.

"Anyway, about two weeks ago, a Cumar scouting force moved into the region. The Spiders engaged them in the usual skirmishes for a couple of days. Puck's forces routinely probe our defenses throughout the summer. We do the same to them. Usually, they would harass us for a week or so before retreating with our troops in cautious pursuit. This time, they only skirmished for two days. The last report we received was that Major Quick was suspicious and had taken a recon force into the Marshes. The next thing we knew Cumar appeared from the south and we were forced to flee. When we found Cumar to our north, it became clear that a full-scale raid or invasion was on. Not good. Not good. So we fled here."

Martinez leaned back and shook his head sadly in obvious anguish.

Entreska hesitantly asked, "So you don't really know what happened to the Dawn Spiders?"

Martinez shrugged, "No. But I wouldn't keep much hope Professor. Admittedly, Chairman Rolf and Major Quick are resourceful leaders and maybe they wriggled out of the trap. But I don't see it. Cumar were everywhere. Too many of them. I'm sorry."

Entreska blurted, "What? Did you say Rolf?"

Martinez sighed in apprehension, "Yes, Professor. Chairman Rolf was inspecting... er... the local terrain. I'm sorry."

Entreska hung her head in despair.

Park Jones put a hand on her shoulder.

Then Entreska said, "I'm sure you had many friends among the fallen as well."

Martinez nodded, "Yes. I'm afraid so. Well. I suppose the way things are going, we won't have to grieve for long. Although I cannot say the same for our families and friends back in Jurasketu."

She said, "We can't just give up. As long as we breathe, we have a chance..."

Martinez snorted, "I suppose. But quite frankly I don't like our chances."

Park laughed, "It doesn't matter. I will fight until every drop of my blood has been spilled and splattered. I will continue until my flesh has been slashed and torn asunder. I will not stop until every bone in my body is broken and split. No one will say we lacked courage. No one will say we lacked determination. No one will say we suffered from indecision... Not that we will care, we will be dead or worse on our way to the Valperium or the Citadel."

Entreska and Martinez had no answer.

The next day brought a decision. They decided to wait as long as they could in Park's canyon. Their disappearance from the Raffin would at least confuse the Cumar and maybe distract them a little. They would rest and plan while the Cumar looked hither and thither. They had plenty of water and probably sufficient food.

The Cumar wouldn't know this part of the Raffin that well. One of the main reasons the Jurasketu Army patrolled so deeply into the Raffin was to prevent extensive scouting of the Eastern Raffin by the Cumar and Immortals. The odds were good that they would not find them. The problem was they couldn't wait out the Raffin Winter. Even with the cave, they would run short of firewood and the air would become nearly unbreathable from the blowing dust. Their plan had little future.

Entreska wondered about the others. She hadn't asked for an update in a long while.

"Can I have an update, please?"

"The second group was set upon this morning. I monitored closely, and I believe all were killed or taken captive. Major Vest's group is drawing considerable attention to the northeast. Several hundred Cumar cavalry chases them."

"The Ruined City?"

"A probing attack was made last night. It was beaten back easily. It is likely that Puck's Army doesn't know the Black Scorpions strength or defenses. The Immortals main force remains camped west of the City."

To Entreska, the Immortals hesitation was interesting. If Mallory *were* Puck's agent, he would have been able to give the Immortals details about the Scorpions' defenses and situation. A forty-thousand strong army would not need to hesitate. They would simply have attacked immediately. Instead, the Immortals were trying to assess the threat before proceeding. Not that she harbored suspicions about Mallory despite his arrest.

She wondered what her father was doing and thinking. He would surely attempt to send a relief force. She doubted it would come in time.

"I suppose that every day that the Immortals wait is another day for my father to prepare or maneuver."

"Is your father sufficiently skilled in the Art of War? Puck will be a formidable foe."

She thought with some derision, *"My father is the best."*

"Then we wish him good fortune and all great speed to be about it, for yours and our sakes."

Entreska suddenly felt enormously tired and slept.

"Yes. Quite. I need some rest."

The fever and chills woke Entreska near lunch time. She was sick, very sick. Lack of sleep, overexertion and worry had apparently done her in. She ached all over. Her joints and muscles hurt terribly with the slightest movement and just hurt when she didn't move. She was given an herbal tea and told to rest. She could not do otherwise. She would simply have to sleep the fever away. Entreska just hoped it wasn't Desert Flu. Desert Flu was usually fatal.

Entreska slept the afternoon and evening in complete delirium. She could recall nothing from the whole time...

The scream brought her awake to a constant chant and pleading in her head.

She thought, *"What the hell?"*

She heard a thud and splash. She smelled fresh blood and horse.

She sat up. It was dark, and she was no longer feverish.

The Voice boomed, "Please wake up. They come. They come. You must flee!"

Entreska heard shouting and screams. She heard swords clash and arrows flutter.

"What is happening? How come you didn't warn me?"

"The fever and delirium prevented communication. There is no time. We tried to give Park feelings of danger, but he simply suppressed them."

Entreska screamed for Park. The din of battle simply increased. She could see people fighting in the moonlight on the south slope. She tried to rise. Her fever was gone, but her limbs remained sore and her strength was missing. She stumbled and then crawled on hands and knees. Pain shot through her sore wrists and sharp rocks pressed into her knees and palms. She shouted for help. There was no answer.

Entreska collapsed onto the rock and rolled over lacking the strength to move farther. She placed her hand against the crystal that rested in her breast pocket.

She felt a chill and then warmth. In fact, the crystal had become hot. Suddenly, a wave of images flooded across her mind as in a dream.

Entreska stood holding the crystal high above her head. Rainbow hued smoke poured from the crystal encircling her in a deep haze. Nothing could be seen or heard beyond the haze. Instead of choking her, though, the smoke imbued her with a grand feeling of euphoria that lasted for ages to be replaced by an incredible desire to taste the crystal. Taste? Yes. She must. Bringing the crystal to her lips, she gently kissed the largest facet and felt as though she must be burned from the heat. But there was no pain. She licked the side. It was unexpectedly sweet... she must consume it. That's crazy. She couldn't eat a hard crystal. Smoke continued to pour from the crystal that glowed moment to moment in a different hue of the rainbow.

She kissed and licked the crystal again. She took a tentative bite hoping not to shatter her teeth, but there was no more resistance than that offered by chocolate pudding and the taste sensation exceeded that of the finest dessert she had ever been served. The mouthful dissolved into liquid almost immediately and she swallowed. More... She consumed the remainder in about a dozen bites each of which seemed to be lighter and sweeter than the last...

A number of torches had been cast onto the canyon's floor. Other torches up above on the canyon rim provided a flickering but fairly continual bright light. Entreska could see a dead horse and Cumar soldier in the pool. She watched with revulsion as two Scorpions fighting near where she lay were overwhelmed and impaled to death by a dozen Cumar wielding their broad-tipped, heavy spears.

Entreska looked to the cave. Two dozen Cumar were slowly pushing their way into the cave leaving a bloody trail in their wake. She saw Park nowhere, but guessed he was dead. Bleeding and broken bodies lay strewn about the canyon floor.

She pulled the crystal from her pocket. Although she felt no pain, the crystal felt like molten iron in her hand. Mesmerized by the sensation, she felt an overwhelming desire to bite into the crystal. Exhausted, knowing that she was going to die soon anyway, she gave into the insane desire and nipped off a corner. The morsel melted immediately into her mouth with the most pleasant of taste. Out of the corner of her eye she saw approaching Cumar, and so she roughly shoved the rest of the crystal into her mouth and it was gone in four swallows.

Then she just rolled over and awaited the end wondering what in the Great Burning Blast she had just done.

Soon, rough hands grabbed Entreska's arms and held her up while her hands and ankles were expertly bound with ropes. A hooded blindfold, that she was certain must have seen previous duty storing putrid cheese, was pulled over her eyes but left her nose and mouth clear. She retched involuntarily and spewed trying to hit the Cumar on her left. She tried to prepare herself for a retaliatory slap or worse, but nothing happened.

In the harsh spitting language of the Cumar, Entreska heard a woman shout, "Do not harm her."

Entreska had learned the language from Murchinda Vuk, a friend and colleague at the Jurasketu Academy. Murchinda was a former high priestess of the Valperium. Entreska had learned much about the Cumar from Murchinda.

The female shouted orders that Entreska didn't quite follow, but she felt the female come close and begin to search her clothes and person, not gently, but not too roughly.

The priestess said, "Hold her tight. I want to examine her for suitability." Then the woman probed Entreska in ways that were uncomfortable and extremely impolite. Entreska tried to struggle against the intrusion but strong hands negated her efforts.

The priestess announced with glee, "She's unbroken. The Valperium will welcome her blood and we will bathe in the glory."

Then in a growl she said, "So, NO touching. If you touch her, I will gladly have your throats ripped out and your innards fed to the cabbage... Understood?"

Or something like that Entreska guessed given that her Cumar wasn't the best. In any case, apparently, the priestess thought she was special. The Cumar chose only the best for their sacrifices to the Valperium, but Entreska did not feel particularly flattered by her captor's appraisal.

Entreska heard a number of barked affirmatives.

A ceramic container pushed against her lips. Then sweet tasting water flowed into her mouth. She drank letting some spill down her chin.

Minutes later, she felt warm, dreamy...

Entreska marveled at the pleasantly warm and humid meadow filled with brightly colored flowers the size of trees. Their scent seeped into her pores and filled her with a hazy energy. Butterflies the size of giant bats flapped here and there. She skipped and danced through the flowers. Suddenly, a small earthquake jerked her about and she fell laughing into fantastically bright blue clay. She rolled around a while before bouncing back to her feet. She climbed a great green stalk and stood in the heart of a purple and white flower. The stalk wavered in a stiff breeze that cooled her body and whipped her wet hair back about her ears.

From her perch, Entreska could see nothing but a rainbow of colors and varying shapes and sizes of flowers. The horizon fell away in all directions with undulating, living color. No clouds defaced the perfect yellow sky. She felt she could rise into the sky on the aromatic energy generated by the infinite field of flowers. So she did. A thermal drew her high up into the sky. There, she spread her leathery, translucent wings and flitted here and there. She discovered another, stronger thermal that she rode ever higher until breaking into a steep exhilarating dive that she transformed into a slow circling glide that brought her back to the thermal. She repeated the process for hours.

Eventually, Entreska grew thirsty. She landed on a thick bush of eight lobes, orange flowers streaked with black. She sat in a flower's center with her legs dangling. Her back rested against a soft, yet firm petal. She licked moisture from the smooth orangeness. Hungry, she tore strips of moist petal into a delicious salad that she munched on while she rocked her legs and lived at peace with the universe...

Some time later a deep shadow came to rest over her. A giant woman with skin a surprising deep shade of green peered down at Entreska with wide green eyes that formed the focal point of a beautiful face. The giant woman smiled in wonderment and bellowed, "What are you doing here?"

Puzzled, Entreska replied, "I don't know. I don't even know where here is."

The giant woman straightened up, adjusted her mint green tunic and brushed her long, fine golden hair from her face.

"Interesting. Here is the Garden of Vorkfest. Are you a faerie?"

"No. At least, I don't think so. I didn't used to be. Until today, I was very much a human, I thought."

The giant woman knelt and examined Entreska more closely without touching. The woman nodded her head having clearly decided something. "I must have seen you flying earlier."

Entreska said, "Yes. That was me."

The giant rubbed her slender jaw. For a giant, she seemed proportioned very much like a normal woman.

Entreska ventured, "May I ask who you are?"

"Yes, you may. I am Heather Moonstalker. The Garden of Vorkfest is my private preserve."

"I'm sorry. I didn't mean to intrude. I will promptly leave if you show me the way."

Heather boomed cheerily, "No. That is quite all right. I get few visitors." Then she frowned, "Actually, I get no visitors. You are the first." A broad smile returned to her face.

Entreska asked, "Are you a giant?"

"No. I was always considered rather short, not that anyone ever dared make mirth over my stature. You are a quaint little creature. What is your name, if I may ask?"

"I am Entreska Nevercare."

Heather's mouth gaped for a moment.

"Oh my. Does Jasmine know you're here?"

Jasmine? A roll of thunder rippled across the yellow sky and then back again. Entreska stared in total fascination for the five or ten seconds that the sound lasted. Then she looked at Heather who seemed at once astonished and delighted. Heather said, "Wonderful. What a wonderful effect!"

In complete desperation, Entreska asked, "What is going on?"

Heather raised a hand to silence Entreska. Heather crinkled her eyes in concentration for nearly a minute. Then she frowned and dropped her hand. "Apparently, you have projected yourself into Evermore. Something I would have rated impossible until now. How did you do that?"

"It was completely unintentional. But I have a suspicion how that I will share if you'll answer a question"

Heather frowned, "Okay."

"What is Evermore made of exactly?"

Heather raised an eyebrow and stared at Entreska for some time trying to apprise something, "Technically that's a secret."

"Um... Well, I can understand that. But I mean is it poisonous?"

"What do you mean?"

"I mean, what would likely happen if you, say, ate some of it?"

Heather smiled, but then gaped with a look of horror. "You didn't? Some or all?"

"Well, all of it actually."

Heather's expression went to stone. Then she smiled in irony, "Ah. Well, that would explain how you projected yourself into Evermore. And explain some other stuff as well. Um... Why did you do that?"

"I saw myself eating the crystal in a bizarre dream even though I was awake. And then I was overcome by an irresistible desire to do as the vision showed. I was suffering from a sickness and not exactly myself. The Cumar were closing in, and I wouldn't escape them. So, there was nothing to stop me I guess."

Heather frowned once more, adjusted her tunic and gently lowered herself to the ground. She sat with feet flat, knees up, arms folded across the knees and delicate chin resting on a forearm. She stayed deep in thought for some time.

Slowly, Entreska began to regain her bearings and started to wonder what really had happened. Thinking about it brought great puzzlement to her mind. She considered everything as it now seemed to be.

Entreska ventured a question, "How can Evermore still exist if I ate it?"

Heather raised her eyebrow, "Evermore is a special example of Wizard's Essence. Wizard's Essence has a number of viable states. The crystal form is best used for transport and storage." Heather paused and giggled, "Although in our case, the crystal was being used for wizard storage."

"Then am I trapped here? Embedded in the Crys- I mean Evermore like you and the others? Do I still have a working body?"

Heather snickered slightly, "You are not embedded in Evermore. Evermore is now embedded in you. It has melded with your body and mind. All wizards are born thusly."

"What? How? How does that work? Do they all have names like Evermore?"

Heather said in a most serious tone, "When a person consumes the Essence, the Essence enters its active state. The act of eating the Essence is called Conjunction. And with training, a person who has Conjoined with the Essence can become a sorcerer. The power of a sorcerer is a function of their skill, temperament and most importantly the purity, quality and amount of the Essence consumed.

"When a sorcerer dies, the Essence remains in the body but will begin to degrade and dissipate in a few hours to days. But if the body is cremated in the proper way shortly after death, the Essence can be recovered and fashioned into a crystal. The recovery is called Redemption.

"Interestingly, sometimes more Essence is recovered from the dead sorcerer than they had consumed to become a sorcerer. This growth seems to be related to the skill, longevity and essence, if you will, of the dead sorcerer. Once refashioned into a crystal, another person with the right temperament can eat the Essence and become a sorcerer. We've always kept careful records of all known Essences. But most go by the name of the most powerful or famous wizard ever Conjoined with the Essence."

Heather then laughed, "But to answer your other question, as to how it actually works, I don't know. Mind you, when I walked among the living, I was regarded as the greatest sorcerer then alive and supposedly knew all that anyone knew about Wizard's Essence. In fact, at the time, I was the only sorcerer who even knew the secrets of creating Wizard's Essence. So, I'm going to presumptuously, at risk of being immodest, claim that no one knows."

With a shrug, she added, "Not that modesty was ever regarded as one of my finer virtues."

Entreska barely acknowledged the witticism. Instead, with this latest incomprehensible revelation, Entreska's mind reeled and crowded with many questions, many imaginings and many implications. But, as often happens, a mind under duress, will find itself curious about seemingly irrelevant details, and so Entreska blurted out, "Can you eat more than one?"

Heather raised both eyebrows and Entreska felt really stupid until the giant woman spoke, "As far as being Conjoined with more than one. That's a touchy subject. Most sorcerers would have claimed that two different Essences are incompatible. And truly most are not. Attempt Conjunction with an incompatible Essence and you will be incinerated in the conflagration that results. However, a Wizard with sufficient power can Conjoin with a lesser Essence of matching purity and quality. Properly trained, a skilled sorcerer can easily recognize the power field each Essence projects, but it takes exceptional experience and skill to recognize a compatible Essence. Fortunately. Otherwise, I suspect the murder rate among wizards would have been even higher."

Entreska gave Heather a quizzical look.

"Oh yes. The very limited supply of usable Essences presents a nasty problem. When a wizard dies, who gets the Essence? Usually, the candidate would be an apprentice of the deceased wizard. Often, one of their children. But the High Wizard Council had the power to veto the choice and set up an open competition if they deemed the chosen candidate unsuitable. Although, more than once, the Council has been accused of deeming a candidate unsuitable when the quality of the Redeemed Essence was particularly high so that one of their favorites would have a chance at the Conjunction in the competition. I suspect that was even true on occasion. The members of the High Wizard Council were but humans after all.

"Anyway, occasionally an apprentice would attempt to hasten their ascendancy by murdering their master. So, typically, the High Wizard Council would always veto Conjunction of an apprentice when the master died under suspicious circumstances. Of course, this policy led to an increase in assassinations in the hopes that the Council would open a competition for the murdered wizard's Essence instead of allowing the intended apprentice to be Conjoined."

Heather paused to allow Entreska time to recover from her look of horror.

"Worse, in addition to assassinations, certain wizard factions, with aims divergent with the Council would occasionally attempt to circumvent the rules entirely and even engage in kidnapping and murder to obtain more Essence for themselves. But because Essences are readily identifiable, factions had great difficulty operating in secret for very long. And openly, no faction could hope to withstand the combined power of an angry High Wizard Council and its many allies. And in the end, the Council always prevailed by either force or fear over those who didn't like the current system."

Entreska was thunderstruck. All her life she had wanted to know if the legendary wizards were real. Incredibly, the events of the past few weeks had culminated in this: she could become a sorcerer. Except very soon her blood would decorate the Valperium and all would be lost.

Heather seemed to sense Entreska's dismay, "You are not dead yet. Events may yet turn in our favor."

Entreska began, "The Voice-"

Heather interrupted, "That would be Jasmine, my dear sister."

Entreska continued, "Oh. I see. Anyway, she explained that the High Wizard Council had been formed millennia ago to prevent the misuse of sorcery. Eventually, they concluded that sorcery did more harm than good and should be entirely suppressed. They decided that no more sorcerers would be trained, and they destroyed all Essences they could find. But they needed a way to ensure that no one could become a sorcerer after all the wizards were gone. So they created Evermore. And the last members of the Council permanently projected themselves into Evermore to safeguard the future."

Heather sighed. "Well, that's not exactly true. They didn't create Evermore. I did. Secondly, I was the one who pointed out that once we were all dead, if someone should obtain a stray Essence and learn how to use it - who would stop them if they proceeded to do great harm whether from malice or a desire to make things better? I thought the argument would squelch their plans. But I was wrong. Instead, they became angry with me and formed this notion that I was scheming against them."

"Were you?"

"Well yes, technically. But only because they had turned into a pack of fools seeking the great evil of imaginary Certainty."

Heather sighed and buried her face briefly in her arms.

"That my dear Entreska is why you now suffer, why your friends have died and why millions have suffered and died at the hands of Puck. Because I could not dissuade them and they pursued their quest unto its horrific end."

Entreska blinked in dismay.

Heather continued, "The Council executed anyone who defied them. They would have executed me as well. But they were afraid to try."

It was Entreska's turn to raise an eyebrow.

Heather smiled, "Powerful though I was, they could have taken me despite the heavy price I would have extracted. But they were really afraid of what provisions I had made in the event of my death. Remember I told you I was the only one then living who knew the secrets of creating Wizard's Essence. Well, for a long time there has only been one such person at any one time, and we were always called the Essence Keeper. The ability to create Essence is a dangerous responsibility, so the ancient keepers wanted to limit the ability. And the Keepers only made new Wizard Essence at the direction of the Council, which typically occurred when a wizard died and the Redemption was either weak or unperformed. While having but a solitary Keeper was effective at limiting that dangerous knowledge, there is an obvious problem. The Keeper had to confer their knowledge to the next Keeper upon their death no matter what the circumstances and yet keep anyone from stealing the secret."

Entreska's eyes widened in anticipation.

Heather smiled again, "A neat trick eh? Not surprisingly, it involved a specially tuned Essence Crystal called an Essence Tome. The Tome was generally placed in a secret, distant yet accessible location. The Keeper attuned their own Essence, through means that naturally are secret, to the Tome. Seven small Essence crystals called Essence Charms that if Conjoined would hardly confer any powers at all and were attuned to the Keeper's Essence and the Essence Tome, were given to worthy candidates, five chosen secretly by the Council but known to the Keeper and two chosen secretly by the Keeper. When the Tome sensed the Keeper's demise, it sent a homing signal to the Charms. Unknown to both the Charm holders and amusingly the Council, the Keeper always ranked the candidates and instructed the Tome to send a stronger signal to the highest ranked candidate still alive. The first candidate to find the secret location would have to negotiate the usual litany of traps and safeguards that presented little problem for a competent sorcerer given adequate notice by the Charm. Once inside, the Tome would project the secrets of Essence Making into the candidates mind and attune itself to the candidate's Essence. At that point, the candidate would become the new Keeper and the other Charms would grow silent. An additional Charm held by the Council would immediately alert the Council upon selection of the new Keeper."

Entreska nodded in understanding and wonderment. But then she had a question, "What would happen if more than one candidate reached the secret location at the same time?"

Heather laughed, "Manipulations and violence have long been an aspect of choosing the next Keeper. And sometimes noble sacrifice as well. The story of my own accession to Keeper was regarded by many as a grand tale in itself. Of course, the very first task for the new Keeper was to reset the Tome and move it to a new location."

"Could someone consume the Tome?"

Heather smiled and tilted her head regarding Entreska carefully, "Yes... But it still would not reveal its secrets until the Keeper died, and it wouldn't reveal them to the wizard Conjoined with the Tome either. Only a charm holder could do so, although a wizard Conjoined with the Tome could make life a bit difficult for the charm holder I would think."

Entreska had the distinct feeling that Heather was holding something back but clearly wanting Entreska to know she was doing so without saying so. Entreska was slightly confused, "Where is the Tome now?"

"I destroyed it."

"How?"

"Very simple. You simply crush an Essence Crystal and scatter the dust into a suitable body of water. Totally unrecoverable. They are actually rather fragile when not conjoined with a human."

"But why were they afraid of the provisions made in the event of your death? It seems that they would know who the new Keeper would be and everything."

"Well, they were afraid I had moved the Tome, deactivated their Charm, issued new Charms to only wizards I trusted and made it so that all the Charm Holders, not just one, could communicate with the Tome and learn its secrets."

'Why did they think that?"

Heather grinned, "Because I told them I had done so."

"Had you?"

"Naturally. I told you I didn't trust them anymore. And so if I was executed, the new Keepers would be unknown to them, and I had instructed them in the event of my execution or unexpected demise to manufacture as many new Essences as possible and directly oppose the Council. I didn't want that to happen mind you for reasons beyond the fact that I would be dead. The death and destruction that would have resulted from such a Wizard War would have been terrible in the extreme with many innocents surely caught in the middle."

Entreska frowned and became downcast.

"So I proposed the creation of Evermore. The Essences of the Council and mine would be forged into a single Essence that would be hidden beneath Duravon. I told them we could give Charms to our agents. We would be able to project power through the Charms to enable enforcement of the *No Sorcery Decree* and perform other deeds important to the Council. Then we make sure all Essences were dissipated upon the natural deaths of the remaining living Wizards, which at the time numbered less than a hundred - or at least so they thought. It was a bad idea, of course, but it seemed distinctly better than all the other courses of action open to me at the time."

Heather sighed and sadly shook her head, "I was weak. I just couldn't bear starting a Wizard War. As things have turned out, of course, I should have started the war. It wouldn't have been any worse than what has followed the rise of Puck. Never mind what the other dark empires, both greater and lesser, have done. A functioning Council would have at least limited the harm if not stopped the horror entirely."

Heather grunted a derisive laugh, "Anyway, the Council, while highly suspicious of my motives, went with my plan I think partly out of their own greed for greater power and longer life even in a pseudo-form. It actually worked quite well really for over a millennium until the Great Blast destroyed Duravon, killed the agents and entombed us."

"All the agents were killed?"

"Not all actually. But since Charms need their attunement renewed periodically, the remainder became useless and the agents despaired. And we've been left waiting for someone to come and rescue us."

Entreska grunted in disgust, "And so I did. But now we'll all be destroyed. I'm sorry. Is there any way to stop Puck without sorcery?"

To Entreska's surprise, Heather laughed, "All things must die. Including Puck. The mighty often grow arrogant in their power and become vulnerable. Besides, we are not done yet. Have you thought about your other problem, besides having your blood splattered all over the Valperium?"

"What other problem? And what does it matter given my main problem?"

Heather chuckled, "Well, according to policy, strictly speaking, the Council should sentence you to death for having Conjoined with Evermore. Of course, if you die, Evermore will dissipate ending whatever one might deem the existence of the Council and myself to be. Of course, they can't actually kill you either since they are Conjoined with you. Technically, I suppose they could drive you to suicide. But that's not too likely with the interference I would raise to protect you. And I suspect, there would be interference from other members of the Council since someone on the Council enticed you to Conjoin with Evermore - because I know I didn't. Obviously, they don't want you to just die taking them with you. Unless they were afraid that somehow Puck would end up with Evermore."

Entreska swallowed hard and thought about dying, she knew the Cumar liked to watch their victims experience significant distress and pain and so they drugged them to prevent them from killing themselves. She was beginning to wonder if she was just hallucinating.

Heather muttered to herself unintelligibly. Then she said in a clear voice, "I wonder.... I believe at least a faction of the Council, if not the whole lot, is trying to seize control of your mind and use you as their puppet sorcerer. It should be repugnant for them to even consider it. But in their extremity I suppose it seems palatable to them. Hypocrites."

"A puppet sorcerer?"

Heather sighed again, "Yes. Although untrained and unaccustomed to being Conjoined with Evermore, in theory, you could wield its enormous power, far beyond that of any wizard ever because Evermore is, by a couple orders of magnitude the most powerful Wizard's Essence ever created. You are now the master of Evermore. The Essence responds to your will, neither I nor the Council can impose our will on you. But if you were voluntarily to allow the embedded wizards to enter your mind, they could wield the power of Evermore instead with all their considerable skill as though they were you - which, in effect, they would become."

"For always?"

"Well, they are a committee. And while I think they are misguided, they are fairly ethical and their intentions good. So, it would seem to be unworkable and improper for them to actually assert permanent control."

Then Heather raised a dramatic finger, "I believe that once that way has been opened, though, nothing other than your death will close it. The Council will be able to assert control whenever they so choose and you will be powerless to stop them. The ancient lore calls the effect an Assumption. It is rightly considered an Abomination. I implore you to not allow it, no matter how dire the circumstances should become."

"I should die instead?"

"I would."

Entreska shrugged, "Sounds like being a slave. And so Abomination it would be to me as well. And so I would always hazard certain death instead."

Heather nodded in grim satisfaction.

Entreska considered the situation further and asked tentatively, "Are you going to be in trouble for talking to me?"

Heather laughed, "Trouble? They will know we talked; you will not be able to conceal much of what you have and will learn. At least, not until you have much greater skill at walling off your mind from them. But don't worry about me, there is not much the others can do except not speak to me for a few decades. Admittedly, Evermore is a lonely place already without being shut off from all conversation. That is why, even considering the circumstances, this particular conversation brings me considerable joy. And since, miraculously, you have become the Master of Evermore, you can talk to me even if they won't. That is, assuming you wish to talk to me."

Entreska laughed, "Wish that I shall. No doubt. But now what should we to talk about?"

"Wrong question. What are we *not* going to talk about is the real question."

Heather and Entreska talked for what seemed to Entreska at least several hours or maybe even days. The sky rippled occasionally but otherwise remained placidly yellow. Heather suggested that only in a dream sleep, an intoxicated state or a special meditative state that has to be learned could Entreska stay this long projected into Evermore.

Heather gave a rather long and detailed account of the history of

Evermore, always pointing out, however, that Entreska might get a different version from the rest of the Council. Entreska laughed and explained she was more than accustomed to trying to reconcile widely differing accounts of historical events in her studies. Entreska took full advantage of the opportunity to query Heather about various details of certain events.

In turn, Heather asked many probing questions about the last 800 years of world history, since she and the Council had been forced to rely on minimal snippets of mind probes. While useful in aggregate to show the general movements of people and technology particularly in the perspective of time, such probes did not provide nearly enough information to prevent the Council from developing what they were sure was a very distorted picture of important events and the political landscape.

Eventually, Entreska became drowsy and the Garden of Vorkfest disappeared, and she found herself bound and lying uncomfortably on the dirty floor of a Cumar wagon rumbling across the Raffin. A wave of sadness at her impending doom wracked her whole body. Then she heard the comforting voice of Heather telling her not to despair. She tried to obey.

The Chairman

Under the bright morning sky, the tattered and blood stained Command Tent of the Dawn Spiders occupied a hillock overlooking the Maw of Hell. Two blood streaked and very weary soldiers of the Dawn Spiders lolled outside the tent pretending to be on guard. More than a hundred dead Immortals and a dozen Dawn Spiders carpeted the area around the tent. Eight slain horses lay scattered amongst the dead. The unsoiled Regimental flag fluttered in the mild breeze.

Glen, Juragi and a bodyguard of twenty rode up to the tent becoming ever more apprehensive as they approached. They picked their way gingerly up the slope through the blood, bodies, broken arrows and discarded weapons. When the weary soldiers started to raise themselves to attention when they realized it was the Grand Marshal, Glen motioned them to remain as they were and thankfully, they slumped back down.

He dismounted smartly despite his own weariness and said, "I was told I could find Rolf here."

The soldiers nodded and pointed to the ruined tent.

Glen stepped into the ruins of the tent expecting the worst and cried out in anguish when he saw a bloody Rolf reposed against a pile of pillows, a bloody sword laying across his thighs. The shout caused Rolf to grip the sword and leap to his feet into a perfect defensive crouch. A moment of confusion was followed by Rolf discarding the sword and staggering into his father's embrace.

Glen held him for a moment, and then pushed him back to examine him for injuries. Rolf weakly patted his chest and said sadly, "I'm fine Glen. I'm fine."

"You don't look fine."

"I've suffered no injuries except to my soul."

Glen sighed. It was an old argument. Rolf hated the idea of giving the orders that condemned soldiers under his command to suffering, injury and death. Rolf even felt deep sympathy for the enemies of

Jurasketu. In a funny way, Glen could not be prouder of his son. How could he decry his son's revulsion of war?

Then again, had Meredith and he raised their children wrongly by emphasizing ethics and humanity? Glen's father had taught him to be hard and cold for the world is unforgiving and cruel. His mother had taught him kindness and tolerance. But he had paid greater attention to his father for the world really is unforgiving and especially cruel. And yet Glen had despised his father for his cruelty. Meredith, his dearest love, had taken him down a path that excised that cruelty - the path of love and kindness. Yet, the hardness remained.

Rolf nodded, "Your presence here would seem to indicate that our efforts were successful."

Glen shrugged, "Saffron is dead and his regiments are no more."

Rolf grimaced, "And Entreska's Expedition?"

Glen shook his head, "Your sister is dead, son. So is Colonel Jones and virtually everyone else in the Expedition."

Rolf stepped back and sat down heavily on a small rug. He folded his arms across his upright knees and laid his face against his arms. Glen laid his hand on his son's shoulder in a small gesture of connection rather than an attempt at comfort. Rolf's soft sobs of sorrow and weariness had an innocent, child-like quality...

Glen deferred the discussion of events past and future until Rolf could have some rest. A supply wagon was brought up to carry Rolf and the two weary guards to the Northern Command Tents where they were sponged of blood, given fresh uniforms and provided with cots for a few hours' sleep.

Meanwhile, the war went on. Glen ordered all the Heavies, the Dawn Spiders, and the 14th Lights to rest until the next morning. The rest of the Lights were pushed into the Blades chasing down fleeing Immortals and racing to the gates of the Centaur Citadel. With any luck at all, all the roads, bridges, fords and supplies between the Maw and the Citadel would be seized before Puck and his generals could even begin to consider a counterattack.

"Juragi?"

"Yes, Glen."

"Order the staff to get some sleep."

Juragi glanced about the Command Tent at the exhausted staff officers and nodded in agreement, "I will do so."

"You too."

"Of course. And you?"

Glen smiled, "I am heading to my tent now before I pass out ruining a reputation for sleeplessness that took decades to build."

Juragi could not suppress a grin, "Indeed. We would not want that."

The warming sun gently brought Glen awake. He felt almost refreshed. *Another day in the Army. Another day commanding troops. Another day defending Jurasketu from its enemies.* Glen bolted upright, slammed his boots on, rubbed the sleep from his eyes and bellowed for his aide. A panicked Lieutenant Eneko collided with Glen as he emerged from the tent frothing with rage. Eneko landed on his back in the sand.

"Why was I not waked?"

Eneko flailed about trying to salute, get up and talk at the same time, "Grand Marshal. You left no orders. Marshal Juragi said to let you sleep."

Glen clenched his fists and shook them in front of his chest. Then, with a look of concern, bent down and dragged Eneko to his feet. Only then did he look around and see that the Command Tents were all gone. All that remained of his headquarters were his personal wagon, guards and horses. Glen relaxed a little. Juragi had put his Army back on the move while letting him get a little extra rest. Rest he would likely need.

Eneko spoke tentatively, "Grand Marshal, shall I have your tent packed up?"

"What? Yes. Right away. Where is Chairman Rolf?"

Eneko pointed to the wagon, "Waiting for you in the wagon."

Before Glen could make a move towards the wagon, Eneko pointed off in the other direction, "A messenger comes from Juragi."

Glen and Eneko waited as the dust cloaked messenger astride a huge black stallion skidded to halt in a cloud of choking dust a few meters away. The messenger, a small young woman, bounded off the horse, ran up to Glen and stood perfectly still proffering a dispatch.

Glen took the dispatch, saluted smartly, thanked the messenger and sent her off with Eneko to see to her needs. He marched off to the wagon and peered inside.

A rested Rolf chirped, "Glen?"

Glen thundered cheerfully, "It is I."

Glen half-raised a hand to ask non-verbally whether Rolf wanted to talk in the wagon or outside. Rolf waved him aboard. Glen assented and clambered up and sat across from his son. Rolf raked back his sweat soaked orange hair which badly needed cutting.

Rolf spotted the dispatch and asked, "Latest news?"

Glen responded, "No idea. Let me see... It's from Colonel Humble...Ha! We've taken the Yellow Pass with no casualties."

Rolf barked, "What? How could it have been left undefended?"

Glen read further, "It was defended. By the Immortals of the Lost Moon. We captured the entire regiment – apparently they had been incapacitated by a sickness that affected the whole regiment except for a few."

Rolf murmured, "That could turn out to be a problem."

Glen continued, "Hmm.... Possibly. Humble reports that he has taken precautions to limit contact with the prisoners and our troops. He also reports that the Immortals blamed it on bad ale or provender since everyone was affected at once. Hopefully that is the case."

Glen took a deep breath and shrugged. "Nonetheless, nothing will stop our advance on the Citadel now. Fortune appears to have turned in our favor."

Rolf cocked his head to the side and smiled, "I can't believe my own good fortune actually. I should have been slain like Jones and Entreska."

Glen nodded grimly, "Indeed. Did Juragi have a chance to divulge how we arrived here?"

Rolf nodded, "He did. He gave me a detailed description of the battle. I think in the annals it will be known simply as The Battle at the Gates of Hell. An excellent plan - although Saffron showed greater skill than I would have imagined. It's a good thing the Dawn Spiders blocked his retreat when they did - he might have actually escaped."

Glen rubbed his chin and chuckled, "Might? Hell. The slippery devil was escaping. But what I want to know is how you managed that exactly."

Rolf took a deep breath and lolled his head to the side a little. "Well. While Saffron showed great skill in nearly escaping the trap - what in the Great Burning Blast was he doing there in the first place? Strategically speaking. From what Juragi told me, his Cumar cavalry were almost completely wiped out scattered as they were across the Raffin. We gamed many scenarios - but this was not one of them. What would be the point of tracking down every last survivor just to be slaughtered by the counterattack that they seemed to anticipate?"

Glen frowned. "I don't know. I've considered it carefully. The only sensible explanation involves the Expedition. They wanted to destroy it. And every single member of the Expedition - no matter what. There must have been a traitor in the Expedition that alerted Puck to its presence. Otherwise, how would they have known they could even successfully find and attack the Expedition?"

Rolf stared out the rear of the wagon, cocked his head, and scratched his neck, "Well. They did deploy forces across the entire Raffin."

Glen shrugged, "Yes. Obviously some came your way. You were going to explain."

Rolf nodded, "Indeed. Let me. Then we'll consider Saffron's motives some more. Oh. Juragi told me to tell you they found his body."

Glen nodded grimly. It was unlikely that Saffron had escaped, but it was always good to know for certain.

Rolf continued, "Anyway. I was inspecting the caverns as we had discussed - although I gathered from Juragi that I had neglected to tell you I was going. Sorry about that. I'm sure I meant to. I really was not engaged in subterfuge."

Glen shrugged, "It is of no matter."

"Major Quick gave me the full tour. I spent a couple of weeks carefully inspecting the supplies to make sure they were holding up under storage like we desire. Which they were quite nicely - as I'm sure you'll be glad to now take advantage of them. Then I spent time joining one patrol or another scouting the area. I visited the salt marshes. I also hiked up the Maw a fair distance. The Maw is a wonder that is certain."

Glen agreed, "I rank it second only to the Black Firs of White Tower in sheer natural beauty."

Rolf bobbled his head in agreement, then continued, "As Summer ended, a Cumar scouting force probed our defenses for a couple of days, then vanished. According to Quick, that was very unexpected for reasons he never explained. On instinct, he decided to push a strong recon troop into the Southern Marshes. The troop was ambushed by a large Cumar force, and Quick was killed along with all but two troopers. Next, to our horror, pickets reported Cumar Banners to our rear. With Quick dead, Captain Fulsark asked that I take command doubting his own skills and the desperate nature of the situation.

"I knew that trying to retreat intact was not going to work. So we either had to scatter or do something unexpected and potentially strategic useful. So, I decided to move to the southwest thinking that the Cumar would never expect a move along the edge of the marshes towards their side of the coast. It worked brilliantly indeed. We edged forward. And then under cover of darkness evaded the Cumar patrols and slipped into their rear."

Glen raised his eyebrows. "What did the Cumar do once you disappeared like that?"

Rolf shrugged, "I don't know exactly. They certainly didn't realize we had slipped behind them. I'm guessing they charged off into the Lower Raffin pursuing our remaining pickets or continuing on to their ordered goals assuming we had been destroyed or scattered. At this point, though, I was left very much to guessing what was going on. The logical thing to do was to swing rapidly northeastward and skirt the Maw up to the Central Raffin where hopefully we could link up with the Black Scorpions. We could also scout the enemy rear. So we did just that."

Rolf shook his head, "To our dismay, however, we found the way blocked by large movements of Immortals. We pulled back into the brush land of the Blades. It seemed like a major campaign was underway. I reasoned that you would mount a counterattack across the Central Raffin as we had discussed. So I decided to continue scouting but try to remain undiscovered awaiting a critical moment to intervene."

Glen nodded grimly, "It would seem that moment came up."

"Indeed. When we saw Immortals retreating in disarray, I realized immediately that you had counterattacked much quicker than I anticipated. I learned from Juragi, our spies had reported Immortal army movements sometime before the Spiders were attacked. He believes messengers sent with warnings to us and the Scorpions were intercepted. Indeed, we received no warning."

Glen held up his left hand, "Yes. I mobilized immediately thinking that the Scorpions and the Expedition were in danger. Sadly, despite our quick mobilization and forced march, we were too late."

Rolf looked away a moment then continued. "I guessed that the Immortals were trying to retreat down the Maw and turn to the sea. With only 800 light troopers, we could not stand and fight, but we could sure slow them down. I sent scout messengers out to find your army that must be pursuing them. After receiving your orders, we continued to skirmish but our horses had become exhausted so our attacks had diminished effectiveness. Worse, the clearly desperate Immortals tried to force their way past us in the darkness."

Rolf paused to gather his thoughts. He wiped his mouth and rubbed his forehead before continuing.

"I echeloned the eight troops from north to south across the narrow plain that separated the Maw from the foot hills of the Blades. I had positioned the Command troop overlooking the Maw to serve as the back anchor. The Immortals would likely push forward along the Maw and then the other seven troops would threaten the Immortal flank slowing them up which should accomplish our goal allowing your army to fall upon them."

Rolf frowned almost in pain. "Unfortunately, not knowing the terrain as well as we would have liked, we had deployed the Command Troop too far forward. An entire Immortal regiment, Immortals of the Frost, blundered into us about two hours after sunset."

Glen took a sharp breath in horror at the thought.

Rolf waved his hand, "It turns out they were way more exhausted than us and could barely fight. We quickly ran out of arrows, but we just kept fighting with sword, spear and axe long enough for the two nearest troops to arrive to help. The battle raged for almost an hour. Finally, the Immortals pulled back and then apparently tried to go west - but then the 1st Heavies arrived and slaughtered them. Scattered groups of Immortals kept running our way all night. We just killed them as best we could. It was horrible. We had fewer horses than troopers - so I remained at the Command tents with a couple of sentries and sent the horses and troopers to find your army. And I apparently dozed off until you arrived."

Rolf looked pensive then said, "Juragi said that the squadron still has 460 troopers. So I guess I did well."

Glen nodded grimly. "You will surely be awarded a Golden Cloak."

The Golden Cloak was the highest award for bravery and service given by the Jurasketu. Glen owned two. Other than Glen, in the 1800 years since the award had been created only Ervin the Invincible had earned more than one. Of course, Ervin had been given seven - the last posthumously. Some say he had deserved several more.

Rolf showed only irritation at the mention. "It is of no matter."

Rolf narrowed his eyes suddenly. "Juragi told me something else."

Glen instantly went on his guard, "Yes?"

"He told me that you have secret orders from the National Council of War and the Grand Debater that give you permission to pursue all the way to the Citadel in the event such an opportunity arises following a Puck attack."

Glen pondered carefully. Rolf knew that couldn't be true. Rolf had argued in favor of such orders before the National Council of War in support of Glen, but the Council had declined citing the many risks. Glen could attempt a transparent lie. He could tell the truth. Either was risky.

Rolf was duty bound to inform Juragi if he thought Glen was contravening the orders of the NCW and more importantly the Grand Debater. If Glen lied, Rolf would go with his suspicions to Juragi who might suddenly doubt Glen's claim. If Juragi did, it would be ugly indeed. On the other hand, if Glen told the truth, what else could Rolf do but inform Juragi?

Rolf seemed annoyed by Glen's lack of response, "Well? Do you or don't you?"

Glen sighed in defeat. "You know I don't have any such orders."

Rolf nodded sadly, "I know... When I questioned the troop movements, Juragi was surprised that I didn't seem to know about the Secret Finding of the National Council of War - being that I'm a prominent member. I covered by saying that it had been debated but not yet approved when I left with the Dawn Spiders. I told him that I had strongly supported the Finding and was pleased it had been approved finally."

The import of Rolf's words slowly sunk into Glen's Web of Thought. Unasked, Rolf had essentially joined him in his violation of orders. Glen was both pleased and disappointed. He smiled then frowned.

Rolf laughed, "You are happy that I supported the lie but angry that I would willfully violate my military honor."

Glen frowned deeper and scowled in aggravation. He always hated the way Rolf would laugh inappropriately at moments of the deepest seriousness.

Rolf laughed some more. "What was I supposed to do Glen?"

Glen shook his head and whispered, "I don't know.... I don't know..."

Rolf murmured, "If you overthrow Pachinko Puck, I suspect the Grand Debater will be compelled to allow you to retire honorably."

Glen snarled, "No. Should I survive the coming battles in victory, upon our return to Jurasketu, I will have to resign in both triumph and disgrace. However, I did not expect to have you riding in the bucket to hell with me. We'll need to come up with a ploy to excuse you from blame."

Rolf smiled, "I think we should worry about winning the necessary battles first. We can consider our personal fates later."

Glen shrugged, "I thought you were the one who always preaches that the follow-up plans are the ones that require the deepest thought and consideration."

"That I do.... That I do... But isn't the ruin of Puck worth our lives and reputation? Besides, the situation seems a bit desperate. Juragi told me that Murok managed to get himself appointed Governor of Tangur. Attempting to take the Centaur Citadel is a very risky move. But if Puck is destroyed or effectively neutralized, Murok will not be able to move against us. Instead, all Imperium troops will be diverted to plunder Puck's Empire before we can. And your position on the Imperium Council will be greatly strengthened. You might even be able to undo Murok's appointment."

Glen nodded. "Yes. Murok's appointment has made this move possible. But the situation is actually not desperate at all."

Rolf frowned, "Glen. I'm not sure I understand."

"No. You do not."

Rolf squinted and scrunched his face unable to quell his anger and frustration without serious effort. "What about Murok having control of Tangur is not a desperate crisis? I believed you were trying to neutralize Puck before Murok can act against us."

Glen frowned and returned to his seat, "I think you have out thought yourself. Think again about what would happen if we neutralized Puck entirely."

Rolf sat back. He brushed the sweat from his face, pulled on his hair and then wiped his hands on his trousers. Then he said, "Oh. As I said, the Imperium would divert all troops to seizing as much of Puck's Empire as they could. Without Puck, the only threat on Zetu to the Imperium becomes the Jurasketu... We would be screwed unless you could achieve something monumental on the Imperium Council. That's possible given that you would have overthrown Puck yourself... But if the Council supported the appointment of Murok – that can't be counted on in any measure."

Glen nodded, "Give it some more thought."

Rolf shrugged, "I suppose you could use that moment to invent an incident and attack into Tangur yourself. If you defeated Murok, you would use your newly enhanced power on the Imperium Council to annex Tangur for Jurasketu and make a long term deal with the Imperium..."

Glen's eyes lit up for a moment, "I actually hadn't thought of that angle. That would likely have worked."

Rolf threw up his hands in exasperation. "Then what is your PLAN?"

Glen nodded, "My plan right now is revenge pure and simple. Puck has inexplicably given us an opportunity to destroy him and I desire that outcome more than anything at this moment. So I have acted."

Rolf, sweating more heavily, blinked and rubbed his eyes to dispel the burning. "But you just said that would be a bad outcome for Jurasketu!"

"No, you said that."

Rolf grunted, "But you agreed with that."

Glen nodded, appearing to enjoy Rolf's discomfiture.

Grabbing his hair, Rolf said, "But Murok is making this possible?"

"Right. By providing an atmosphere of desperation, I can achieve my revenge and Puck's destruction with well-motivated troops. Revenge only carries troops a short distance – desperation will push troops to achieve well beyond anything they thought themselves capable of doing."

Rolf pursed his lips, "But isn't that short term thinking?"

"Revenge usually is."

Rolf closed his eyes, "Okay. You did say that Murok's appointment is not a crisis. Why not?"

"Ah. Yes. Why not? Can you think of any reason that would be?"

Rolf opened his eyes and thought deeply for a moment before sarcastically saying, "Murok had a sudden realization that his implacable hatred for you and Jurasketu was deeply wrong and he is a changed man?"

Glen shook his head, "Murok has not changed. I can assure you. Consider everything you know about Murok."

Rolf froze for a moment, then leaned back and stared hard at Glen, "You and Murok are cousins, born a month apart and were very close friends before a major falling out when you decided to become an officer in the Jurasketu Army. He proclaimed you a traitor. He has advocated that the Imperium take direct control of Jurasketu for decades. Rumors have circulated for years that his faction has been behind the numerous attempts on your life."

Rolf paused thoughtfully... "But I've always suspected you knew they were coming. Your spies within the Imperium are clearly good and have never been exposed even once. Murok has long desired the lucrative Governorship of Tangur but you have always been able to block him. But now, some of your allies have betrayed you."

Rolf paused and smirked, "I bet your former allies are going to soil themselves but good if we overthrow Puck. They will find themselves in a rather awkward situation."

Glen nodded calmly.

Rolf continued, "But I don't understand. How could the Imperium Council conduct important business as appointing a Governor without allowing all members to attend?"

Glen shrugged, "It was a scheduled meeting. Members routinely are absent and I had already given the Zatta Buruza my voting instructions by messenger. The Raffin Crisis obviously precluded my attendance. The meeting was called while you were off exploring in the Lower Raffin and so we hadn't discussed it."

Rolf nodded, "Right. Hmm... Anyway. I've always been bothered by Murok's personality. He constantly blusters and threatens but he has never actually done anything rash that mattered. He is totally conservative and seemingly bides his time in a way that runs counter to his apparent personality. Another thing, you always seem to know the minds of your enemies on the Imperium Council, particularly Murok's. You have always claimed cunning and knowing Murok when he was young to explain your clairvoyance. I think there is another explanation for these facts."

"And that would be?"

"Murok and you are secret allies and the animosity between you was a complete sham from the beginning."

Glen smiled, "Really? That's a rather bold leap."

Rolf grunted. "You always seemed to know exactly when and how an assassination attempt would occur. So you have to have information from inside Murok's faction."

Glen demurred, "There have been attempts I wasn't expecting. Someone tried to poison me autumn before last at the formal Imperium Council meeting."

Rolf rolled his eyes, "Okay. So one of twenty-four attempts was unexpected. Exception proves the rule. Murok never does anything strategically rash which means his bluster and impatience is clearly an act. You always seem to know what he and his allies are going to do. And now you are not the least bit upset by his appointment as Governor."

Glen sat up, "Oh. I'll show my displeasure at the next meeting of the Imperium Council."

Rolf sneered, "Doubtful. You have been planning this move for some time. There is no doubt."

Glen frowned, "It was a more recent idea actually."

"Ah. You admit it."

Glen smiled, "Of course. I'm mildly disappointed in you and pleased with myself that you weren't able to see the deception sooner. I guess you trusted me too much."

Rolf sighed.

Silence.

Rolf spoke quizzically, "Then what is the plan?"

"Let me explain..."

Deliverance

Mallory studied the terrain carefully but with a casual manner often adopted by those with his great skill and experience. Tall brown grass bent to the will of the North wind. Squat, spiky shrubs huddled in depressions to escape the relentless winds. Pitiful, twisted trees dotted the slopes here and there. The eastern foothills of the Blades while sustaining life seemed only forlorn and sad compared to the beautiful starkness of the nearly lifeless High Raffin. Worse, the Blades offered even less cover from interested eyes than the Raffin where at least the dunes limited vision. They would have to continue their journey by night.

Mallory turned to Entreska who stood beside him studying the terrain with seemingly more care but less confidence. She looked at him expectantly.

Mallory came to a sudden decision and spoke with certitude, "We should change our plan. Instead of trying to return you to Jurasketu immediately, I want to return to my ship. I think you should see it. I have equipment there that can be used against Puck."

Entreska blinked. "Didn't you say your ship crashed on Wokometu? Two days travel from Port Deliverance?"

Mallory frowned, "I did. And that is true."

Entreska said with a deep stain of incredulity, "Then how do you propose to get there?"

Mallory shrugged, "Well. You see. The kindly folks who transported me from Port Deliverance to Zetu so I could scout Puck's lands promised to retrieve me. I'm sure they would be glad to transport you as well on my say so."

Entreska scowled, "I can't imagine them waiting all summer off the coast – how and when will they know where to meet you – us. And who else but pirates or warships would risk plying Puck's coast without his permission?"

Mallory smiled, "We arranged a series of locations and dates. The next one is but 15 days off near the mouth of the Wrything River. We could make it there in plenty of time if we don't dawdle."

Entreska shook her head, "Pirates?"

"Well... Strictly speaking, I would think so. But they docked openly in Deliverance."

Entreska pushed back her hood and brushed back her hair with her hands. "The Lords of Deliverance are passionately neutral and often allow safe harbor to the mischievous. So long as you are well behaved in their purview, what you do elsewhere is of no concern to them. Who are these pirates?"

Mallory looked around as if somebody could be listening. Entreska almost panicked in surprise and looked nervously about. Mallory muttered an apology and said, "The *Inky Darkness* skippered by Buck Jules."

Entreska's eyes went wide, "Great Burning Blast! How in the hell did you manage to hire the most famous ship on the planet?"

"I didn't hire them actually. Captain Jules simply agreed to help me since we shared a mutual goal."

Entreska was still goggle-eyed. "Mutual goal?"

"The demise of Pachinko Puck."

Entreska nodded, "I hadn't guessed that Buck Jules would favor such an enterprise. Not entirely surprising though. Do you know the full story of the *Inky Darkness*?"

"When Captain Jules realized I had never heard the story, he regaled me with what he claimed to be a complete and unencumbered version. To his credit, he spared no opprobrium for his grandfather. When I asked around, the publicly known details matched up with his version anyway."

Entreska smiled sardonically, "A rather sordid and hence memorable tale."

Mallory shrugged, "Indeed. Does that change your opinion of my plan?"

Entreska wiped dust from an eye and nodded, "Yes. My new objections turn to how exactly are we going to slide across the edge of the Blades without getting cut?"

"Well. Much the same as before. We travel at night using Darkglasses. More importantly, we are going to move to the western side of the Blades where water is plentiful and so are trees and brush to hide our movements. And if anyone threatens us – I kill them."

Entreska grimaced and looked back and up towards the towering heights of the Blades. "Very well. Better cover and likely fewer troops, right?"

Mallory nodded and was glad that she recognized the logic of the plan.

They made excellent time despite having to make a detour to find a decent spring to load up on water for the ascent that night. They wouldn't be able to use any of the lower, easy mountain passes since those would likely be guarded. They would have to troop through a difficult high pass that Mallory had selected using his high-resolution topographical map of the entire globe. He summoned the images into his Darkglasses and mapped out what looked like a reasonable path through the Blades to the shore near the Wrything Delta. But the map didn't show Immortal or Cumar troop positions, wild animals or water quality. They would have to determine that for themselves as best they could.

It took one night of a relatively difficult 20-kilometer trek up the sloping, stony terrain to reach a position about a kilometer from their intended pass. Mallory and Entreska had to lead the desert ponies on foot, which left them quite exhausted. The night air grew increasingly colder as they climbed. After a brief rest before dawn, Mallory established his Virtual Watcher at maximum setting so they could sleep without posting watch. The Watcher antenna, a 60-meter long string of thin wire, had to be played out relatively linearly and hence couldn't be used while moving – disappointingly so Mallory always thought.

A Virtual Watcher can detect the presence of humans and beasts up to three kilometers away depending on the terrain. Supposedly, the Watchers detected the unique and recognizable electromagnetic signatures emitted by all creatures. Watchers can be tweaked to recognize known signatures like those of Mallory, Entreska and their desert ponies as 'friend'. Usefully, though, it could alert if so configured when the known signatures entered or left a designated watch region.

While finishing the setup, Mallory noticed that Entreska appeared dubious of the Virtual Watcher. He said, "I can assure you that it works perfectly. I would be happy to demonstrate if you would like. Come here."

Entreska approached cautiously. Mallory started to hand her his Darkglasses and then made a somewhat momentous decision. Rubbing his pate harshly, Mallory retrieved his smaller spare set of

Darkglasses from an armored pocket on the duffel bag.

He handed the spare Darkglasses to Entreska. "Here. Put these on and tap the side twice lightly in quick succession like this."

Mallory demonstrated on his own Darkglasses. When he did so, the transparent Watcher Monitor appeared in his upper right vision. Entreska tentatively took the glasses and put them on. Then she lightly tapped the side but her second tap was too slow. Two more failures were finally followed by success. Her mouth went slack.

"Do you see the red marks?"

She nodded.

"Notice the labels. Horses. Me. You."

Entreska was agog. "How does it know my name? And the horses?"

"Oh. I told it the names. Otherwise, you would have been labeled by recognized type and encounter number. Er... in this case... Human Female 10453. The Watcher remembers every encountered animal and I can assign names to any that I wish."

Entreska just nodded.

"Anyway. I'll explain all that later. You sit and watch. I'll move out of the protected region – it'll flash and beep quietly as currently configured."

Mallory moved up the slope about 100 meters. He found a vantage to scan back down the slope and out into the Raffin. Then he returned. He found Entreska nodding, obviously impressed.

"So this will keep us safe?"

Mallory laughed seditiously, "No. We'll just have the privilege of being awake when something comes to kill or eat us."

When Entreska frowned, Mallory added, "Likely as not, I'll kill the something first of course – given the advantage of knowing it was coming."

That just made Entreska frown even more.

Then she said, "The High Wizard Council says they will detect soldiers or beasts for many kilometers distant. The Virtual Watcher is not really needed."

It was Mallory turn to frown at that. While he believed her story, he wasn't about to trust an artifact that might very well really be a magical prison for a bunch of disembodied wizards. Maybe it was an unusual technological artifact that was more than it seemed. That was another reason to return to his ship. Entreska needed a deep medical analysis. Instead of saying he didn't trust the wizards, he said, "Well.

We'll be doubly warned then."

Entreska took off the Darkglasses and started to hand them back. Mallory waved her away.

"No. You keep them. Just don't lose them. I'll show you their most important function after I scout the pass."

"I won't lose them. Most important? They do more?"

"Much more."

They awoke in the early afternoon. Leaving an anxious Entreska with the horses, Mallory scouted the pass by foot during the afternoon. To his relief, the pass was devoid of any sign of past or present human activity. He was not surprised the pass was unused and unguarded. It was impassable to wagons, easily defended and at sufficiently high altitude to have dangerous, unpredictable weather. The Immortals likely wasted no troops to patrol the pass unless they knew an Army was heading for the pass.

He returned before dusk. They decided to eat and then pack up for the ascent. Mallory dreaded the night ascent of the pass that stood 3200 meters above sea level. The howling wind would die down – but it was going to be brutally cold.

They spent an hour packing everything up. Then they climbed up and over the pass in the bone-chilling cold, traveled several kilometers down into the much warmer but still chilly autumn forests on the other side and finally made camp under the canopy of towering, majestic evergreens Entreska called White Fir. Mallory gave her a puzzled look at the name since the trees had dark gray bark and dark green needles. Entreska explained with a laugh that they are the dominate tree on the northern slopes of the White Mountains.

Exhausted, they slept peacefully most of the day behind the shield of the Virtual Watcher and the High Wizard Council. Diffuse clouds spread over the horizon and cloaked the sky in a somber winter gray. Mallory awoke first and with deliberate stealth making no noise, prepared the horses for travel. Entreska woke suddenly almost in a panic.

Entreska shivered in the cool evening air. She looked around. "Why didn't you wake me? I would have helped."

"You were sleeping so peacefully I thought you deserved a few extra winks. You told me yourself you didn't exactly sleep well most of the summer."

Entreska smiled in relief, "Indeed. Sleep. I could use a bit more of that."

Mallory watched carefully as she gathered her blankets and stowed them aboard her chosen horse that she had named Daffodil. Mallory thought about the paths ahead. In theory, road travel was faster, but once he factored in the time lost avoiding roadblocks, skirting villages and cowering from enemy patrols, going directly cross country was probably safer and quicker. This was especially true since he had the technology to avoid getting lost and to navigate around impassable and dangerous terrain without backtracking.

Mallory estimated that they would need to average something near 50 kilometers per day to reach the rendezvous point three days in advance. He wanted to have plenty of time to scout the area once they got there. On horseback, that pace could be achieved easily assuming they could find or steal adequate supplies and avoid too many delays from natural and man-made obstacles. He planned to push them along fairly hard at least in the early going. Entreska simply nodded when he told her.

After a couple of hours, a steady, light snow began to fall. Soon, the world was a beautiful glowing white with a hint of blue and red under the light of the moons. Mallory had to smile in delight at the unqualified beauty of the scene. Yet, he cursed silently at the deep tracks in the snow that would likely remain visible for some days given the cold conditions. Hopefully, no patrol would think it suspicious enough to raise a general alarm and make their journey more exciting than desirable. Eventually almost 20 centimeters of snow covered the valley.

During a break Entreska hesitantly said, "You said you were going to show me the most important function of the Darkglasses. Would now be a good time?"

Mallory popped his lips quietly. He looked up at the night sky. Then he bobbled his head.

"Let's wait until we make camp. It'll take a while."

Entreska obviously disappointed simply nodded.

Despite the snow, benefiting from the downhill grade, the lack of enemy patrols and local inhabitants, they traversed 70 kilometers the first night. Although they had seen no one, several small, identically built cabins with small adjoining corrals dotted the landscape every few kilometers. Mallory could tell via his Darkglasses they were unoccupied and investigated the first couple to determine their purpose. Both cabins had a single room, chimney, wood floor swept clean and nothing else. The cabins weren't big enough to sleep more than four people – so it had to be some kind of summer lodging for loggers or hunters.

Mallory and Entreska took advantage of a cabin for shelter from the snow during the first day. Once the horses were safely put in the corral, they made a small fire in the chimney relying on the Watcher and Wizards to provide warning against discovery.

While chewing the dried fruit and nuts that had been salvaged from the Cumar, Entreska paused suddenly, swallowed and asked, "Do you keep a personal diary?"

Mallory had been concentrating on chewing and was taken off guard, "What?"

Entreska waved a green hand, the right one, "You know. A private record of your life and thoughts."

Mallory shrugged, "Oh. I only do - or rather did - mission reports. And those were only written some time after the fact. And according to my former commander, my reports were notoriously fallacious."

Entreska half-smiled and said, "So you never write down your thoughts and memories?"

Mallory shrugged, "No."

"Ever?"

Mallory shrugged "Not ever. I prefer to remember things the way I want them to have happened rather than how they actually happened. Memories have to be carefully aged to allow them to reach their potential. Keeping accurate records has a nasty way of spoiling good memories."

"Like your mission reports?"

Mallory laughed, "Not at all. Those contained no truths. They were just outright fabrications. Memories are more subtle than that. The truths contained therein justify the thoughts and actions of the here and now. And that applies to all memories. Even to memories of things that were learned rather than lived as may be."

Entreska frowned.

Mallory ventured, "So. Is keeping a diary common practice among Jurasketu?"

Entreska shook her head. "No. Only a few. But unlike your purposeful disdain, mostly from lack of desire or purpose I think."

Mallory sensed disappointment in Entreska, "Do you keep a diary?"

"Yes. But it's mostly thoughts related to research rather than a purposeful gathering of thoughts."

This made the disappointment seem incongruous to Mallory if not downright confounding. "Why did you ask if I kept one then?"

"My father places great importance on them. He keeps careful records of damn near everything. He has often sorted them into books that he has published."

"Everything I've been told gives me the idea that your father is a great man. You must be proud of him."

Entreska looked wistfully at Mallory and muttered, "I suppose I am. Funny how that would be."

Mallory merely nodded in outward approval. Inwardly, he was wondering if Entreska was mentally well. Then he decided – how could she be? How could anyone bear such trauma as she had suffered and survive mentally intact? When he reached his ship, a full mental workup in addition to a physical examination was definitely in order for poor Entreska. Hopefully, she would cooperate.

Mallory then realized that she had been consciously or unconsciously comparing him to her father. His impression was that he had not done too well on that one. In fact, he was feeling that Entreska wasn't happy with him at all.

"Are you not happy with me?"

"What?"

"You seem a bit disappointed in me or something."

Entreska's face showed obvious confusion and consternation. Mallory was thinking himself a fool for even mentioning it. But then Entreska's face softened and her eyes became downcast.

She nodded her head, "I suppose I am."

Mallory gestured wide and said, "But why?"

She snorted a half-laugh, "Stupid eh? Not to mention ungrateful. But it turns out you are a warrior rather than the engineer that I had envisioned you to be."

"Oh."

Silence.

"I'm really neither. I'm more troubleshooter – in the worst sense of the word - than a noble warrior. I'm sorry. Truly I am. Perhaps I am less than I could or should be."

Entreska shook her head, "No. I'm the one who should apologize. And I ask your forgiveness. You deserved greater thanks than I gave for saving my life. Forgive me."

Mallory sighed and sat back, "There is nothing to forgive. But if your thoughts haunt you as they sometimes do me, all is forgiven past, present and future."

Quiet.

Mallory then asked, "Isn't your father a great warrior?"

"Indeed."

"Then why would my status as a warrior, ignoring my claims otherwise, be disappointing?"

Entreska smiled, "Didn't you catch how I said it was funny that I had so much pride in my father?"

Mallory shrugged sheepishly.

Entreska muttered, "That pride exists despite his accomplishments as a warrior."

"Oh. I see."

Mallory looked away deep in thought. He wished he were a noble warrior. No, that wasn't right. He really wished he had gone ahead with a career in microbiology – he had spent years getting his advanced degrees. He really liked manipulating bacteria, fungi, algae and viruses. He had written his master's thesis on modified yeasts. He had always told himself, just another couple of years, retire and then find a nice, quiet research job. Maybe even find a wife. Just like an ancient Roman legionnaire.

Mallory noticed that Entreska was studying him with some concern. She caught his eye and said, "How about we talk about something else."

Mallory laughed, "No. It's okay. Would it help if I told you I started out to be a microbiologist?"

"A what?"

"A microbiologist is a scientist who studies bacteria, fungi, algae, viruses and other microscopic life."

"Mi-cro-scop-ic?"

"Indeed. I think now is the time."

"Time for what?"

Mallory smiled, "To show you the most important function of the Darkglasses."

"Oh. Yes. Let's do that."

Mallory pulled over his duffel bag. "The Darkglasses provides a visual display for my computer woven into my duffel bag."

"Computer?"

"A computer is a ridiculously fantastic device invented hundreds of years before I was born. It changed everything. One of those changes is that vast stores of knowledge are available in moments.

Put your glasses on. In a moment you'll see what I see."

Mallory switched his glasses to shared mode. He showed her microscopic images first – bacteria, cells, viruses, fungi. That impressed her. For almost an hour, he went on to explain how bacteria and viruses caused disease. How cells divided. Everything he could squeeze out in a short time. Eventually Mallory detected some signs of renewed respect from her that made him wish more strongly that he had become a pure scientist. Of course, they would never have met if that had been the case. *But whatever. Wishes are like that.*

Although she actually had more questions about microscopic life and disease, he waved off the questions and showed her more. He showed her the satellite images he had taken of the Earth. Then it was Old Earth. Then it was spaceships and engines. He showed her a mélange of videos and pictures from across the years of himself, his proud looking parents and vibrant younger sister, Melissa. He showed her a kaleidoscope of cities, artwork, alien landscapes, stars, and anything and everything he could think of that he thought she would find interesting. It was probably the wrong thing to do considering her vulnerable state of mind – but it would definitely give her a better understanding of what he had been telling her. She was almost beside herself.

Four hours later Mallory finally stopped the show.

"We can look at more later – we have a long way to go yet and we need some sleep. Plenty of time for me to show you more and allow you to explore on your own."

Entreska removed the glasses with wonder and awe beaming from her face. "Yes... yes... later..."

Mallory studied her carefully and recalled an ancient story he had read about an isolated tribe in the old Amazon rain forest before the rising seas had turned the basin into a vast salt marsh. A linguist/anthropologist from Old New York City had visited the tribe to make some record of their language and culture. Over the months, a gregarious young woman of the tribe had managed to learn a good bit of English from him and asked if she could visit New York with her young boy. He reluctantly agreed to take them thinking she would be overwhelmed by the modern world and become homesick very quickly. Instead, she didn't want to go back.

Using his government connections, he arranged that she could stay. She learned to read and write passably enough, got a menial job that paid enough to have a small apartment for her and her child.

The linguist had been certain that she still would eventually become homesick but he was wrong and so asked her why she didn't want to go back. The woman had been incredulous and proclaimed that everything in New York was better than the Amazon – everything being food, shelter, clothing, healthcare, hygiene, personal safety and most importantly education and opportunity for her child. The lesson Mallory had taken was that the woman had instantly recognized the practical power, value and potential of the modern world.

Amusingly, one of the great features of the modern world was despite its vast complexity, for an ordinary citizen, most of that complexity was hidden behind a veneer of convenience and continuity. Indoor temperatures varied but a few degrees summer to winter. Quality, safe food of all types was available with utter disregard to seasonality. Communication and entertainment was available instantly and effortlessly. Things that kings of old would have given heaps of treasure to have could be had by anyone and everyone for just a mere fraction of a day's pay.

Millions had thrown all of that away to found the Primitive Colonies. Mallory wondered how many would now trade their current lives for the modern one like the tribal woman had. Of course, this Earth wasn't particularly Primitive anymore. Entreska's descriptions of the Jurasketu economy seemed to describe a society heading towards industrialization. He could make that happen in short order if he wanted and if he ignored the fact he was duty bound not to do that. But that duty seemed to be lost in the mists of time. *Duty.* Mallory's thoughts returned to the problem at hand – returning safely to the ruins of his starship.

By the end of the second night, they had moved into lower and more southerly parts and so the temperatures rose above freezing. They located and sheltered in another cabin the second day. Mallory was thinking they had been very fortunate so far. The third night they had progressed another 20km when they were stopped by a major road running east to west. The road itself posed no obstacle. It was the long wagon train and a regiment of Immortals using the road that night.

Mallory spent some time observing to estimate the number of soldiers, auxiliaries, and supplies. He found his mouth watering at the sight of more than two dozen heavily built wagons pulled by teams of six huge horses each. The wagons were loaded high with small 60-liter barrels of Tarfun Stone Brew. To Mallory, of all the privations of life in the field, the lack of beer ranked among the worst.

Upon returning to where Entreska and the horses had been hidden after scouting the road, Mallory said with a mild hint of admiration, "Well. You and your wizards were right. There is indeed a regiment of Immortals marching up the road."

Entreska nodded, "They are heading for the Yellow Pass."

Mallory summoned the satellite images into his Darkglasses and noted the road indeed led to a wide pass nearly 35 kilometers due south of their current location. "Yellow Pass?"

"Yes. The pass is flanked by high cliffs of yellow sandstone on the east and west. The Yellow Pass."

"Ah. I can see that. Very yellow indeed."

Entreska looked as if he was crazy. "You can't see the pass from here." Pause. "Can you?"

Mallory removed the glasses, turned and said, "What?" He tapped his Darkglasses. "The satellite images I showed you earlier."

Entreska threw up her hands. "That's right. I'm not used to that yet."

Mallory smiled. Then he said, "I wonder why Puck is sending more troops into the Raffin."

Entreska shrugged. "Maybe he's not. Maybe they are to defend the pass."

"Against what?"

"My father. A large Jurasketu force is moving across the Central Raffin so the wizards tell me. I guess a vain rescue attempt. Puck's generals are likely just being prudent should my father mount a deep raid in retribution. I hope not."

Entreska closed her eyes and hugged her knees.

Mallory frowned. He put a soft hand on her shoulder. She covered it with one of her own. They said nothing for a while. His frown changed to a sigh as he found it increasingly hard to disbelieve in Entreska's wizardry.

"How long before the Jurasketu Army reaches Duravon?"

Entreska sighed. "Oh. They have moved quickly. Probably another two or three days I would guess."

"Hmm... Would the Yellow Pass be a good place to attack if they decided to raid into the Blades?"

Entreska frowned, "Er... Yes. My brother Rolf says it is the least defensible pass in the Blades and must be defended in force by quality troops. The High Pass further north than the one we stole through is the shorter route from the Centaur Citadel to the Northern Raffin and the Needle's Eye is the best route into the Southern Raffin. Which is why I surmised the Immortals are being sent to defend it."

Mallory shook his head in wonder, "For a pacifist, you sure know a lot about military matters."

Entreska laughed, "A Professor of Ancient History is required to understand military matters. Of course, it's not like I had any choice. It was either be able to talk soldiering or get left out of many a dinner conversation growing up."

Entreska became pensive and looked down.

Mallory tilted his head in concern, "Are you going to be okay?"

Entreska looked up, "Mostly not. I was just thinking how I became well versed in logistics and moving large groups of people from just such conversations and how without that confidence I wouldn't be where I sit now."

Mallory nodded in understanding. "I'm sorry. I wish I could have done something."

Entreska waved her right hand, the green one, "I know."

Mallory said, "I could do something now."

"What do you mean?"

"Will your father attempt to raid into the Blades?"

"I don't know. I am necessarily not privileged to his operational parameters."

Mallory scowled at her use of military jargon. It was not impossible the jargon had developed independently. The survival of English nearly intact into Jurasketu, certainly argued for a sustained tradition of universal literacy. Persistence of military jargon would be reasonable if some of the founding colonists were former soldiers. *Still, what did she mean by that?*

"Operational parameters?"

"The Jurasketu Army answers to the Debaters. The National Council of War agrees and approves in advance what the Army can do for a given tactical or strategic situation. Most of these operational parameters are public since they must be known to all soldiers. Others are secret. Whether or not my father can risk regiments to raid deep into Puck's territory would be something secret."

Mallory laughed, "I see. But would he if he had permission and opportunity?"

Entreska considered for a moment and said, "Yes. And maybe even if he didn't... Have permission that is."

"Does he often take such chances?"

Entreska looked surprised, "Take chances? No. He leaves almost nothing to chance. But he is not paralyzed by fear that he is taking unknown chances either. Although I suspect he is regretting letting me convince him that the risks of the Expedition being attacked were remote."

Mallory nodded, "I suspect so... Anyway. I could give him tactical advantage."

"How so?"

"Disrupting the defense of the Yellow Pass."

Entreska gave him the Eye of Suspicion, "And how could you accomplish that?"

Mallory shrugged, "I don't know yet. It would seem I have a few options. Although most would involve violence that you wouldn't likely approve."

"I suspect not. But I have no claim over you. If anything, you have a claim over me for saving my life."

Mallory nodded gloomily. He felt deep possible guilt. He had become increasingly worried that Puck had been after him. If that was true, the tragedy was his fault in no small measure. Hopefully, one day he would know the answer. Then again, maybe not knowing was better should the answer prove not the one he wanted. *Did it matter?* He hadn't caused the tragedy purposefully or neglectfully. Even if it was his fault, his course of action was the same: eliminate Puck and his enablers.

Mallory considered the matter of disrupting the defense of the Yellow Pass the rest of the night. He let Entreska explore his computer archives as best she could while he planned. Killing the command staff would probably be the simplest, easiest plan. If what former Immortal Craig Henderson had told him was true, the Immortals were well-disciplined, so the junior officers were likely competent replacements and Puck could probably send up adequate senior officers. So such a plan seemed less effective the more he considered. He really shouldn't do anything that would delay their arrival at the Wrything Delta. Any attempt to disrupt the defenses could easily take two days just in travel time. Time they might not have if other delays arose. But Mallory wanted to help. Mallory felt compelled.

On a whim, Mallory checked his copious supply of tiny dried yeast packets. They had been an indispensable component of the modern world since the dawn of the Biotech Revolution in the 21st century.

These specialized genetically engineered yeasts could produce vast quantities of various useful chemicals simply by growing the yeast in an easily prepared broth containing cellulose or food sugars as could be found locally. Most of the chemicals could be easily extracted by distillation, filtering, cooking or combination of such. A number were merely precursor chemicals that had to be mixed together to produce the intended useful item. Others required fancy purification techniques detailed on the package. Some required trace elements to be added to the food stock. A high percentage of the chemicals were a menagerie of useful field medicines including antibiotics, cortisones, antivirals, vitamins and analgesics. Others were organic solvents and fuels. He was particularly fond of the epoxies, explosives and toxins.

Most modern colonies and small settlements relied on the special yeasts to meet their pharmacological and industrial chemical needs at a mere fraction of the interstellar shipping cost that would be required to maintain adequate supplies of just the most common items. The uncommon items simply wouldn't be available when really needed given that the ordering and shipment of goods took minimally months, often years being limited to the speed and vagaries of interstellar transportation and communication.

It was a strange dichotomy. On any given modern planet, communication was instantaneous across the breadth of the world. But communication between planets was limited to the stored electronic mail delivered by random starship. Interplanetary communication could at best be described as slow for Ancient Romans. Ironic that the invention of interstellar space travel enabling starships to cover vast distances in weeks and months had put basic communication between star systems back to the Dark Ages. Mallory laughed out loud bemused by the irony.

Entreska asked, "Is our situation that funny?"

Mallory turned around, embarrassed, "What? Oh. Sorry. No. I was laughing at a private joke."

Entreska nodded and asked, "What are you looking at anyway?"

"Yeasts"

Entreska looked around doubtfully, "Where are we going to get flour?"

Mallory chuckled, "I'm not going to make bread. Although, you know, I should add some premium bread yeast to my standard package.... These are special yeasts. I used some to make the epoxy for the bridge."

Entreska's eyes widened, "Oh yeah. The epoxy. Where did you find such yeast anyway?"

Mallory smiled and patted the packets, "You don't. It's genetically engineered. All these are."

Entreska brightened, "That's right. The DNA stuff you told me about."

"Right. It was actually a fluke that I had the epoxy yeast in my pocket. I had grabbed my standard medicinal set but the epoxy pair got mixed in by accident. We could have built the bridge anyway – but the design would have been different and taken much longer with the extra woodwork required. Puck's Army would have been upon us before we had gotten across I imagine."

Entreska nodded sadly. "What can your yeasts do besides make epoxy?"

Mallory shrugged, "They make medicines, fuels, poisons and some other useful stuff."

Entreska looked at Mallory pensively. "Should we go back? And try to find my father? We could give him Puck's troop dispositions."

Mallory rubbed his ears in aggravated thought. "Hmm... Seems like a good idea. But the risks are very grave. We could end up chasing him all over the Raffin. It'll take at least six days for us to reach him if he remains in the Duravon area. And that's assuming your wizard ghost or whatever friends are able to provide the best advice to help us avoid Puck's pickets and patrols. And then we'd have a lot of explaining to do that will likely prevent us from reaching my ship for months."

Mallory cocked his head suddenly and smiled briefly. "Besides I have a plan to disable the defenders of the Yellow Pass. We need to return to the last cottage we saw a few kilometers back."

It only took two hours and a displeasingly large portion of their food rations that they had salvaged from the Cumar to brew up five kilograms of Enguard, a fantastic medicine that kills virtually all parasitic worms – adult, larvae and eggs - with 100% effectiveness with just a single therapeutic dose. But that effectiveness comes with a small price – it leaves the patient extremely weak and fatigued requiring two to three days of bed rest plus at least another week before vigorous activity can be attempted. After a few minutes of heat pasteurization to kill the yeast and other unwanted microbials, Mallory filtered the product through a cloth and let it dry spread out on a warmed, clean bread board thoughtfully provided by the absent cottage dwellers.

Mallory refused to explain until the product was complete and looked like the pictures in the medical dictionary of the Galatica Encyclopedia – better known as the Encyclopedia of Damn Near Everything. While he waited for the product to dry, Mallory studied every entry on beer barrels to come up with a plan to dose the barrels. Eventually, just before noon, Mallory announced the Enguard was ready with a silly flourish.

Entreska barked out, "Finally. Now would you please explain the plan?"

Mallory smiled, "This is Enguard. It is a famous medicine for parasitic worms. Just one dose kills virtually all known worms regardless of life stage – adult, larvae, egg. It readily dissolves in alcohol and is virtually tasteless. It's perfect. The recommended dosage is 10mg. We have enough product to dose 5000 liters of ale."

Entreska raised her arms, palms upward, "And so?"

Mallory frowned, "And so I plan to dose a wagon load of Tarfun Stone Brew belonging to the Immortals."

Entreska stared in puzzlement, "Worms? I've never heard of anyone having worms. And if they did, wouldn't making them go away improve the Immortals health and help them to fight better?"

Mallory flicked an eyebrow, "Once they recover."

"Recover?"

Mallory smiled sardonically, "Indeed. Being tough, trail-hardened soldiers, they will probably only be completely incapacitated for two days and after another ten days they might be able to manage a brief outburst of moderate activity every so often. It's a brutal side effect. But should more than serve our purposes."

Entreska's face went slack.

Mallory rubbed his ears in thought. "There is the tricky bit, however."

Entreska recovered and said, "How exactly do you plan to get that in the ale? It'll be heavily guarded against illicit consumption. And it would seem a little problematic to open and reseal 50 barrels of ale without somebody noticing. Don't you think?"

"More like 80 barrels actually."

"Fifty. Eighty. What's the difference?"

Mallory shrugged, "Need to make sure we down the whole regiment. The barrels are 60 liters each of Tarfun Stone Brew. So I need to put 600mg in each. I think I'll swipe a barrel though..."

Mallory licked his lips at the thought.

"Great. I still don't see how you get the medicine in."

Mallory laughed, "You've never worked in a tavern have you or paid much attention eh?"

Entreska was getting a little annoyed. "No. I mean I like ale as much as the next girl, bwa...ait! Ale barrels are vented before you drink them! Tarfun Stone Brew needs a day for best drinking. Everyone knows that now that I remember."

"Indeed. I just pour the Enguard into the shive holes of the barrels that are being vented. I just gotta be careful not to lose the spiles in the process. I suspect the venting ale will be covered in a tent – but no matter. I'll be a ghost to the guards."

Entreska smiled, "That is almost evil. What if my father fails to attack, though?"

Mallory shrugged, "Too bad. But it is the best I can do without killing them."

Entreska said, "Could you?"

"Sure. There is even still time. I can make several medicines that if I overdosed the ale would prove fatal to most of the regiment."

Entreska frowned, "That wasn't what I meant actually. Well, what next?"

Mallory grimaced and clenched his fists in self-admonition. He kept failing her tests. Of course, why should he care? Mallory decided to not answer himself just now. "Well, I'm going to leave you here. I'll take Dandelion and ride up to where the Immortals are setting up camp. I'll dose the ale as soon as I can and return. If your Wizards warn of approaching trouble, send your horses away and try to find a good hiding spot. Hopefully, I'll be able to return and rescue you again. Here. Put this in your pocket."

"What is it?"

"It's a tracking device. I'll be able to find you if I'm within a 1000 meters of it."

Entreska briefly fingered the small plastic device that was the size and shape of a small coin, and then she slipped it into her pocket. She breathed heavily.

Mallory rubbed his ear harshly and said, "I know. I don't want to leave you alone either. But it can't be helped – you'd be in more danger if you went with me. It's clear these cottages aren't used in the winter. You'll be safe."

Mallory decided to ride most of the way in daytime. The evergreen forest provided sufficient cover until he was close to the Yellow Pass. He covered the forty-kilometer distance in good order at a leisurely pace. There was no reason to arrive at the pass before nightfall. The backside of the pass would not be heavily patrolled so he wasn't overly concerned, but he dismounted and tied off Dandelion in a secluded spot with a nice patch of grass for him to munch on.

Mallory reconnoitered the Immortals encampment at the pass for a couple hours to learn their positions and map out his route to the ale tents, which luckily were located at the rear near the road. Apparently, the Immortals were very well disciplined, since a detail of only two bored looking guards watched over the ale.

Mallory mulled the possibilities. He didn't want to kill or incapacitate the guards since that might bring suspicion onto the ale supply – so this was going to be tricky. As a precaution, he put the silencer on his 5mm automatic and held it ready. He easily slipped past the guards and entered the ale tent from the rear under a loose flap. There he worked the barrels near the rear first. Then he waited awhile until he thought the guards were lightly dozing. Then he carefully worked the barrels near the front keeping the automatic ready to down the guards if something went wrong. The process took nearly 90 minutes and he was sweating uncomfortably in the cool air from the tension and exertion.

Once he was done, he exited the tent the same way he came in and then came face to face with a dilemma, the unopened ale storage tent. The barrels of ale weighed 70 kilos each. He could heft one and carry it 1500 meters back to his horse. He stared for an uncomfortably long time and decided he was contemplating sheer foolishness. He turned to leave and saw two amused sentries who Mallory swore must have just been magicked into that position. Both were armed with small crossbows that were raised and pointed at his chest.

The shorter of the two spoke confidently and softly, "And just what do you think you are doing?"

Mallory instantly realized that in the darkness, his dark skin and special camouflage clothing would make it impossible for the sentries to see him clearly. Obviously, they thought he was a wayward soldier trying to sneak into the ale tent for an extra ration. This meant the two sentries would die. Very disappointing in the sense that the whole purpose of this mission was to avoid killing them, but he could not escape with them alive. They could not have anticipated his next actions.

In a static ambush, movement and accurate aim is the key to survival. Mallory had spent many hours learning to fire on the run in an ambush. As Mallory fired the first shot, he jump-stepped quickly to his left and turned sideways to dodge the expected bolts. The crossbows twanged and fortunately missed as he made his second shot. The first shot hit the taller man dead center in the throat. The second shot caught the shorter man just above the right eye. Both fell dead in a heap.

Mallory quickly scanned the area. He heard voices in the distance. Although his shots had been silent, the crossbows had made loud, distinctive noises unlikely to be ignored by experienced soldiers. Thinking quickly, Mallory picked the shorter man's body up and carried it to where Mallory had been standing. He grabbed a bolt from the man's belt and rammed it into the bullet hole. Then he went back to the other body, grabbed another bolt and grimly rammed it into the other bullet hole. Stupid, but it might confuse the issue long enough for him to make good his escape. He took off at a run counting on the camouflage and darkness to conceal him. Near the tents, his tracks would be indiscernible amongst the trampings of many soldiers from the previous days.

He could hear a bit of a commotion back at the ale tents, but he wasted no time looking. He reached Dandelion in about 7 minutes and rode off into the night. He reached the cottage just before dawn.

A worried Entreska greeted him and asked the obvious.

He just said, "It is done."

"Any trouble with the guards?"

Without hesitation, Mallory said, "None."

Entreska ordered Mallory to take sleep while she groomed and put up his exhausted horse. Mallory threw himself down on his bedroll and didn't awake until dusk.

The High Wizard Council

Entreska sat and stared at the sleeping Mallory huddled under his thermal blanket. Like many, Entreska had always loved tales of high adventure. She particularly loved the wilder, darker and deadly ones to the open chagrin of her parents who didn't seem to enjoy such wanderings of the imagination. Entreska suspected they had witnessed too much death and destruction. The reality of her own high adventure knotted her insides and seemed to be crushing her like a vise.

War had destroyed her life and ended the lives of many of her friends. An ancient artifact had transformed her into a living rainbow and crowded her head with the voices and vexations of wizard ghosts. A man claiming to be from a distant past with knowledge beyond imagining dragged her across the wilderness. She felt a surreal mix of calm excitement. She had learned things of stunning implications. The wizard ghosts provided her with perceptual knowledge of her surroundings to a distance not even dreamed possible. It was all a bit too much. *Great Burning Blasted too much really.*

She needed to reassert control of her destiny. *Somehow.* She waited for commentary from the wizards... But none came from indifference or in silent mockery.

Her thoughts drifted...

Assert control she thought. On that whim, she shed her own thermal blanket and pulled back her sleeve to bare her left arm. She studied the swirling colors that swam across her smooth skin. Assert control. She concentrated on a lavender swirl that extended from the back of her elbow to the base of her wrist. She imagined it darker, bluer. Nothing happened. She focused her will. She willed it to be so. Nothing happened. She tried harder. Nothing happened. Nothing.

Entreska rubbed her now cold arm, shimmied the sleeve back down and drew the blanket tight around her. Entreska wondered on the silence of the Voice.

The Voice responded readily enough to her requests for information regarding disposition of forces across the Raffin and gave her regular reports about anything and anyone nearby. Actually, sometimes, Silas Hurme, called the Second Voice, would provide the information when Jasmine was resting or otherwise occupied. But their ability to read her thoughts seemed to have become limited to some extent. She tried to visit Heather daily to give her updates and receive coaching. She could only communicate with Heather by projecting herself into Vorkfest. Heather speculated that either the Council was preoccupied trying to decide what to do and so wasn't monitoring Entreska's thoughts very closely. Or Entreska was subconsciously using the power of Evermore to block them. Or the Conjunction had imposed limitations on them. Heather rated the latter two most likely. For herself, thinking back, Entreska had become convinced that the last was the reason. The limitation had seemingly arisen immediately following the Conjunction; Entreska just hadn't noticed it right away.

Despite the limitation on knowing her thoughts, the Council clearly could hear and see everything that Entreska could see and hear. It seemed they could still sense her emotions. Neither she nor the Voice had commented on the change. In a slightly aggravating way, she felt a near constant feeling of agitation from the wizard ghosts. Even more interestingly, they had yet to comment on the information provided by the Darkglasses.

"He lied."

Startled, Entreska said aloud, "What?"

Mallory stirred, but did not open his eyes.

Regaining her composure, Entreska thought *"What?"*

"Mallory has freshly smeared blood in several places on his clothing. He is unhurt as best we can tell. Didn't you notice?"

Entreska frowned, *"I wasn't paying close attention apparently."*

The Voice sighed audibly. "Owens is a dangerous man."

Entreska chuckled silently, *"Indeed he is."*

"This is more serious than I think you suppose."

"More serious than life and death? The future of civilization?"

A wave of anger was suddenly broken by an unseen rock into a shower of kindness. But Entreska did not miss the anger.

"Well. At least you understand the dangers. I think the time has come for you to meet the rest of the Council. I will bring an image into your mind. The image will be that of our Tea Room as we call it - a rather fancy receiving hall actually. If you focus strongly on the image and imagine yourself there – you should be able to project your mind into the Tea Room as if you were there."

Entreska hesitated a moment. Heather had been preparing her for this moment since her first meeting following the Conjunction twelve days ago. Heather was rather puzzled by the fact the Council had failed to ask for this personal meeting immediately. It seemed to be an indication of internal strife on the Council. Heather said the Council wasn't speaking to her since she had refused to answer any of their recent questions and subsequent accusations, so she had no way of knowing what they were thinking at this point.

Entreska took a deep breath and thought, *"Bring the image."*

A smooth, glossy black marble statue of a stylistic naked woman standing with legs together and arms spread wide filled her mind. The woman's almost non-face looked to the sky. Entreska followed the statue's gaze to a puffy gray nothingness. A sudden ripple of azure followed by a counter ripple of dark purple marred the gray but they faded quickly leaving Entreska and the statue to stare once more into nothingness. Entreska stared at the gray for what seemed like several minutes before examining the statue in greater detail. The raised, round base rested on large, white square tiles that seemed to extend to the horizon. Suddenly, the distinctive aromas of several varieties of teas and fresh cakes wafted over Entreska. She turned towards the pleasant smells to see an ornately carved marble archway that opened into a darkened room. The flower and branch motifs extended into a white mist that obscured the outer boundaries of the arch. Entreska covered the few steps quickly and then cautiously passed through the archway.

The room beyond was immense, at least 20 meters long by 10 meters wide. The ten-meter high ceiling was barrel vaulted with square wooden panels trimmed with a simple lattice and a clear oil or wax finish allowing the light colored grain to glisten in the lamp light. The five-meter high walls were paneled with vertically placed, very wide tongue and groove boards stained uniformly a dark red. A heavy ebony stained wood plinth topped the walls. The other end of the hall had an archway similar to the one she had passed through. Beyond that archway was diffuse yellow light and a patio with a low stone bench.

Lining the walls stood black marble statues, carved in a variety of styles each depicting a person engaged in a different activity. Each piece was clearly the work of a different master sculptor. She let her gaze sweep across the statues ignoring the middle of the room. Ancient ghost wizard imaginations apparently included a lot of fine sculpture. Yet, she had a vague feeling of being familiar with this room.

Bright colored sofas, overstuffed chairs, small wooden tables, large wooden tables, a few granite tables, spluttering oil lamps, tea services, plates of cakes and wizards were scattered about the room in a rather haphazard fashion. The ten wizards remained in various stages of repose drinking tea or munching cakes. The eleventh sat cross-legged, forearms resting on knees on the low stone bench on the far patio. Clothing seemed to be held in low regard by the Council.

None of them moved. They just stared curiously at Entreska. For a brief moment, she panicked and looked down to see if she was clothed. Instead, she was surprised to find herself wearing her standard expedition tan blouse, trousers, proper undergarments, stockings and boots and not the baggy, ill-fitting Cumar outerwear she had been forced to loot. When she looked back up, their expressions had changed to slight smiles.

Entreska quickly scanned the group. Five wore nothing. Three wore only short, plain white skirts. Two wore colorful but simple tunics. One sported trousers striped in shades of the rainbow. And no footwear was in evidence. Entreska supposed that any semblance of modesty had evaporated long back in the hundreds of years the wizards had been trapped together. In a way, it was surprising that any of them bothered with clothing at all. Entreska took a deep breath and looked around more carefully.

Heather had spent several hours describing each wizard in great detail including appearance, personality, character, sorcery skill and history. Heather also had much to say about each wizard's motives, thinking processes and trustworthiness but readily admitted that was more subjective in nature and that Entreska would have to make up her own mind on such matters.

Entreska's gaze fell first on The Voice, Jasmine "Jaz" Moonstalker. Her smooth silver skin, black eyes and short, shiny black hair all glistened in the lamp light. She looked much like Heather, athletic, trim, a handsome face and short but with slightly rounder hips. Heather described her as kind, very wise and yet naively idealistic. She had disdained clothing even before entering Evermore. Entreska smiled warmly and Jasmine nodded.

Findaryle "Daryl" Dustwhipper sported dark blue skin, blue eyes and short, spiky pink hair. His Zattan features fit well with his tall and lithe frame. He always used his considerable powers sparingly and with great subtlety to achieve his somewhat mischievous aims. Heather said he cared only for himself and was to be feared. He covered himself in a white skirt.

The Second Voice, Silas Hurme was a thick, muscular man who loved to fight armed and unarmed. His soft pink skin, winsome gray eyes and bushy dark red hair belied his hard-edged attitude. Heather liked him and described him as scrupulously honest, ethical and extremely dangerous to offend. He wore the rainbow trousers.

Rhenda "Rat" Rattleskone had bright yellow skin, cheerful brown eyes and long cascades of purple hair. Rhenda appeared to be very unathletic and somewhat overweight. Heather described her as overly friendly, highly manipulative, a lousy ally and a worse enemy. She wore a bright, mottled red tunic.

Lee Yultz, the lone wizard on the Council of Valruk descent, had orange skin with thin black stripes, green eyes and no hair. Lee was long-limbed, tall, limber, quick and strong. He constantly goaded Silas into arguments that they often settled with a wrestling match although Lee usually lost. Lee tended to believe all plans will lead to ruin. Heather considered him her best friend on the Council and admired his courage if not his wit. He wore nothing.

Urzeldamay "Zelda" Rooker hailed from a now long extinct tribe on Wokometu. She was small, lean and wispy with brownish-gray skin, soft brown eyes and brown hair. Her hair changed to yellow to green to brown to white with the seasons. She constantly lamented the demise of her tribe, complained bitterly about their fate and generally whined and moaned. She was no one's ally or enemy. Her powers, however, were well-tuned and she was often called the Dream Maker. She wore a brilliant yellow tunic.

William "Billy" Smith had deep red skin, black eyes, and deep blue hair. His large, unathletic bulk was deposited on a sofa. He could be best described as lazy, slow and extremely powerful. He laughed constantly at everything and never seems the least bit unhappy, ever. But he was not to be trusted. He wore a white skirt.

Diana "Dee" Hurosa had lavender skin with pink streaks, blue eyes, and shiny dark lavender hair with pink streaks. She had strong, muscled arms and legs. She proudly displayed her large, gravity ignorant breasts and never wasted effort on choosing clothes. She favored style and wit over substance. She was exquisitely competent but not particularly original. She valued her status and power caring nothing for others. She would make an excellent ally if given the right incentives.

Baxatom "Tom" Furth had chocolate brown skin streaked with gray, brown eyes, gold and green hair. He was lean but awkward and unathletic. His only visible emotions were slight frowns and slight smiles and those don't seem to be consistent with external events. At 485 years, he had been the oldest wizard then living when Evermore was created. He spoke only rarely and then only in riddles. Most thought he had gone daft a century before Evermore including Heather, but no one had come up with the courage to dismiss him from the Council – and so here he still was. He wore a white skirt.

Stanley "Stan" Black had blue-green skin, blue eyes, deep purple hair. He was lean, strong and tall and probably the most quick, agile and athletic of all the council. His mental acumen was exceptional as well and was well regarded as being charming, humorous, sympathetic and humble. He disliked confrontations, greatly desired consensus and always tried to make everyone happy. He wore nothing.

Toviel Baker, the eleventh wizard, perched unmoving, apparently meditating on the patio, was from the Deliverance river valley. She had perfect gold skin, deep green eyes, emerald green hair and an absolutely perfect lean body. She was aloof, wary, never offered an opinion and kept to herself. She harbored deep, mysterious powers that she rarely used. She always supported Jasmine and Silas and was always known for efforts on behalf of the less fortunate. She wore nothing.

The wizards just continued to stare and smile placidly while Entreska looked them over. Heather had armed Entreska with several conversational gambits, but Entreska ignored that advice for the moment. She said, "Well?"

Jasmine nodded and said, "Indeed. Welcome to Evermore. Would you like to sit?" She indicated a nice lemon colored chair to Entreska's left that faced the room. Entreska shrugged and relaxed into the chair. Entreska was nervous but not fearful.

Entreska began with a disarming lie, "It is nice to actually meet you in person and see what you really look like. Putting faces to voices so to speak."

The wizards nodded politely along with a few polite dismissive waves. Early on, Heather had conjured images of all the wizards and so she already knew them quite well, but she asked, "Introductions?"

Jasmine spoke quickly, "Of course." She proceeded to introduce each member of the Council, extolling their great accomplishments and virtues in life, and their continuing contributions over the centuries of isolation in Evermore. Entreska paid scant attention having heard most of it from Heather. She simply exchanged glances with the wizards as they were introduced. All were obviously on their best behavior as would be expected.

Finally, Jasmine indicated Toviel on the patio, "Toviel is currently scanning the outside world. We all take turns with scanning duty – anywhere from a couple hours to about 16 hours."

Entreska nodded. Heather had explained that the spirit wizards did not need food or water and their powers of focus were almost unlimited – except inexplicably they all still needed about four to six hours of spirit sleep every day or their powers, focus and energy would fade precipitously.

Then, to everyone's great surprise, Baxatom Furth spoke up suddenly, "Entreska. Once you understand what you are, you shall be Invincible. Evermore is Mighty Indeed. Its power will encompass you and your life will extend into untold millennia. Do not let the boredom of it all turn you away from Love. You must love all the world. Or you will wreak ruin upon it." Then he smiled, picked up a cup of tea, nodded and quietly sipped away ignoring the stares of his fellow wizards.

The unexpected comment brought ruin upon Entreska's conversational plan that had involved elaborate verbal sparring with the vastly more experienced wizards. She had expected to be outmatched and so had planned to ask their advice concerning Mallory, Puck and Jurasketu. She wasn't really interested in their advice, but she wanted them to reveal themselves and allow her to learn what they would tell her about the history and nature of Evermore. It would be interesting to see if they tried to twist the truth that she had learned from Heather. Or at least thought she had learned. It was entirely possible Heather had things a bit mixed up. Or had lied. This encounter might put Heather's story to the test as well. Entreska was deeply interested in what the powers of the wizards really could be if they would admit it.

But that plan was all ruined. Baxatom had steered the conversation directly and probably irrevocably to the relationship between

Entreska and the Council. Entreska decided to dispense with sparring and simply start throwing stones. "I am deeply curious. Who brought the vision into my mind? The one that compelled me to be Conjoined with Evermore."

This brought a number of surprised looks and glances at one another. Then Findaryle Dustwhipper, with a puzzled look, asked, "Are you saying that Heather didn't?"

Lee Yultz snapped, "How could she? The only place to Externalize is from the Patio of the World."

Stanley Black spoke soothingly, "Maybe Daryl presumed she has a way to overcome that limitation. She hasn't revealed all the secrets of Evermore that is certain."

Lee just snarled in retort.

Jasmine asked Entreska, "Heather claims she did not?"

Entreska shook her head, "No. And I believe her. She seemed quite shocked at what had happened."

Everyone chuckled.

Jasmine smiled, "Entreska. My sister is skilled in all the arts of theater, sorcery and storytelling. It is almost impossible to distinguish her real emotions from her conjured ones. I suspect she doesn't even know the difference once she decides to play a scene."

Everyone nodded in silent agreement.

Jasmine continued, "That being said. I don't see how she could have been responsible. If she could Externalize from her private quarters or garden, she would have done so long ago and we would have known it. I am certain of it. It was clearly one of us. Silas had been monitoring and called us all to the Patio. Only Daryl and Billy failed to join us before the Conjunction occurred."

Slightly puzzled, Entreska asked, "What does that mean?"

Billy Smith spoke next, "It means that one of the nine members of the Council who stood on the Patio at that moment has brought us to this current situation. Technically, Entreska, what you did and what one of us induced you to do is a capital crime under the jurisdiction of the High Wizard Council. Fortunately for you, we are in absolutely no position to enforce that law now or ever - given current circumstances."

Billy paused and turned to Jasmine, "I formally request an immediate vote on a full and unrestricted pardon for Entreska. So she'll be more likely to cooperate more fully with us without fear – real or imagined."

Jasmine frowned. She looked at the expectant faces of the wizards and then said, "Very well. Does anyone object to taking a pardon vote at this time without debate?"

No one moved or spoke.

"Very well. All those in favor?"

To Entreska's amusement, all eleven raised their hands. Heather had been right. They would quickly grant her pardon in hopes she would be a more benevolent master.

"Pardon is granted to Entreska Nevercare."

Entreska smiled and said, "Thank you. What about the inducer?"

Jasmine scowled as Billy spoke again, "I suggest we grant the trifler amnesty in exchange for a confession and maybe their motive. Jasmine?"

"Very well. All in favor of granting amnesty for a full and complete confession including motivation to the... inducer."

Everyone raised their hands including Entreska.

Then everyone looked around waiting for a confession that never came. Jasmine and Billy both seemed particularly nonplussed. Most of the others seemed amused.

Silas Hurme rubbed his nose and sighed, "I guess your curiosity won't be satisfied anytime soon."

Diana Hurosa muttered, "We could speculate instead. Shall we?"

A chorus of hoots and grunts followed and Billy could be heard to say, "I've had enough speculations this century. Especially yours."

Diana simply smiled and picked up a pastry.

Entreska twisted her mouth. She wasn't making much progress so far. So for a lack of better ideas, she said, "May I have a tour?"

Jasmine looked around, shrugged and said, "This is pretty much it. There's the Patio of Infinity behind you, the Patio of the World at that end, and this is the Tea Room."

"Tea Room?"

"We presume the architecture is an invention of my sister – although she refuses to comment. But this room is essentially unalterable by any of our powers. If we try to move the furniture more than a short distance from its current arrangement – it fades back to near its starting place. Tea and pastries constantly replenish themselves as consumed and certainly do not go stale or cold. Essentially, it is always tea time in Evermore. So we call it the Tea Room or just the Hall."

Entreska smiled. She already knew that. And that Heather had done it as a joke.

Lee chuckled, "And some of us call it the Hall of Eternity – but not because it never changes..."

Lee was deluged with laughter and boos.

Entreska gestured around, "Well. How do you reach your private Halls and gardens?"

Rhenda Rattleskone barked, "What? Heather didn't tell you?"

The wizards glanced briefly at Rhenda and then turned to Entreska. Entreska rolled her eyes and shrugged. "Well. Yes. I was just checking I suppose."

Rhenda raised an eyebrow. "Then again. Heather has never seen any of our private quarters or gardens. Why shouldn't Entreska see them?"

Entreska realized moments later that a number of the wizards were obviously engaged in telepathic communication. Oddly enough, none seemed interested in making mental contact with her. She tried making telepathic contact with Jasmine. Nothing. She tried harder. Nothing.

Silas spoke suddenly, "Entreska. Are you okay?"

"What? Yes. I'm fine. And call me Tresh."

Silas raised an eyebrow. "As you wish. If you like, I can show you my quarters first. And then one of the others can do the same. I'm sure it will satisfy your curiosity."

The others all made the same offer except for Jasmine, Baxatom and Toviel who was otherwise occupied. Entreska nodded. "Well. I don't have a lot of time. How about Silas and then Lee, if no one objects?"

Urzeldamay Rooker spoke in apparent objection, "Don't you think you should be more wary, Tresh?"

"Why? Wary of what?"

Jasmine interrupted, "Well. Zelda was once held prisoner by Daryl. You see, in here, our powers are normal. Our private quarters seem to give us greater power and in our private gardens, we are the supreme being if you will. We can manipulate the gardens to our will with ease and without the usual fatigue. The rest of us objected, of course, and Daryl was ostracized. Eventually, Zelda was released and all was forgiven. As you can see, we are all friends now." She smiled sincerely and swept her arms around. The others all smiled on cue.

Entreska managed not to laugh at the "friends" comment. Heather had told her all this as well. Before the incident, the wizards had visited each other's gardens regularly except for Vorkfest – Heather's garden. No one trusted her. She had been unsure if Entreska could be held prisoner. Entreska had offered to experiment, but Heather had declined saying the as yet uncontrolled power Entreska could potentially wield in an attempt to break free might tear Vorkfest asunder and destroy her garden irreparably. The whole conversation now took on new meaning in light of Baxatom's comments about her powers being so strong she risked losing her humanity. It was all very odd and scary.

"I will see your quarters anyway, Silas."

Silas smiled politely and walked over to statue of a kneeling man sharpening an axe. He said, "Here. Put your hand on the statue. Doesn't matter where."

Nothing happened and Entreska frowned.

Silas caught her expression, "I have to touch it as well and activate it – it responds only to me."

Entreska pulled her hand back from the statue in surprise as the light dimmed suddenly. Silas and the statue were unchanged. The walls, statues, ceiling and floor were unchanged. Otherwise the hall was empty – no sofas, no tables, no wizards, just marble tile floor. Looking back, the Patio of Infinity seemed unchanged, but the Patio of the World now looked out onto a dark, old growth forest.

Entreska frowned and turned to Silas.

Silas shrugged and said, "Disappointing eh?"

Entreska nodded. Heather had told her the private quarters replicated the Tea Room but that each of the wizards decorated their version at their whim.

Entreska gave a quirky smile, "No furnishings?"

Silas shrugged again, "I don't spend much time in here. I'm either in my garden or in the Tea Room. You'll find most of the others do the same. While I can summon almost anything I might desire, summoned things here and in the Tea Room require significant effort to bring into existence and then more effort to maintain including my trousers. I have to renew their existence every morning."

Entreska scowled causing Silas to laugh.

"Sometimes I don't bother. In my garden, I can effortlessly wear whatever I wish. And sometimes I do. Anyway, unless we want a private meeting and the other parties don't wish to be trusting, we typically don't bother to maintain anything in our private halls. A few don't trust the private Halls either and only conduct private meetings out on the Patio of Infinity."

Entreska nodded. She had learned something new. Heather had glossed over this aspect. Heather never allowed anyone into her private hall or garden and refused to visit the other private halls.

Then she said, "Has anyone visited your Garden since the Zelda Incident?"

Silas smiled, "Yes. Many times actually. Everyone except for Daryl and Zelda. Daryl doesn't trust me and Zelda still hasn't gotten over it I presume."

"Is Daryl justified in his fear?"

"No. But I think it would be impossible to convince him the danger was not real."

Entreska nodded. "When I have more time, I would like to visit your gardens."

Silas betrayed no hint of disappointment and said, "I would be glad to show you when you will. I'm sure you'll find my gardens pleasant and the denizens friendly."

Entreska nodded absently. Then she changed her expression and said, "What exactly is the Infinity?"

Silas frowned. "I assume you mean the one accessible from the Patio of Infinity? Rather than a nebulous Infinity that existence inhabits."

"Yes. The Patio."

Silas frowned deeper. Then he turned aside and spoke slowly, "We don't know. Heather claims she does not either, but as was pointed out by her dear sister, what is true and what is theater is not always discernible with her. And mind you, I've always *liked* Heather. But she manages to blur reality and fiction with a relish that I find disconcerting. Entreska. I mean Tresh. While I cannot honestly counsel you to trust the High Wizard Council, I can say, very honestly and earnestly, be careful how much you trust Heather. And Mallory as well. He is an even deeper enigma than the sum of all the other mysteries that lay before the world."

Entreska said, "I may be young and lack the deep experience of the Council and Heather, but as you say, it would be dangerous to trust you, the rest of the Council, Heather or Mallory. So it will be my own counsel I shall keep – not that I particularly trust myself either."

Silas quirked a brief smile and said, "Then you are wise indeed."

"Perhaps. We shall see."

Silas replied, "Maybe. Events have a nasty way of making the wisest decisions turn out wrong."

"My father is less sanguine in that regard."

"With my apologies, I would say your father is dangerously arrogant."

Entreska smiled, "He is very dangerous that is true. And very arrogant. But what I mean is that he does not believe in wisdom. For him, wisdom means trusting instinct and experience. He believes that is a poor substitute for seeing the truth of something. He is not a fool. He knows that the most well-reasoned decision can be beaten by a decision made by a throw of the dice."

Silas grinned, "Very good. Then I retract my criticism. I would say, instead, that he is particularly wise."

Entreska laughed but then her thoughts returned to the Infinity.

"Has anyone ever ventured into the Infinity? To explore?"

"Yes. Several attempts. I once walked for an entire year. I counted over 30 million steps into the endless gray nothingness before I gave up."

"Did it ever vary?"

"The sky roiled and changed but the tiles went seemingly to Infinity."

"Could you have been going in circles?"

Silas crinkled his face in thought, "I'm not entirely sure. I used a sorcerous method of path marking. And it appeared to be working when I tested it by retracing my steps. But then when I gave the enterprise up, I sighed and started the long journey back. Except after a few steps the statue and arch came into view and within a few minutes I was back here. Mind you, that was a relief since there is only so much endless nothingness paved with white tiles one can take. But it was also terribly disappointing, I mean, apparently I had gone nowhere even though I'm fairly certain I never crossed my own path."

Entreska nodded sympathetically.

Silas sighed, "Tresh. It is difficult for us. Even after the many long centuries, we chafe at our pathetic existence. It's just a horrible mind game gone awry. It's amazing we haven't all gone completely mad. My body never changes except in my private garden where I can be a fire-breathing dragon should I choose. That's probably why we don't go crazy – our minds cannot break because they are merely echoes of our own imaginings. We are just vibrant dreams blending with the slow turning of the world across seasons indifferent to our strivings for relevance."

Entreska's expression gave way to concern.

Silas noticed and smiled, "Sorry. My despair at not understanding this place sometimes leaks out at odd moments. I was quite crazy before I became a Spirit of Evermore. And this place hasn't helped. Shall we return?"

"How?"

"Just touch any of the statues and you'll be back in the Tea Room."

Entreska did so. Silas followed shortly thereafter.

Toviel Baker had been relieved by Billy Smith. Lee Yultz and Daryl Dustwhipper were having a very loud shouting match that Stan Black and Jasmine were desperately trying to referee. The others had retreated to the set of sofas closer to the Patio of the World. Silas avoided the shouting wizards and steered Entreska over to formally meet Toviel Baker. Toviel nodded almost imperceptibly and offered Entreska a cake quietly extolling its virtues. Entreska politely declined and went to observe the Patio of the World.

Suddenly, Entreska felt a powerful jolt as though being buffeted by a gust of wind. She stumbled forward and saw Silas careen past her onto the Patio of the World crashing into Billy Smith who had somehow held his position. The two tumbled onto the stone and bounced back up cursing. Entreska turned to learn what had caused the jolt.

Broken and scorched furniture was scattered across the hall. Two statues had been toppled and broken. Teapots lay spinning and rattling hither and yon. A fine dusting of pulverized pastries covered everything including the four wizards who all lay torn, bleeding and insensate from multiple, very serious-looking injuries. Entreska looked back to see what the others were doing. Rhenda lay prone and unmoving. Silas and Billy slowly checked themselves for injuries apparently not yet aware that others were seriously hurt.

Tom emerged from behind a pillar and stared at the mess, hands on hips. Diana spent time looking herself over. Toviel, unhurt, ran to the crumpled wizards across the hall. As Entreska watched in fascination, Toviel stopped and knelt before Jasmine. Toviel touched her own forehead with her right hand, bowed her head and held her left hand over Jasmine. Within moments, the blood and gore washed away and Jasmine was restored. Jasmine heaved herself up to a sitting position and began breathing heavily while rocking back and forth, hands pressed on the side of her head. Toviel moved on to the others, treating Stan, Lee and Daryl in turn. After few moments, all three were sitting up, rubbing themselves and moaning loudly.

While Diana attended to Rhenda, Silas and Billy swept past Entreska to join Toviel. Tom stepped up beside Entreska.

Tom muttered, "Children."

Entreska turned to him, "What?"

"A bunch of children fighting where they ought not."

Entreska simply nodded.

After a few moments of silence, Entreska asked curiously, "Can any of you die here?"

Tom quirked an eyebrow, frowned slightly and then smiled faintly, "Probably not. Except possibly... No. Never mind. I would think not."

"Then how did the four suffer such severe injuries such that Toviel needed to heal them. What if they had been alone without care?"

Tom shrugged. "One of us would have found them and given them aid."

"Only here in the Hall."

Tom shrugged again, "True. But not important. Injuries, including fatal ones seem to resolve themselves in about 10 days."

"Resolve?"

Tom smirked, "Return to prior condition before injuries."

Incredulous, Entreska asked, "So, there have been fatal fights or rather fights that would have been fatal?"

"Only after we learned that fatal was not."

Entreska leaned back, "Oh?"

"After only 80 years of being in Evermore, Zelda despaired one day and publicly stabbed herself to death in ritual fashion out on the Patio of Infinity."

Entreska scowled in horror.

Tom sighed, "Yes. In that time, I would have counted it as one of those things that I would rather have not been present to witness..."

He continued after a pause, "Horrified, we dragged the body to the side, out of sight, on the Patio of Infinity while we decided what to do with the body. Eventually after a long argument over who was to blame other than Zelda herself, we agreed that I would entomb the body in my private hall. Except that it turned out, we couldn't get the body out of the Hall. Ha. So much for that plan."

Tom smiled faintly and Entreska laughed nervously.

"So, instead, we just left it out on the Patio. Fortunately, the body didn't become putrid. Being merely a Spirit of Evermore, we reasoned that was not cause for immediate alarm and grateful for the lack of bad odor."

Entreska nodded. "Then what?"

"About five weeks later, we noticed the body had vanished. After some discussion, we determined that no one had checked on it after the first week. There is little reason to visit the Patio of Infinity for reasons that would be obvious had you spent any time there. But then another week after that despite many plausible theories explaining what had happened to the body, Zelda shows up, completely whole, but even more depressed than ever complaining that she couldn't even kill herself and that this was Hell as ever it was."

"Great Burning Blast."

Tom nodded, "Indeed. Indeed."

Entreska was still puzzled.

Tom noticing the puzzled look on Entreska's face added, "Since death has yet to achieve permanence for us, the temptation to test the limits of our wizard skills has proven too strong despite constant pledges to eschew violence in argument, sport or revenge."

"Wonderful."

Heather hadn't explained any of this. She wondered why not.

"Yultz. Lee, that is, gets slain at least one or twice a decade arguing with Daryl, Diana or Billy. Everyone else except myself has been slain quite a few times. Well. Not counting Heather."

"What? You've never been killed? Why not?"

Tom replied evenly, "I don't get into arguments. And I don't lose tests of wizard skill either. Nor, I might add, does Heather."

Entreska quirked an eyebrow, "Get into arguments?"

Tom gave her a sidelong glance, "Sorry. She does get into arguments. I only meant that she doesn't lose tests of wizard skill."

Entreska smiled slightly, "Well. Then who would win a test of skill between you and her?"

"We would not test each other so."

Bemused, Entreska asked, "Why not?"

"Heather doesn't engage in tests of wizard skill for sport."

Entreska decided that further evasive answers would prove futile and let the matter drop until she could corner Heather.

Entreska took a deep breath and said flatly, "Heather says that I am invulnerable in Evermore. What do you think?"

Tom shrugged, "If Heather really believes that to be true, I would not doubt her knowledge on such matters."

"She would possibly lie about that?"

Tom smiled slightly, "Everyone lies."

Entreska gritted her teeth, "Would she lie about something like that, though?"

Tom frowned slightly, "Heather is a capable and effective deceiver. But I've always thought she only deceives for good purpose. In some sense, deception is a vital skill for The Keeper."

Entreska nodded, looked at her left arm and gave a momentary start. The lavender swirl had become darker and bluer.

Tom said, "Are you alright?"

Entreska replied with a smile, "Yes. I'm fine. But you'll have to excuse me I need to be going. Thank you."

Tom waved a hand, "Good luck. And say hello to Heather for me."

Entreska faded back into herself. Or something like that. Once her vision cleared, she bared her arm and indeed the lavender swirl had changed.

The Imperium Council

Imperium Council meetings traditionally took place in a specially made, large desert tent that comfortably accommodated fifty people. Sewn in a complex layered pattern of fine silks, in the desert wind the tent shimmered with an effervescent splash of color. The colors represented the melding of many small tribes into the Invincible Zattan Imperium. Glen didn't think it was so invincible but naturally kept such opinions to himself for obvious political expediency.

Glenmorgan detested formal meetings of the Imperium Council. Admittedly, he detested the informal meetings as well, but he particularly despised the formal meetings. The informal meetings were always held wherever the Zatta Buruza was holding court. The formal meetings, however, were by tradition and law, held biannually, on the autumnal equinox at the ancient ruins of Zatta Urazar, the supposed birthplace of the Zattan forebears. The ruins were really nothing more than a few dozen badly worn shaped stones with illegible glyphs scattered along the apparent shoreline of a lake that had dried up long ago.

A small detachment of the Zattan Royal Guard constantly watched over the remote, desolate area ostensibly to prevent desecration of the site but in reality to keep potential assassins from scouting the site or making local preparations in advance of a formal meeting of the Imperium Council. Over the centuries more than a few Councilors have had their memberships terminated at one of the formal meetings. The Zatta Buruza always suffered a significant loss of prestige and potentially power whenever a Council member died at a meeting, so security was extremely tight.

The formal meetings of the Imperium Council were intertwined with a week long ceremonial event at Zatta Urazar attended only by members of the Council and the wife and minor children of the Zatta Buruza. The ceremonies were orchestrated by the Zatta Fenyal, a Council member responsible for oversight of the Zattan religious establishment.

The Zatta Fenyal provides erratic and highly personalized control of Zattan religious tradition – if it could be called that. The Zatta Fenyal and lower ranking shamans were expected to constantly modify their ceremonial performances to please the Zattan Spirits with their creativity, cunning and craft. In parts of the Zattan Imperium, locals would attend Zattan ceremonials for the entertainment value alone while continuing with their own, very static religious traditions. As basic policy, the Zattan were perfectly content for locals to continue their own forms of worship. The Imperium had often used suppressed religious groups as spies and allies to expedite conquests and so granted religious freedom to such groups in exchange for their invaluable aid.

Glen rested on an array of purple silk cushions in the center of the tent and quietly drank dark boiled coffee sweetened with brandy and sugar. A Royal Servant offered him dried fruit and nuts, but he demurred. He had arrived early so that he could have a day's rest between the stress of travel and the stress of the meeting. That meant an extra day of wearing the stupid if expensive and comfortable blue and silver Council Robe that the Royal Guard had given him after taking away his own clothes and possessions.

For several decades now, at both informal and formal Council meetings, Council members were not allowed their own servants, aides, weapons, clothes, bodyguards or even medicines. The Royal Guard supplied all food, clothing, medicines, bodyguards and servants for the duration of the meeting. All this was particularly galling, thought Glen, given that the Royal Guard answered directly to the Imperium Council and not the Zatta Buruza. After four nasty deaths at a meeting, the Council had unwisely voted unanimously to make the Commander of the Royal Guard personally liable for a security failure at a Council meeting which would lead to the Commander's certain dismissal and likely execution barring a Royal Pardon. The natural consequence was the ridiculous security precautions. By arcane Council rules, a ruling could only be reversed by a vote with at least the same margin as the original ruling and invariably a few fearful members would vote against the change. Admittedly, their fears were probably justified.

As his custom, Glen traveled to the meeting accompanied by most of the Swamp Rats as his bodyguard. All council members typically were accompanied by a military bodyguard, but most numbered no more than a hundred. Other Council members constantly objected to the perceived violation of Zattan sovereignty by the Swamp Rats, but the ancient rules were perfectly clear – a Council member could travel anywhere in the Imperium accompanied by a trusted, personal bodyguard no larger than the 1st Royal Guards Regiment which numbered about 3500.

Glenmorgan recalled with a chuckle the time he had decided to take a vacation at Yuz on Lake Orlan in the Tangur province. He had taken the Swamp Rats as his usual bodyguard. Erwin Ironhide, the Governor of Tangur, brought up forces and besieged Glen and the Rats. Glen could have easily slipped the siege and escaped but his whole purpose had been to taunt Ironhide into a stupid mistake. Sure enough, a threatening letter from Garrick Farseeing, the 53rd Zatta Buruza, arrived within two days forcing Ironhide to withdraw in total humiliation.

Of course, the joke had been on Glen a few years later when Garrick suffered an untimely and many thought unnatural death. Garrick had no Royal children, and so the Council had to elect the Zatta Buruza from the available First Blood Royals and had ultimately chosen Harvey Quickfingers, whom Glen regarded as capable and competent. The problem with Quickfingers was that he was Ironhide's older brother. While they did not agree on policy so much, the brothers were quite close and so Quickfingers allowed Ironhide excessive latitude to pursue his 'interests' which mostly centered around an implacable opposition to Jurasketu independence and included numerous unsuccessful plots to assassinate Glen.

Harvey Quickfingers conducted Council Meetings in a cheery, disarming way that annoyed Glen to no end. During meetings, Quickfingers would often idly strum on a small guitar while lounging on the large mass of pillows needed to support his massive but not quite obese bulk. When anyone made a dramatic point, he would add emphasis with a loud, hard double strum on the guitar and then smile innocently while looking around for the source. Then he would scan the Council with his black, almost lifeless eyes looking for reactions that varied from amusement to annoyance to outright anger.

Quickfingers once told Glen in confidence that only the best conspirators could keep their emotions concealed in such situations and so it was a perfect means to identify them. This amused Glen greatly in that he rarely bothered to keep his emotions concealed – only his conspiracies. Nevertheless, Glen never underestimated the extremely patient Quickfingers. The Zatta Buruza always had a deep understanding of the tribal and global political situation. His knowledge of military and economic matters proved time and again to be equally insightful. For his part, Quickfingers openly admired Glenmorgan for his legendary martial and survival skills.

Glen was still thinking and sipping his coffee when his cousin and sworn enemy, Murok Firemaker, strode up, apparently also an early arrival. Murok resembled Glen in many ways: lean, strong, bright green eyes, and wavy brown hair. Yet, Murok's facial features were hard where Glen's were soft.

Murok smiled darkly. Glen nodded and smiled mockingly in return.

Murok waved a hand, "Is the coffee good?"

"The Royal Guard does not serve anything of low quality."

Murok shrugged and briefly scanned the tent, "Undoubtedly."

Silence.

Glen noted the discomfiture of the nearby Royal Servants and a couple of Royal Guards who looked ready to intervene should an altercation arise. Glen sat stone-faced attempting to look like he was feigning unconcern.

Glen spoke finally, "A bit early for you, isn't it?"

Murok nodded, "A bit. I saw you brought almost the entirety of the Swamp Rats. Why do you insist on that grave provocation?"

Glen laughed, "Better to be a provocateur then a rotting corpse lying on a mountain road."

Murok stated flatly, "All paths lead to death."

Glen laughed again, "Indeed. Do you have any new banter to entertain the Guards and Servants?"

Murok smiled faintly and looked sidelong at three servants who decided to scatter at that moment. "Actually. Harvey wishes to speak with us in his tent. He sent me to fetch you."

"Really? You don't seem like an errand boy type to me."

Murok chuckled, "No. Consider me an ambassador then if it eases your conscience."

Glen curled a lip, "What does Harvey want anyway? This isn't another of those, 'Play nice boys' talks is it?"

Murok shrugged, "I don't know. He seemed pretty serious for some reason. Does the Grand Debater tolerate your insolence as well as the Zatta Buruza?"

Glen chuckled, "She chooses to simply ignore anything other

than my performance of my assigned duties. She couldn't care less about my attitude. Competence has its privileges. Maybe you should try it sometime."

Murok adjusted his robe and tugged at the beautiful but barely functional sandals supplied by the Royal Guards, "I might. Change can be good occasionally. Are you coming or not?"

Glen sighed, "Very well. I suppose I must."

Glen rolled over backwards onto his feet to show off his agility, but then had to retrieve a lost sandal. Annoyed, he followed Murok to the tent exit. Murok exited nonchalantly past the two Royal Guards standing on duty. Glen, however, hesitated to make sure there wasn't an ambush waiting. This visibly annoyed the guards who stepped into the entrance and pointed to show that everything was clear. Glen, shrugged, muttered a half-hearted apology and walked warily outside. An escort of ten Royal Guards waited for him along with a smirking Murok. No one spoke during the mere 100-meter walk to the Royal Tent, although not surprising with the winds beginning to howl.

The Royal Tent was essentially a miniature version of the Imperium Council Meeting Tent. Looking very serious, Quickfingers sat cross-legged and arms crossed on an array of pillows. He motioned for Murok and Glen to sit on pillows uncomfortably close together and facing him.

Murok started to speak but was stopped by a raised hand. Quickfingers nodded to the guards who reluctantly left the tent. Quickfingers tapped his left arm with his fingers for a long time and just stared at them.

Finally, he sighed deeply and whispered, "This meeting is just us. You two and me. No one else. Understood?"

Glen looked around, smiled, then shrugged and leaned forward, "Of course, Harvey. What is the matter?"

Not to be outdone, Murok leaned in and said, "Only between us, Harvey."

Quickfingers glanced from Murok to Glen and back again to Murok. Then he said, "You two have just got to stop trying to assassinate each other. It is an intolerable distraction."

Quickfingers snarled as Murok and Glen both shook their heads and opened their mouths to protest. Quickfingers muttered, "My spies report no less than three active plots against you, Murok, and five against you, Glen."

Privately, Glen was nonplussed. He knew of six plots against Murok, but only four against himself. Hopefully, the three mentioned by Quickfingers were amongst those six. For himself, however, an active plot left unaccounted was not usually regarded as a good thing.

Glen shrugged, "Surely there are plots unknown to yourself, Harvey. Your spies can't know everything."

Quickfingers looked even more annoyed, "I said 'at LEAST'. Speaking of which, can you at least look concerned? I'm serious. This has really gotten out of hand."

Quickfingers stood up suddenly. "This is what I'm going to do. I want you two to stay in my tent until whatever crazy ceremony Robert has dreamed up for tomorrow night. Although I can't actually command that you settle your differences peacefully, I can command that you try. And if either of you comes to harm, I'll have the survivor or survivors executed as fighting is expressly forbidden in my tent. Food and drink will be brought – but you may not leave until tomorrow night. You have complete privacy. My guards will keep their usual distance and certainly not allow anyone else to get close. Understood?"

Glen and Murok bowed slightly.

Quickfingers bellowed for his servants and exited the tent.

Murok smiled at Glen who put his hands behind his head and leaned back onto the pillows.

Glen whispered, "Do you suppose anyone is listening or watching?"

Murok shrugged and then got up to inspect the tent walls that thrummed with the stiffening evening winds. Then he carefully checked all the possible and impossible hiding places within the tent. He appeared to find nothing, and so came and sat back down in a huff.

Murok whispered, "As long as the winds continue, which is the usual case this time of year, if we keep to a whisper, it would be impossible to hear us. But I think we shouldn't look too friendly in case someone does manage to get a glimpse of us talking. So let's pretend to bicker and argue the whole time instead of just most of the time as we normally would."

Glen smiled, then nodded serenely and whispered, "Agreed. So I got word that Jen gave birth last month and that you finally have a granddaughter."

Murok laughed in faked derision. Then he whispered, "Yes. That makes six grandsons and one granddaughter. But Jen says she won't have another and Ravia has already stated enough is enough. What about you? Still just the five granddaughters?"

Glen smiled. Then he whispered, "Yes. Catrinja's two daughters and Rolf's three. Entreska and Zemfrekis might eventually get married and have children – hopefully in that order. Not that I care, my granddaughters are wonderful and plenty enough for me."

Murok murmured, "Indeed. Hopefully, we'll give them a worthy future."

Glen nodded and spoke extra softly, "Somewhat fortunate that Harvey insisted we be alone together. With all the extra security, arranging a meeting was looking difficult."

Murok practically beamed, "Exactly. But fortune had nothing to do with it. I planted the idea with Robert who enthusiastically put the suggestion into Harvey's head. Since Harvey desires greatly that we kiss and make up, he jumped at the plan."

Glen shook his head in admiration, "You are such a clever bastard."

"That I am."

"Are there really five active plots to kill me?"

Murok shrugged. "I only know of three."

Glen frowned. "I was aware of four... Great."

They spent the next two hours feigning an argument while making sure they were caught up on the stuff too sensitive to leak to each other's spies.

Dinner arrived. A warm and hearty soup of meat and vegetables served with crunchy white bread and washed down with Tarfun Stone Brew from a small keg. As Zattan custom demanded, they ate in peaceful contemplative silence.

Sipping his post-meal, second draft, Murok stared at Glen wistfully and then became stern and said in a firm whisper, "Glen. It is time. The next phase of the Grand Plan must be executed."

Glen raised an eyebrow, "What Grand Plan?"

Murok smirked, "The one you and I have been working on."

"You mean our belief that somehow if we maintain a balance of interests on the Imperium Council, we can prevent it from destroying Jurasketu directly or indirectly? With the faint hope that one day, we can steer the Zattan towards the ideals of individual liberty protected by a strong system of democracy?"

"That one."

Glen rolled his eyes, "The idealistic dreams of the young and foolish that have turned into the muddlings of the old and cynical should not be confused with Grand Planning. And hadn't we decided to avoid any more serious moves until we brought Rolf and Jeruk into our secret?"

Murok tried and failed not to smile, "Perhaps. The Imperium is becoming stronger. The danger is growing. And we may not be able to establish the trust between Rolf and Jeruk that you and I enjoy. And we are getting old."

Glen sighed, "I know. Maybe we should have involved them sooner?"

Murok smiled, "That would have been risky before we had a proper measure of our children as adults. If they had proved unworthy, we would have been faced with the undoing of all our efforts. Fortunately, Jeruk and Rolf have exceeded expectations. Has Rolf figured it out yet?"

Glen smirked, "No. Not yet. Jeruk?"

Murok shook his head, "Not yet. I've been dropping extra hints to see if he starts guessing. I can see he is slightly puzzled by some things. Ironically, he has always been annoyed by my unyielding hatred of you and Jurasketu."

Glen whispered, "I wonder how upset he'll be with you when he finds out the truth?"

Murok shrugged, "He is paranoid, tough, clever and dangerous. But he wants everyone to live happily ever after in peace and harmony."

"Hmm... Are you sure he is up to the task?"

Murok wobbled his head, "That is partly why we need to move on to the next phase. Once he sees where we are headed, it will tighten his resolve."

Glen nodded in agreement.

"What about Rolf?"

Glen grimaced and smiled, "Rolf is much the same as Jeruk. He wants peace and harmony. Funny how our offspring turned out eh?"

Murok chuckled.

Glen continued, "And meanwhile Rolf constantly frets that I don't seem to be doing enough or worried enough about the Imperium. I assure him constantly that I am."

Murok nodded. "Well? Do you agree or not?"

Glen pursed his lips, stood and muttered. "I need to think. Keep up the show."

Glen shook himself to loosen up. He grabbed another draft of Tarfun Stone Brew and a soft, dessert pretzel. Then he proceeded to pace around the tent alternately sipping, chewing and staring at Murok.

Murok sat comfortably but glared in response to keep up the show. After about fifteen minutes, Glen settled back into his pillows.

Glen looked around, smiled, and whispered, "So who should assassinate Ironhide?"

Murok flashed a smile, "My faction will do the deed, but I'll blame you. I'll get that Valruk bastard, Gormali, to do it. He thinks Ironhide cheated him on a gambling debt, so he'll have extra incentive. He's mercenary to the core and won't likely fail. He'll need preparation time, though."

Glen nodded, "He's an evil bastard indeed. How come no one in your faction has suggested he try me?"

Murok looked around in apparent anger, then laughed loudly, but whispered, "Several times. He refused. He says you must be protected by a demon to have lived so long. I mean he has a point, how many known failed attempts on your life have there been?"

"Twenty-two."

"And the assassins?"

"All killed or captured and executed."

"Does that count the ones we foiled before they even got close?"

"No. That would add another thirty or forty to the total."

Murok became thoughtful for a moment, "How many attempts have been made by Jurasketu?"

Glen shrugged, "None."

"Why not do you suppose?"

"I am clearly regarded by everyone as loyal to Jurasketu."

Murok frowned, "Very true."

Glen shifted around his body position to remain comfortable, "Okay. So we take down Ironhide. How do we arrange for your election as Governor of Tangur? You only have eight votes. You need three more. Ten are definite against you. Harvey, Ironhide and Robert are the only ones who are not a member of our opposing alliances. With Ironhide dead, you can't get the third vote even if we managed to convince Harvey and Robert to support you."

"Robert would support me with a small inducement of flattery and treasure."

Glen shrugged, "Okay. So you have nine votes. Still need two more. I don't see Harvey supporting you since he considers you an instigator."

Murok smiled, "Yes. But if he suspects you of the crime – maybe he'll back me just to spite you."

"Harvey might think you set the whole thing up because he would know you might think something like that up. And he would be right."

Murok shrugged, "Quite possibly."

"And even then – you would be short Ironhide's vote. Him being dead. His wife is not royal blood so can't be elected to the Council and his son, Burke, is too young. So Harvey will probably put forth his crazy Uncle Rufus as a caretaker until Burke is old enough. Opposing the Zatta Buruza over that would be impossibly dumb."

"Rufus hates me."

Glen muttered, "Exactly my point."

Murok stood and paced around shaking his fist in pretend anger or maybe real anger – Glen wasn't entirely sure. Glen and Murok thought for a while. Then Murok glared at Glen to the point that Glen became uncomfortable. Murok grabbed more ale and some nuts on the way back to his seat. He shook his fist at Glen a couple more times.

Then he whispered, "I have a plan. Almost too clever by half. Quentin and Jenna only back you because they fear you more than they fear me."

"I've been generous in rewarding their loyalty."

Murok shrugged, "Maybe. But what if you leaked word that you planned to kill them? Then if I happened along with an offer of money and protection in return for their support for election as Governor."

Glen scratched his neck, "They are not to be trusted."

"Which is why my protections will be largely inadequate when you have your revenge. This will be particularly poignant when I leak word that you had not planned to kill them at all and that the story had actually been cooked up by me. The irony will be complete when Harvey feels the pressure to pass over their children for elevation to the Council when their treachery and stupidity is revealed against the background of their misuse of Council monies and fraudulently depriving the Zatta Buruza of tax money raised in their provinces."

"Everyone on the Council does that. Well, except me. And Robert. But he's a fool and I'm not normal."

"Of course, but we'll have irrefutable proof of their stupidity. That will provide the pressure and cover for Harvey to appoint his loyalists that have positive feelings towards you and so you'll naturally support his choices."

Murok rubbed his hairy arms, threw up his hands in mock exasperation and took another stroll around the tent. Glen stretched for a bit until Murok came back and sat down.

Glen sighed, "Very well. You have made it possible for you to gain the Governorship of Tangur but keeping the balance of power on the Council apparently in my favor. What would be the next step in this new chapter of the Grand Plan?"

Murok laughed, "Well. You obviously could assume control of the Highland Province. Barry is completely loyal, not particularly ambitious, and so wouldn't complain, right? This would appear to check any unapproved move I might attempt from Tangur. I would very much fear the dire threat to my right flank from your Zattan forces there."

"But I would have to retire from the Jurasketu Army to do that."

"Departing your post while still alive may give the Valruk and Puck pause during the transition. You would continue to be able to block any official movement to war by the Imperium. Also, you could, in theory, still step forward and retake control of the Jurasketu Army should need arise. And everyone knows your successor would listen to your counsel. Don't underestimate the fear you provoke."

Glen wobbled his head in grudging agreement. Then, Glen looked at Murok and smiled, "You are right. The Imperium is becoming too powerful. We have many ambitious and clever leaders. One of them will eventually get the idea to disband the Imperium Council – by force, murder or diabolical manipulation. And then nothing will check the ambitions of such a Zatta Buruza who will no doubt be tempted by the riches that Jurasketu represents. And all our work will be for naught."

"It gives me no pleasure to be right."

Glen nodded, "Doubtless. We actually need to fracture the Imperium without fomenting open civil war or inducing sufficient weakness to allow Puck and the Valruk an opening."

Murok frowned and whispered, "And you thought our original dream was idealistic and foolish?"

Glen ignored the comment and continued, "If we create permanent regional entities bonded together for defense against external and internal enemies but otherwise committed to their own independence, then I think it could work. We preserve the Imperium Council and even a weakened Zatta Buruza. Jurasketu, Tangur, ancient Zattan, and the Western provinces renamed as Norazetu could form the regional states."

Murok sneered, "Puck would sense weakness and almost certainly attack to regain his lost provinces."

Glen nodded, "The plan is predicated on weakening Puck first."

Murok cocked his head, "And your plan for that would be?"

Before Glen could answer, there was a shout from the entrance of the tent barely heard over the increasingly loud winds. Glen and Murok stood, looked at each other, shrugged and Glen approached the entrance. A grizzled looking servant accompanied by two bored Royal Guardsmen had appeared bearing another keg of ale and more pretzels. Glen accepted the interruption with slight annoyance and the servant brought the ale and pretzels over to the low serving table.

Murok looked furtively at Glen who was eyeing the guardsmen and the servant carefully. Murok turned towards the guards and waved his left hand behind his back to signal to Glen that something was wrong. Glen edged toward the tent entrance and looked out, he then bellowed at the officer in charge of the tent guard detail. The servant and two guards jumped and turned to look. The officer, a smartly turned out, young captain with bright eyes and wavy black hair, entered the tent with four more guards following Glenmorgan's directing arm.

Murok took the lead and barked, "Captain Deathdealer?"

"Yes. Lord Murok. What is the problem?"

Glen smiled inwardly that Murok always seemed to know everyone's name. Even people he had never met.

Murok growled, "Who is this servant?"

The servant who had been impassive suddenly looked very nervous, looking down and casting a sidelong glance at Murok.

Captain Deathdealer made a puzzled look at the servant. "I do not know. Master Brighteyes!"

A scarred, older man stepped up, "Sir?"

Deathdealer sternly pointed palm up at the servant and said nothing.

Brighteyes chewed his lip a moment, "Sir, he is not a member of my staff."

Deathdealer motioned with his finger and two guards quickly

moved forward and pointed swords at the servant who dropped to his knees looking near tears with his hands wrapped around his middle.

Deathdealer looked around and pointed suddenly at the two guards who had escorted the servant into the tent. Four more guards drew swords and moved towards the two nervous and protesting guards. Deathdealer yelled for them to be silent.

Next, Deathdealer motioned for the general alarm to be raised. Soon, more Royal Guardsmen, Quickfingers and the Royal Guard Commander, Colonel Walter Deathwright, arrived all looking highly aggravated.

Colonel Deathwright looked to be nothing more than sinew and bone wrapped in a pale, flaky skin. His dark, bloodshot eyes bulged from his wizened face making him look like some nightmarish, animated corpse. Despite his appearance, Glen knew him to be an efficient and effective commander with a wicked sense of humor.

Glen and Murok sauntered over to join them.

Deathwright said flatly, "They both seem to be alive. I thought the whole idea was that they would kill each other and the problem would be solved?"

Quickfingers turned and snarled, "You know damn well that wasn't the idea."

Murok and Glen smiled as Deathwright rolled his eyes in response.

Deathwright looked around, spotted Captain Deathdealer, and beckoned him to where they all stood. The servant and two guards were all on their knees, ankles and wrists roped securely together. A guard each held them steady with a firm hand on a shoulder.

Deathdealer jogged over, saluted smartly, "Colonel, I-"

Deathwright held up a hand, halting the young officer mid-sentence. "Grand Marshal. Would you care to give your version of events?"

Glenmorgan looked around. "Simple enough. Servant and guards shouted that fresh pretzels and ale had been brought. We let them in without much thought. It turns out that no one seems to know who this servant is. And-"

Murok blurted, "I do actually."

Everyone nearby said, "What?"

"His name is Fred Redcap. He once worked for my father who caught him stealing and subsequently exiled him."

Glen turned to Murok, "Do you know everyone and their brother?"

"No. But I never forget a face or a name."

Deathwright rolled his eyes. "Interesting. What was he trying to do when he was arrested?"

Glen shrugged, "Delivering ale and pretzels as I said. He was acting suspiciously, so I summoned Captain Deathdealer which was when we established that neither the guard detail nor the Chief Royal Servant knew who he was – which makes him an imposter. Although with Murok's help, we now know who he is – but we don't know what he was doing unless..."

Glen pointed at a burly guard standing near the pretzel and ale table. "You. Carefully, pull a half-draft of ale from the barrel on the right. Yes. That one. Wait. Use gloves and be careful not to spill any on yourself. And bring it over here."

The guard, who had moved enthusiastically initially at being singled out by Glenmorgan, changed into a very cautious ale server. The guard gingerly brought the mug to Glen who then pointed towards the kneeling servant.

"Would our imposter servant now revealed to be a Mister Redcap care for some ale?"

Redcap muttered, "No thank you sir. I'm not thirsty."

Glen smiled, "No. I insist."

Redcap said, "Sir. I don't want any ale."

Glen raised an eyebrow and glanced back at Murok, Quickfingers and the Royal Guard officers who all nodded knowingly.

Murok crinkled his forehead and said, "We both drink ale. So it would appear that he was trying to poison us both."

Quickfingers glared at Deathwright who seemed oblivious.

Quickfingers barked harshly, "The Council will have your head for this one."

Deathwright calmly intoned, "Nonsense. The governing Council Order quite clearly states that unsuccessful plots should not be held against the Royal Guards."

Quickfingers clenched his fists and yelled, "It was only unsuccessful because Murok and Glenmorgan were doing your job."

Unruffled, Deathwright proclaimed, "Harvey. Security is everyone's job."

Quickfingers closed his eyes for a moment, "Well. Regardless. I want an investigation of all foodstuffs and ale. Use these three as test subjects."

The two imprisoned guards and Redcap remained impassive at the Zatta Buruza's order. Glen nodded furtively to Murok knowing that meant the poisoning was likely limited to the delivered ale.

Deathwright nodded, "Yes. But do you wish to discover who Redcap's employer is?"

Redcap whimpered.

Quickfingers shook his head, "He is not a professional. He won't know his true employer. We would have to assume his employer is an enemy of both Glen and Murok: Puck, my brother Erwin, whomever... Unless, of course, it is Glen who would have known to avoid the ale."

Quickfingers glared at Glen who shrugged innocently and silently agreed with his assessment of the likelihood of discovering Redcap's real employer. He also agreed that Ironhide and Puck would definitely head the list. He wondered if Redcap counted as two known plots, one known plot or was not among the list of plots Harvey or Murok knew about. In the chaos, Glen took an opportunity to poke his head out of the tent and smiled at the scene. A light mist enveloped the moonlit valley of Zatta Urazar.

The Velvet Sea

Mallory squatted and carefully cooked the nice, spicy sausages he had acquired from a farmer the previous morning. He had already brewed up a steaming pot of tea. Like every fall morning, bitter cold air rolled down from the central Wokometu highlands spreading frost and light fog over their forest encampment ensconced just above a beautiful trickling creek. Mallory felt buoyant. He had always rather enjoyed cool weather camping.

Entreska emerged from the woods, stopped to pat her unremarkable but sturdy, light brown horse named Daffodil, on the nose. In triumph at being given attention, Daffodil cast sidelong glances at Mallory's massive dark brown horse, Dandelion, and the mottled, dour packhorse, Violet. Dandelion and Violet snorted in disgust.

Entreska grunted a good morning and growled, "Is the tea ready?"

Mallory replied pleasantly in the affirmative and proceeded to pour two cups of the herbal tea.

Entreska took hers and huddled under the thermal blanket Mallory gave her and slowly sipped the tea while cycling between a placid expression and a deep frown.

The remainder of their trek across the Southern Blades to the signal cave in the Melted Hills had been completely uneventful. Both Captain Buck Jules and Mallory had been pleasantly surprised to find each other at the cove given the number of variables that would have prevented either from being there. Favorable winds had allowed the *Inky Darkness* to carry them and their horses west across the Bay of Lydaron in just three days to Deliverance where the *Inky Darkness* would await Mallory's return.

Entreska looked away in thought and then asked, "How long will Captain Jules wait for us?"

Mallory shrugged, "He promised a minimum of 14 days."

Entreska nodded, "I believe you can trust him."

Mallory chuckled, "You are just saying that because he liked your book. I think you found him charming. I can say he certainly seemed interested in you."

Entreska rolled her eyes, "I'm not romantically interested in middle-aged pirate captains. No matter his interest in my books or me."

Mallory smiled, "Anyway. I agree. He has proven to be a reliable ally so far."

Mallory congratulated himself for trusting Captain Jules and his capable crew. It would have been very embarrassing if not ultimately fatal had the *Inky Darkness* failed to appear at the rendezvous from inability, malice or indifference. And the promise of additional help from them seemed to be solid.

Entreska quirked her mouth, "How far did you say this valley was from here?"

Mallory looked up in surprise. "Oh. Not far now. Let me check..."

Mallory requested his relative position from his duffel bag. He said, "Fourteen kilometers southwest from here." He pointed generally in the right direction, although in the dense woods it was a meaningless gesture.

Entreska scratched her cheek. "Hmm.... Didn't you say the valley was deserted?"

"I did. Because it was. Why do ask?"

Entreska shrugged, "Well. The Council seems to think there is about three thousand or more folks in that valley."

Mallory concealed his immediate agitation. Entreska had proven capable of perceiving numbers and even intentions of peoples over many kilometers distant. Her powers of perception were amazing. Whether or not it was the Council rather than her "own" powers made little difference to Mallory. It was clear that the crystal she claimed to have eaten had given her the powers in addition to her rather striking rainbow appearance.

"What? You're kidding. I don't see how that's even possible."

Entreska nodded, "Yes. I'm afraid so."

Mallory rubbed his forehead, "Um... Unless it was a military force?"

Entreska shook her head slightly, "No. Nothing like that. Adults, children, many different sorts. Undisciplined. Like a small city."

Mallory just stared at her slack jawed. "I won't be able to believe that unless I see it for myself."

Entreska shrugged, "Well. Let us go see then."

Mallory sighed, "Yes. But first have some breakfast..."

After breakfast, they broke camp loading most of the equipment, water and food onto the annoyed looking Violet. And off they trudged through thicket and up hillsides until late morning when Mallory stopped them while leading his horse up a particularly steep hill. He moved up ahead and took out his detached rifle scope to survey the upper hillside for several minutes.

He returned and whispered, "There are three armed men patrolling that ridge."

"Why?"

"Well, our destination is the valley just over that ridge."

"Oh. That would be bad, right?"

Mallory sighed, "Truly. It would seem you are right."

"Yes. The Council was right."

Mallory glanced all around and pursed his lips in strategic thought.

Entreska raised an eyebrow, "Well, what are we going to do now?"

Mallory looked toward the ridge and nodded. "I'll need to see what's in the valley. We need to retreat to a suitable spot, make camp, and then tonight I'll hike back up for a look-see."

Camp was made and Mallory spent a few minutes establishing the Virtual Watcher – Entreska had given up saying the Council would keep watch. He also made sure Entreska knew what her possible escape routes were should someone approach. The afternoon passed with another long lecture circuit of Entreska explaining the intricacies of some obscure Wokometu tribal group and Mallory explaining yet another aspect of basic biochemistry. Night fell and Mallory departed leaving Entreska to sit in the tent and fret while she watched the icon labeled Mallory zigzag southeasterly across the elaborate virtual map displayed for her by the Darkglasses.

Mallory trudged up the hillside through the cool night air. Even without his Darkglasses, Mallory would have seen more than a dozen small fires along the ridge and the glow of a large encampment from the valley on the other side. With the Darkglasses, he could see that two or three armed men were attached to each fire along the ridge.

Mallory simply observed for an hour and noted that the men did nothing more than huddle at their fires. Apparently, active patrolling at night did not excite them. A brief afternoon rain shower had dampened the leaf covered forest floor allowing Mallory to tromp noiselessly up the hill to the top. The two smallest moons had risen in the East but their pale red light was nearly lost in the glow of several hundred campfires covering the high valley below.

Mallory found a clear vantage point to observe the valley with his detached rifle scope. Mallory jaw went very slack as he looked for the remains of his starcraft, the *Velvet Sea*. Instead of eight square kilometers of quiet high mountain meadow, at least three thousand people occupied the valley.

Incredibly, an elaborate three-story wooden temple-like structure complete with a fancy high-pitched curved roof had been erected near the center where the *Velvet Sea* should have been. An extensive wooden stockade had been erected around the temple building easily enclosing an area 200 meters across. A trench with breastworks extended around the entire southern end of the once pristine meadow and about 40 meters of forest had been cleared away beyond that. Most of the people appeared to be living in randomly positioned family-sized tents located inside the defensive perimeter. The northern end of the meadow had been plowed and planted with now harvested crops. Armed and partially armored men patrolled the perimeter and the stockade. A wooden building located on the northern end of the defensive trench appeared to serve as the main entrance gate.

Mallory double-checked his position in disbelief. Minutes later he spotted the remnants of the HE drive in the far southeastern corner. The rest of the *Velvet Sea* should be where the temple building was located.

Mallory mouthed highly abusive curses to himself as he continued to scan the meadow become religious center - because that could be the only possible explanation for the transformation. Someone or someones had seen the crash and/or found the wreckage and had interpreted the event as one of major cosmological importance. Maybe, Mallory thought, they might be right from this little world's frame of reference. Mallory reckoned that the haphazard layout of the tents indicated that most of folks in the valley were really pilgrims. The armed men here and there were essentially local militia most likely organized by whomever had built the temple in what had to be record time as only five hundred days had passed since he had left this valley after the crash.

Mallory sighed trying to see how his short term plans were

anything but totally ruined. He had no decent long range plans to ruin at this time but if he did, he was certain they would be quite ruined as well.

Mallory continued to carefully observe the valley for over an hour before returning to camp, although he had to avoid two actively patrolling men on his side of the ridge. Mallory smiled and frowned at that discovery since it meant that the guardians of the valley were a bit more professional than they had first appeared and that it might mean greater difficulty for himself.

In the firelight, Entreska listened patiently to his description of the scene in the valley, only occasionally asking questions. When a very miserable looking Mallory finished talking, Entreska simply asked, "What now?"

"I must reach the wreckage of my space craft. I need the equipment contained therein."

"But how? I suppose you could just ask permission."

Mallory rolled his eyes.

Entreska bobbled her head, "Yeah. Not likely hun? Still, you could gain the confidence of the Temple leader, priest, priestess or whomever. Or at least bribe or threaten them in a suitable fashion..."

"Hmph. That's seems terribly time-consuming at best, fatal at worst. Erm... I wonder if I could simply get them to all leave in a panic."

"Panic? How so?"

Mallory considered the various ways, imagined General Lang laughing at his supposedly clever plan that inevitably would end in blood everywhere, and then said, "Never mind. It would likely risk too much violence."

Entreska narrowed her eyes. "Oh. Yes. Please never mind that."

Mallory scowled. "Well, maybe those folks are all corrupt, evil and miscreants of the worst sort. I mean, they did steal my starcraft. They could be sacrificing children inside that temple at this very moment."

Entreska rolled her eyes in dismay.

Mallory sighed. "Okay. Slaughtering a bunch of religious zealots without proof of criminal behavior while probably in the best interest of society is not the most ethical choice in this situation."

"Well, we won't know until we gather a bit more information will we? Why don't we pose as religious zealots, I mean curious pilgrims? If we're lucky we'll get a look around, talk to some folks, you know, do some spying."

Mallory was skeptical. "And if they are unfriendly, do I get to shoot them? It could turn into a terrible massacre."

Entreska sighed but showed no anger, "I would imagine folks come and go with regularity. Being curious pilgrims, why don't we station ourselves on the road to the temple, wherever that lies, and ask comers and goers? Of course, maybe I should ask the questions. You don't look like a pilgrim."

"Why don't we say you are a wayward princess seeking religious fulfillment, and I am your faithful bodyguard, Bonecrusher Bart?"

Entreska smiled and said, "Bonecrusher Bart, eh? I always wanted to be a princess. Let's do it."

Mallory scowled. He was only joking. But then again, it wasn't the worst plan actually. Still, it would have to be slightly more convincing. "What kingdom are you princess of anyway?"

"Oh. That's easy. I am Princess Sky of Berhelen, errant daughter of King Olvik and Queen Joy."

"And where is Berhelen?"

"In the mists of the East. It's from a popular storybook tale actually. Olvik and Joy as well. Princess Sky is their errant daughter. Of course, the story doesn't have a Bonecrusher Bart, but this is obviously a new adventure for the princess - so why can't she have a new bodyguard?"

"Um... I don't mean to cast doubt on your subterfuge skills, but it seems to me that pretending to be a popular fictional character won't likely fool anyone. And does Princess Sky have hair and skin swirling with all the hues of a rainbow?"

Entreska pouted, "No. But remember I'm seeking religious fulfillment. Maybe I was the victim of an errant religious ceremony or unwanted demonic sorcery?"

"I'll say. At best, though, they would mark us for delusional but harmless. At worst, they would suspect us to be delusional and a danger to society."

Entreska smirked. "True. True. But then, who would dare disrespect a delusional princess with Bonecrusher Bart standing by to punish bad manners?"

Mallory laughed softly but deeply. "But won't they say things simply to try and make us happy?"

"Well sure. But if we phrase our questions with the right dose of curiosity and skepticism, they would likely tell us the truth not knowing our true intentions."

Mallory didn't think the plan would be very effective, but Entreska's silly cover did make them appear to be nothing more than buffoons. Should anyone in "authority" question their presence, he would seize the opportunity to detain and question them. After pausing to give the appearance of due consideration he nodded agreement. "Time for some sleep. In the morning, we move..."

The thick forests surrounding the valley showed a beautiful palette of fall reds and golds. A low ridge delineated the northern end of the valley. When Mallory had crashed here, there had been no roads or major trails leading into the valley. Now, a wagon trail had been cut through the forest running across that low ridge and winding down toward the coastal plain. They had to hike all the way around the valley, avoiding pickets and patrols, to locate a good spot on the trail in the forest below the ridge line.

To Entreska's annoyance, Mallory insisted upon spending an entire day scouting the road from a distance to determine the patrol pattern which turned out to be simply an early morning ten-soldier patrol that started from the mountain valley and apparently relieved an outpost lower down whose former occupiers then marched back up the road to the valley arriving near dark. Mallory adjudged the outpost likely lay about 10 to 15 kilometers distant - although he mentioned to no one in particular that a one day sample might not be enough to make a definitive judgment.

The patrols directly escorted no pilgrims, and individual or small groups of pilgrims moved up and down the road all day. This surprised Mallory and gave him pause. This meant that the pilgrims perceived no immediate threat to their safety. This cast the defensive measures at the temple and the associated patrols to be merely precautionary. Combined with his other observations, Mallory concluded that the temple guardians were likely professionally trained and led or even a professional military unit that, for whatever reason, wanted to appear to be no more than a hastily assembled militia. Mallory had a bad feeling about that but didn't share his feelings with Entreska or the horses.

Mallory decided to avoid contact with the temple guardians for now and so they waited until the morning patrol passed by them before moving into the spot they had chosen. The spot, just off the wagon path, was a nice mossy clearing with a couple of large flat boulders and a nearby brook. They tied their horses to a downed tree and set themselves up on the rocks to wait for the next batch of pilgrims. They planned to depart before the return evening patrol made its way up. They had missed some pilgrims, but avoiding the patrols seemed to be the wiser course for now.

They did not have to wait long. A wizened, deeply tanned old man hobbled down the path assisted by a stout but clean-featured young woman. They wore blue woolen traveler cloaks, sandals and tunics of gray wool. They stopped in surprise when Entreska hailed them having not seen her or Mallory until just then.

Entreska said in Jurasketu, "Hello. Good Pilgrims. I am Princess Sky."

Brushing back her auburn tresses the young woman said, "Er... Hello."

Entreska smiled happily and lightly touched her own chest. "I am a Pilgrim as well." Then pointed to a bored Mallory, "And he is my bodyguard. I have heard grand rumors about the valley above. Can you tell me whether or not they are true?"

The old man stared hard at Mallory and then Entreska, and back again. The young woman blinked with disbelief.

"Who did you say you were?"

"I am Princess Sky of Berhelen and my bodyguard is, ahem, Bonecrusher Bart. But despite his name, he is very polite to those who give him no cause to act otherwise."

The woman turned her head to the old man but kept her eyes mostly fixed on Entreska and occasionally glancing over at Mallory. Not even imagining that Mallory was an accomplished lip reader, she whispered, "Grandfather. What should I do?"

The old man looked all around before answering in a lower whisper, "Humor them." The younger woman and the old man pulled themselves up straight and put both hands briefly over their hearts in the common sign of respect for persons of merit including those of royal blood. Mallory covered a snort of derision with a mild coughing fit.

The young woman spoke soothingly, "What rumors has the Princess heard?"

Entreska paused and said, "That those who are sick will find healing. Those who are in turmoil will find calm. Those who are in anger will find peace. But I have not heard what god will make these miracles and what the price will be. I am ever skeptical. Many false religions and fraudulent priests have I encountered in my journey to seek the True Way."

Mallory clamped his right hand over his mouth pretending to cover a yawn to keep himself from bursting into laughter. The woman and her grandfather glanced at Mallory but nodded solemnly in thoughtfulness at what Entreska had said.

"There is some truth in the rumors you have heard. My grandfather was crippled with arthritis and could no longer walk, but the Healer has made him well."

Entreska raised her blue eyebrow, the left one, at the old man.

The old man coughed and laughed, "It is true. Although I'm still an old man of sixty-three. And so 'well' is somewhat a relative term."

The woman spoke again excitedly, "I saw many others cured. But some the Healer said she could not help."

"She?"

"Well, her voice is that of a woman and everyone referred to her as a she. We never actually saw her..."

Mallory upon hearing the word "Healer" lost his mirth for a few moments, but then could not stop himself from chuckling softly.

"Then how did 'she' cure your grandfather?"

The old man said, "Temple Students carried me into a special room like nothing I've ever heard spoken of much less seen. The enamel surfaces instead of being hard and cold were supple and warm. The leather surfaces were hard, cold and clean instead of being pliant and warm. I was laid on a low enamel table. The Healer spoke kindly to me even though I could not see her and told me to relax. The Students left the room, closing the sliding door with a sucking thud. Then I fell asleep almost at once, when I awoke, after what I'm told was only a few minutes, the arthritic swelling had vanished. Still, it took almost six weeks before I could actually walk properly again. But the arthritis is completely gone. No pain, no swelling. My muscles are weak still from the long years of disuse, but I get stronger every day."

Entreska seemed deeply cheered by the story, "And what of the price?"

"We were asked for nothing but our good will and to do for others as we could. Grandfather insisted on giving them our donkey as a gift which they accepted with gracious reluctance."

Entreska smiled, "Hmm... We, bless us, are in good health. Is the Healer accepting more students?"

The younger woman looked at her grandfather who nodded for her to answer, "Well, the Healer is, I think, a spirit or angel, maybe a god, although the Temple Guardians sharply reprimand anyone who refers to her as anything other than the Healer. The Temple Guardians don't seem to need any recruits, although your bodyguard would probably be welcome to work anywhere brawn was needed."

Mallory twitched in annoyance but held his tongue. He would take his brains over his brawn anytime. Firearms, knives, skill and abundant transport easily made up for a lack of brawn. There is no substitute for brains.

"The Temple has a Medical School run by Temple Guardian Physicians who train new physicians and associates. The Healer has taught the Physicians things wonderful and new I am told. I saw many pilgrims who claimed to be made better by the Physicians or the Healer herself like my Grandfather. I know a few folks apply to become Students at the school. But I don't know how many they accept as students or anything more than that though. They have something they called Counseling for folks who have troubles of the mind. I know even less about that. I'm not really certain you will find the religious fulfillment you seek. They seemed to be concerned solely with healing and very little with telling people how to live. Sorry."

"No need to be sorry. It is hard to argue with health and peace of mind. And being allowed to live as you would like, I suppose. You have been more than helpful. Thank you."

Then Entreska smiled and pointed to their horses, "We have poor provender but we would be happy to offer you lunch."

The old man shook his head and patted his tummy, "No. No. We've already eaten. Good day and good luck."

"Same to you and thanks again."

Mallory and Entreska said nothing until the two pilgrims had disappeared down the trail. Mallory sat deep in thought.

Entreska walked over and said, "See? That worked well. They are not religious zealots at all - just a bunch of physicians."

Mallory tilted his head and frowned, but did not reply. Then he scowled... He half-closed one eye... He rubbed his right thumb against his index finger... Entreska widened her eyes and looked around waiting for Mallory to say something.

Finally, Mallory sighed heavily and said, "Well, it is both good and bad. The good is that Vanessa controls the situation and most likely the Temple Guardians and Physicians are taking orders from her. The bad is that Vanessa controls the situation and is giving orders and conducting activities in serious breach of numerous important laws and regulations. She may presume that I might take a hostile stance to her actions and therefore may not give me a friendly reception."

"Vanessa?"

"Besides myself, I had three crew members. The other two, Julia and Henry were killed. Vanessa survived. She is, in fact, a healer of incomparable skill, knowledge and equipment."

"Crew? Why didn't you mention that before?"

"Well, it's a bit hard to explain what she really is, actually. She's not fully human like you or me - although she once was. The same was true of Julia and Henry. I was the only true human on the *Velvet Sea*. And so I simply wanted to show you. I thought it would be simpler that way."

Entreska stood blinking in understandable bewilderment at the latest incomprehensible thing that Mallory had said. Mallory smiled faintly and shrugged in apology for her predicament. The Temple Guardians might react poorly to his arrival. Mallory knew that if Vanessa was going to be hostile, she could easily provide the Guardians with a quality likeness of him that made pretending to be Bonecrusher Bart worthless. Mallory grunted in dismay.

Mallory shrugged again and said, "Let us question some more pilgrims and possibly clarify the picture a little before we act in haste."

Entreska nodded and stared up the trail.

Six more groups of pilgrims passed by their spot by mid-afternoon.

A solitary young man arriving ignored them and hurried off up the trail in apparent fright.

Next, a young boy, his mother and grandmother departing told of the miracle that had cured the boy of a wasting illness.

Then, a clearly downcast yet hopeful mother and father carrying a very sick young boy of about eight, with four healthy older children leading a pack mule, came down the path. They had no useful information but were encouraged by Mallory and Entreska to continue to the Temple.

A large family departing, brimming with joy, told a tale of restored eyesight, relief of back pain, removal of a disfiguring scar, and a repaired tooth. They only spoke Gurwoko - a local language that Entreska fortunately spoke well that sounded vaguely like Spanish to Mallory.

A departing wild, unkempt looking young woman and her unhappy parents were wisely left unquestioned by Entreska. Mallory speculated she suffered an incurable mental defect most likely.

Lastly, two brothers departing claimed the older was cured of a disabling knee injury. The brothers only spoke Gurwoko as well.

After watching the brothers literally skip down the path and away, Entreska turned to Mallory and said, "Pretty consistent, don't you think?"

"Indeed."

"What now?"

Mallory sighed. "I'm not sure. Vanessa will welcome us gladly if she believes I won't punish her for severely breaking the law as she has done."

Entreska narrowed her eyes. "You wouldn't, would you?"

Mallory breathed deeply. "While her intentions appear to be clearly to the good, her actions are essentially unforgivable breaches of regulation, ethical code and law that she and I are bound by duty and oath. We are to limit our contact and involvement with the local populations strictly to what is needed to accomplish our assigned mission. Furthermore, we are absolutely forbidden from explaining who and what we are. And clearly we cannot allow our knowledge or technology to be given to the local populace."

Entreska barked, "But you've done all those things!"

"Indeed I have."

Entreska stopped laughing and narrowed her eyes, "Why would you break an oath and duty like that? And then hold Vanessa accountable? That doesn't seem fair."

"Did I say I would punish her?"

Entreska frowned, "Well, no..."

"Naturally I would not. But I need to impress upon you the gravity of the circumstance. On several occasions, I have hunted down and... er... brought to justice... such persons who violated the Law Against Contact. In fact, it's one of my specialties."

"You killed them didn't you?"

"Not always. Most simply had no intention of being taken alive. Breaking provisions of the Law Against Contact is a capital crime, the punishment is rarely less than lifetime confinement."

"Great Burning Blast. But then, why have you broken that law yourself?"

"Isn't that obvious, Tresh? Everything I told you is as I believe it to be. I crash-landed here after a deep space accident that apparently has dumped me several millennia beyond my own time. Who knows now what laws or government has authority if any? I can't go back. I can't leave. But I can make things on this planet better, so I shall try. Besides I've always thought allowing a bunch of zealots to permanently impose a largely primitive lifestyle on the population of an entire planet totally stupid."

After Entreska gave him a painful stare, he hastily added, "If this planet is really a Primitive World gone askew, mind you. And, in fact, if it's not a Primitive World - then neither Vanessa nor I have broken the Law Against Contact anyway. But I think you can see why we would have to presume it to be so."

Entreska sighed and nodded seemingly convinced, but leaving Mallory with some doubt. The conversation returned Mallory to the Time Problem. Maybe Entreska was right. Maybe this world wasn't a "failed" Primitive World after all. Possibly a small group of colonists had landed here and then been cut off from the Big Organized Star Systems. Although that begged a question, B.O.S.S. kept close track of all inhabitable planets. In fact, Star Scouts roamed far and wide throughout the Milky Way or maybe they didn't anymore? Could a galactic calamity have turned everything into chaos producing uncharted, unmonitored colonizations? Mallory considered the lack of monitoring particularly damning.

He stared at the beautiful blue cloudless sky and wondered if there was anyone left out there at all. It seemed implausible that the entirety of 250+ worlds had been destroyed or so damaged that interstellar space flight had not been re-established within a few decades. But what if it had? Then he and Vanessa represented the most valuable resource in the human universe. Mallory sighed. If only he had bothered to take a transmitter with him. Of course, the range was about 5 km tops, and except the day he left and the last two, he had never been anywhere close to anyone with a receiver. It would have been stupid to carry one instead of something more useful like ammunition.

"Mallory? What if you wrote a letter to Vanessa?"

Mallory looked blankly at Entreska for a moment and then his face brightened. "Ah." Then he frowned as he thought of the problems.

Entreska confused by his reaction said, "Is that a bad idea? Can Vanessa read?"

"What? No. No. No. It's a great idea. And yes Vanessa can read. I'm just trying to think how to make it work properly."

"Oh. Why wouldn't it work?"

"Well, first of all. Remember, we assume that Vanessa believes I mean her harm. A letter may seem like a ruse. She may simply send her Guardians after me. Or pretend to play along. The letter needs to be convincing."

Entreska and Mallory sat thinking with contorted faces for a few moments. Then Entreska shrugged and said, "Why don't you confess that you've broken the law and you're convinced the Big whatever no longer holds sway?"

"Big Organized Star Systems. And yes... That should work."

Then Mallory's gaze turned to the trail and his eyes widened. Ten mounted Temple Guardians, eight men and two women were proceeding down the trail in good order and spirit. Mallory tried to conceal himself by hunching over and by scratching his face in what he hoped was a bored, unconcerned fashion.

The Guardians barely gave Entreska and Mallory a second glance. But then the hindmost soldier, a woman with long red hair braided six ways shouted something causing all the soldiers to stop. She quickly dismounted at which point it became clear she was very tall and strong for a woman. She didn't draw her weapon, but instead pointed at Mallory.

In a firm but quiet voice, she said in perfect Jurasketu, "Citizen. Please stand and show yourself."

Mallory sighed and stood up, hands open at his sides. "Yes?"

The woman gaped and then in a gleeful yet tentative voice she said, "Colonel Owens?"

Mallory scratched the back of his neck absently and said, "That would be me."

The woman smiled warmly and said, "I am Captain Tamara Tallrider. The Healer has long expected you. We were told to keep sharp lookout. And give you an important message."

Mallory noted that the soldiers seemed to go out of their way to look off their guard, hands in plain view.

"And that was?"

Captain Tallrider drew a deep breath, licked her lips in thought and said, "The message is this: 'The Healer will always know you as Her kind and generous commander no matter what and that the Healer will do anything to protect you. And also that the Healer wants to speak to you.' We are to bring you to the Temple at once. Will you please come with us?"

Mallory looked at Entreska with a what-in-the-world expression and shrugged, "Of course. I have come to see the Healer. I was afraid I might have difficulty when I saw the Temple. Apparently, my fears were unwarranted."

That's what Mallory said, but he did not think his fears unwarranted at all and that Entreska's clever idea had just been soldiered away. Vanessa clearly was sending him a message that she knew he might be upset, but that he should not fear her. She knew him quite well indeed. She was predicting he would be forgiving which would be very true. But what if this was just an exceptionally clever ruse...

Tamara hopped slightly with excitement. "Excellent."

Tamara motioned at her troop and looked sidelong at Entreska and stammered, "Do you and your... er... companion need any help gathering your belongings?"

Two dark haired, dark eyed, clean-shaven men dismounted and stood at either side of Tamara in a relaxed fashion, but to Mallory's experienced eyes, they were clearly ready to spring into action given the slightest reason. They were both clearly younger and slightly shorter than Tamara who looked to be in her early thirties.

Mallory smiled slightly as Tamara stared at Entreska who shifted her stance uncomfortably. "No. We can manage. We were just having lunch. Are you Zattan?"

Tamara raised an eyebrow in slight surprise at the question. "My mother is Zattan. Does that matter?"

Mallory shrugged. "No. I was just wondering."

Tamara narrowed her eyes and said, "And I was just wondering who your companion is?"

Mallory looked at Entreska briefly who was looking apprehensively back and started to invent a name but was distracted by the Guardian on Tamara's left, who was staring at Entreska and had developed a puzzled look on his face, then his mouth fell open and he said, "Professor Nevercare?"

Everyone looked at the Guardian in bafflement.

Tamara barked, "Professor what?"

The Guardian immediately stood at attention. Then pointed stiffly at Entreska and said, "Captain. I'm dead certain that woman, despite her... uh... exotic body paint... is Entreska Nevercare, Professor of History and Antiquities at the Jurasketu Academy. I took one of her courses just two years ago."

Entreska looked helplessly at Mallory who immediately leapt

to the conclusion that the Temple Guardians were the professional military unit he had guessed. He said, "Uh. Yes. That's right."

Entreska straightened, "Yes I am. And I remember you. Hilmore Troutdale, isn't it?"

"Yes, Professor."

Entreska nodded with approval, "You were a good student as I recall."

"Yes, Professor. I received top marks." The Guardian beamed with pride.

Tamara seemed greatly taken aback by this exchange. She shot an angry look at Troutdale and then turned toward Entreska, "Entreska Nevercare? The daughter of the Grand Marshal?"

Entreska flourished and said, "At your service."

Tamara crinkled her forehead, "What are doing here? With him? And may I ask why you have painted your skin and hair that way?"

Entreska sighed and her eyes showed a grim sadness, "A horrible disaster. He rescued me. It's not paint."

"Disaster? What sort?"

Mallory held up a hand towards Entreska, "Don't answer that."

Entreska snapped her mouth shut and stared at him.

Tamara gaped in puzzlement, "Why not?"

Mallory raised an eyebrow, "Well... Before we answer your questions, I need to know more about your relationship to the Healer and, moreover, where did you learn soldiery."

Mallory noted that the mounted Guardians tensed up considerably, hands positioned to grab their weapons, orienting their horses. Tamara and the two Guardians on her sides remained impassive leading Mallory to conclude they were confident, unafraid and very skilled. He could easily kill them all, of course, since he had a 5mm automatic ready for quick draw and they had only swords, spears and bows.

Entreska began to look very nervous.

Tamara noted that with a sidelong glance and said, "The Healer said you might be suspicious. She also said that you are a paranoid and extremely dangerous warrior and that I should not, under any circumstance do anything that might provoke you to violence. And so I want to give you my assurance, we mean you no harm nor certainly the daughter of the Grand Marshal."

Mallory smiled slightly, "Paranoid and dangerous I am. But I'm not too easily provoked." Entreska gave a disapproving glance at

Mallory who grimaced somewhat guiltily in return. "Anyway. So, then you are a unit of the Jurasketu Army?"

Tamara sighed and nodded.

"What unit? How long have you been here?"

Tamara sighed, looked around at her troopers and said, "We are a detachment of the Black Scorpions: two-hundred fifty-three in all. I am their commander. We've been here 400 days."

"Hmm... Interesting... How did you end up taking orders from the Healer exactly?"

Tamara smiled, "The Healer doesn't give orders. The folks running the Temple are all volunteers and at her insistence, it is run democratically. I command the detachment under the authority of the Jurasketu Army. We protect the Healer, her followers and the pilgrims because well... it seemed the right thing to do. We still operate under our own orders, but we don't really have much say except in deciding some defensive measures and keeping limited order amongst the pilgrims. The Physicians conduct law, order and policy by consensus and the occasional vote."

Mallory raised an eyebrow.

Tamara nodded and continued, "We were - and still are - involved in secret reconnaissance of this region when we stumbled upon the Temple. I quickly realized its importance, informed my superiors who indicated we should keep the Temple under close watch."

Mallory threw back his head and laughed. "Are your superiors aware of how literally you took that order?"

"Erm.... Not entirely. I've indicated that we've infiltrated the Temple and that we are taking efforts to prevent our enemies from doing the same. And the Healer knows all this as well. Does that satisfy your questions about who and what we are doing?"

"In the main I would think. What else did the Healer tell you about me?"

Tamara shrugged, "Not too much really. Are you really the Healer's commander?"

Mallory sighed quietly, "Yes. I really am."

Then surprising himself he said, "But having been absent for a while, I am not entirely certain how she would take my reappearance. Admittedly, her message seems a bit reassuring."

"Mmm... Doubts about your conduct as commander?"

Mallory laughed, "Yes. I suppose so."

Tamara grunted in amusement and then said, "I think she has

genuinely missed you."

Mallory took immediate heart from that observation. "Fair enough. I suppose we should answer your questions as well. But, er... some of our information might be a little sensitive in nature. How much do you normally share with your troops?"

Tamara cocked her head around to glare at her troopers. They tried hard in vain not to smile. Tamara grinned in return and said, "As much as I can. Certainly more than most commanders. These guys are the best of the best, and deserve to know more. Certainly, I keep a few secrets as all military commanders must."

Mallory nodded and became stone-faced and very solemn. "I think Entreska should explain the horrible disaster."

Everyone turned expectantly and apprehensively to Entreska.

"This will take a little while. I suggest we sit."

Tamara motioned for her troopers to dismount and gather around posting two troopers as lookouts though close enough to still hear Entreska speak.

Entreska's eyes became downcast and misty as she slowly explained the disastrous fate of the Expedition and the Black Scorpions complete with a litany of recriminations. Tamara became increasingly distressed as Entreska recounted the tale. Soon, Tamara, Entreska and the troopers were in tears. Mallory did not cry but his countenance had become very grim indeed.

Entreska continued on with her rescue by Mallory. The rescue seemed to cheer Tamara and the troopers a little. And judging from their glances, the story further inflated their opinion of Mallory the Dangerous Warrior.

The Fylurian Ethic

Tamara, Mallory and Entreska rode three abreast through the wide main gate of the defensive wall. They continued down the muddy main avenue toward the Temple. The rest of the soldiers followed through the gate but then turned right to the main stables.

Entreska turned towards Mallory and said, "Wow. Your description of the Temple was totally inadequate."

Tamara turned sharply and barked, "What? Owens has been here since the Temple was built?"

Mallory smiled, "No. I just observed it from the eastern ridge line the night before last."

Tamara stiffened slightly and looked towards the ridge clearly upset. Finally, she said, "I see."

They rode on for a few more minutes. Along the way, various pilgrims and Temple valley denizens stopped whatever they were doing and stared at the strange appearance of Entreska and Mallory. The few Guardians that dared to stare were intercepted by glares from Tamara and quickly found something needing their immediate attention.

At the Temple Entrance, Tamara said, "I'm sure the Healer would wish that you take residence in the Temple. The Temple stables will have room for your horses. Groomsmen!"

Two smiling young women and an earnest young man trotted out of the nearby stable door. They were garbed in heavy leather pants, knee high brown boots and loose, short beige tunics. Entreska patted a nervous Daffodil on the neck and told her to be good for the stable hands. Dandelion snorted in irritation at having the ride apparently cut short. In contrast, Violet clearly was glad to be heading for a stay in a nice, comfortable stable.

Expecting a large open interior with a central gathering space, Entreska was very surprised to find the Temple was laid out more like a luxury inn. The entrance was essentially a lobby with elegantly carved wooden benches, a few chairs and a large finely crafted table manned by an older man wearing a simple white tunic, dark blue trousers and cloth slippers. His bushy white hair, bulging blue eyes, wrinkled smile and body language made him look permanently shocked with surprise.

Tamara smiled warmly at the man and said, "Jake. Tell Ursula that Colonel Owens has returned and I'm taking him to speak with the Healer."

Jake glanced at Owens. He then stared at Entreska and said, "As you wish Captain. I will tell her at once."

Without otherwise moving, he turned his head towards an open door on Entreska's right and bellowed, "Ursula! Captain Tallrider is here with a Colonel Owens! They are going to speak with the Healer!"

Entreska cringed. Tamara rolled her eyes. Mallory smiled.

Ursula, an older woman with warm brown eyes, clean ivory skin and long gray hair tied into a ponytail, poked her head out from the doorway. She smiled with even and intact but yellow teeth. Then she bounded out into the lobby. She wore a dark blue knee length skirt, a sleeveless, bright lavender blouse that was tucked into the skirt and matching cloth slippers. She wore no jewelry other than a gold medallion hanging from a short gold chain necklace.

Ursula stepped forward and pointed with a flourish, "And so this is Colonel Owens?"

Tamara nodded. Mallory bowed and spread his hands in the Jurasketu fashion of formal greeting. Entreska did the same.

Ursula reciprocated to them both. Then she stepped back and gave Entreska a look over. "And who are you, may I ask?"

Entreska nodded, "I am Entreska Nevercare. Professor of History and Antiquities at the Jurasketu Academy of Learning."

Ursula nodded obviously impressed. "I am Ursula Valcott, Chief Physician for the Temple of Healing. Um... Why have you painted yourself like that? Is that the latest in Jurasketu fashion?"

Entreska laughed softly, "It is not paint. And I didn't do it myself. But making it a new fashion might solve the problem of constantly answering that question."

Ursula shrugged slightly in embarrassment, "Sorry."

"No. No. It is okay."

Ursula nodded and then said to Mallory, "Well. Colonel Owens. The Healer has spoken highly of you."

Mallory frowned, "I doubt that."

Ursula smiled and gave him a strange look. "She has. Really. Anyway. I am certain you and her need to talk. Come. I'll show the way."

Ursula skipped behind the table and over to an ornate wooden door on the opposite side of the room from which she had emerged. Ursula pressed her hands together and bowed before turning the handle and beckoning them to follow.

Mallory followed immediately. Entreska and Tamara hesitated, but an annoyed Mallory waved for them to follow which they did. Entreska was last to enter the room. Ursula, Mallory and Tamara stood to the outside of the building looking towards the interior wall – that was entirely unlike the other three walls which were horizontally planked with whitewashed, relatively thin, tongue and groove boards. The interior wall bulged towards them with an unbroken, black wax-like finish.

Mallory folded his arms and contemplated the wall for an uncomfortably long time. Entreska tried to feel what he was thinking. Heather had been encouraging her to test her skill and ability in mind reading. But Entreska couldn't be sure that the feelings she thought she was reading weren't just her imaginings. And worse, for Entreska, reading someone else's internal dialogue seemed completely wrong on a number of levels. Ursula and Tamara showed no concern whatsoever and just stood idly by, Ursula smiling innocently and Tamara holding a neutral, military expression.

About the moment that Entreska couldn't bear the wait any longer, Mallory spoke, "Well. Vanessa. What do you have to say for yourself?"

Ursula and Tamara turned towards Mallory with very puzzled expressions. Entreska looked around wondering how Vanessa would manifest herself. Then Ursula blurted, "Who is Vanessa?"

Entreska answered, "The Healer."

Mallory nodded. Tamara and Ursula looked over at Entreska with mild surprise but said nothing further.

Although Entreska had become accustomed to digital images and video from using the spare Darkglasses, she still jumped when the image of a pleasant female face of indeterminate age appeared on the black surface of the interior wall. Neither Tamara nor Ursula seemed surprised by the appearance of the face and simply shifted their stance and gaze. Entreska took this as a good sign and relaxed.

A silky smooth voice said, "Welcome back, Commander Owens."

"Cut the crap."

The face turned towards Entreska. "How does she know my name?"

Mallory looked briefly at Entreska, "I told her."

The face smiled, "I see. It would seem we both have some things to explain."

Mallory nodded, "And many things that neither of us can explain."

Vanessa smiled wryly, "Do you mean like how this planet has recorded history going back millennia?"

"That would be one."

Vanessa smiled in a motherly manner, "That would make us a little more lost than we first realized, don't you think? And beyond all applicable law."

Mallory responded sternly, "Laws are of no concern to me. I'm more interested in your seeming disregard for my orders."

Vanessa became placid, "I did what I thought was right to preserve myself and the remnants of your command. You gave me full discretion instructing me that my preservation was paramount – I can play the recording if you like."

Mallory laughed, "That won't be necessary."

Mallory turned to Entreska, Tamara and Ursula. "I need to speak privately with Vanessa. Uh... I mean, the Healer. I am going to enter my ship. It should only take a couple of hours. Please."

The three women nodded resignedly.

Mallory gestured at the face. "Vanessa. If you please."

An outline appeared in the black surface and a door sized panel slid back inside the ship revealing a small white room. Mallory stepped inside. The panel slid back into place with a soft snick.

Tamara and Ursula looked at Entreska.

Entreska shrugged, "Don't look at me. I have no idea what he is up to."

Tamara gestured towards the door and the three of them returned to the entry hall. In the hall, Ursula invited them into her spartan living quarters for tea and cakes.

They readily accepted.

Ursula looked Entreska over in a kindly way and said, "So how did you ensnare Colonel Owens exactly?"

"Pardon?"

Ursula smiled, "I'm sorry. I meant to ask how you came to be travel companions."

Entreska laughed, "We met in desperation. First his. Second mine."

Tamara chimed in, "You can tell her. I had planned on telling her the whole story anyway. It would be better first hand if you don't mind."

Entreska nodded at Tamara then launched into the entire emotional story again. Tamara and Entreska ended up in tears again. Ursula stayed stoic throughout the tale with occasional words of comfort.

They sipped tea in silence for a bit and then Entreska asked, "So, how did you come to be the Chief Physician of the Temple?"

Ursula frowned unexpectedly, "I am a lifetime disciple of the Fylurian Ethic. Until a year ago, I lived a comfortable life as a respected private physician catering to the healing needs of the citizens who came from all over Tarfun to my place in Vamour Sylenz. I thought I was a learned, humble and wise physician. But you know what?"

Entreska reflexively said, "What?"

"I've since discovered I knew almost nothing."

Entreska nodded, "I know that very feeling recently."

"You are still young. I am old. It is a hard thing to discover that a lifetime of dedication and study was completely worthless. And totally wrong about almost everything."

Entreska bobbled her head, "Everything we know is either wrong or incomplete."

Ursula looked down and slowly shook her head, "There is wrong. There is incomplete. And there is completely and totally wrong. This was the latter. Anyway. For almost three months, I heard amazing reports of miraculous cures being offered by a brand new temple of healing that had opened up two days travel west from Deliverance. In my ignorance, I immediately suspected the work of charlatans. So, I went to see for myself and gather sufficient evidence to officially denounce the temple."

Entreska smiled, "I guess you were convinced otherwise."

Ursula laughed, "Indeed. After a week of travel, I reached the temple. I purposely examined some of the pilgrims before and after they received treatment. The results were simply astounding. I requested an audience with the Healer. Of course, that was an even more astounding revelation, as you might have guessed."

"I know. But then what? What did the Healer say?"

Ursula smiled wryly, "The Healer questioned me extensively

on the general state of healing knowledge and mine in particular. At the end of the interview, I begged her to impart some small part of her skills and knowledge so that I could return to Vamour Sylenz and give this knowledge to others for the benefit of all. To my great surprise, she then asked if I would consent to become Chief Physician and then establish and run a school at the temple to train physicians with exactly that goal – the benefit of all. I accepted without a second thought or consideration of how all-consuming such a task would become."

Entreska frowned, "Do you regret accepting then?"

"Are you joking? I just wish I were younger with more vigor and time to devote to the task."

Entreska smiled and noticed Tamara smirking. Then a dark thought occurred to Entreska.

"Tamara? With the reputation of miracle cures, don't you think brigands or more dangerously, one of the local city-states will attempt to seize the Temple for themselves? Deliverance could easily launch such an operation I would think. Admittedly, you have defenses and given the terrain would make an attacker pay dearly – but I can't imagine they realize the quality of the defenses and would likely assume the temple is poorly defended."

Tamara took a deep breath. "You are perceptive. Brigands we fear not. A sizable company of mercenary Cumar attempted to raid the valley as the temple was under construction. We slaughtered them. They were not expecting a well-ordered militia and certainly not a militia backed up by a company of elite veterans. I'm confident that example will discourage the brigands and other amateurs."

"Very good. But what about a real army?"

Tamara looked to Ursula who smiled and shrugged, "The Deliverance physician community has many members in training here. So does the Tarfun League. I recruited students from all the neighboring cities and provinces. They even pay tuition. Since the various students have almost certainly reported back to their home rulers that the Healer is not human and by definition supernatural, those rulers would naturally assume a naked grab of the temple by force would not please her and that the miracles and training would cease. And most of them would have to fear the ill-favor of the Healing Spirits."

Tamara nodded in agreement, "We also think that even if despite all that a force moved against us, the others would intervene to preserve our neutrality and usefulness."

Entreska nodded in admiration, "Matters seem to be well in hand then. Assuming Mallory doesn't upset them somehow..."

Tamara rubbed her arms and said, "For someone who follows the Ultherian Ethic, you sure seem to have a deep interest in military matters."

Entreska laughed, "Consider who my father and brother are. I could not help but learn something."

Tamara shrugged, "Doubtless. Of course, forgive me."

Entreska shook her head, "No apology required."

Ursula raised an eyebrow, "Ultherian? Hmm... And who is your father?"

Tamara stated, "Grand Marshal Nevercare."

Ursula squinted at Entreska, "Really? That is a bit ironic though. I hope it wasn't from resentment."

Entreska laughed again, "No. I love my father. Truly. My devotion to the Ultherian Ethic is honest and true. It is the path of peace and deep learning. Not far from the Fylurian in most ways I would say."

Ursula pursed her lips in thought for a moment, "You pursue the theoretical. We stay practical."

Entreska smiled, "There is nothing more practical than a good theory."

Ursula laughed, "You are quite right. What I was trying to say is that our Ethics make good allies."

Entreska nodded, "Yes. That is what I meant as well."

They both turned to look at Tamara who had cleared her throat, she fixed her gaze on Entreska and spoke slowly, "What can you tell us about Colonel Owens?"

Entreska smiled, "He is not from this world."

Ursula nodded, "We know. The Healer told us."

Entreska continued, "What else has the Healer told you about him?"

Tamara chuckled, "Almost nothing. He is her commander. He is human like all of us. Brilliant, skilled and exceptionally dangerous."

Entreska frowned, "But what has the Healer told you of their civilization?"

Ursula shrugged, "Nothing beyond the healing arts. It is rather frustrating in that regard. Speaking for myself, I have a great many questions I wish the Healer would answer."

Entreska nodded in sympathy. Scratching her neck, she said,

"Mallory has shared a number of things with me, but I don't want to reveal anything unless he says it is okay."

Ursula frowned, "I was right. You are smitten with him. Yet he is a warrior. Followers of the Gudarian Ethic are not usually compatible with your philosophy. Are you comfortable with that?"

Entreska almost blurted out that she was not smitten with him, but it would have been a lie. She slumped back in her chair, instead, and considered what Ursula had just said. She closed her eyes, the obvious pain evident on her face.

The older woman simply said, "Sorry. I wasn't trying to upset you."

Entreska waved her hands, "No. It's all right. Or not actually. And no, I am not comfortable with that. I think in the end, it would prove to be an ill-fated romance."

Ursula paused to think and said, "I'm not an expert in matters of romance, but if I were you, I would keep an open mind."

Entreska paused in thought for a bit, nodded wondering about the contradictory advice Ursula seemed to be giving and said, "Okay. I will."

Ursula shrugged and said, "Besides, if you are not careful, you might have competition." Ursula winked at Tamara who narrowed her eyes and took on a clearly mock miffed look.

Entreska laughed, "She certainly would be a better match."

Tamara laughed, "Doubtful. Our egos would likely clash."

Ursula measured Entreska carefully for a moment then asked, "What are your plans?"

"Mine? Mallory said he needed some things. Then we are going to return to Zetu."

"And do what?"

"Mallory has plans to dethrone Puck."

Ursula and Tamara both gave looks of surprise then deep concern.

Ursula asked, "How exactly?"

Tamara snorted, "Probably superior weaponry."

Entreska nodded, "Special equipment, armor and weapons."

Ursula looked stern, "How can you countenance helping him?"

Entreska shrugged, "I owe him my life so I will do what I can to protect him. In reality though, I am more of a hindrance than a help. And I cannot prevent him from doing what he wills."

Ursula said, "You could employ reason."

"He is not so easily swayed. Remember we are friends not lovers."

Ursula nodded with a frown.

"Will he succeed?"

"Mallory seems determined enough. He certainly has the skills and tools required for the job. I expect him to be successful."

Tamara queried Entreska extensively about recent events in Jurasketu and beyond. Tamara and Ursula provided news about the goings on in Deliverance, Tarfun and the various city-states of Wokometu. The conversation was finally interrupted by the sudden appearance of Mallory a couple of hours later.

Mallory smiled at the expectant faces, "My conversation with Va-I mean, the Healer, is concluded. Entreska, if you care to join me, I plan to leave tomorrow morning."

Entreska felt and looked modestly hurt, "Of course I will join you."

"Very good."

Tamara spoke up, "Colonel?"

"Yes?"

She spoke earnestly, "I wish to accompany you with a few of my best."

"What? Why?"

"We know Western Zetu quite well. My unit has spent many years secretly scouting Puck's empire. I think you would find our knowledge and support valuable."

Mallory narrowed his eyes, "I suspect other motives. And I usually work alone. But the assistance of skilled warriors in traversing hostile territory cannot be refused. I will grant your request. At the very least, it will allow us to bring more horses and hence more equipment and weapons."

Tamara smiled, "Excellent. I and a hand-picked team will be ready early tomorrow. Any assistance you need this evening to make preparations is yours for the asking."

Ursula gaped at the unexpected exchange, "How can you leave us?"

Tamara turned and said confidently, "Lieutenant Thurman is perfectly capable of handling command duties in my absence. A military campaign against the Temple is highly unlikely with the approach of winter."

Ursula breathed deeply obviously stressed by the latest developments, "Very well. I cannot force you to stay."

Tamara added, "Please don't worry. And quite frankly, a plan with a reasonable chance of destroying Puck is worth the small risk that my leadership would be decisive."

Ursula sighed, "Hopefully, we will not need that leadership while you are gone. Colonel, I hope you understand the value that Tamara will provide. And I charge you with returning her to us in one piece."

Mallory smiled, "My plan is to return us all in one piece. I can assure you I am not careless with my own life or others."

Ursula raised an eyebrow, "Let us hope your skill matches your desire."

Mallory laughed, "Indeed. Let that be true."

Tamara laughed in response while Entreska and Ursula frowned.

Entreska continued conversing with Ursula while Mallory hauled enough stuff hidden in boxes and satchels to load up five large draft horses. The process took nearly three hours with Mallory, Tamara and a draft master supervising the provisioning process. They would leave before dawn. A messenger had already been sent ahead to warn Captain Jules that he would be providing passage to horses and a dozen soldiers. Entreska wondered if Captain Jules would be annoyed or just bemused. She decided upon, bemused, reflecting upon Jules' reaction to Mallory's survival story and claim of a plan to destroy Puck.

Later that evening, she pressed Mallory on his plans. Mallory vaguely responded that he was still formulating his plan and that the defenses of Puck's fortress would have to be scouted anew when they reached the Centaur Citadel. Entreska expressed concern at how could he achieve his goals without killing a lot of people both soldiers and innocents at the fortress.

Somewhat irritably, Mallory said firmly, "I will finalize my plans once I am there. I will aim to keep the killing limited."

And then it happened. She didn't mean to say it. It just came out. Entreska shouted at Mallory, "Don't you understand? I cannot love you if you continue to kill people!"

In utter surprise, Mallory barked, "What?"

Entreska clasped her hands over her mouth. Her eyes went wide in shock at what she had said.

Mallory shifted partly to the side and stared down in thought for a moment.

Entreska turned away and burst into tears.

Mallory sat quietly for a moment and then just said, "Oh. Oh."

Entreska sobbed.

Mallory took a couple of deep breaths and tentatively said, "Do you mean to say that you would love me? That is, if I stopped killing people?"

Entreska hesitated between sobs and said, "What?"

Mallory fumbled with his words for a moment and said, "I mean. Could you, would you love me if I stopped doing what I am trained to do?"

Entreska stopped crying and said quietly, "You are right. I cannot ask that of you. I am being foolish. I take back what I said. Please. I am clearly exhausted. I need to rest for the journey tomorrow. Please. Go."

Mallory stiffened slightly, "Oh. Yes. As you wish."

He stood and turned to leave, looked back to say something, but changed his mind and left quietly.

Entreska resumed sobbing. She cursed herself. Romance was the last thing she needed right now. She did want Mallory to end Puck's reign and the overt threat he posed to Jurasketu. How could she even think about jeopardizing that by asking Mallory to abandon his Ethic for hers and her love? Worse, how could she wish him success in a way that didn't follow her Ethic? She didn't have time to reflect on the complex shape her life had taken. She decided to cry for a while longer and hope sleep overtook her instead.

Entreska sat and stared at the darkness.

"Entreska?"

Entreska said aloud, "What?"

Entreska closed her eyes realizing that the speaker was the Second Voice, Silas Hurme. "Dammit."

Then she thought, *"Sorry. I mean – what do you want?"*

A feeling of parental kindness that her mother would have exuded sloshed about her mind. She smiled. Heather seemed to be right about Silas and his good character. "No apology needed. I perfectly understand. Can you return to the Tea Room for a conversation?"

"With just you?"

"No. The Council wishes to discuss some matters with you."

Entreska snarled inwardly. She would rather sleep but instead said, *"Yes. A moment."*

Entreska had projected herself several times onto the Patio of Infinity since her first time in the Blades. With each time, it took less effort and time to appear there. She also discovered she could change her garments as she wished. Her ridiculous swirling skin tones clashed badly with most of her choices so for several visits in a row she had settled for pure comfort and complete modesty with a loose fitting long sleeved black blouse and gray striped pantaloons. Both garments were made from unnaturally soft cottons and somehow magically woven without seams. She went barefoot like the wizards.

Jasmine, Silas, Stan, and Toviel were perched on the sofas waiting for Entreska. Baxatom, Daryl and Lee were conversing quietly off in the back corner. Diana was on duty sitting out on the Patio of the World. Billy and Rhenda were not present. Zelda sat off to the side staring darkly at nothing.

Entreska feigned deference and politeness, "Good afternoon, my dear friends of the Council. What would you wish of me?"

Jasmine rolled her eyes, "Enough with that nonsense. What do you think of Mallory's plans?"

Entreska shrugged, "May I sit?"

Annoyed, Jasmine gestured with a silver arm towards a chair.

Entreska took her time, sat demurely and quietly observed the wizards. Toviel sat unmoving like a golden statue topped with a green wig. Stan pressed his fingertips together holding his hands close to his washboard, blue-green stomach. Silas sat with pink arms folded across his chest. They waited patiently for her response.

Entreska finally spoke, "He seems confident. You see what I see and hear what I hear, so you know as much as I do about him and his civilization."

Stan spoke, concern obvious in his manner and voice, "You mean as little. This Healer--"

"Vanessa."

"--Vanessa. She has her own agenda it would seem."

Entreska stroked her shoulder, "Agenda? More like a mission to relieve suffering. You could say that Mallory has taken on that same mission by going after Puck. So I wouldn't say they have different agendas at all."

Silas spoke over something Stan was about to say, "I thought you disapproved of his plan."

Entreska nodded, "I strongly disapprove of violence, yes. But that doesn't mean I think his motivation is wrong. Right motive. Wrong method."

Silas said with a smile, "Do you have a proposal to get rid of Puck without violence?"

Entreska sighed, "Not as yet. No."

Stan frowned and said with apparent sincerity, "That is disappointing."

Entreska slightly threw up her hands, "Yes. Indeed."

Then there was a shout. Everyone looked over at Zelda who had stood up. She yelled, "Violence? I'll show you violence."

Zelda stepped forward, raised her arms and exploded with a deafening boom into a horrible cloud of red, brown and white.

The four wizards and Entreska were covered in a fine, wet mist of what had been Zelda.

Silas bellowed, "By the Ashes of My Ancestors."

Stan rolled his eyes, "Gah. What was the point of that?"

Jasmine muttered curses while tossing her tea aside.

Toviel just sighed heavily and looked back to where Zelda had been.

Entreska retched slightly and let forth a low guttural, "Great Burning Blast."

They all turned to look at Tom who stood with his hands slightly extended towards them and a deep, hard scowl on his face framed by his wild green and gold hair. Daryl and Lee had stepped back in opposite directions from Tom in obvious surprise.

Daryl barked in laughter, "Ha. Stupid bitch. Good show Tom. That'll teach her a lesson."

Tom twitched slightly, tucked his head back in towards his right shoulder to look at Daryl, and then snapped his right hand upwards. The gesture coincided with another booming explosion. This time Daryl vanished in a red, blue and white spray that ended up covering the back wall in a thin layer of reddish blue paste.

Tom snapped his head back forward and snarled, "Maybe he'll learn to keep his useless trap shut."

Lee said, "Boy. Uh... Easy Tom."

Tom turned slightly to stare at Lee, "You need not fear me."

Jasmine, Silas and Stan moved towards Tom but stopped in their tracks after a few paces when he fixed his gaze on them. All three assumed the same stance: feet apart, shoulders and head back, hands raised in front of chest. Entreska became aware of a strong undercurrent of something that could be best described as magical humming.

Tom grimaced and said, "Zelda was going to strike at Entreska. And I'm certain Daryl goaded her into the attempt."

Stan looked at Jasmine who looked sidelong back and nodded.

Silas sneered, "You don't know that."

To some surprise, Toviel spoke, "I was monitoring Zelda's mind because I was worried about her. She definitely intended to harm Entreska. If Daryl induced her to do so, though, I didn't discern anything like that."

Tom spoke, "Satisfied?"

Silas dropped his hands and reluctantly said yes.

Jasmine and Stan quickly followed suit.

Tom remained alert for several more seconds and then relaxed his stance and posture as well. He then contemplatively surveyed his grisly handiwork and then with a glance towards Entreska wandered over to a clean chair on the far side of the room to enjoy an éclair and some, fresh steaming tea.

Entreska tried in vain to shake off the Zelda dust. She looked around the room at the unbelievable gore and very uncomfortable looking wizards. A few moments later, Billy and Rhenda appeared asking what happened. Jasmine started to answer but Entreska interrupted her with a bark.

Entreska stared at the wizards in turn and finally said, "This is utter madness."

With that, she faded from the room and a few minutes later ignored a somewhat feeble plea to return from Jasmine. Despite her exhaustion, Entreska struggled to sleep. Thoughts raced through her mind. She had managed to add sexual tension to a somewhat difficult circumstance and relationship with Mallory. She had to consider her new found relationships with Tamara, Ursula and the Healer and where they would lead. Meanwhile, it was becoming increasing apparent that the High Wizard Council was infested with madness. She couldn't trust any of them. But she couldn't exactly get away from them either. She was trapped. What if Baxatom was right that she might live for centuries? Heather had confirmed the possibility when Entreska had put the question to her. There would be no escape.

At first light, Mallory and Entreska joined Ursula for a welcome breakfast of scrambled eggs, bacon, dried fruits, oatmeal and tea prepared by Ursula herself. Tamara had insisted they eat while she and her soldiers readied the horses. They ate quickly and quietly, then sipped tea and talked a little.

Entreska was thinking it was time to get going when Mallory looked over at her and said, "If you are willing, I would like the

Healer to examine you briefly before we go."

A stifling wave of thick, black smoke billowed through her mind and only dissipated when she summoned a stiff breeze. That was followed by a chorus of voices shouting dismay and dire warnings.

Entreska muttered, "Shut up. Just shut up."

Mallory and Ursula stared at her with grave concern.

Entreska closed her eyes and shook her head, "I'm sorry. I was talking to the voices in my head."

Ursula raised an eyebrow, but Mallory simply nodded.

Entreska looked Mallory in the eyes, "Yes. How long will it take?"

Mallory shrugged, "No more than 10 minutes or so I would think."

Entreska nodded, "Okay."

Mallory stood, "Come then. Ursula? Can you inform the Captain we will be a few minutes late?"

Ursula nodded assent.

Entreska had to continue fighting the voices while Mallory led her to the black wall and into the strange white room. He directed her to sit in a surprisingly uncomfortable chair. Mallory summoned Vanessa who appeared on the wall facing Entreska.

Vanessa nodded, "Good morning. Colonel, for this particular testing, you need to leave the room."

Mallory simply nodded and exited the way they had come in.

Vanessa smiled warmly and said, "Colonel Owens spoke to me at length about you and your various troubles. He thinks that I might be able to provide you some answers. While I am very curious to see what the scans will reveal, I have serious doubts about my ability to provide you with useful information. I also have reservations. Normally the scans are completely harmless and carry no risk. But from what the Colonel has told me, I cannot be completely sure of that in your case. Given that, I will need your explicit permission to do the scans. Do you grant that permission?"

Entreska mulled that over while the voices in her head continued to wail fire and smoke at her. Then she nodded and said, "Granted."

Vanessa nodded, "This won't take long, dear. Ready?"

Entreska nodded again and waited patiently for some indication the examination had begun. She was disappointed. Instead, for several long minutes Vanessa simply stared at her and the voices in her head switched from anger to wails of despair.

After about an eternity of only five minutes, Vanessa announced,

"Okay. Done."

Entreska, incredulous, asked, "That's it?"

Vanessa frowned, "Yes. I have to analyze the results. That I'm afraid will take some time in your case. Hopefully, I'll have an answer by the time you return."

Entreska furrowed her brow, "Oh. I was hoping maybe you could give me some advice."

Vanessa shrugged, "I can. You have to embrace, tame or succumb to the madness. And avoid mangoes, you are allergic to them."

Entreska muttered, "Okay thanks. Wait – what the hell are mangoes?"

Vanessa said evenly, "A tropical fruit. Probably not found on this planet. So never mind."

Then Entreska asked, "And how does one embrace madness exactly?"

Vanessa did a slight head bobble, "I suppose I meant that you have to make yourself fully aware of your madness and think through and around it. Taming is always the first choice, of course."

Entreska smiled, "Sound advice I'm sure. But the advice I wanted was about Colonel Owens."

Vanessa's expression became neutral, "Yes?"

Entreska stammered, "Can I trust him? Is he really who he says he is?"

Vanessa studied Entreska keenly for a few moments, "Colonel Owens belongs to a semi-secret military outfit that specializes in handling troublesome individuals."

"You mean he kills them."

Vanessa smirked, "That is his usual method. Yes. Did he not tell you this?"

Entreska took a deep breath, "He did. He called himself a Troubleshooter."

Vanessa smiled, "Exactly that. He shoots troubles. But whatever connection we had to that organization appears to be lost deep in both time and space. He has stated that he believes himself no longer obligated to that duty and is now at liberty to live as he would like. Entreska, he has killed and killed. He desperately needs healing of a type I cannot provide. I think your love and patience could lead him down a new path."

Entreska frowned, "Is he that fragile?"

Vanessa shook her head, "Fragile? No my dear. He is not fragile at all. He knows himself and the world quite well. But he despairs of that knowledge. It chills his soul... He needs your warmth. It would give him purpose."

The Voices wailed with more vigor.

Entreska closed her eyes and pressed her fingers against her temples to massage them.

Vanessa spoke encouragingly, "He has revealed himself to you as who he truly is. That means he believes in you. And clearly trusts you. Can you trust him? That depends on you. He definitely won't betray you. But he is at a dangerous crossroads. He could very well break your heart should you give it to him."

Trakora Runk

The bonfire roared and sparked. The orange glow and smoky haze smothered the stars and lesser moons. The drummers pounded away intoxicated by the heat and smoke. The giant White Fir climbing the valley walls loomed above the stone paved circle that measured nearly fifty meters across. Hundreds of Zattan adults dressed in loose-fitting, colorful shirts, trousers and sandals sat cross-legged around the entirety of the circle.

At the west end of the stone circle, Glenmorgan stood completely naked. The heat from the bonfire and the midsummer temperatures bathed him in sweat. He breathed slowly to control his excitement. At the completion of the upcoming ceremony and rituals, he would be accepted as an adult Zattan. He would be free to choose a mate, allowed to own property and afforded all the other rights and privileges that belonged to an adult Zattan. He would have the duties as well, but everything has a cost so complaining about that would be simply adding to the total cost.

For the three nights of Midsummer Festival, across the Zattan tribal realms, other teenagers would be enduring various ceremonies and rituals all generally called the Zatta Revark. The Torra Makur or Stone Circles of Life were one of the very few Zattan religious traditions that had endured across the centuries. This particular circle was known unimaginatively as the Torra Glennur or High Grove Circle. It was used exclusively for Royal Revarks. Most circles would host multiple Revarks over the course of each evening of the Midsummer Festival, but the Torra Glennur would have just one this year.

Glen's ceremony included the Trakora Runk, an extremely expensive and dangerous ancient ritual that was alleged to give protection against sorcery. Given that there was no living memory of anyone actually being a proven victim of sorcery, the ritual had fallen into deep disfavor except with the hardcore traditional Royals.

His father, being a hardcore, traditional Royal, had insisted over the protests of his mother who was, well, not.

Glen was ambivalent. Many claimed that Pachinko Puck was indeed a wizard. Most claimed it was just a legend perpetuated by the senior commanders of the Immortals who were the real rulers of the Centaur Citadel. The Legend of Pachinko Puck was just their idea of a joke to taunt the ambassadors of Jurasketu, Wokometu and the Zattan. Glen's father and his clever cousin Murok thought otherwise. But Glen had been taught to avoid unnecessary risks - and the dangers of Trakora Runk were quite real.

He had been mostly raised in Endurance where his father had been the long time ambassador of the Imperium Council to Jurasketu. He had lived as a Zattan full time for only two years now. He had to prove he was as tough and courageous as any Zattan. Enduring the danger of the Trakora Runk would help his reputation in a way worth the risk. His mother constantly counseled against too much ambition perhaps simply to counter Glen's very obvious burning desire for fame, glory and power. His father, however, counseled him to seek allies, power and strength while being wary of everyone and everything.

Glen waited trying to show the patience and nerve that the ceremony required. The Zatta Fenyal, Kendra Cloudreader, motioned for Glen to move into the center of the circle to where she stood beside a wooden altar laden with various jars and strange implements. He purposefully walked forward, hands held low, palms up and slightly crossed as he had been instructed. He stopped and held himself motionless when she raised her hand.

Kendra Cloudreader was relatively young, at age 32, and just appointed the previous year to be Zatta Fenyal. Her shamanic skills were already legendary, however, long before her appointment. She was also widely regarded as beautiful, but she claimed youth, presence, high office and fine clothes simply created an illusion of beauty. Glen thought she was just being modest which in his mind made her all the more admirable. She stared at him for a very long time while he breathed slowly and deliberately waiting for the ceremony to officially begin.

Finally, she fluffed up her purple, gold trimmed robes and boomed in a loud voice, "Glenmorgan, son of William Stormbreaker and Allison Summer, are you ready?"

Glen, as he was taught, spoke less loudly, "Yes, Zatta Fenyal. I am ready."

She nodded and looked around. She loudly asked, "What name have you chosen?"

He whispered, "Nevercare."

She smiled briefly and whispered, "Interesting."

Then she spread her arms wide and boomed, "The candidate has chosen Glenmorgan Nevercare! What say the Gathering?"

The gathered Zattan muttered momentarily then roared approval.

She nodded and proclaimed, "The name is accepted. We will proceed."

She motioned for Glen to close his eyes and mouth, spread his legs and raise his arms. She proceeded to pour an entire jar of a secret herbal oil over his head. She used a soft brush to spread the strangely cool oil until he was completely coated. Next, she randomly tossed various powders of blue, white, black, red, purple, yellow and green onto him until he was fully caked. She clapped when she was done which meant he was allowed to bring his arms back to his center and open his eyes. The oil interfered with his ability to sweat so he had to pant heavily to dissipate the heat.

She motioned downward. He dropped down onto both knees, placed his hands on his thighs and bowed his head. She placed her left hand on his head and spoke a long liturgy in Archaic Zattan that emphasized the responsibilities that an adult Zattan must bear without complaint. Finally, she withdrew her hand.

She said quietly, "Look at me."

Glen dutifully looked up into her smiling face.

She whispered, "Don't pretend. Be who you are. If you don't like yourself, you should change you. That is your sacred charge."

Glen, slightly surprised by the unexpected admonishment or advice since it seemed to be both, simply nodded assent.

Kendra raised her arms again and facing the crowd walked in a wide circle around Glen. The crowd chanted an Archaic Zattan encouragement. She returned to face Glen and motioned for him to rise. He rose carefully keeping his hands in his center.

She nodded to the crowd and spoke, "Now come the Tests of Strength, of Touch and of Endurance. Bring forth the Axe and Block."

The Tests were not just a mere formality. One failure meant two years mandatory service as a laborer in the Imperium Engineers building roads. Two failures meant four years in the stone quarries. Three failures meant eight years and most likely death in the mines.

Two red and blue robed shamans brought forth a large block of Black Fir and placed it near the Zatta Fenyal. Then they brought a large battle-axe and with an informal bow placed it into Glen's waiting hands. With a nod from Kendra, Glen stepped forward, laid the axe head onto the block to measure the distance. With a deep breath, he drew the heavy blade up and back. Without hesitation, he stepped forward with a smooth and powerful stroke and brought the axe down onto the block. His mighty grunt and the impact coincided with a loud crack as the block split neatly in two. The crowd roared with approval.

Kendra smiled at Glen and nodded. The shamans retrieved the axe but left the split wood where it lay.

She waved the crowd to silence and bellowed, "Bring forth the Basket and Pillow!"

Glen breathed deeply. This was extremely difficult. The shamans brought forth a small basket that contained a small pillow and held forth the basket towards Glen who picked up the pillow with both hands and bowed. To Glen's amusement, the pillow had been scented with mint and cinnamon. The shamans retreated and placed the basket five meters distant and then backed away. Kendra nodded with a face of stone.

Glen breathed deeply, spread his legs and performed deep knee bends while swinging the pillow back and forth between his legs. Glen worked to pace his breathing to match the swinging pillow. Once he had the breathing perfectly in time with the swinging pillow, he let it fly with no spin or tumble. It landed perfectly in the basket with an audible plump. The crowd roared. Glen straightened up and breathed a sigh of relief.

Kendra smiled again and silenced the crowd.

She looked at Glen, smirked and barked, "Now the test of Endurance. Bring forth the Sand Glass."

The shamans brought forth a glass bottle filled with black sand and a special glass stopper. Then they brought forth a small table with a wooden stand for the Sand Glass. She took the glass and held it high so the crowd could see.

She projected her voice, "The Candidate needs to complete twenty-four laps of the circle before the sand runs out."

With that, she placed the glass on the stand angled down. Instantly, sand started to trickle. Glen wasted no time, sprinted to the edge of the stone circle and began a fast trot. Twenty-four laps was approximately 3800 meters. Under perfect conditions, he could easily run that in 7 minutes *[13 standard minutes]*. The Sand Glass was filled privately by the shaman leading the ceremony and so not necessarily a standard amount. In this case, he knew Kendra liked him and wanted him to succeed, but she also knew he was a very good athlete. The shaman would look foolish if he completed the run with too much sand to spare. He would have to really run rather than jog. But caked with oil and powder, he could easily overheat and so he had to keep his pace reasonable or risk heat exhaustion.

The crowd began a low sonorous chant in Archaic Zattan that was meant to give encouragement to someone attempting a difficult task. Glen maintained a heavy pant trying to move as much air in and out of his lungs as he could. After a couple of minutes, he could feel the sweat displacing the oil and powder in his hair and begin to run down into his eyes. The sting was almost unbearable and he had no way to relieve it. He mopped his forehead occasionally with his hands, but he was afraid that would just remove the powder there and allow the sweat a quicker run. Instead, he tried to shake his head every half lap to reduce the buildup. Barely able to see, he just kept running and running while losing complete track of how many laps he had completed.

Suddenly, Kendra shouted, "Done!"

The crowd roared approval.

Glen stopped, staggered around, shook his head, squeezed his eyes open and shut several times, and tried to find the Zatta Fenyal. Eventually, a shaman brought a wet rag that he used to clear his eyes. Despite labored breathing and nausea from the heat exhaustion, he gamely trotted over to Kendra and dropped to his knees in proper position.

She nodded and whispered, "Well done."

One of the shamans brought him a small jug of water that he gratefully accepted and quickly drained. The Zatta Fenyal turned to the crowd and chanted something soothing in Archaic Zattan he didn't recognize. The crowd joined in and the sound filled the valley for what seemed like several minutes. Finally, she waved the crowd to silence. His breathing was no longer labored and the nausea had dissipated.

She looked at him and said just loud enough for the crowd to hear, "We are nearly done. Do you still wish to endure Trakora Runk?"

Without hesitation, Glen said, "Yes, Zatta Fenyal. I wish to endure

Trakora Runk."

She nodded grimly and shouted, "The Candidate will endure Trakora Runk!"

The crowd remained silent except for a few mutterings of open disapproval.

The Zatta Fenyal walked to the altar and regarded the various jars. She sighed deeply and selected a glass one holding a luminescent blue liquid. She motioned to the shamans. They brought forth chains and leather cuffs. Then they prised up a stone slab in the center of the circle that revealed another stone with an inset that had been set with a heavy brass bolt and ring. Glen rose and approached the shamans as he had been instructed.

The shamans attached the leather cuffs to his wrists and ankles with bolts. Then they fed the chains through the rings on the cuffs and then bolted them to the heavy steel ring. Glen jerked on the chains to prove they were soundly attached. He hoped they would not be needed.

Kendra approached and whispered, "This is your last chance. Do you wish me to proceed?"

"Yes. Proceed."

She nodded and held the glass aloft and paraded around for everyone to see before returning. He breathed steadily. His father, a great warrior, had trained Glen constantly from a young age in the arts of combat, strategy, endurance and control. As he had been taught and diligently practiced, he opened his mind such that he would be completely in the zone where his mind enveloped his body and the external world. In that state, all stimuli and thought became subsumed in the seamless expanse of the Immediate where past and future cease to exist. In that zone, pain and other distractions were reduced to mere motes in the infinity.

The bottle touched his lips. He opened his mouth and swallowed rapidly as the airily sweet liquid poured. Kendra stepped back and stared with evident deep concern. Glen breathed deeply. The mixture blended into his existence and expanded until it stained the entirety of the Immediate. Glen retched involuntarily. Then everything exploded in purple flames.

The flames subsided just licking at the edges of infinity. Purple steam rose all around Glen and swirled upward. A dark purple goo began burbling up through the stone between Glen and the Zatta Fenyal. The bubbling goo slowly took shape into a giant human-like form. The Demon flexed its limbs as the bubbling slowed and stopped. It scowled at Glen and then bellowed. Kill THEM. Kill them ALL. They are laughing at your suffering. They should PAY. It raised its arms urging Glen to act.

Glen slowly looked around. The Zatta Fenyal and everyone else just stared watchfully at him oblivious to the Demon. Glen continued to breathe slowly still deep in the Immediate. But the Demon continued to bellow and taunt. No one else seemed to notice its existence. Eventually, the Zatta Fenyal stepped right through the Demon, approached Glen closely and whispered, "Glen. Are you alright?"

Hallucination. Mere hallucination. The Madness of the Trakora Runk. Madness... Ignore. Ignore... Dissolve. Dissipate... Clear. Clear... Empty the mind. Empty. Empty... Glen closed his eyes and willed the Demon into a cloud of wispy purple smoke as it wails faded into the night. "Fine. I'm fine."

She sighed in relief and spoke quietly, "Good. For a moment there, I thought you had been taken by the Trakora Runk Madness."

Glen dropped from the Immediate and looked around. He shook his head confidently, summoned what his father had told him about his own experience and spoke in a low voice, "No. The potion seemed to course through me and then expand outward, around and wrapped itself around me like a veil. Hopefully, that is the protection I was seeking."

She smiled, "Or you have a very active imagination."

Glen smiled back, "Or that. You are not a believer?"

She muttered, "Belief and imagination are not mutually exclusive."

Glen nodded and shook the chains.

The Zatta Fenyal motioned to the shamans who rushed over to remove the cuffs. Glen stepped aside, and the shamans replaced the stone and returned the chains to their supply chests. Glen knelt before the Zatta Fenyal. She raised her arms and paced back and forth a few times.

"It is done. Glenmorgan Nevercare. Welcome to adulthood."

The crowd roared approval.

Glen bowed his head in acknowledgment.

The Zatta Fenyal motioned for him to rise, smiled and whispered, "All done. Except for your bath."

While the shamans started cleaning up, she escorted him off the stone circle to a square platform where four servants waited with buckets of warm water, soap and washing rags. Twenty minutes of hard scrubbing were required to cleanse the oil and powders from his exhausted body. They toweled him dry, and he was given back his clothing. Glen reflected for a moment in amusement that unlike many tribes, the Zattan didn't use any visible symbols of his transition to adulthood. No tattoos. No scars. No jewelry. No special clothing. It would simply be known by those in attendance and recorded in the official Zattan records. Claiming Zattan citizenship without being in the official records was punished with a brutal public execution, so it wasn't really an issue.

By the time he was cleaned and dressed, everyone had left the Circle to engage in the traditional, post-ceremony celebratory feasting and drinking at their tents scattered on the other end of the valley. Glenmorgan could hear music, singing and a cacophony of feasting noises. The Zatta Fenyal had already cleaned up and left. Per custom, the shamans hurried off leaving Glenmorgan alone with his thoughts and the Circle.

Glen walked to the center and looked around. He sighed and deepened his breathing. Having not actually considered the moment before, he suddenly wondered what others had thought during this special time alone. *Feelings of relief? Triumph? Daunted by the prospect of a lifetime of adult responsibilities? Freedom? The ability to create a family? Wondering what other people think at such times?*

Glen laughed to himself - not likely the last one.

Glen continued to scan the valley. The bonfire had been timed to burn out by the end of the ceremony and was now reduced to mere spluttering embers. Other than that, there was nothing but the summer breeze and gently swaying trees. He was alone, unless, of course, an assassin lurked in the shadows. Glen laughed at that. Instead of triumphant thoughts, he turned his mind to assassination.

At his father's insistence, Glen had thoroughly studied the theory and practice of Zattan assassinations. Subconsciously, he would assess the potential for an assassination attempt wherever he might be. He called his current assessment into conscious thought for deeper consideration. The post-ceremony alone time would, on the surface, seem like a perfect time to effect an assassination of a very unwary target still basking in the glow of the elevation to adulthood.

Admittedly, the valley had undergone the usual security sweep and had a standard security cordon, but virtually any Zattan adult citizen could attend the ceremony. An assassin could use the chaotic flow to the celebratory gatherings to steal away from the crowd to effect a murder that likely would go undiscovered a sufficient time for the assassin to blend back into the celebrations and avoid suspicion.

But finding a Zattan assassin to murder a teenager on sacred ground during a sacred ceremony was probably impossible and a non-Zattan would never be allowed near the place. And he didn't know of a single instance across the centuries. With that, Glen dismissed the thought but looked around wondering if his father had stationed hidden guards anyway in clear violation of tradition. Glen snarled, his father always visibly showed strict adherence to Zattan traditions but would often violate the most scared of them covertly for the slightest advantage. Glen hated that style of thinking.

There was a sudden shout back behind him. Glen turned into a defensive crouch.

From the edge of the Circle, the purple Demon charged at him, lunging to and fro, fists clenched. Glen planned to dive away from the attack, but when the Demon neared attack range, it did a handspring and vaulted high above and over Glen's head.

Incredulous, Glen straightened up and turned to face the Demon.

The Demon twisted mid-air and landed solidly on its feet facing Glen bellowing with laughter. Now! Now is the time... They will be drunk and in high spirits. You can kill them easily like wheat before a scythe.

Glen spat, "I will not. Find another to haunt."

The Demon laughed and laughed. I am born of your mind. I am forever chained to you. Accept and be guided for I can see far.

Glen summoned the Immediate to clear his mind and banish the Demon.

But the Demon simply stood and smiled wryly while wispy purple steam slowly rose from its limbs and head. I am the Immediate. Just kill them and all will be calm and peaceful. You'll see.

Glen took a deep breath and then cleared his mind with a tornado that swept away the Demon whose howls of laughter faded into the night. Glen dropped to his knees and rubbed his face. He clenched his fists and rose slowly while releasing them. He let his anger flow out through his fingertips as he stood.

Glen looked around grimly once more. It was the Madness. There was just no other explanation. The Madness of Trakora Runk was irresistible. The records were unequivocal. No one who exhibited the signs lasted very long before suicide or murder took them. He was now doomed to a short and inglorious life. Ambition had destroyed him even before he had gotten started.

Glen closed his eyes. He should probably just kill himself now and save himself the suffering. He snarled. Maybe he should go on a killing spree of his enemies before being killed in some epic fight. He sighed. He had no real, personal enemies. That would be madness. He sighed. He could go on a suicide mission to slay Puck or some other infamous person. That would at least be glorious in failure and productive in success even if the end would be the same for Glen. He sighed.

Glen opened his eyes and looked at the hazy summer night sky. The smoke had largely cleared and the stars were visible again. The scattered moons and dying fire sketched a weird pattern of his shadows on the stone. For a long time, he marveled at the pattern and wondered for how much longer he would have time for quiet contemplation of the wonders of living.

Finally, he took a deep breath. He was now Glenmorgan Nevercare. He would not give up so easily. Maybe others had survived by controlling and hiding the Madness. If anyone could, he could. He could channel the urge to kill towards those who would thwart or hinder his path to fame and glory. That was the way of a Zattan Royal as his father had taught him.

There was no doubt that his path to fame and glory had become more difficult. But he had no choice but to find a way to tame the Madness. He would need all his talents and skills to find that way.

A Crossing of Plans

Mallory intently observed the two dozen mounted troopers moving cautiously up the road below them for ten minutes through his detached rifle scope before sitting up in surprise. He turned to Entreska and Tamara and said, "Those appear to be Jurasketu."

He handed the scope to Tamara who immediately identified them as an element of the Swamp Rats. Murmurs of surprise and excitement filled the whole of their little troop. Mallory nodded to Tamara who headed down on foot to greet the advancing Jurasketu troopers. Mallory snapped the scope back on his rifle and watched warily, rifle ready, as Tamara approached the troopers who had halted and assumed a defensive formation.

The patrol leader, a stocky, balding man, showed mild surprise and excitement when Tamara pointed to herself and up the hill where they were hiding. Mallory couldn't see what she said, but he saw the patrol leader frown, shake his head negatively and then apologize. Tamara became agitated at his response and started yelling at him. Though obviously pained and continuing to apologize, he kept firmly refusing to do something Tamara wanted. Finally, she flung her arms up in frustration, turned and gave the signal for Mallory, Entreska and her troop to emerge from hiding.

When they reached Tamara who stood hands on hips facing them, she said, "Master Troop Leader Secret Mission Warwick won't tell me what he's doing here. And he insists they must finish their patrol up to that ridge..." She paused to point and then continued, "...despite the fact I told him we just came from there and we saw no Immortals or Cumar, alive or dead. Then and only then, they can escort us to their Troop Force headquarters where he thinks his dear Major might tell us what's going on."

Warwick shifted uncomfortably in his saddle. The two groups of soldiers tried to hide their amusement.

Mallory laughed softly. "I guess we'll just have to wait then."

Tamara turned and shooed Warwick on his way. Warwick waved his troopers forward.

The Black Scorpions murmured amongst themselves obviously speculating on the presence of the Swamp Rats. Mallory refused to discuss it saying only that they would know in good order and that they should rest for now.

An hour later, the Swamp Rats returned. Four hours later heading into dusk they arrived at the extremely well kept Troop Force command tent to meet with Major Kyle Young. The Major was a robust, tall and handsome man in his late thirties with short, sandy hair, exotic green eyes and an infectious smile that spread across his lean, smooth face. He stood, hands clasped behind his back, eyeing them carefully.

When Warwick realized that Mallory and Entreska had entered with Tamara, his face registered surprise and he just stood pointing at them. After an awkward silence punctuated by the slight rustling of the evening breeze against the tent, Major Young cocked an eyebrow and said, "Yes, Warwick?"

Warwick recovered from his shock at the breech in etiquette, and saluted, "Sir. This is Captain Tamara Tallrider of the Black Scorpions. I don't know who these other two are. She refused to reveal anything beyond her name and Command Token."

Young smiled and spoke in a polite, yet booming voice, "Captain. I am Major Kyle Young, and this is my chief aide, Lieutenant Resluck." He pointed to a dark haired, dark eyed, sharp featured man who wore an unchanging sullen expression, standing behind the map table. Resluck did nothing to acknowledge the introduction.

Young continued, "Captain Tallrider. Due to the sensitive nature of the current tactical situation, I'll need more proof beyond your Command Token that you demonstrated to Warwick. Cipher Verification is necessary."

Tamara sighed and nodded, "Very well. If we must. Since you are the host, I must verify your identity first."

Young nodded curtly, "Naturally."

Mallory was intrigued and very surprised. He watched intently as Tamara reached under her shirt and pulled out a small, thick book no bigger than her palm. She then flipped along in the book for about a minute.

Tamara asked, "Identity?"

Young replied, "D - F - 3 - 4 - 1 - 5 - 6 - 6 - 4 - 9 - 8 - 7."

Tamara nodded, "Right." Then, she pulled forth a numbered die, cast it and wrote down the result. She repeated this 10 times. She then handed the result to Young.

Young smiled, then sat down with pencil and paper and made a set of calculations that took him nearly five minutes. Then he wrote the answer on a clean piece of paper and handed it to Tamara along with the pencil. Then he burned the papers he had used to make the calculations. Tamara sat cross-legged on the ground, made some calculations on her paper and nodded when they were complete.

"Verified."

Mallory was stunned. They appeared to be using an asymmetric cipher to prove identity. He guessed that each officer memorized their private key and the small books that they carried held a serial number associated with a name and the corresponding public key. Once he established the complexity, the remarkable speed and validity of the verification algorithm they were using he likely would have a vital clue concerning the planet's puzzling history.

Then, Tamara encoded a random list of numbers chosen by Young using his own numbered die. Young successfully decoded it some minutes later thereby proving to him that she was indeed Captain Tallrider. Mallory and Entreska had remained standing in silence for the full fifteen minutes the verification procedure had taken.

Young spoke smoothly, "Sorry about the delay. I have responsibility for this district, so now I must ask you to report your mission and plans. And please explain your companions."

Tamara glanced at Mallory, who nodded slightly, "Major. I command a detachment of the Black Scorpions operating in a sensitive area of Wokometu. I have crossed the Bay of Lydaron and come here at the behest of my companions. We didn't expect to find Jurasketu troops in this area and so our mission may in fact change depending upon what you tell us."

Young did not miss the fact that Tamara had seemed to defer to Mallory. The major narrowed his eyes and glared at Mallory, "Who are you?"

Mallory smiled warmly and instead of instinctively giving a false name said, "I am Colonel Mallory Owens."

Young frowned with a distinctly puzzled expression and replied, "Colonel? I do not recognize the name. What army has your loyalty?"

Mallory chuckled, "You perceive correctly, I am not Jurasketu. Sadly, my former army is no more and hence my rank is reduced to nothing more than an honorific. However, Entreska Nevercare is my great friend, and hence I am a firm ally of Jurasketu."

"What? Entreska Nevercare is your friend?"

Entreska spoke firmly, "Yes. He is my friend. A great friend indeed. And he has saved my life more than once."

Young stared at her and stammered, "Entreska Nevercare? As in, the daughter of the Grand Marshal?"

Tamara, Mallory and Entreska all nodded immediately in agreement.

"Then, why have you painted yourself like that?"

Entreska fumed, "It's not paint, dammit. And I didn't do it myself."

"Sorry. No offense meant. How did you get to the other side of the Bay of Lydaron?"

Entreska frowned, "The usual way - by ship."

"I mean, why?"

"Colonel Owens needed to obtain some things we needed."

Young sighed deciding that his line of questioning was going nowhere and turned to Tamara, "Captain Tallrider. What are your present plans?"

To Young's obvious dislike, she glanced at Mallory who again nodded slightly and then she replied, "We plan to visit an end to Pachinko Puck."

Young raised an eyebrow, "Well, you'll need to hurry along if you want to beat the Grand Marshal to that happy goal."

Mallory, Entreska and Tamara in unison cried, "What?"

Young smiled, "The Grand Marshal with an army of more than a dozen regiments took most of Puck's capital about five days ago, and is besieging Puck's fortress atop the Centaur Citadel. The Swamp Rats are protecting the southern flank. Some Mountaineer regulars protect the northern flank. Puck's Army never expected the massive counterattack that the Grand Marshal mounted in response to the attack on Entreska's expedition...." Young trailed off in sudden sadness.

Entreska sighed heavily and asked tentatively, "Major. Were there any survivors?"

Young grimaced, "Last I heard 23 Black Scorpions and two students. And, as we now know, yourself. There might be a few others who have or will turn up. We know several were captured by the Cumar and later killed when the Cumar themselves were destroyed.

Most of the Black Scorpions including Colonel Jones fought to the death near Duravon. We have located most of the bodies of the students and workers in the Lower Raffin. We may never find them all."

Entreska and Tamara clearly struggled with their emotions. Mallory remained stoic and tried to brighten things by saying, "At least they have not died in vain. Maybe we will be able to honor them as the last victims of Puck's evil reign."

Everyone nodded.

Young continued for a good hour explaining in exhausting detail how the campaign had unfolded until now. Mallory, Tamara and Entreska occasionally interrupted with questions especially when they learned Rolf had led a troop force of the Dawn Spiders during the campaign. Entreska explained the movements of the students and Black Scorpions before their demise. And then she explained her rescue and escape to Wokometu without mentioning that she and Mallory had met before he rescued her from the Cumar. Additionally, Mallory, Tamara and Entreska had agreed upon a false and vague cover story for the events in Wokometu and forestalled any press for details by saying that they couldn't give any further details because of the sensitive nature of the detachment's mission.

Young concluded the explanation with, "So, Captain Tallrider. What are your plans now?"

Again, to Young's obvious annoyance, Tamara glanced at Mallory, who tilted his head. Then, she stated flatly, "They are unchanged. We will ride to the Citadel and assist the Grand Marshal in concluding Puck's end and join the celebration if that is already achieved."

Mallory and Entreska nodded firmly in agreement.

Young arched his eyebrows, frowned and nodded. "Very well." Then he turned to Entreska, "Um... Do you realize that everyone thinks you are, well, dead?"

Entreska nodded grimly, "That is likely."

"Should I forward this news to your father by messenger? It will likely take four days for you to reach the Citadel. I can get a message there by lunch time tomorrow if you like."

Entreska hesitated a moment and then said, "No. Let me surprise my father in that."

Young nodded with a half-smile, "Very well."

They took dinner in the Command Tent.

Mallory thought carefully about all the things that Craig

Henderson had told him about Puck and thought that the Grand Marshal must be a mighty general indeed. Mallory had some nagging doubts, though. Mallory had used Henderson's information to carefully scout the Citadel and had mapped the eleven secret escape routes from the fortress. He knew that there were no others.

He wondered if the Grand Marshal would place sufficient precautionary guards to counter that obvious likelihood - even if the Jurasketu did not know their exact locations. He wanted to relay the exact locations of the exits to the Grand Marshal. But he was afraid. If the Grand Marshal had already gathered that intelligence through other sources, then the exits would already be covered and patrols mounted against unknown but likely exits. And so Mallory need not tell him. If the Grand Marshal did not have that information, then it would be extremely suspicious for Mallory to have it - especially in such detail.

They covered the remaining 150 kilometers to the Citadel in four long days that grew increasingly colder as they moved north and achieved greater altitude. They topped the southern end of the horseshoe ridge that surrounds the Citadel and worked their way along the ridge until they reached the heights above the Citadel proper. The Jurasketu Army apparently occupied the entirety of the ridge and most of the city below. Using his scope and naked eyes, Mallory carefully observed the terrain.

The Fortress entirely covered a crag that jutted out from the base of the horseshoe ridge approximately centered between the wings of the ridge. The top of the crag was only half the height of the horseshoe ridge, but the western, northern, and southern edges were sheer granite rising 400 meters from the valley floor. The crag top ran 500 meters west to east and between 40 and 60 meters north to south depending on the section. The negotiable eastern edge was connected to the horseshoe by a narrow, sheer-sided descending ridge line that dropped sharply down to the base of the horseshoe. A narrow, winding road paved with stone and lined with protective stone walls provided the only access from the valley to the crag. An imposing gatehouse 20 meters high and four gleaming square towers all over 30 meters high defined the narrow crag. Ten-meter high double walls connected the towers. They had arrived near lunchtime and so the noonday sun reflected off the pearly white walls of the towers. Banners of purple and gold snapped and rippled in the stiff breeze atop the towers.

Several smaller gatehouses and Imperial buildings were scattered along the crag anchored by another massive gatehouse 25 meters high and 70 meters long that guarded the base of the crag. Barracks, warehouses, markets, imposing Imperial buildings and palatial mansions were ensconced into the mountainside. A huge plume of black smoke billowed from the front of the massive gatehouse and covered the top of the northeastern ridge in dense smoke.

The once gleaming white buildings of the city were now smudged with black and gray. Hasty barricades had been thrown up in the streets using furniture, logs and stones. Several buildings were burning. The unclaimed frozen corpses of Immortals and Cumar lay scattered in the streets and on the rooftops. Mallory reasoned that the Jurasketu Army had taken the city by storm before an effective defense had been mounted and were now stymied by the defenders of the Fortress on the crag. He would soon break the stalemate.

They were escorted to the Army Command tents. Messengers seemed to be constantly running hither and thither. A verbal altercation occurred between their escort and the Command tent guards. The shouting did not cease until a large man wearing a distinctive beret came out and demanded an explanation. Entreska, who had pulled her fur-lined cloak down around her face to avoid questions and stares, shouted, "ROLF!"

Rolf turned to look for the source of the familiar voice.

Entreska, who was standing next to Mallory, threw back her hood. "Rolf. It is me, Entreska."

Rolf edged forward trying to decide what he was seeing and then he bounded forward to embrace Entreska. Then he stepped back, "Why have you painted your face like that?"

Entreska said, "Never mind that. What are you doing here?"

Rolf sighed heavily. "Right now. Wishing I wasn't. Please come inside with me and I'll explain. I'm more than a little curious how you survived I might say."

Rolf gazed over her escort, stopped briefly on Mallory, and barked when he saw Tamara, "Captain Tallrider!" He paused in thought and then continued, "Shouldn't you be across the Bay of Lydaron?"

Tamara smiled, "Events have carried me to this side I'm afraid."

Rolf nodded grimly, "You should join us as well."

Tamara and Entreska both pointed to Mallory. "You'll want him too."

Mallory smiled and nodded when Rolf turned to apprise him

once again. Rolf put his hands on his hips and said, "Who are you?"

Entreska spoke first, "He is the reason I survived. And he's also the reason we're here now. His name is Colonel Mallory Owens. We need to speak to Father immediately."

Without taking his eyes off Mallory, he said, "That's a bit of a problem just now, that's one of the things I need to explain."

Entreska's expression of wonder changed instantly to one of deep worry, "Why? What's happened? Is Father all right?"

Rolf motioned stiffly towards the tent from which he had emerged, "I'll explain in there. Captain Tallrider and Colonel Owens may join us."

The Command tent guards seemed somewhat nonplussed by the latest developments and seemed to only grudgingly stand aside. Tamara ordered the Black Scorpions to locate warm shelter, stow their gear and find food. Rolf ordered the guards to hold messengers and visitors until further notice.

Inside the tent, Rolf indicated five folding chairs arrayed haphazardly against the side of the tent where they could sit. A large table piled up with maps and documents occupied a third of the tent. Three gray-haired, thin, haggard-looking senior officers stood peering at the maps and documents. Rolf introduced them as Marshal Tang, General Urkiza and Colonel Humble. They nodded politely but otherwise said nothing and resumed studying the maps, pointing and whispering. After Mallory, Entreska and Tamara were seated, Rolf talked privately with Marshal Tang for a few minutes after which Tang grunted and returned to the maps.

Rolf sighed and spoke quietly but firmly, "Yesterday morning, the Immortals General Walton emerged from the Fortress claiming that Puck was dead and they wished to surrender if the Grand Marshal would allow them to go free. The Grand Marshal certainly didn't want to lose anyone taking the Fortress, so he readily agreed. Naturally, we were suspicious of a ruse, and we insisted that the Immortals abandon the Fortress and bring out Puck's body. General Walton agreed without hesitation and returned to the Fortress. An hour later nearly a thousand Immortals marched out bearing a body on a litter.

"Until we identified the body and searched the Fortress, we put the Immortals with our other prisoners, mostly other Immortals and a few wounded Cumar. The body matched what little we knew of Puck's appearance but it was hardly definitive, so we decided that a thorough search of the Fortress would provide a little more certainty.

"Marshal Juragi insisted that he would lead the search personally and make sure no traps or other nasty surprises had been left behind by Puck and the Immortals. He took six full Troops of the Swamp Rats up the crag to the Fortress. They advanced cautiously up the crag, deploying a Flight or two to man every defensive point. This meant they reached the Fortress proper with only four Troops. Then they went inside. About an hour later, Juragi himself returned saying everything was clear and safe and that the Grand Marshal should come inspect it for himself.

"The Grand Marshal, ever suspicious, told me to stay here and assume command while he and Juragi continued to poke about the Fortress. They then went back up to the Fortress. About two hours later a messenger comes to my tent bringing a message from the Grand Marshal asking the senior officers and myself to join him for a toast to our victory in Puck's so called Hall of Reverence."

Rolf paused dramatically and said, "But the Grand Marshal had told me explicitly and privately that under no circumstances must I personally enter the Fortress in the event a trap or surprise went undetected. My father would never forget having said that. So I indicated very well and that we would be along within the hour and the messenger departed. I told the senior officers that trouble was afoot and to be aware the possibility that Marshal Juragi was a traitor and the Grand Marshal had been taken prisoner by a not-so-dead Puck. And then we waited. After the hour passed, a different messenger arrived with a message supposedly from the Grand Marshal expressing the Grand Marshal's anger at having his orders ignored and demanded we follow the previous instructions immediately. I detained that messenger. And then waited some more."

Rolf stopped to take a draft of Tarfun Stone Brew.

"I doubled the guard over the Immortal prisoners and ordered all regiments to full alert. I had already ordered elements of a heavy regiment to occupy the lower gatehouse prepared for anything. Within the hour, the Fortress gates closed and Immortals emerged from secret tunnels all along the crag. A number of Swamp Rats were killed or captured. Forty escaped back to the lower gatehouse. Several hidden incendiaries at the lower gatehouse exploded not long after the Swamp Rats were attacked setting it ablaze as you can see and we had to abandon it. That is the current situation."

Tamara and Entreska were clearly stunned and distressed by the news. Mallory meanwhile was frightened by the shocking treachery of a senior Jurasketu officer. Henderson had claimed that Puck could control a person's mind through sorcery. Mallory hadn't believed him, of course, but now he wasn't so certain. It seemed to be a terrible coincidence.

A brief smile crossed Mallory's face as he reminded himself that the armored helmet he had brought was supposed to block or cancel certain quantum mechanical effects that theoretically could be used to influence or read his thoughts despite no one ever having demonstrated a working device capable of doing anything of the sort. He had always considered that to be typical military specification overkill. But now he wasn't so certain. In any event, this complication would make killing Puck much trickier, if in effect, he had to rescue Entreska's father and dozens of Jurasketu soldiery, too.

Mallory's original plan, before ending up at Duravon, had been deceptively simple. He would have attacked on a dark night. He would have donned his special electro-gel body armor and helmet that makes him virtually invulnerable to attack. He would have killed anyone who crossed his path and blasted any obstacle away with bullets, grenades or demolition charges. He also had brought non-lethal NK gas to incapacitate large troop concentrations and very effectively guard his rear as he fought his way up and through Puck's fortress. He didn't really expect to kill Puck directly. Not that he wouldn't given the chance, but he expected Puck to flee in the face of his ferocious and unstoppable assault. Puck would use one of his secret exits and blunder straight into the multi-layered demolition charges Mallory would have positioned at each of the escape holes and could remotely monitor to make sure Puck was indeed blasted into oblivion.

The carnage would likely have been immense, but Mallory could muster little sympathy for Puck's soldiers. The slaves in the fortress were another matter. The simple and safest tactic would be to kill anyone and everyone along the way - no telling which slave would be driven to try and impede his way leading to unforeseen disaster. He would have felt pity for them. He always did for both the innocent and the guilty that ended up as casualties, but mission success and more importantly, his own survival was paramount.

A year ago, that's exactly what he would have done without a second thought. But now he wouldn't be answering to just himself or the laughter of General Lang, he had to answer to Entreska and her reasoning on the matter. Her logic had been unassailable, either he was of good character or he wasn't. The question was - did he care. Certainly, he cared that she cared about it. He wanted her to judge him to have good character; otherwise, she would not love him. He wanted her love. But she could only judge his words and deeds, not his actual thinking. What if he simply acted in ways that represented good character for purely utilitarian reasons - at least while anyone was watching? Would that be good enough? It seemed like a lie, even treachery. But then if he wasn't of good character that shouldn't bother him, should it? Of course, if one cannot be of good character, why bother with the pretense? Freedom lies in the exercise of one's true character, however muddled or pure.

Entreska nudged Mallory, "What are your plans now?"

Mallory whispered back, "Unchanged. Puck must die. Your father's efforts have become tangled, so I must step to the fore and effect the necessary events."

Entreska narrowed her eyes, "How exactly? You promised to explain in detail when we got to the Citadel. Well, we're here."

Mallory whispered, "Can we trust your brother and his aides?"

Entreska frowned and motioned to Rolf who leaned in close. Entreska whispered something in his ear. Rolf scowled, straightened up and looked back at the staff table where Tang, Urkiza and Humble had stopped whispering and now stared at Rolf, "I need ten minutes alone with my sister and her companions please."

Tang suppressed a snarl, shrugged and left the tent smartly followed by the Urkiza and Humble who did not look back.

Entreska turned to Mallory, "Explain your plan."

Rolf, Tamara and Entreska stared intently at Mallory who managed a faint smile.

"I'm going to kill Puck and hopefully rescue the Grand Marshal and the other prisoners."

Rolf stifled a laugh into, "Bwa... how exactly do you plan to accomplish that?"

"With some planning, skill, guts and an enormous advantage of technology. I'm almost certain of killing Puck. Rescuing your father and the others is much trickier. Puck may order them killed before I reach them. He may have already killed them. I will need some assistance to effect the plan rapidly. We need to do some preliminaries tonight under cover of darkness. Then I can mount my assault tomorrow night."

Rolf gaped, "Alone? In the dark?"

"Yes."

If it weren't for the nods of agreement by Tamara and Entreska, Mallory was sure Rolf definitely would have burst out laughing at that answer.

"How can you do that? Are you a sorcerer?"

"Not sorcery. Better weapons and armor than anyone would imagine possible. My P24 Electro-gel Body Armor and J7C Battle Helmet are virtually invulnerable to even most of my own weapons - never mind the primitive sorts used by Puck's soldiers. And my weapons will destroy any barrier and will incapacitate anyone who dares to get in my way."

Tamara said, "P24 what?"

Mallory smiled, "You would like it. It's wicked stuff. It is several layers of a special gel between fabric. Essentially the armor is soft and flexible until a blow or missile hits the outer layer when it instantaneously crystallizes to dissipate and deflect the attack. The crystallization is localized and temporary allowing the wearer to move with great freedom and safety even under a hail of blows. It's not foolproof against everything. But it is damn amazing stuff."

Tamara nodded dreamily clearly gathering the moving freely and safely bit if not the other details.

Entreska was grim, however, and said, "Incapacitate? You mean kill, do you not?"

Mallory frowned, "Actually, I was planning to use a non-lethal poison gas to render Puck's soldiers unable to fight. So, except when I need to blast through doors and walls, few will die I would hope."

Entreska sighed heavily. Mallory did not take this as a good sign. She had said clearly she could not love him if he killed. But she had to be torn. She wanted Puck's reign of terror to end. And worse, her father was Puck's prisoner. She lowered her eyes and nodded her understanding.

Rolf frowned showing numerous creases across his forehead, "What weapons and armor? You seem to be under equipped at the moment."

"Tamara's Black Scorpions who accompanied me across Lydaron have graciously carried my equipment, weapons and ammunition for me."

Rolf cast a sidelong glance at Tamara, "Really?"

Tamara shrugged, "Five pack horses worth of stuff."

Mallory sensing the wrong kind of interest from Rolf added, "Only I can work the weapons, however."

Rolf narrowed his eyes, "I see."

There was a commotion outside the tent. Rolf barked in anger and strode to the tent flap. He disappeared outside. The shouting stopped and then a man wearing a fur cloak stepped in closely followed by Rolf. Entreska snapped out of her grim countenance and jumped to her feet to meet the man with a hug shouting, "Zeke!" while he shouted "Tresh!"

Zemfrekis stepped back and regarded her a moment then turned to Tamara and said, "I ran into your troopers Captain Tallrider, and they told me you had brought Entreska back from Wokometu with them. And so I came here as fast as I could."

Tamara saluted smartly in response.

Zemfrekis regarded Entreska for a moment, "Why–"

"It's not paint. And it wasn't my doing."

Zemfrekis nodded and said, "Right. How did you get to Wokometu? We thought you were dead. We found Riska's locket on a Priestess of the Valperium on the High Raffin. She and the rest of her six dozen Cumar comrades had been slaughtered in a most mysterious fashion."

Entreska frowned and pointed at Mallory, "Colonel Owens rescued me from those very Cumar. He killed them."

Zemfrekis gaped and stared at Mallory, "What do you mean? By his lonesome? How?"

Rolf asked, "I'm guessing using weapons and armor unimaginable to us?"

Zemfrekis gave Rolf a puzzled look.

Mallory chuckled, "Actually. I only had my rifle. But they couldn't see me coming in the dark and I don't miss at close range very often."

Zemfrekis puzzled look changed to one of realization then back to puzzled, "Who are you? And what the Great Burning Blast is a 'rifle'?"

"I am Colonel Mallory Owens. But my army is no more. I have transferred my loyalties to Jurasketu because of my friendship with Entreska and concordance with its ideals of liberty."

Rolf and Zemfrekis stared at Entreska who muttered, "He talks like a Debater. But what he says is true."

Mallory continued, "And a rifle is a very handy missile weapon. And I have tools to see in the dark."

Tamara went to fetch some of Mallory's equipment and weapons so he could show Rolf and Zemfrekis. Entreska explained, once more, the sad fate of her expedition, her rescue by Mallory and journey across the Lydaron and back. She also maintained the fiction that her first contact with Mallory had been the rescue. Her explanation that Mallory had come from the stars and crash landed here by mistake was met with total bewilderment by Rolf and Zemfrekis. When Mallory tried to explain further, they just shook their heads in disbelief.

Rolf summoned Tang, Urkiza and Humble back to listen to Mallory's plan to kill Puck and rescue the Grand Marshal. Mallory had not protested knowing that his otherworldly origins would not stay concealed for long. Already over a hundred members of the Jurasketu Army knew. After he killed Puck in the manner outlined in his plan, he would be very uncomfortably famous. He would have great difficulty disguising his appearance not to be recognized for good and for ill. There would be many who would want to use him for good and for evil. The enemies of Jurasketu would be expected to try desperately to kill him. The friends of Jurasketu would be angry because they would expect him to solve all their problems and naturally, he would be unable to do so. Others would fear him and want him controlled or killed. He would be a hunted man. A dangerous and very deadly hunted man, but hunted nonetheless.

Mallory took a nap to prepare for the evening work of booby-trapping all of Puck's escape holes. Although completely exhausted, Mallory insisted on setting powerful demolition charges at the still blazing lower gatehouse before taking his rest. He slept for most of the day in a tent procured for him and his equipment.

Contingency Plans

Entreska put her hand on Tamara's shoulder and asked, "How is it going?"

Tamara nodded behind the Darkglasses, "Pretty good. Our troops have moved into the Second Tower. The Third Tower is finally clear. He's about to attack the Fourth Tower. No action at any of the escape holes."

Entreska frowned, "Could Mallory have missed one?"

Tamara shrugged, "I don't know. He seemed pretty confident."

An explosion flared in the Darkglasses partially visible to Entreska. Tamara had the Darkglasses on full speaker so Entreska could hear the explosions, clatter of arrows and gunfire.

Entreska turned away and went to select a pretzel to gnaw on. She couldn't bear it. The whole spectacle was very distressing.

Mallory's voice blared out, "Dammit."

Entreska cringed.

Gunfire barked.

Tamara muttered, "Blast. No. Run."

Then Tamara jumped up and cried out in horror. She took off the Darkglasses and covered her face.

Entreska screamed, "What? What has happened?"

Tamara turned, waving the Darkglasses, and whispered, "He fell. He fell off the wall."

Entreska covered her mouth. Then steeling herself asked, "Is he still alive?"

Tamara regained her composure, put the Darkglasses back on, tapped the frames a couple of times, rubbed her face in concentration, and finally said, "I don't know. The signal appears to be lost. That doesn't mean anything. We lost the signal each time he went into the basements of the towers. So..."

Entreska slumped to the floor.

Meanwhile, Tamara summoned Zemfrekis from the nearby

command tent and informed him of the latest developments. Zemfrekis gave Entreska a sorrowful look and left the tent at full speed. Tamara continued to stare into the Darkglasses without saying anything further to Entreska.

She had not been to the Wizards' Tea Room nor Vorkfest since the horrific killings ten days ago of Zelda and Daryl – however temporary that might be. In fact, she had ignored virtually everything the Wizards said/thought/felt to her. She curtly thanked them for the periodic tactical updates of human presences near and far but otherwise made no response to their entreaties.

She couldn't realistically ignore them forever anyway, her needs were direct and the moment approached desperation.

"Can you find him?"

The Voice replied calmly, "We are searching already, but the search is necessarily indirect. Once he put on his war helmet, his mind totally vanished from our view."

"J7C Battle Helmet."

The Voice spoke in a slow, measured tone, "Entreska. Rolf's troops might be vulnerable to Puck's powers. And so we fear they will not be able to complete the task of killing Puck if they approach too close."

"What about the contingency plans that Rolf and Mallory concocted?"

The Voice admonished, "Well, they don't ensure Puck's death, and they almost certify that your father and the other prisoners will die. And Owens if he's still alive."

Entreska sighed.

The Voice continued, "Yet, Owens and Rolf have given us an opportunity that is unlikely to arise again."

"And that opportunity would be?"

"The opportunity to approach within a hundred meters of Puck. He would then be within range of sorcery powerful enough to subdue or kill him."

"You can take him at that range? I thought you said your powers were limited and that he was sufficiently powerful enough to deflect your attacks."

"That is still true."

Entreska's mind flooded with bafflement. A weird feeling of grim amusement penetrated the bafflement and sloshed here and there.

"I don't understand."

"If you were to allow us to assume control of your mind, we could wield our full powers through you. Puck would be little match for our skill and power."

"How is that possible?"

The Voice chuckled, "You allow our thoughts to become yours. And they will. And then we'll be you with our skill and experience wielding the considerable might of Evermore."

"And after you take down Puck? Then what?"

"We relinquish control. And your thoughts are your own again."

"Will I remember everything that happens?"

"Most definitely. I daresay the experience may be somewhat disconcerting. And so this is not a path you should choose lightly. But the need is great. The opportunity may not arise again anytime soon and so many will suffer and die if Puck cannot be stopped."

Then she heard Heather's voice but only briefly. And then an unintelligible argument punctuated with growls and shouts filled her head. Entreska definitely found *that* disconcerting.

"Stop it. Stop it. I command you to stop."

The shouting and arguing continued...

Entreska sucked in her breath, focused her mind and thought hard. *Silence!* This time Entreska felt the power of her command flow throughout the Essence bound to her body. And silence ensued.

She sighed. *"That's better. Now, I want to hear what Heather has to say. So she will speak and no others."*

Heather spoke with a trace of amusement, "Excellent. You are a natural. Can you join me in Vorkfest for a brief and private conversation?"

Entreska didn't hesitate. *"Certainly. The Council will please excuse me. Silence is lifted the moment I enter Vorkfest."*

She instantly and smoothly projected herself into Vorkfest.

The sky of Vorkfest was a collision of pink and yellow with streaks of each color penetrating deep into the other's territory. A pungent, warm wind billowed over the endless field of purple and white flowers. Entreska stretched her leathery wings and immediately took flight soaring high above the field scouting for Heather. Entreska spotted Heather's standard off to her left, so she circled and made an effortless descent towards the simple wooden platform Heather called home.

Heather sat on a pillow sipping wine from a cup and eating cheese with hard biscuits from a low wooden table. Heather smiled as Entreska approached and landed gently on the table. Although Entreska could actually assume any form she wanted, she liked the faerie from her first visit to Vorkfest. She absolutely loved flying. The original faerie was uncomfortably small, though, so she had increased her height to 25 cm in this incarnation. Heather offered her a bit of cheese, which Entreska tasted and then ate finding the flavor mildly tangy.

Entreska asked, "Do you even need to eat?"

Heather laughed, "No. Not at all. But I find the sensation pleasant, so I do. And no, the wine is not intoxicating either. Quite annoying really. Can't be intoxicated. The endless sameness can be difficult sometimes. It's a wonder the Council and I are still relatively sane."

Entreska raised an eyebrow, the green one.

Heather rubbed her jaw and muttered, "Well, we seem relatively sane anyway..."

"The Council claims they can subdue or kill Puck and rescue my father and the other prisoners. I only have to temporarily surrender to their will. Is this what you warned me about? And that I shouldn't let them."

Heather sighed, "Yes."

Entreska waited for Heather to continue, but she did not, so Entreska asked, "Would that really work? I mean could they really subdue Puck that way?"

Heather nodded, "Definitely. They would squash Puck like a bug even if his strength and skill were double that of the greatest wizards who ever lived. Evermore wielded by any single member of the Council would have incredible reach and irresistible power."

Entreska nodded in resignation. Then she asked, "Is what you said before true?"

Heather sipped her wine, "True? Which part?"

"The part where once I gave them access, I wouldn't be able to prevent them from asserting control the next time they wanted it."

Heather nodded, "While it is possible you might be able to resist them, I would be very surprised if you could. Once that path has been opened, it will not be easily closed. You would be at their mercy. It's possible I'm mistaken about their collective character. Maybe they would refrain from taking control without your permission no matter the circumstance. But you would always be under that threat."

Entreska frowned, "Why didn't Jasmine mention that?"

"Two possible reasons. One, she hasn't realized that will be the case. She may think the second time will require your active desire. Second, she has recognized the effect, but didn't want to frighten you, since she could not imagine taking control without your permission. Sooner or later, though, they would know and will begin to imagine. And your mind will be in peril."

Heather's expression became wistful, and she continued, "I fear eventually they will succumb to the allure of the Assumption. All with good intentions, of course, but then there will be nothing to stop them. And since they would have committed an Abomination, they will need to rise above their crime by becoming something superior and not subject to simplistic human laws and standards. They will give themselves a promotion to Angels, Archangels, Benevolent Spirits, Defenders of the Faithful or whatever sounds suitably impressive yet implies goodness and humility. Once no longer subject to any law or ethical standard, they will be free to commit untold horrors and abominations in the name of the Good."

Heather narrowed her eyes and looked deeply into Entreska's eyes, "And they will. I know them all too well. They will. Nothing Puck can ever muster will approach that catastrophe. He will fade and die. But Evermore is mighty indeed. When your body falters, and should the Redemption be done properly. They will be able to claim another body. This time, there will be no resistance, and they will be able to force the Assumption. And so the horror will continue for millennia."

A sudden stream of tears poured forth from Entreska who wiped futilely at them and nodded resignedly, "I won't. I understand."

Heather frowned and reached out to caress the faerie. After a while, she said, "There is another possibility."

"Yes?"

"It is risky. But it holds the possibility of achieving all our goals. Removal of Puck. Rescue of the prisoners. And no Abominations."

Entreska stemmed the flow of tears, "What is it?"

"You confront Puck and subdue him. Admittedly, your skill is limited as yet. But you are definitely talented and as I said - Evermore is mighty. It would be tough. Puck is skilled and very powerful. If you make a mistake, he could easily defeat and kill you."

Entreska looked about darkly, "If I were to fail, would he be able to perform the Redemption?"

"Possibly. He may have the skill and knowledge. But it would only be his doom. Once returned to the Crystal form, at such close range, we would take him."

Entreska began to feel hopeful but scared.

Heather went on, "But the wisest and safest path is to simply withdraw now. After sufficient training and practice, you could more easily defeat Puck. In fact, I believe that with just two years of hard training, Puck would have no chance against the power you would wield. Of course, in some respects, the effort would be greater, you would have to find your way through hostile territory and get close enough to Puck without him stealing away and forcing you to chase. That is always a dangerous and risky proposition without an army arrayed to protect your flanks and rear. I guess you might be able to arrange another military expedition. Puck's forces have been seriously depleted and so it will take a while for him to rebuild.

"Of course, he might go into hiding..."

Entreska coughed, "Enough."

"Sorry. Of course, you do have some distinct advantages right now that you won't likely have later."

Entreska raised an eyebrow, "And they are?"

Heather laughed, "Puck won't be expecting you at all."

Entreska laughed hesitantly, "I suppose not."

"And despite his experience subduing minds, he's never actually fought a real wizard duel."

Entreska shrugged, "Neither have I."

"Ah. But I have."

Entreska swallowed, "Explain how I will subdue him."

"First, you must tell Rolf to wait at least four hours."

Vorkfest faded suddenly.

"Entreska?"

"What?"

Entreska found herself looking into Tamara's concerned face.

"Are you okay?"

Entreska jumped to her feet and seized Tamara by the shoulders, "Yes. I'm fine. Listen. You need to tell Rolf to delay the contingency plan. Tell him I have an alternate plan. But I need four hours to prepare. And then I'll be coming up to the Third Tower."

Tamara looked around not sure what to say or do.

Entreska felt a bit of desperation welling inside her at Tamara's hesitation. "Please, Tamara. Puck isn't going anywhere. This is important, dammit. I need that time. It could be a disaster if Rolf attacks now. Please trust me."

Tamara breathed heavily.

Entreska felt an uncontrolled effusion of urgency radiate from inside her. Tamara nodded suddenly, "Yes. Of course. I will send a message immediately. But I will say Mallory is still fighting despite his fall. Otherwise I'm afraid he will not listen."

Entreska shrugged in agreement. Then a feeling of relief suffused the tent and Tamara summoned a messenger. Entreska projected herself back into Vorkfest. This time landing virtually on top of Heather who remarkably did not appear overly startled.

Entreska resumed her place on the table where she eyed Heather suspiciously, "Did you influence Tamara?"

"No. My apprentice. You did that."

"Oh my. That's not right. I didn't mean to do that. I--"

"It's alright. You'll learn to control that soon enough. It's not your fault. Real apprentices all received training prior to being Conjoined. You had no such benefit. Anyway, that is not our agenda this moment. We must get you ready for Puck. Fortunately, the baby steps I've been teaching you these last few weeks before the incident in the Tea Room are the basic foundation for what I must teach you now..."

An hour later, she had to interrupt her training to deal with a suspicious Rolf who had turned up at the monitoring tent with Zemfrekis. Rolf's troops hadn't heard a single shot since Mallory fell off the wall and so Rolf was convinced Mallory was dead or incapacitated. Scowling, Rolf asked Tamara several questions to which she had very poor answers. Rolf became enraged and began shouting angry accusations.

Entreska cut him off, "Leave her alone, Rolf. I can explain."

He turned and waited with an expression of incredulous expectation.

"Captain Tallrider was just following my orders."

Rolf looked back at Tallrider who stood feet apart, hands clasped behind her back and looking very dejected. Then he returned his gaze to Entreska, "Since when did officers in the Jurasketu Army start taking orders from you?"

Entreska, from sheer nervousness at her impending duel with Puck, giggled and said, "Since I became the second living sorcerer on the Raffin."

Rolf's head rolled slowly to the left in bewilderment, "What?"

"As I've explained to you many times, wizards issue orders and folks will obey despite themselves."

Rolf ran his hands slowly through his hair in utter confusion and shouted, "Entreska, what are you talking about? There are no wizards."

"Yes. There are. Exactly two. Pachinko Puck and me. I asked Captain Tallrider to ensure that you delay your contingency plan. But since I am now a sorcerer, admittedly somewhat lacking in proper training just yet and can't exercise proper control over my powers, I infused the plea with enough sorcery, purely inadvertently, such that she couldn't resist and did as I wished."

Rolf looked back at Tallrider who continued to stare grimly at the other side of the tent. He then turned back to Entreska and laughed, "Powers, eh? Well, if you've got such powers, why don't you just march up to the Fourth Tower and try out your powers on Puck?"

Entreska's expression changed to stone and she sighed, "That's exactly what I intend to do. That's why I wanted you to hold up your attack."

Rolf's incredulous, exasperated expression changed to one of horror, "WHAT?" Then he flapped his arms wildly and said, "Even if you have these powers and can stare down Pachinko Puck. How in the Great Burning Blast are you getting close enough without getting killed by his troops, eh?"

Entreska smiled, "I was kind of hoping you could help with that. I don't need to get that close either. Just twenty or so meters away I think will be sufficient. In fact, we'll be able to duel just fine from different rooms of the tower - no need to make eye contact or even see him at all. I can feel him. I can feel his presence now."

Rolf stared for a long while and then whispered, "You're serious aren't you?"

"Yes."

Rolf sighed and took a chair. He strongly massaged his forehead with his fingers. After about a minute, he looked up and said, "If I let you do this and you get killed, do you have any idea what Mother will do to me?"

"Don't tell her. She thinks I'm dead already."

Rolf tilted his head and nodded with slight bemusement, "That's right. I've not made any recent dispatches since I wanted to keep Father's capture secret at least until we know his fate. Can you really take down Puck in some kind of sorcerous duel?"

Entreska considered the question with a sigh.

The Voice spoke in her head, "Risky. Very risky. If you let us, we will carry the day with certainty. Defeat Puck. Save your father. And save Jurasketu."

Heather's voice boomed in her head, "Entreska can take him herself, thank you very much. With both hands tied behind her back even."

The Voice snapped, "Like that matters in a wizard's duel."

Heather just laughed.

Rolf said, "Well, can you?"

Entreska looked him hard in the eye, "I can do it, Rolf. Just get me into the Fourth Tower. I need another two hours to prepare."

"Okay. I only have you to lose. And as you say, you're already dead."

Entreska chuckled, "Indeed."

Of course, she thought, it's a whole lot easier to joke about death than actually go running after it. And neither Uncle Val nor Mallory would be there to save her this time.

Tamara spoke, "Sir. I would like to lead the team to do that."

Rolf said, "Nice try. But no. You need to continue watching the monitor in case Puck does flee and survives the booby traps somehow. Or if Mallory reappears."

Crestfallen, Tamara sat back down and hid behind the Darkglasses.

Rolf turned to Zemfrekis, "When Tresh says she's ready, bring her to the Third Tower. We're well positioned and so I don't think we'll get caught off guard this time by any of Puck's tricks. So, she can have more than two hours if she wants. Puck's not going anywhere."

"Yes, sir."

Rolf frowned, "That would be, Rolf, my little brother."

Zemfrekis smiled, "Yes, Rolf." After a pause, Zemfrekis asked, "Do you think Puck will kill Father?"

Rolf spat, "Only in spite. Upon Puck's death or defeat, Father's guards will likely have orders to kill him. Hopefully, they will decide not to follow those orders and plead for special treatment after their surrender."

Zemfrekis nodded grimly. Rolf hugged Zemfrekis and Entreska and then left.

Entreska asked Heather, *"Can I stop them from killing my father?"*

Heather spoke softly, "We'll try. But I doubt you'll be in any condition to do much of anything for several hours after you defeat Puck."

"A Wizard Duel is that draining?"

"Rarely, but this one will be."

Entreska sat down on the floor and assumed a meditative position.

She looked over at Tamara and said, "I need to resume my training but don't hesitate to rouse me."

Tamara raised an eyebrow, "How exactly would I do that? You seemed to be in a deep trance. I tried to rouse you several times by calling your name and shaking you. You only came out when Rolf entered the tent and started shouting."

Entreska shrugged, "Oh. Then try a bit of shouting."

Tamara shrugged in return, "As you wish."

Entreska projected herself into Vorkfest for the third time and to her surprise she found herself perched perfectly on the table. Heather showed no surprise this time.

Heather stated with a hint of admiration, "You're getting better at that."

Entreska nodded with uncertainty, "Apparently. Hopefully, that bodes well for the rest of the day."

Heather nodded and launched into a long theoretical explanation of wizard duels. Entreska simply listened, shifting her feet and slowly spreading her wings occasionally. Finally, Heather concluded and announced that they would do some exercises and then Heather would make progressively stronger attacks against Entreska for training purposes.

Entreska nodded and then upon sudden reflection asked, "How long did you say duels usually last?"

Heather shrugged, "Often many minutes between competent wizards."

Entreska deeply furrowed her faerie brow, "Are duels in Evermore different?"

Heather smiled, "No."

Entreska looked even more puzzled, "You spoke theoretically about subduing and crushing the mind, but the three wizard duels I've seen so far manifested as extreme physical violence."

Heather chuckled, "A powerful and well-trained wizard is highly resistant to mind attacks. She can divert the energy into her body away from the mind and thence directed harmlessly into her surroundings or re-channeled into a counterattack."

Entreska snapped her wings open and closed in slight frustration, "But Baxatom destroyed Daryl and Zelda in an instant why couldn't they resist longer?"

Heather flatly stated, "Baxatom's skill and power far exceeds their considerable skills. Sufficiently skilled and powerful wizards can flood power directly against the mind and body in a fashion that creates an almost instant overload if the target cannot react fast enough."

Entreska's eyes widened, "What if the target can react fast enough?"

Heather smiled, "Then the targeted wizard redirects the energy into a pressure wave of energy that scatters in all directions that often clobbers everyone nearby."

Entreska rubbed her face and took a gulp of wine, "Aha. That is what happened in the first duel I witnessed, right?"

Heather nodded, "Yes. Tom gave me the details."

Entreska paced back and forth on the table and then fluttered around for a few seconds, before landing back on the table. "Isn't that a dangerous tactic then?"

Heather raised an eyebrow, "Yes. Particularly if friends, allies and innocents are nearby the target."

Entreska narrowed her eyes, "Then Baxatom was being reckless?"

Heather shook her head, "No. Only one existing wizard has sufficient skill to resist an overload from Baxatom."

Entreska smirked, "Is that why he said you would never fight each other when I asked who would win a wizard duel between you and him."

Heather chuckled, "He said that?"

Entreska nodded.

Heather looked into the distance, "Could be. I actually thought it was because we were such good friends."

Entreska became more serious, "Will I learn to do that? Can Puck do that?"

Heather nodded and then shook her head, "Eventually. And probably not. But all the more reason to engage Puck at a distance in case he has somehow developed such an ability. Fortunately, the Deluge Attack, as it is called, is not even possible at anything beyond a few meters."

Entreska nodded in relief at that.

Heather raised her arms, "Come. Enough talk. Time for training and sparring."

Entreska resumed the training. It concluded an hour later with Heather saying, "More training will only do harm at this point."

Entreska arose from her trance state and informed Zemfrekis she was ready.

The Hall Of Reverence

Glenmorgan's spies had always reported that Puck was disheveled at his best and a complete sloven the rest of the time. Apparently, deep in that unrepentant slob lurked an appreciation for exquisite works of art, craftsmanship and high quality furnishings. All kept in a perfect state of tidiness and cleanliness.

Puck's enormous combination banquet hall and throne room that he had ostentatiously named the *Hall of Reverence* featured one meter square, mirror polished unique granite tiles laid out in a checkerboard pattern of various dark and light shades representing almost every known source of granite across four continents. Intricately carved marble columns lined the room and supported enormous gently curving beams of Black Fir stained deep red that arched upward to form the high-pitched roof. Incredibly vivid murals depicting various scenes of legend and myth covered the plaster walls between the columns.

A collection of long, elegant tables, each uniquely designed and beautiful, lined either side of the hall. Dozens of extraordinary carved wooden chairs were neatly arranged under the tables. Luminescent ceramic vases holding fresh flowers of all types adorned each table. At the north end of the hall, a slightly raised dais held a small dinner table and a single high-backed wooden chair. While clearly of exceptional craftsmanship, the table and chair were of a simple design and very plain in comparison to the banquet tables and chairs.

A series of high, glass paned windows at each end of the hall provided a surprising amount of light throughout the day. Expensive oil lamps positioned on chest high plinths on each of the support columns that lined the hall supplemented the daylight and were kept lit throughout the night.

Steam supplied, radiant floor heating kept the hall surprisingly warm, dry and comfortable. A good thing since Glen had been stripped naked and his manacled wrists were chained to an eyebolt attached to a tripod mounted on a heavy wooden cart. Rotating shifts of extremely bored guards kept watch over him. He was provided water whenever he asked. The smell of urine pervaded the cart. He had been given no food since his capture two days ago. Apparently, Puck did not want him to expire prematurely, but otherwise Puck had paid him no attention. No questions. No curses. No gloating. Nothing. In fact, Puck had gone about the business of conferring with his advisers and generals as though Glen wasn't there. This, of course, meant that Puck was most certainly planning to torture him to death.

Although the situation was hopeless, Glen had decided to remain silent and avoid a beating that would likely result from an outburst. He wanted to keep his mind clear and his body relatively intact in case an opportunity arose for action. He also needed his strength to deal with whatever torture Puck had in store. Not that it really mattered in the least, but Glen didn't want to give Puck any satisfaction. Admittedly, Puck was going to save him the humiliation of a public trial before the Debaters for disobeying the explicit orders of the National Council of War.

The worst part was that the ancient rumors were true. Puck could seemingly read and control minds. He had somehow turned Juragi into a traitor. Glen could not fathom any other explanation for what Juragi had done. Yet, despite the apparent treachery of Juragi and the capture of the Grand Marshal, Puck and his officers still faced a desperate military situation.

Rolf had sufficient force and supplies to maintain the siege through the winter months. Rolf also had the skill, forces and position to destroy any relief force that dared to venture near the Citadel. Aware that Puck might have secret escape tunnels, the Jurasketu Army had deployed forces to prevent any escape. Normally, Glen would have rated Puck's situation as hopeless, but Puck's extraordinary abilities clearly gave him a chance that no one else would have.

When Puck wasn't conducting business, Glen tried to nap despite the discomfort of being chained to the wooden cart...

Glenmorgan awoke mid-afternoon to the bemused stare of Puck draped across his dining chair with arms and legs akimbo. Puck was, as his usual custom, clad in a pair of battered sandals and a stained, ragged, ostensibly white nightshirt that hung loosely from his gaunt frame. His supple, elaborately tattooed purple skin and uncombed, wild orange hair but elegant features and impish smile gave him the appearance of something mischievous from a child's fairy tale. Glen met his bright green eyes but remained impassive.

Puck smiled without a single wrinkle, "Tell me, Grand Marshal. Where does your power to resist me come from?"

Glen cocked his head in thought. Glen had been prepared to ignore all questions including innocent ones since those were simply purposed to draw him off focus. Glen's pride and confidence went before his caution and he decided to engage Puck in conversation after all.

Glen shrugged, "What do you mean?"

"Your mind, your very presence is invisible to me. Why?"

Glen chuckled, "I have no idea what you are talking about."

Puck nodded, "Indeed. You are the third Zattan of royal blood that I have encountered with that ability."

Glen shrugged, "Is that unusual?"

Puck stroked his face, brushed back his orange hair and said, "You would be exactly the third person I've encountered with this ability."

Glen said, "How many Zattan royals have you ever encountered? Maybe it is a blood trait we all share."

Glenmorgan knew that Puck had met with Zattan diplomats of royal blood more than a few times, had captured and executed a few more and there were at least two Zattan traitors that had entered Puck's employ over the centuries. The unexpected treachery of Juragi cast those Zattan traitors in a new light, however.

Puck shook his head, "I have encountered more than a few dozen over the decades. So it would seem to be uncommon. You are the first to be directly within my power, though."

Glen shrugged.

Puck pressed his fingertips together and then cast his hands forward maintaining the connection. He smiled briefly before turning his face to stone. "Yet, we will need to discover your secret before I release you."

Glen raised an eyebrow, "Release? As in, released from my earthly burdens?"

Puck smirked, "It seemed a bit rude to say it like that."

Glen tucked his head back, "When did niceties creep into the mind of Puck?"

Puck smiled, "You cannot provoke me. I will not let you escape with a quick death. I will gain your secret. Decades are days for me. Days are mere minutes."

Glen snorted, "I'll have to admit that I am curious."

"About what?"

"How exactly do you expect to survive? While cunning, capturing me doesn't seem to have changed the military position very much. In fact, if days are minutes, I would guess you have mere minutes to live. Yet, you seem rather indifferent."

Puck laughed, "You mistake indifference for rationality. Either I will survive or I won't. Getting all emotional about life just muddles the mind wouldn't you agree? And quite frankly, for a dead man, you aren't showing much emotion."

Glen tilted his head, "I only get choked up about children and animals."

Puck snorted, "Hardly. You seem to forget I can afford quality spies. And it is hardly a secret that you are clearly unable to check your emotions. But now I wonder... Is that all an act? Are you in reality a cold-hearted bastard that only uses emotional outbursts for tactical purposes?"

"Don't you?"

Puck laughed, "Your spies could have hardly missed the fact that I never show any real emotion except mirth."

"True. And I will have to give you credit for the mirth."

Puck smiled, "I will give you a secret, though, for free. I haven't felt anger in a long time. Rational mirth only."

"Then you are truly blessed to be free from the flush of hot temper."

"Blessed indeed."

Glen stared for a bit... "Yet, you hate Jurasketu."

"Hate is such a strong word. In reality, I just foster dislike of Jurasketu. The idea that ordinary folk should have a say in how they are ruled is obviously foolishness."

"You dispute its success?"

Puck laughed, "It succeeds despite itself."

Glen shrugged and then stared at a haggard, but otherwise nondescript soldier who had appeared at the entrance to the hall. He approached Puck quickly but with visible trepidation.

Puck raised an eyebrow, "Yes?"

"Sorry to disturb you, Lord Puck. Captain Wallis reports that the Black Skinned Man was just sighted from Tower Three coming over the southern rim. He was accompanied by twenty soldiers and several pack horses. They were promptly escorted to the Jurasketu

Command Tents."

Puck looked to the southeast and said, "Interesting. Anything else?"

"No, my lord."

Without turning, Puck muttered, "Dismissed."

The soldier backed away and practically fled the hall.

Puck continued to stare in the direction of the Jurasketu Army for over a minute.

Glen finally broke the silence, "Black Skinned Man?"

Puck turned back with a rueful look and said, "Yes. A particular man sporting very dark, black skin has been sowing chaos across both sides of the Blades for more than a year. I assumed he worked for you."

Glen hesitated to answer for a moment and gave Puck a sidelong glance. One of Colonel Jones' last reports had mentioned the appearance of someone that at least vaguely matched that description. Jones had raised the possibility that this person – Mallory Owens – was a Puck spy. This recent evidence, however, pulled apart that web of thinking.

"Doesn't remind me of anyone that works for me. Do you know his name? Maybe I would recognize it."

Puck shrugged, "If I knew his name, he would already be mine."

"Too bad. But if he causes you that much concern, I would have to applaud his efforts whomever he calls his master."

Puck laughed vigorously then said, "If he doesn't work for you, shouldn't you be worried given that he is in your camp?"

Glen frowned, "No. I only worry about things I can do something about. And right now that is a very short list."

Puck laughed even louder, "You are even more entertaining than my spies have led me to believe."

Glen rolled his eyes and shook his head.

Puck continued, "So tell me..."

Glen proceeded to evade or ignore Puck's questions for rest of the afternoon before Puck ordered dinner for himself. After eating, Puck left the Hall. Glen went back to napping...

Glen suffered a sharp spasm of pain in his shoulder when he jerked awake from a loud curse. The high windows allowed only the pale gloom of moonlight so the muddy oil light dominated the hall. Distant cursing and yelling filled the night. His two guards were highly agitated since they had strict orders to stay put and watch him. They shifted nervously and cursed loudly every so often when something clattered near to the hall.

A few minutes later, Puck entered the Hall, strode purposely to the dais and unceremoniously draped himself across his chair. He glanced at Glen and smiled ever so slightly. Two servants hurried out from an alcove and placed a pitcher of citrus water and a bowl of fruit on his table. Moments later, Puck's senior advisors and their aides, all of them looking very worried, came running into the hall in various states of undress and hustled over to the dais and started shouting at each other. An entire squad of Immortals appeared in full battle gear including spears and took up a position near the main entrance after detaching two soldiers to guard the servant's entrance.

Neither Puck nor his advisors seemed to understand the attack. Glen listened closely and discerned something about poison smoke that had disabled the entire watch shift and all the soldiers who had rallied to duty quickest before the officers realized what was happening and held the rest back.

A huge explosion had completely leveled the Lower Gatehouse extinguishing the defensive fire. Jurasketu forces could be seen forming up to attack the ramp. Two more explosions were reported a number of minutes later at the Second Tower. An officer reported that the access tunnels to the other towers were still impassable due to the poison smoke. More minutes passed and an officer reported Jurasketu troops advancing up the ramp to the Upper Gatehouse.

The strange thing was that despite reports of some kind of fighting going on – no one had spotted Jurasketu forces except those advancing up the ramp. Puck seemed curiously unperturbed by this while his senior commanders were more understandably completely freaked out. Puck ordered his commanders to prepare to defend the Fourth Tower room to room.

Sometime later, Glen observed Puck's most senior advisor, a short, balding and portly man whisper something serious to Puck who sat up in his chair and laughed, "I'm not going anywhere. You'll see what happens when they get closer."

About an hour into the attack, an explosion outside the tower rocked the Hall. A few minutes later, an excited officer came running to make a report. The officer, named Captain Bearclaw, was tall and athletic with bright blue-gray eyes and blonde hair. Despite his excitement, he maintained formal etiquette.

The Captain spoke, "Lord Puck, thirty Immortals charged the

Interloper and overwhelmed him. He killed twenty but was driven over the courtyard wall."

Puck nodded, "Excellent Captain Bearclaw. Bring the body here."

Captain Bearclaw barked, "Yes, Lord Puck."

He turned to leave and then hesitated suddenly unsure, "Lord Puck, did you say bring the body here to the Hall?"

Puck looked askance, "You have an objection?"

Horrified, the Captain said, "No. Of course not, Lord Puck. Just wanted to make sure I heard correctly. I'll make proper arrangements to avoid soiling the floor."

Puck smiled, "Of course. Whatever is required. And be certain to gather up his equipment and bring that as well."

A relieved Bearclaw replied, "Yes. Lord Puck."

Puck cast a glance at Glen who simply shrugged and otherwise remained impassive.

A few minutes later, Captain Bearclaw returned with a desperate look of fear in his eyes.

Puck rolled his eyes and said, "What now Captain? Where is the body?"

The Captain sighed heavily, "Lord Puck, the Interloper fell onto the roof of the well house which collapsed. The body apparently dropped into the well. When we started clearing the wreckage so that we could rig up some ropes, we were fired upon by Jurasketu archers in the Third Tower and were forced to take cover."

Puck laughed, "Never mind that. We can get the body later. We have graver matters at hand. We need to evict the Jurasketu now that their Champion is defeated."

The advisors and Puck argued vigorously for many minutes about how to accomplish that task. Finally, a bold plan involving secret tunnels, mountaineering, and fighting skill to be executed at dawn was agreed upon. Puck dismissed his advisors to effect the plan or sleep depending on their function. Puck, however, stayed and simply stared at Glen who said nothing and ignored the stare.

Eventually, Puck spoke, "I can discern many dozen Jurasketu soldiers in the first three towers. But I couldn't see that Interloper."

Glen smiled, "And?"

Puck nodded, "The Interloper must have been the Black Skinned Man. I could sense him in the distance – then he disappeared. If it's a natural ability, that would be impossible. So that casts doubt on how you evade my abilities. It cannot be natural born. Yet, it cannot be something you would wear – otherwise you would have lost the ability. So it must be a medicinal... Although I suppose it could be a rare spice or delicacy."

Glen laughed, "Brandy?"

Puck smiled, "Hardly. But despite the terrible annoyance, the Interloper has provided an important clue to the puzzle. So the question arises, how long will it take for the effect to wear off?"

Glen muttered, "Well... If it's more than a few days, you'll have to feed me or I'll expire before the experiment can conclude."

Puck tapped his fingers, "Indeed. Disappointing. I'm beginning to think you have lied to me."

Glen rolled his eyes, "Everyone lies."

Puck nodded, "True enough. But, in this case, the Black Skinned Man, must have been provided with the proper concoction before embarking on this attack. Which can only mean that, you and someone on your staff knew it would block my abilities."

In frustration, Glen barked, "What are you talking about? If I had known and had possessed such a concoction, wouldn't I have given some to Juragi? And avoided all of *this*?"

Puck nodded again, "Hmm... Quite true."

Puck began tapping his fingers again and stroking his lips. After a few minutes, he said, "What if the concoction doesn't work on everyone? That would explain your lack of caution and arrogance making your capture all the easier. You thought it would protect you and your senior staff."

Glen sighed, "Invent whatever fantasy you will. I know nothing."

Puck looked away and then back at Glen, "You're right. That doesn't make any sense."

Glen muttered, "I'm so glad we sorted that out."

"But what does? Great Burning Blast!"

Puck stood up and began laughing maniacally for a long spell that ended with him slumping back into the chair.

"Of course. Of course. That presence is a wizard. The wizard could very well likely have some power or knowledge to hide a person's presence. Very likely. And so you must have set me up. Zabala was right. He is fat and stupid but has a great intuition for such things. Too bad I rarely pay him mind. Bravo. Grand Marshal."

Glen tried to remain impassive. Puck had clearly reached that point of desperate madness that overcomes people trapped in impossible circumstances. Glen had long trained himself to face destruction of his own plans and life with complete placidity. Proper desperation requires calmness of mind, body and spirit otherwise the execution will invariably fail.

Puck continued with his rant, "Yes. You and the wizard set me up by making me think I had set you up. Nothing else explains your sudden appearance at Duravon with half the Jurasketu Army just at the right time. That fool Saffron never had a chance. And even before I learn of his defeat, I felt your army march on the Citadel. Incredible. How long has this wizard been your ally? It had to have been at least five years. And you kept this completely from my spies. Bravo. I say. Bravo! Grand Marshal."

Glen shrugged not sure what emotion to show. He wanted to say he had no idea what Puck was talking about. But it seemed better for Puck to be deceived and confused to help whatever plans Rolf had set in motion. A Rolf plan tended to be complex with multiple threads of strategy with multiple alternatives for when things inevitably went wrong. Sometimes Rolf's plans counted on something to go wrong because the enemy would necessarily attempt to exploit the situation and naturally fall unsuspecting into one of his counter stratagems.

A strange thought twisted through Glen's Web of Thought. Could Rolf had set this situation up? A multi-year plan that culminated with the sacrifice of his sister Entreska to draw Saffron into a military disaster? Rolf loved Entreska dearly. He couldn't have consciously planned for that. Glen snarled at himself. He was just hungry and desperate. Rolf had done nothing.

Puck continued with more ranting, "My stupid generals underestimated the size of your army claiming you couldn't possibly have so many ready for a sudden dash across the Raffin. And with winter coming, the Raffin supply lines would be blocked and your army would perish in a siege. So we should just fight a delaying action and wait for your army to crumble in the winter.

"I certainly didn't want to abandon my beautiful capital if I could help it. So I summoned four of my seven regiments guarding the northern lands as reinforcements. But, again, bravo Grand Marshal. A sizable Zattan raiding force had appeared to threaten the rice and potato harvests and all seven regiments had to meet your perfectly timed diversionary attack. So I was trapped and almost defenseless."

Glen smiled at that. He had indeed arranged that diversionary attack. He also had set in motion a disinformation campaign that claimed there was a disinformation campaign attempting to trick

Puck's field commanders. Since a surprise winter attack by Jurasketu forces on the Citadel could not be remotely believable, Puck's regimental commanders made the logical choice of ignoring the summons as a Zattan trick. Once they realized their mistake, Glen wondered if they would defect fearing execution. But Puck seemed way too happy that he had been trapped. And he was seemingly defenseless.

Puck stood up again suddenly and cheerfully said, "Don't go anywhere. We're not done talking."

Glen glared. Puck smiled. Puck then trotted the length of the Hall and out the main entrance to leave Glen contemplating the events leading up to that very moment.

Rolf may not have created the situation where the Expedition and Entreska would be brought to ruin and death, but he sure knew how to take advantage should that terrible event arise. Rolf had gotten Glen to change the basic strategy for defending against late season attacks on the Raffin. Rolf just happened to be in place with the Dawn Spiders ready to provide the perfect flanking force to ensure Saffron's complete destruction. Without hesitation, Rolf supported Glen's deception of Juragi and the drive to the Centaur Citadel.

Wait... A setup? For what? A trap for the rescue force? If that had been the intention, it had been the worst execution imaginable. Admittedly, there is no way Saffron could have anticipated the size and speed of the relief force. Glen shook his head. No. The only logical conclusion was that Saffron's goal had been the complete destruction of the Expedition. The Web of Thought hummed for a long time.

Glen suddenly shouted, "Great Burning Blast!"

The guards, Immortals and advisors all turned to stare at Glen.

Glen ignored them.

Puck had somehow set up the Expedition. One of the surviving Black Scorpions had told him that Entreska had located a special room in the ruins of the Duravon Archives complex. Immediately following a brief investigation of the room, Entreska announced the Expedition was done for the year, and then the Cumar attacked two days later. Saffron's deployment now made sense. The Immortals were there to provide a protective base for the Cumar while they went after the Expedition.

Puck must have known or believed something of special value existed in the ruins of Duravon. He must have believed that wizard stuff like some secret wizard book or artifact was there. Maybe there was an entire trove of valuable artifacts and books. Entreska claimed just that in her book. Glen's spies regularly reported that Puck was always looking for lost ancient wizard knowledge. This something would have required a major excavation to find. As the Expedition demonstrated, finding the building required many weeks of exploring and digging in the desert. Obviously, Puck couldn't hope to mount such a large-scale operation inside Jurasketu territory unmolested. So he needed a proxy. And somehow he had supplied Entreska with enough information to allow her to do the rest of the work for him using her knowledge and skills.

Why not just wait for her to return with the artifacts to Jurasketu and steal them more easily then? The Jurasketu Academy wasn't that heavily guarded. A carefully planned, researched burglary of the campus seemed more certain of success than a wild chase across the Lower Raffin. But what if Entreska had recognized and understood their importance and requested the Jurasketu Army safe keep the items? Should that happen, Puck's chances of stealing the artifacts would be reduced almost to zero. Attacking the Expedition after it located the artifacts seemed the better option. That would explain why they had relentlessly chased the Expedition across the Lower Raffin.

What had Entreska really found? Had she even found anything other than some empty room? And what had the Cumar done with whatever she might have found? Entreska probably had some warning, and so it seemed likely that Entreska would have hidden anything she had found to prevent the Cumar from capturing it. Until recently, Glen wouldn't have cared. Ancient artifacts were interesting and valuable academically but not important militarily. Glen had always scoffed at Puck's reputation for Wizard powers. Not anymore. And so it was possible the ancient artifacts or even just books of Wizard secrets could make Puck more powerful.

Would Rolf eventually realize that Entreska might have found something that needed to be safeguarded or even destroyed? *Possibly. Possibly not.* Rolf couldn't know that Puck had set things up. And he probably would not likely guess that Puck's real target was an ancient artifact. Glen breathed deeply. He needed to come up with a way to let Rolf know or somehow guide him to that conclusion so he could find whatever was lost and post strong guards in the right places.

Some time later Puck returned looking ever bemused. He

sauntered across the Hall from his private entrance and flopped himself onto his chair never taking his eye off Glen. He stared for several minutes. Glen remained impassive.

Puck spoke finally, "Your Wizard is coming. Apparently, she thinks I'm ripe for a confrontation."

Glen raised an eyebrow, "She?"

Puck nodded, "Indeed. I can sense gender easily usually. Although she reads somewhat ambiguous."

Glen dropped his chin keeping his gaze on Puck, "No fear?"

Puck smirked, "Need I remind you that I have trained myself to have only one emotion, and that would be mirth. Fear and anger I leave to others."

Glen shrugged.

"I will crush her, of course."

Glen narrowed his eyes, "You have defeated a Wizard before?"

Puck shrugged, "No. Never had the opportunity. But no mind - that I could actually feel - has withstood me before. She can't have more experience than I at crushing minds. I'm not restrained by ethics which means I have had plenty of opportunity to refine my skills."

Glen wondered who this damn Wizard was and why his spies hadn't been any better than Puck's at noticing such an important person. She was definitely bold since she had to know Puck's reputation.

Puck tapped his fingers together.

"Hmm... Your Wizard must have been the one who educated your daughter then eh?"

Daughter. Entreska... Dead. Puck... A loud bellow emanated from the main entrance to the Hall... The Demon, arms down, fists tightly clenched, came stomping across the Hall to stand a couple of meters before Glen. The Demon bashed itself on the head twice before extending its left hand and index finger at Glen's chest. It then extended its right hand to point at Puck. It then turned sharply and swung its left arm to also point at Puck. It snapped its head back to look at Glen. Well? DESTROY! LAY WASTE! KILL! Glen clenched his fists and shouted in despair. The Demon snarled at Puck and vanished suddenly...

Glen flailed about in his chains and then went limp in tears.

Puck jumped up and shouted, "Great Burning Blast!"

Glen sobbed. Glen heard Puck yelling something unintelligible. Glen looked around. Puck was staring at him mouth agape. Puck paced around Glen's cart twice before returning to his chair. Glen closed his eyes and breathed deeply.

Puck said quietly, "What did you just do?"

Glen opened his eyes and glowered at Puck, "I did nothing."

Puck laughed, "A wizard like presence appeared near you and when I tried to probe - it vanished."

Glen started to say something sarcastic but held up and went slack jawed. Puck must have sensed the Demon somehow... The Web of Thought snapped. Rolf had some plan underway and apparently, he had recruited some Wizard as an ally. Now was the time to distract Puck...

Glen sighed, nodded and intoned, "It is a Demon bound to my Soul. It protects me."

Puck's eyes widened and a smile crossed his face, "I'll be damned."

Glen laughed, "That makes two of us."

Puck stared at Glen, "What kind of protection?"

Glen thought for long while, "The usual kinds."

Puck ignored the evasion, "How did this come to be?"

Glen took some time to compose an answer, "An ancient and secret ritual commonly done to Zattan of Royal birth. Less commonly in recent years."

Puck clapped his hands, "Now we're getting somewhere. What is this ritual?"

Glen raised an eyebrow, "You do not already know about this particular ritual?"

Puck smiled and shrugged, "Humor me. Maybe I want to test the quality of my spies. Besides, Zattan rituals tend to mutate wildly - even the ancient, secret ones like Trakora Runk."

Glen nodded, "That would be the very one. I will give you the full description."

They were interrupted by the return of an agitated Captain Bearclaw who came trotting into the Hall.

"Lord Puck! Twenty or more Jurasketu using a tortoise crossed from the Third Tower and fought their way into the Anteroom before we could finish blocking the doorway. Fortunately, we have solidly blocked the interior door. We believe it will take several hours at least for them to hack their way in. More than fifty Jurasketu are forming up outside the Third Tower as reinforcements."

Puck nodded calmly while staring off into the distance, "Yes. I see their Wizard is likely preparing to cross. A confrontation seems inevitable."

"Orders? Lord Puck."

Puck chuckled, "Our plans are unchanged. If anything, this may make them more vulnerable to our counterattack. But reinforce the Main Hall should they somehow force their way through the block sooner than expected."

"What about the Wizard, Lord Puck?"

"I will handle her once she reaches the Anteroom."

"Yes, Lord Puck."

Bearclaw smiled taking on the confidence present in Puck and exited the Hall in a slow trot.

Puck turned back to Glen, "Where were we? Oh yes. You were going to describe Trakora Runk for me."

Glen spent several minutes describing the ritual in detail. Puck stood the entire time and asked no questions letting Glen complete the story uninterrupted. After Glen finished, Puck nodded sagely and returned to flop back down onto his chair.

"Some unknown concoction eh?"

Glen shrugged, "I'm sure it is known to the priests who made it - but they don't share their secrets."

Puck bobbled his head, "So you don't know. That is no matter. I had no clue the ritual was connected to this unusual ability. Now that I do - I can focus on finding that particular secret. Challenges are the stuff an interesting life is made of."

Glen shook his head sadly. He was also very puzzled that Puck seemed to have taken Glen's sudden loquacity without question. He was gaming Puck - had he just been gamed somehow? Puck was so used to compelling anyone to talk he must have forgotten that Glen was speaking voluntarily. Amusingly, Glen had spoken the truth deciding that deception might subconsciously alert Puck to Glen's true motive - distraction.

Almost on cue, Puck stiffened suddenly, sat up, leaned forward and muttered, "Ah. It begins..."

Glen watched in fascination as Puck closed his eyes and his face became clouded with concentration. This continued for a very long while. After a few minutes, something caught Glen's eye and he looked over at the private entrance a few meters away. The two guards stationed there jerked and collapsed face down where they stood. Glen's assigned guards straightened up and snapped out their swords as they yelled in alarm.

Oddly, the doorway blurred slightly. Glen blinked and shook his head thinking his vision had gotten out of whack. To Glen's shock, the blurry area rapidly moved towards him. As the blur came closer, Glen realized it was actually a warrior wearing some kind of helmet that totally encased his head but had no slits for vision or breathing. Puffy clothing covered the rest of the warrior's body and he appeared to be unarmed except for some small object carried in his left hand. The warrior's helmet and clothing just happened to match the coloration of the floor and entranceway. That combined with the puffy clothing had made the warrior appear as just a blur. Glen glanced over at Puck whose face had gone from contorted to suddenly placid but seemed to pay no notice to what was happening.

The warrior, with an obvious limp, rushed forward and a moment later, Glen's guards jerked and fell face down just like the first two. Four Immortals broke ranks and rushed forward only to collapse in a sprawling tangle of limbs. The remaining Immortals and advisors faced with this new apparition and with Puck doing nothing suddenly decided on a new career path and fled the Hall.

The warrior moved cautiously, arms raised, putting Glen and his prison cart between Puck and himself.

Glen, overcome with wonderment blurred by lack of food and proper sleep, blurted out, "Who are you?"

The warrior replied in a surprising clear and calm voice, "I am Mallory Owens."

Puck continued to ignore them.

An Army of One

Late in the afternoon, Mallory awoke and under the watchful eyes of Tamara, Entreska and Zemfrekis he checked out his weapons and set up the monitoring screens in the spare Darkglasses. During the brief voyage across the Lydaron Bay Mallory had trained Tamara in using the monitoring screens, and he had quickly showed her some of the advanced functions. The monitoring screens would let the Jurasketu Army know exactly where he was and whether or not he became disabled by some accident or attack. Mallory convinced Rolf that if something bad were to happen to him, the damage and disruption he was going to wreck upon Puck's defenses was going to be so extensive that Rolf could likely launch a very successful assault on the Fortress and effect victory anyway. Toward that end, Rolf had assembled a rested and capable force of four heavy regiments and several troops of Swamp Rats.

Besides the escape routes, Craig Henderson had given him many details about the Fortress which Mallory had carefully recorded and studied in some depth. He knew the First Tower provided barracks for 500 Immortals who served as the Fortress garrison. The Second Tower held a dining hall, junior officer quarters, and a brothel stocked with slave girls. The Third Tower held apartments for senior officers and other high level administrators. The Fourth Tower, reserved solely for Puck, his concubines, and some select bodyguards, consisted of opulent bedrooms, baths and the *Hall of Reverence* which Puck used as a throne room even though he claims no titles and insists everyone simply call him 'Lord Puck' - that being everyone that's actually allowed to talk to him. A complex tunnel network lay beneath the Third and Fourth Towers with spurs off to the other towers and the Upper Gatehouse. The tunnels held weapons, stored food, treasure, boxes of imperial papers, and prison cells

The most likely place for finding the captured Jurasketu would be in those tunnels, but Mallory couldn't be certain and would need to make a methodical search. Additionally, he needed to avoid a chance injury that would derail the mission never mind his life. Therefore, he had crafted a plan of action that would eliminate all effective opposition.

Mallory had already decided upon taking an indirect route into the Citadel. He would approach from the northern spur of the horseshoe ridge keeping him and his team in the darkness out of the moonlight. Two Black Scorpions would carry the industrial cable launcher he had brought. The powerful unit fires a rocket that pulls a microfilament climbing cable up to a thousand meters high. Upon impact, the soft rocket cone would give way to a rocket driven barbed tip called a Climbing Spear that typically embedded its half-meter length entirely into the target surface: metal, rock or masonry.

He would remotely blow the charges at the lower gatehouse. Simultaneously, he would launch the cable rocket at the Second Tower. Next, he would launch NK gas from the valley floor blanketing the crag from the lower gatehouse to the Fourth Tower. He didn't expect the gas to affect many troops inside the towers, but he wanted to disable anyone keeping watch and manning defensive positions between the lower and upper gatehouses. He also expected many to run and look for the source of the explosions and be overcome. Although NK gas dissipates harmlessly after about 20 minutes, anyone exposed would be completely incapacitated by long spells of retching and severe vertigo lasting for many hours.

Then, he would use a motorized climbing box attached to the climbing cable to ascend the 400 meters in literally seconds and then penetrate the tower with special shape charges designed for masonry. After clearing the Second Tower of unfriendlies and dropping NK gas, he would then haul up boxes of ammunition, more NK gas, and his spare rifle just in case the one he carried failed, although he hoped that inconvenience would not arise. From there, he would thoroughly gas the First Tower and then move back through the Second Tower to the Third and Fourth.

He expected that securing the first and second towers plus the gatehouse at the top of the crag would take at least 15 minutes, possibly thirty. Then, battling his way through the larger third and fourth towers would take 20 minutes if the defenders panicked as he expected or upwards of two hours if they fought grimly room to room. Mallory advised Rolf to begin his assault no sooner than thirty minutes after he gassed the First Tower. Tamara would monitor

Mallory's progress and keep Rolf apprised of the situation. Rolf's troops should stay one tower back from wherever Mallory had progressed or they might be caught in the NK gas or accidentally shot by Mallory.

Night fell and the two large moons hung low in the southern sky and eerily backlit the four towers upon the massive crag. The small blue moon high in the eastern sky spat sparkles of pale blue light onto the tops of the towers. On the valley floor, Mallory carefully donned his auto-camouflaging P24 Body Armor and the J7C Battle Helmet. The helmet provided an artificially enhanced false color field of vision including infrared contrasting useful in fog, smoke, and darkness. The helmet and armor provided complete filtration against toxic gases both mundane, exotic and in this case the NK gas plus about an hour's supply of generated oxygen for anoxic conditions.

He used the radio transmitter to inform Tamara he was moving into position and he switched on the video feed and tracking data to the monitoring screens for Tamara. Six Black Scorpions followed Mallory carrying the cable launcher and four boxes containing the extra ammunition, NK gas, spare rifle and a limited assortment of useful gadgets and tools. They stopped about 300 meters from the base of the crag. Mallory surveyed the crag using helmet vision enhancement and then carefully aimed the cable launcher at the base of the second tower. He stepped back ordering the Black Scorpions back with him.

He mentally issued a command. A thunderous explosion erupted from the Lower Gatehouse producing a huge fireball that quickly grew into an eerily glowing yellow and red mushroom cloud rising hundreds of meters into the air. Moments later following another mental command, the cable launcher burped. A mere second later, a small puff of dust erupted from the base of the Second Tower accompanied by a distant thud. The climbing box reported that the pressure sensors in the Climbing Spear showed a good insertion that would easily handle the climbing loads.

The Black Scorpions grabbed the cable launcher and the supply boxes. They raced for the base of the crag directly below the Second Tower. Meanwhile, Mallory skillfully began launching NK gas rockets from his rifle, manually loading each one. He managed to fire an entire case of 24 NK gas rockets in about two minutes. Only the last one landed off target sailing completely over the crag and landing on the southern valley floor. Mallory was perturbed by the unexpected miss and briefly checked the rifle over, but didn't fire another. NK gas is dark gray and invisible against the night sky but the enhanced battle vision provided by his helmet allowed Mallory to discern the faint signs of the gas and he was satisfied the coverage was adequate and so took off running to catch up with the Black Scorpions.

Five minutes later, he was checking and securing his gear making sure his climbing tools and supplies would be properly accessible. Then he slung his rifle over his shoulder and stepped into the harness attached to the motorized climbing box and attached the line to the second position of the box which could actually accommodate three lines. Forty seconds later, he was hanging against the stone face of the Second Tower. He looked right and left. He could hear shouting and the clanging of gear from inside the towers. He could also hear numerous moans and cries for help. He could hear someone retching above on the wall to his right. Up close against the masonry, Mallory didn't like the quality and state of the workmanship and suddenly became hesitant about attempting to blow a hole into the tower afraid he might cause a catastrophic failure.

Mallory breathed heavily and checked his watch. He had about another 10 minutes of free action before the NK gas dissipated and he could potentially come under attack. Something heavy dropped or thrown from the tower or walls could prove harmful if not fatal in his current position. He made a decision to simply ascend the wall to his right and enter the Second Tower that way.

He reversed the climbing box and descended 10 meters onto the rocky crag. The towers and walls had been built a couple meters back from the moderately sloping edge of the crag probably to ensure longevity against erosion of the cliff face and need for a more level foundation for the masonry. While still in his harness, Mallory let out slack from the climbing line as he carefully worked his way over to the wall that rose 10 meters at a slight backward angle and was topped with parapets. Mallory spent a few moments wondering whether the ancient parapet would withstand the strain of a small grappling hook. Then decided he would just take his chances.

Mallory pulled out one of his two 10cm grappling hooks with an integrated 100-meter microfilament line and simply hand tossed the hook on top of the parapet. He tugged carefully until the hook set itself hard against the masonry. Then he ran the microfilament line through the first channel on the climbing box. Next, he set the main line to passive reverse hold and the grappling hook line to positive slow pull. After a few moments, the slack was taken up and Mallory rose up the wall until he was just under the parapet. He could hear multiple sources of retching and moaning coming from the wall. Next, he ran some additional slack onto the main line. Then after a moment or two of heavy breathing and mind clearing exercises, he clambered over the top, catching momentarily on his rifle, and dragged the climbing box over with him. He released the harness and studied the scene.

Nearly twenty soldiers, some obviously geared up for guard duty, the others only partially dressed were crawling and retching along the 60-meter length of the wall. The wall was actually a double wall 15 meters across with a series of raised platforms in the center. He noted two trap doors near the center. He would have to investigate those when he came back to the First Tower. The doors into the First and Second Towers at either end of the wall were closed. Next, he detached the grappling hook line from the climbing box. Then he pulled additional slack on the main line and wrapped the line around two iron hooks conveniently placed along the northern parapet wall. Setting the climbing box for auto-descend he lowered it over the side with the harness still attached.

While he waited for the Black Scorpions to load his extra ammunition, NK rockets and weaponry into the harness and send it up to him, Mallory scanned for any signs of trouble and noted that 14 minutes had elapsed since he had laid down the NK gas barrage. The door to the First Tower opened briefly followed by horrible vomiting sounds before someone managed to shut it. Four long minutes later, his supplies arrived. He had to struggle a little to guide the climbing box and harness containing his supplies over the edge of the parapet. He detached the harness from the climbing box and dragged the boxes toward the door of the second tower occasionally kicking a retching soldier out of his way. Mallory manually armed a NK rocket and rolled it toward the First Tower along the wall. It went off with a harmless poof but poured out fresh NK gas to cover his rear while he cleared the Second Tower.

He left the supplies a few meters from the heavy wooden door of the Second Tower, and he slapped a small masonry shape charge on the door near the latch. He moved back to his supplies, readied his rifle and blew the charge. The muffled explosion blew the latching mechanism into the tower. The wrecked door swung back slowly as dust and smoke billowed out. Mallory fired an NK rocket through the opening and then began dragging his supplies along. He hesitated at the doorway. His battle vision allowed him a clear view despite the dust and smoke. Several retching soldiers littered the room along with many overturned tables and chairs.

The dining hall spanned the entirety of the tower - nearly 20 meters across. The floor was heavy wooden planking. Enormous exposed beams supported the floor five meters above him. Mallory spotted the wooden closet jutting out from the wall on his right that enclosed wooden stairs leading up and down. He noted with satisfaction that the heavy wooden door opposite him that led to the connecting wall with the Third Tower was already barred and secured.

He looked back and noticed a lone archer peering down into the darkness from the top of the First Tower most likely unable to see anything but his comrades writhing on the wall. Mallory ignored him and entered the Second Tower dragging his supplies with him. This room would be his base for the assault on the First and Second Towers.

He could hear shouting above, so he warily approached the stairwells. Heavy iron bound wooden doors with sophisticated ceiling and floor pin hinges allowed the doors to swing out but remain difficult to break down or prize open.

Quickly, he went back and placed a mine in the doorway he had just blown and placed another mine behind the other tower door. The mines were equipped with alarms that would silently alert him to human presence and provide a video feed whereby he could decide to blow the mine if warranted. Satisfied his rear was properly secured, he returned to the stairwell.

Mallory hesitated for a moment on whether or not he should test to see if the door was locked and barred. He decided he needed to see what was below first. Calmly, he pulled a very thin but stiff line of black optical cable from a pocket and clicked one end into a port on his helmet. While kneeling to the latch side of the door, he snaked the cable under the door. He saw empty stairs leading down to a closed door at the bottom. He frowned. He went around to other side and repeated the process. Same result, empty stairs leading up to a closed door. He stowed the optical cable and stepped back to briefly consider his next move. The retching and moans from outside on the wall had intensified - not surprising considering the double dose of NK gas he had delivered. Through the moans he could hear orders being shouted above and so decided to go up first.

He positioned a small charge on the lock to the door leading upstairs and backed away. He tapped his remote, blowing the charge. The door opened slowly. Mallory bounded forward, pushed the door aside with the toe of his boot and took aim having selected his precious armor piercing rounds. He hated using the hard to replace rounds, but he didn't want to put himself in the awkward and vulnerable position on the stairs necessary to placing another door charge.

His first shot severed the top hinge pin. The bottom hinge pin took two before breaking. The fourth shot shattered the latch. Four more shots shattered the bar on the right allowing the door to open slightly, then lurch off the frame and fall edgewise against the outer wall before flopping over and skidding to the floor with a thunderous bang. Before the door had finished falling, Mallory had snapped an NK round into the manual load slot and fired the round through the opening.

Shouts of anguish were followed by weapons clattering to the floor accompanied by the thuds of bodies. Mallory scanned the stairs with his enhanced battle vision carefully checking for booby traps. He saw nothing suspicious. He took a deep breath and vaulted up the stairs. Nearly 40 soldiers lay convulsing on the floor. Arrows, throwing rocks and some weapons were heaped in the center. He kicked away a kneeling soldier who lunged at him. The room occupied only half the tower. A fine wooden wall running east to west divided the tower level.

The retching soldiers cowered out of his way as he strode to the wall. No doubt in the oil lantern light he presented an extremely frightening visage. He pulled the elaborately carved pocket door open that provided entrance to the other half of the tower. The large room contained dressing tables, upholstered chairs and at least ten four poster beds with silk curtains in vivid colors. Two biers positioned at either side, vented to the outside, provided warmth. Fine embroidered pillows and small inlaid tea tables were scattered randomly throughout the room.

Mallory surmised that the two dozen young women dressed in flowing silk robes and cowering in the back corner were slaves. Most covered their faces with their hands. The others who dared to look showed eyes wide with fear. Mallory sighed and said nothing as the NK gas flooded in from the other room and the poor women began vomiting and collapsing to the floor.

He returned to the stairwell and found the door leading to the third level unlocked. He opened the door and saw two soldiers coming down. Instinctively, he fired a six round burst killing both instantly. He silently chided himself on the fact that the NK gas would have gotten them if he had just stepped back. In any case, he stepped back and loaded a NK round, then leaned back in and fired the round through the open doors into the third level. Ten seconds later, he bounded up the stairs and found a mixture of soldiers and officers and another finely appointed room full of cowering slave women all of whom were retching in the back.

The fourth, fifth and sixth levels contained sleeping quarters for the officers and some slaves but no soldiers. The tower battlement held ten retching soldiers and officers, a mounted spyglass, an assortment of maps plus a modest supply of rocks for dropping on besiegers. Mallory scanned the other towers and walls for signs of activity. He saw nothing. The original barrage of NK gas would have dissipated by now, but Mallory didn't feel the need to add more at that point. He descended the stairs down to the dining hall. He blew the door going down, blasted the door at the bottom away with armor piercing rounds and dropped an NK round into the room below which turned out to be a storeroom with just a few soldiers and slaves - all now retching and moaning on the floor.

The level below that contained a cistern and a very well hidden set of four trap doors that only barely showed up with his enhanced battle vision. Mallory used his optical cable to peer into them without opening them and saw tunnels dug into the rock that likely connected to the network of tunnels that supposedly honeycombed the crag. Mallory pondered for a few moments what to do about them before remembering his cans of two-part super-expanding foam epoxy. Smiling at how often the stuff comes in handy, he sprayed the base into the slight crack around the trap doors and then spritzed the setting agent over that. Within seconds, foaming epoxy turned iron-hard and locked the trap doors permanently in place. Admittedly, the doors themselves could be hacked through, but that would take many minutes from an awkward position inside the tunnel. Certainly long enough for him to complete clearing the First Tower and begin clearing the Third Tower.

Mallory took a moment to engage his drinking straw and suck down half a liter of water. Then he tromped back up the stairs to go clear the First Tower. He scanned the battlement and noted the retching soldiers had moved about some, a few had crawled into the wrecked dining hall where he stood. Surprisingly, he saw several archers now posted at the top of the First Tower and peering out of the windows on the third and fourth tower levels. His most recent drop of NK gas appeared to have been blown away by a stiff breeze that had arisen whilst he had been down in the basement of the Second Tower.

He radioed Tamara and informed her that the Second Tower was cleared. He was going to tackle the First Tower next. She noted that Rolf had moved a heavy regiment into position at the base of the crag ready to move on his signal.

Mallory decided to simply walk out onto the wall and see if he drew any fire. He simply strolled along until he reached the trap doors near the center. Nothing happened. The archers on the top shifted around now and again, but obviously they couldn't see him in the darkness augmented by the chameleon-like body armor and helmet. He had intended to deal with the trap doors on the way over, but decided to simply use the foam epoxy and seal them.

Mallory decided to blast the First Tower's recessed door from a distance since he reasoned that the murder holes for the door might be manned unlike the Second Tower. The only question was a rocket grenade or waste more armor piercing rounds. Mallory sighed and decided upon the grenade because it would blast anyone manning the murder holes, although more soldiers would likely die. He crouched behind a raised platform, manually loaded the rocket grenade and fired into the door and ducked.

The blast blew the door apart and blew masonry chips all over the battlement. Mallory slapped a NK round into the rifle and fired it into the opening. Next, he loaded and fired two more NK rounds sending one each into open windows on the third and fourth floors of the First Tower. Mallory jumped up and sprinted through the damaged opening.

The center of the main floor was a day room for soldiers and now in total disarray with five dead and dying soldiers lying amongst the overturned tables, chairs and scattered cards. Another twenty soldiers and slaves lay injured and retching. A barracks lay to his right behind an open door. To the left was the stairwell just like the Second Tower. It took Mallory about ten minutes to clear the rest of the tower which mostly consisted of barracks and large caches of arrows, oil and rocks. The basement had a cistern and hidden trap doors like the Second Tower. Mallory sealed the hatches with more epoxy foam and returned to the main floor.

The Upper Gatehouse proved quicker since it only had two small guard rooms that had avoided the initial barrage of NK gas. Instead of killing or gassing the remaining guards - he used the epoxy foam congratulating himself for not just shooting them. He didn't use the NK gas because he wanted Rolf to start advancing to properly secure everything Mallory had cleared so far. Mallory informed Tamara that Rolf could begin his advance now knowing that it would take them at least ten minutes to reach the First Tower by which time the residual NK gas would have dissipated. Although she had witnessed by monitor everything that had gone on, Mallory asked her to pointedly inform Rolf of the sealed trap doors and their implications plus the unfortunates sealed in the guard rooms in the Upper Gatehouse.

From the vantage of the Upper Gatehouse he could see that the Lower Gatehouse had been reduced to a pile of rubble and the fire had been blown out as he had planned. As he watched, Jurasketu scouts began clambering over the still smoldering ruins. Rolf's supporting moves were underway.

Mallory trotted back through the First Tower and over to the Second to reload, check his equipment and plan his next moves. He double-checked the monitors of the secret escape routes, but they showed no activity which surprised Mallory. Possibly Puck wasn't aware that anything was greatly amiss yet. Maybe he had been taking a midnight stroll and had been gassed in the initial barrage. Mallory muttered a hope that he could only be that lucky. Twenty-seven minutes had passed since the initial barrage, so he was happily on schedule and no major problems had yet developed.

He wanted a peek at the Third Tower before he made his assault. He mounted the stairs and thanked his battle helmet for its secondary ability to screen out noxious odors since the second and third floors were thick with vomit and bile from the retching soldiers. He carefully surveyed the Third Tower and the connecting double wall. The double wall held about thirty sprawled soldiers totally exhausted from retching and struggling against the vertigo for many minutes. The parapet atop the tower showed no activity.

The windows of the third and fourth levels showed two or three archers peering warily out. Mallory zoomed into their faces and saw the obvious fear, yet he could sense their grim determination to fight until the end no matter how hopeless. This dashed Mallory expectation of the remaining defenders panicking and fleeing. He no longer had the advantage of surprise and shock. Of course, the defenders still didn't have any realistic hope of stopping him unless they got an opportunity to get lucky, and so that meant he would have to proceed with caution to avoid any such opportunity.

He pumped a round of NK gas through a window on each the third, fourth, fifth and sixth floors of the Third Tower. He aimed over the heads of the archers posted at the windows not so much to avoid killing them as having the round hit them and bounce back out. Then, he returned to the main level and picked up the door mines. Next, he unbarred the door leading to the Third Tower and opened it.

He moved up slowly along the wall towards the Third Tower searching for the hidden trap doors he was expecting. Indeed, just like the wall connecting the First and Second Towers, four trap doors were positioned near the wall center. This time, Mallory decided to sneak a peek inside the hatches using his optical cable. The two hatches on the north side both dropped into a long, barren corridor that appeared to dead end in both directions. The two hatches on the south side both dropped into a similar corridor, but four soldiers lay sprawled on the floor after one of them had most likely peered out of a hatch not long after the initial barrage. Mallory guessed that hidden trap doors provided egress at either end. Anyway, he saw no advantage to operating in a narrow corridor with no room to maneuver. Mallory sealed the hatches with foam epoxy. Then he loaded a rocket grenade and blasted the door to the Third Tower. He followed that with a NK rocket through the still smoking entranceway. Except for the main floor that contained an officer's lounge now strewn with debris and bodies, the other floors held a series of posh apartments just as Craig Henderson had described them.

Mallory threw NK gas rockets onto the twin walls connecting the Third and Fourth Towers and into the courtyard below. Clearing the nearly fifty apartments took a protracted and exhausting thirty-four minutes. Mallory had to launch more NK rockets into the courtyard, onto to the walls and even the main floor of the Third Tower. Mallory had been forced to kill eleven Immortals. Another ten minutes was spent clearing the basement levels of the Third Tower.

Mallory returned to the Second Tower to take a breather and restock his ammunition belts. He was met by a couple dozen Swamp Rats advancing from the First Tower. They were securing the retching soldiers as prisoners and taking up defensive positions throughout the tower. Mallory could see Jurasketu heavy infantry peeking out from the windows of the First Tower and manning a makeshift barricade at the destroyed entrance to the First Tower.

Then Mallory returned to the Third Tower, there he surveyed the courtyard and walls. The NK gas had dissipated, but only retching and moaning victims were present. Since Mallory expected heavy resistance inside the Fourth Tower, he decided to conserve NK gas and opted to simply mine the north door and precede out the south door of the Third Tower. At the wall midpoint, he loaded and fired a rocket grenade to destroy the entrance to the Fourth Tower.

Next, he reached for a NK gas rocket, but he was distracted momentarily by a nearby metallic tinkling. He looked around but saw nothing. He then loaded the NK rocket and fired. But nothing happened. Annoyed, Mallory turned the rifle sideways to see what was wrong and immediately saw that the control housing had fallen off and was nowhere to be seen. Mallory muttered a mild obscenity and looked around for a moment. He would need to go back and get his other rifle.

The dust and debris had settled in the entrance way and Mallory could see four heads peering out. He could also hear shouting coming from inside the Fourth Tower. Mallory reached back, pulled out another NK gas rocket and proceeded to perform the manual arming procedure. At the very moment he lobbed the rocket towards the entrance, a dozen swordsmen burst forth from the ruined entrance and charged towards him. One of the soldiers accidentally kicked the gas rocket that then hit a prone, moaning soldier and took an odd bounce right over the wall and off the crag.

Mallory barked, "Dammit." He quickly drew his 5mm sidearm and fired several shots in quick succession dropping six soldiers literally at his feet. The remaining six got tangled up in the pile of bodies and Mallory shot them as well. He heard the distinctive twang and whoosh of bows and arrows coming from the upper levels of the Fourth Tower. A shower of arrows began falling all around Mallory. Several prone soldiers got skewered and cried out in agony. Four of the heavy arrows hit Mallory, but his protective armor absorbed the blows although he was staggered a little. A quick glance at the armor revealed why they had been able to draw a bead on him. Blood and dust had so encrusted the armor that the auto-camouflage feature was virtually useless.

Tucking his relatively vulnerable hands into his body, Mallory turned to run back for his spare rifle and time to clean off his armor. As he turned, he felt a sharp blow against his right shin and then a clatter. A moment later, a strong hand seized his ankle. Mallory suddenly realized to his horror he had forgotten to epoxy foam seal the trap doors on this wall. A burly soldier had partially emerged from the nearest trap door and had taken a swipe at his leg. The impenetrable armor had deflected the sword blow and the awkward angle had wrenched the sword from the soldier's hand, but Mallory had stumbled from the impact allowing the soldier to seize his ankle. Mallory shot the man twice in the head, but the delay proved troublesome. Now, he had to deal with seven more soldiers emerging from the other trap doors and partially blocking his escape. Worse, he could hear another sortie from the Fourth Tower on its way.

He only had two shots remaining in the 5mm, so he shot the two soldiers nearest the courtyard side of the wall and he took off running to that side while pulling out a fresh clip. Unburdened, rested and unimpeded by prone incapacitated soldiers, he should have been able to sprint right past the remaining soldiers. Instead, he was intercepted.

In desperation, Mallory beaned the first soldier with a well-aimed throw of the ammo clip leaving the soldier stunned. Mallory then deftly stepped past an overly aggressive sword lunge aimed at his midriff and punched that soldier hard just under the arm with the empty 5mm automatic that left the man gasping for air. Mallory grabbed the man's collar and yanked him into the path of the next two. One fell onto the gasping man and lost his sword in the process. The other jumped back. The fifth and last one made a powerful overhead strike that Mallory avoided by stepping in and twisting his body just a centimeter out of the way, and in one continuous motion, Mallory snaked his hand up behind the soldier's head, pulled, turned and extended sending the man flying aided by the momentum of the strike. The flying man crashed into the stunned man, and they both toppled over the relatively low courtyard side wall and hurtled to the courtyard below with a horrible scream that ended abruptly with a resounding double thud.

The fourth soldier had recovered his footing, advanced and, despite the examples of his comrades, made an all-out slashing attack. Mallory slid slightly to his right and forward. With perfect timing, he reached under the man's left elbow and simply added a subtle turn and push sending the man crashing head first into the base of the wall where he lay still either unconscious or dead.

The motion of avoiding the attack had carried him close to the fallen third soldier who seized the opportunity to leg sweep Mallory who twisted and easily rolled out and back up right next to the man's head. Mallory stomped on his biceps leaving him wailing and writhing in pain.

Mallory glanced back to see another dozen soldiers rushing out the damaged entrance of the Fourth Tower. Mallory quickly grabbed for another ammunition clip and stepped back – and put his left foot directly into the grasp of the second soldier who while still prone had regained his breath. Mallory immediately kicked the man in the ear with his right foot. The man howled in agony but instead of letting go as Mallory expected – the soldier reflexively clamped and twisted, badly wrenching Mallory's knee. Ignoring the pain, Mallory leaned down and clocked the man on the back of the head with the 5mm. The man went slack.

Mallory jerked his foot free, stepped back and turned to run. Unfortunately, the left knee failed to cooperate and instead collapsed causing him to totter backwards and with a mumbled curse, he tumbled backward over the courtyard wall. As he fell, Mallory kept his cool. He twisted his body to avoid hitting headfirst, tucked his hands into his center still holding the 5mm, and relaxed for the impact. The only other thought he had on the way down was, *"Oh man. This is gonna hurt"*.

An Attack of Conscience

They arrived at the Third Tower just after the 17th hour to find Rolf dozing quietly in the ruined officer's lounge under the watchful eyes of General Urkiza and four Swamp Rats. Forty more Swamp Rats rested near the stairwell wearing universally sullen expressions.

Zemfrekis laughed, "How can he sleep at a time like this?"

Without opening his eyes, Rolf snarled, "Not very well apparently."

Rolf stood, stretched, rubbed his eyes and looked over at the four flights of Swamp Rats. Nodded his head in their direction and turned back to Entreska, "Okay, Tresh. Here's the plan. Owens blasted the South Entrance door of the Fourth Tower before he fell off the wall."

Entreska cringed.

Rolf muttered, "Sorry." He continued in a quiet, firm voice, "Two flights of Rats will use a tortoise formation to rush the doorway. Once they secure the entrance, the other two flights will use a tortoise to escort you over there. That puts you within thirty to forty meters of any point within the tower. That's what you need right?"

Heather said, "Yes."

Entreska said, "Yes. That should work. I can feel him now. He is on the main floor."

General Urkiza raised an eyebrow. The four Swamp Rats remained impassive from either discipline or practice at ignoring conversations. Entreska gave Rolf a look of doubt as to whether she should have said that.

Rolf looked around and grinned, "It's okay. I had to tell them. They think I've gone daft, of course. But no matter, they are accustomed to Father's eccentricities. Mine seem mere trifles by comparison. Ready?"

Entreska breathed deeply twice and said, "Yes. I'm ready."

"Master Troop Leader Bellowes, you may begin when ready."

Word was quickly passed to the upper levels. A shower of arrows rained from the Third Tower onto the Fourth. Then the clatter of return fire began hitting the Third. A supply of quilted, multi-layered large shields designed for siege work had been brought up to the Third Tower. The Swamp Rats grabbed the special extra-heavy shields and lined up at the door. Then they began inching their way out and slowly formed up the tortoise just outside the door. One Swamp Rat took an arrow in the thigh and had to be pulled back. One of Rolf's guards took his place. After five minutes the tortoise was formed up and moved forward across the wall. Sixty heavily armed members of the 4th Heavies arrived from the Second Tower and crowded towards the door to begin forming up another tortoise.

Entreska remembered the hatches that had proved Mallory's undoing, "What about the hatches?"

Rolf shrugged, "We pushed wooden pallets laden with sand bags onto the hatches an hour ago. It'll take a good long while for anyone to break through that."

Entreska smiled. She felt a distant hint of amusement coming from Puck.

"Does he know I'm here?"

Jasmine replied, "Yes. But he may only think it's the Crystal of Evermore if he recognizes its signature which is possible. But he probably doesn't have the benefit of sufficient experience to tell the difference from the Conjoined form - especially in the case of Evermore."

Heather added, "My sister is correct. That is why we need to get as close as possible before you attack him in earnest and show your powers. Otherwise, he may be put on guard prematurely. Of course, he thinks something is going on. It'll be interesting to see what he does."

Jasmine said, "That will likely depend on how much he actually knows about Evermore. Yet. Wait. Something isn't quite right. I can now sense an additional wizard presence."

"What? How is that possible?"

A chorus of voices uttered various forms of surprise and confusion. Then foamy waves of disagreement splashed back and forth over Entreska's mind for an eternity of several seconds.

Jasmine finally said, "I take it back. It is not a wizard presence. It is something of different order."

Entreska felt a deep mental sigh of puzzlement.

"I don't understand."

Jasmine gave a hollow laugh, "Of course not. This is entirely unexpected."

"But what is this presence?"

Jasmine hesitated and said, "Technically?"

"Technically. Metaphorically. Really. Whatever."

Jasmine stated flatly, "I've personally never encountered one. It is a rare occurrence. But Silas, Heather and Tom all confirm that the presence is indeed what is called an Infestation."

"That doesn't sound pleasant. But what does it mean?"

Jasmine hesitated then said, "An Infestation can occur when someone ingests unpurified Wizard's Essence. Consuming impure Wizard's Essence can offer protection from all forms of sorcery. The Keeper can probably explain it best. Heather?"

Heather spoke almost wistfully, "The practice is called Immutation, and it was widely employed in the distant past before the formation of the High Wizard Council which banned the practice on the grounds that it was dangerous and unnecessary."

Entreska sensed more than one source of derision.

Heather continued, "Yes. Very dangerous to those with sorcerous abilities. Immutation makes the individual's presence indistinct and essentially clouded to our sorcerous abilities. We can vaguely sense them at close range, but we cannot properly focus on their presence rendering them virtually immune to any sorcery."

"Virtually?"

Heather continued, "Depending on the impurities, preparation and amount ingested, the protection can vary from partial to total immunity. Partial immunity can be overcome if a sufficiently powerful wizard can lay hands on the protected individual."

"Then what is an Infestation?"

Heather continued, "What causes an Infestation is not known, but rarely, some combination of impurities, preparation, excessive amount and the individual, create what can be best described as a shadow presence. The Infested individual's presence is typically totally invisible and totally immune to any sorcery from any wizard. But the shadow presence, the Infestation, haunts the mind of the unfortunate victim with visions and voices exhorting violence that naturally drives the victim crazy. Most soon kill themselves to escape the horrific visions. The rest eventually succumb to the visions and go on violent rampages that are hopefully kept short by the quick and merciful killing of the unlucky victim."

"Would Puck know this?"

Jasmine answered, "A very good question. Very likely. It is even more interesting that Puck would employ such a person."

Heather laughed, "Since the person is likely violently crazy, maybe Puck would simply find such a person both interesting on a Wizard level and useful on a mundane level. And interestingly enough, an Infestation is only detectable when actually active and most Infected individuals will only show the shadow presence briefly and sporadically."

Jasmine barked, "The presence is gone. That was quick. Or not. I really don't enough experience to judge how long an episode should last."

Heather intoned, "Usually not very long was what I was told..."

"Tresh, are you okay?"

Entreska startled, said, "What?"

Rolf looked at her with some concern, "You seemed to have drifted off."

Entreska sighed, "Sorry. I was conversing with the Voices in my head."

Rolf said, "Ah. As I was saying, fortunately, the Fourth Tower wasn't really designed to repel besiegers. So, the Rats will be successful."

Rolf was correct. The Swamp Rats plowed straight through the doorway. Over the clatter of arrows, Entreska could faintly hear the screams of the dying Immortals and Swamp Rats. Apparently, her sensitivity was increasing because she could sense their deaths in the Essence Web as Heather had described it. Worse, she felt them not as dying wails like she would have expected but like a delicious, sweet chocolate that melts away in the mouth with a ruinous bitter aftertaste. Heather had also mentioned that wizards avoided living anywhere where death was a common occurrence within a few hundred meters.

Entreska focused on Puck. She felt no fear only mirth. That frightened her.

The Swamp Rats signaled that the anteroom was secured. They had suffered two dead and four injured, but they were ready. The 4th Heavies maintained their tortoise but did not advance. The other twenty Swamp Rats plus Entreska formed their own tortoise on the left of the Heavies and shuffled forward to the Fourth Tower.

Entreska crouched in the center and flinched each time an arrow clanked off the heavy shields held above her head. Other than that, all she could hear was the creaking of leather and armor punctuated by the groans and grunts of the Swamp Rats. She pushed through the ruined doorway and grimaced at the scene illuminated by lamp light. Blood soaked bodies of a dozen Immortals were stacked against the right hand wall. The dead and injured Swamp Rats lay to her left. Everything was streaked or splattered with blood. She slipped and nearly fell as she moved into the room, but strong hands on either side kept her upright.

Swamp Rats crowded into the room protecting her from all sides.

Heather's booming, but soft voice prodded, "You'll want a stool."

"Master Troop Leader, is there a stool?"

Indeed there was, but the soldier who brought it forth and, despite Entreska protests, pulled his fur cloak off to clean the blood away. Then he presented the stool as though it were a great gift. Entreska thanked him and sat across it in a rather undignified working position. She adjusted her cloak against the bitter cold and tried to clear her mind.

Puck was close, very close.

Instead of stabbing at him, she imagined herself encircling his mind as Heather had suggested. She could feel him applying pressure against her thought tendrils. She allowed Puck to press as hard as he liked, gently giving way but strengthening all the while...

Many minutes passed as this game continued... Suddenly, he viciously twisted one of her tendrils. Heather had warned her, but the pain was sharp, she gasped in agony. That was her signal to squeeze.

Entreska imagined Puck's mind crushed under the weight of his dark deeds. Puck stabbed at a tendril. Then he twisted another. Then he yanked brutally on yet another. Almost unendurable pain wracked her mind and body; she gasped, flailed and groaned, but she did not falter. She felt the strength continue to flow like an upwelling hot spring. She imagined the tendrils searing Puck. She squeezed. She burned.

She could feel the panic rising in Puck's mind. She braced herself for the worst. Puck relaxed... She squeezed tighter. Then she screamed as Puck stabbed directly into her mind seeming to open a horribly cold dark hole in the center of her head. The hole seemed to be freezing her mind as though it was some kind of billowing cloud of hellish black ice.

Her mind was going numb, and so she thrashed her thought

tendrils. She imagined Puck being slammed onto a huge iron anvil. Then an enormous hammer swung by a blood-splattered Valentine Jones squashed Puck's head like a melon. The head reformed. Jones snarled, raised the hammer directly over his head and slammed it down again, his feet leaving the ground as it squashed Puck's head with a sickening meaty squelch. Yet, the head reformed anew. Bellowing in anger, Jones smashed down the hammer three times in quick succession. This time the head reformed somewhat misshapen.

The dark hole crystallized and then shattered. A tornado of heat melted and dispersed the crystal shards... Jones kept battering Puck's head until finally the anvil cracked and the hammer's handle splintered.

Entreska went back to squeezing, tightening. Puck relaxed again possibly trying to ready himself for another counterattack. Then she became lost in memories not her own... Snow-covered fir trees on a steep mountainside... Enormous brewing vats... Autumn wheat fields stretching across a river valley... A crystal blue lake reflecting puffy white clouds... The imposing stonework of a huge dam... Children wrestling in the grass... A warm embrace of slender arms and soft kisses... Then nothing.

Puck was gone. She grunted in surprise and fear. She searched. Nothing... She widened the search... Nothing...

"Heather! He's escaped! Where did he go?"

An overwhelming sense of relief flooded across her mind.

Heather's patient, soft voice seemed to echo, "He has not escaped. He is dead."

"Oh."

Silence.

"That's not the way you said it would happen."

"I know. I have no explanation. But congratulations, my apprentice. You won."

Entreska pulled her arms to her chest, leaned back her head and slumped from the stool onto her knees. Strong arms pulled her to her feet.

A worried voice asked, "Professor?"

Entreska opened her eyes and nodded, "It is over. Puck is dead."

"What?"

"I said it is over. Puck is dead."

A deafening, spontaneous roar filled the chamber. The cheer rang louder and then turned into a booming chant, "Puck is dead. Puck is no more. Puck is dead. Puck is no more..."

To Entreska, the chant seemed to grow louder with each rendition, but then she realized that all other sounds of fighting had died down almost completely. Then the chant was picked up by the Jurasketu forces in the Third Tower. Soon, seemingly the fortress, town and surrounding ridge lines echoed with the chant.

Entreska sighed deeply and then suddenly jumped up.

Master Troop Leader Bellowes barked in surprise, "Something wrong Professor?"

Entreska in a desperate, commanding voice said, "My father. We must find my father. Open that door!"

Without waiting for orders from Bellowes, several Swamp Rats pulled out their hand axes, stepped forward in front of the two ranks guarding the door and started whacking away.

Heather's smooth voice seemed to fill her head, "Envision the door reduced to sawdust."

"What?"

"Imagine the door as sawdust. See it. Believe it."

"What about Puck's Troops?"

"Feel for yourself."

Entreska concentrated, ignoring the loud ax blows, and scanned beyond the door. Nothing. *"No one there."*

"They fled when Puck was destroyed. Now the door. Sawdust. Feel it. Make it true."

Entreska barked loudly, "Stop. Wait."

The men continued.

Entreska turned to Bellowes, "Make them stop."

Bellowes croaked an unbelievably loud, "BELAY THAT."

The men halted and turned with puzzled looks. Bellowes motioned for them to fall back. Entreska nodded thanks. She drew in her focus. Then out to the door. Dust. Wood made into dust. An eternity of about ten seconds passed and the thick wooden door shuddered suddenly. It sagged from its hinges, creaked loudly and then toppled onto the floor where it exploded into a blast of dust and wood fragments.

Heather proclaimed, "Done. Very good. Eventually you'll be able to do that in a blink of an eye - but that was amazing for a first try. You're a natural."

The revealed corridor was oil lit but completely empty. The five-meter long corridor ended in a tee with a beautiful wooden door that had been left ajar. Bellowes, shield held high, stepped forward and bolted through the door and down to the intersection. After looking right and left, he waved for his troops to follow. Several Swamp Rats, shields still up, followed and quickly formed two files behind their leader. Next, Bellowes stepped across, pushed the door wide with his foot and sprang back.

Entreska could see that the room behind the door was actually a large hall - where Puck's presence had been. She could feel nothing in the room. But she could feel the unit of the 4th Heavies moving towards them.

"*I feel no one in the hall. Do you?*"

Heather answered, "Nothing. No one."

When nothing happened, four Swamp Rats each, deployed into the right and left corridors. Then the rest, led by Bellowes rushed through the door and formed a protective semi-circle. Unintelligible shouts came from deep in the hall. Bellowes shouted something equally unintelligible back.

Entreska waited nervously.

Suddenly, the Swamp Rats rushed out of sight except for Bellowes who turned to look back towards Entreska.

He smiled and hollered in obvious joy, "The Grand Marshal! Colonel Owens! Alive!"

To the horror of the remaining Swamp Rats, she lurched forward barely avoiding their outstretched hands and ran down the corridor. Bellowes, apparently convinced all was well or not willing to stop a Wizard, simply stepped aside as she ran past into the Hall of Reverence.

She paused but a moment to take in the magnificence of the Hall and instead focused on the tableau near the far end. Mallory, encased in helmet and padded armor, was kneeling by her naked father who was sitting on a wooden cart of some sort. A purple-skinned man with bright orange hair, who could only be Puck, lay face down on the dais near an overturned table. Two soldiers lay motionless near the far door. Two more motionless soldiers lay near the cart. More dead soldiers lay between her and them. The muddy oil light gave the scene a dreamlike quality. She sprinted over to her father.

Several Swamp Rats clattered past her and across the Hall, took up a defensive position, and then peered into the far doorway. Moments later two flights of the 4th Heavies burst into the Hall and took up defensive positions surrounding the dais, Mallory, Entreska and her father. She could hear Bellowes screaming orders.

Mallory was in the midst of unlocking the manacles binding her father's wrists. Mallory's hand signaled her to wait while he completed unlocking the manacles. She stopped a few meters away. Her father, eyes closed, rubbed his wrists for a moment before opening them to look around. He scanned the Hall and did a sharp double take at Entreska.

"Tresh?"

"Father!"

"How? Why?"

To Entreska's horror, her father went to stand up but his legs failed to cooperate and he fell flat on the floor with a loud whack. Mallory attempted to catch him, but he also seemed to be having a leg issue and he flailed at air and crashed to the floor as well. Four Swamp Rats, who had trailed Entreska, brusquely shoved her aside and stepped forward. They picked up the Grand Marshal who was muttering dark curses, gave him a cloak, grabbed a nearby chair and set him down.

Meanwhile, Mallory was helped up by a Swamp Rat and given a chair as well. He took the moment to take off his helmet. He winced in pain then sighed deeply. But then he looked over at Entreska and broke into a wide smile.

Entreska was conflicted for a moment about whom to embrace first and opted for her father while beaming a smile at Mallory. Her father held her tight and finally released her with a deep sigh and smile.

"I thought I had lost you. In fact, that is why I am here."

Entreska puzzled said, "What are you talking about?"

"I came to bring revenge upon Puck for your murder."

Entreska was even more puzzled, "You don't do revenge. Not strategic."

"The Demon thought otherwise."

Entreska frowned and stared over at Puck.

Her father spoke again, "I have two questions for you though."

"Yes?"

"Why have you painted your body and hair like that? And who is this Mallory Owens?"

Entreska laughed, "It's not paint. And I didn't do it myself. As for who this Mallory Owens is - that's a bit complicated. But he is a valuable ally."

Mallory snarled, "So now I'm just an ally?"

Entreska stepped over and gave him a hug around the neck and sensuous kiss on the forehead.

Mallory frowned, "That seems better."

Her father smiled and said, "I think she likes you. You had better be careful. She always gets want she wants. Very smart and persistent, she is."

Mallory shook his head, "I wish. I'm afraid I use violence to solve problems. So I'm off the list."

Her father nodded, "I know the feeling..."

Entreska ignored them and went over to look at Puck's body.

Heather spoke clearly, "The body must be destroyed promptly and the ashes soaked in water and flushed into the ocean or a river."

"I know. I'll arrange that shortly."

Entreska knelt and examined the body. A pool of blood lay beneath the head. Grimacing, she turned the head to see two bullet holes in the throat and that both eyes had been shot out. She looked back at Mallory who shrugged. She nodded sadly.

Mallory spoke, "I'm sorry. My plan didn't go well. But I did manage to kill Puck in the end. And even save your father somehow. It was weird though. Puck seemed to be catatonic. He was oblivious to my presence."

Entreska smiled wanly, "You are forgiven."

"What?"

Entreska shook her head sadly, "You are forgiven. He was catatonic because I was trying to kill him. We were locked in a Wizard Duel."

Mallory and her father simultaneously said, "What?"

Heather intoned, "That explains things. You were going to win, though, in a matter of seconds."

Entreska ran her hands through her hair. "I was winning the duel. I think it would have been over in a few moments when you shot him."

Mallory frowned, "I thought that was a bit too easy. I'm sorry. If I hadn't screwed up earlier or gotten here a moment sooner. Well... Technically, I did kill him. So you didn't."

Entreska shook her head, "No. I was going to kill him. I cannot pretend otherwise."

Mallory nodded sadly while she stepped back from where Puck's body lay and walked over to stand near Mallory. She traded glances with her father.

Her father spoke warmly, "Tresh, your courage and sacrifice is undeniable. It will not be forgotten."

Entreska looked around the hall in a bizarre combination of despair and elation. She turned her back and began to cry. She slumped to the floor cross-legged and sobbed uncontrollably.

Jasmine tried to comfort her, "You did what you had to do. And you succeeded against all odds."

"Shut up."

Silence.

Minutes passed...

"Tresh?"

It was a different voice but familiar.

"Tresh?"

She looked up. It was Rolf. He had a deep look of concern. She looked around. Her father was quietly sipping steaming soup from a bowl. Mallory had stripped off his armor and was enjoying a tankard of ale with his left knee propped up on a cushioned stool.

Rolf smiled, "Your crazy plan worked. But Colonel Owens' plan apparently worked too. Which leaves me a bit confused."

Her father barked, "You're not the only one."

Mallory added, "Failure is madness. Success is genius."

Her father muttered, "I like that. Can I use that?"

Mallory shrugged, "Of course."

Rolf smiled clearly suppressing an outright laugh.

Rolf extended a hand, "Are you okay, Tresh?"

She took the hand and pulled herself up. "No. But I'll just have to get over that."

Rolf nodded. He looked over to her father and spoke gravely, "Glen. We found Juragi. He's dead along with all the other captives. I'm sorry."

Entreska looked over at her father. He just stared for a moment, took a deep breath and then returned to sipping soup.

Rolf was silent for a long minute and then turned to Mallory. He asked, "I don't understand. How did you get up here? We thought you were done when you fell off the wall. Did you suffer just the knee injury in the fall?"

Mallory laughed, "The knee injury caused the fall - not the other way around. Anyway, I plummeted into the well house, but the roofing apparently was overdue for replacement and I crashed down into the damned well. They assumed I was dead of course. But my armor is completely sealed against water as well as gasses so I didn't instantly freeze to death. Better yet, the auto-camouflage had been disrupted by dirt and blood and needed a good wash that the well water accomplished in fine fashion. It did take me a better part of an hour to work my way up by the ropes with the bad knee and through the wreckage at the top. Then I had to hide and rest a while after all that exertion. I also needed to take medicine for the knee and wait for that to have an appreciable effect."

Entreska asked, "Did it?"

"Not really. I'll be needing reconstructive surgery for certain - it is trashed. Anyway. I tried to find my way back to the Third Tower, but I got completely turned around. By mere chance, I blundered onto stairs that led me to here."

Rolf looked puzzled. "We heard no more shooting. How did you evade the guards?"

Mallory waved the small 5mm automatic. "It's completely silent. It does require a bit more accuracy because it doesn't penetrate armor so easily. The automatic camouflage and darkness helped because I could get really close and I rarely miss at close range."

Rolf nodded in admiration.

He turned back to Entreska. "What now?"

She pointed at Puck and said, "We have to properly dispose of the body. His Essence is still dangerous. I will need assistance."

Rolf glanced warily at the body and looked across the hall. "Bellowes!"

Rolf looked back to Entreska and said softly, "We have accomplished a mighty deed. I just hope we can survive the aftermath."

Entreska nodded, "That is what we have you for."

Heather added, "And you. Do not underestimate your power."

"Silence. I'm not in the mood to talk about power."

The Grand Debater

Glen smiled grimly when he sighted the black veined, green marble walls of the Aruskile Garden, the official residence of the Grand Debater. The military coach pulled up to the expansive entrance with typical precision and halted smartly. The driver, a ruddy, rotund old Master Troop Leader named Hawkins no longer fit for the field, lustily barked out the destination. Glen wasn't sure whether Hawkins was trying to be helpful in case Glen was napping or just being obnoxious. As it was, he didn't wait for a valet to open the door, and instead he leapt out. An annoyed military valet ran up, came up short, saluted and stood in obvious dismay at having failed to perform his door opening duty for none other than the Grand Marshal. Glen hid his amusement, returned the salute casually and directed him to inform the Steward that he was here to see the Grand Debater. The valet nodded and quickly vanished.

In short order the relatively young Steward, Colonel Mendoza, appeared squinting slightly into the mid-morning winter sun making his rugged features even more unhandsome than usual. His uniform and hair both appeared to be crisply pressed, however, and blocked off his lean torso.

Mendoza showing apprehension said, "Sir, I'm sorry. We weren't expecting you. The Grand Debater is at the Chambers having breakfast but is due to return shortly. I have sent word that you await her."

Glen nodded and said, "When are you due to return to field duties, David?"

"Next spring, sir. I am to assume command of the 17ᵗʰ Lights. Please, this way."

Mendoza led Glen into the sumptuously appointed foyer, and they quickly tucked into the official receiving room. Mendoza summoned a butler who brought him cakes and a steaming pot of tea. Glen nibbled a cake and sipped the delicious mild tea. Mendoza excused himself after some more awkward pleasantries.

Glen sighed heavily after the Steward left. After 34 years' service and 17 years as the Grand Marshal, his own stewardship of the Jurasketu Army was at an end. He had defeated Puck in a brilliant campaign that had nearly ended in disaster except for the quite unexpected heroic actions of his daughter and her strange friend. He smiled to himself. He could at least be proud of that.

The cost in lives had been dear including that of his dearest friends, Valentine Jones and Juragi. But, objectively speaking, the losses were much less than he had imagined would have been required to achieve the destruction of Puck and his empire. In many ways, it was a miracle.

There, however, had been other difficult costs. Entreska had sacrificed her own beliefs to help kill Puck. She ignored the arguments that she hadn't really killed Puck because Owens had finished him off actually. In a funny way, her refusal to allow them to excuse her conscience made Glen prouder than the many things she had done to deserve praise.

Glen's own price for victory was grave. He had invented authority to risk a significant fraction of the Jurasketu Army in the campaign to the Centaur Citadel. It didn't matter that it had succeeded. Failure might have doomed Jurasketu. Such a risk was not his to take on his own authority. The National Council of War and the Grand Debater had to approve such a risky campaign as that. Worse, Glen had lied to his senior commanders and hence to the soldiers, that the Council had granted him such authority when it had done no such thing. There could be no other description of his actions other than high treason.

That was why he sat waiting for the Grand Debater. He had written his resignation letter and detailed confession to ensure that he alone would bear responsibility. He would face the courts martial, confess and make clear it was a moment of weakness in himself rather than a systemic fault of the Army. He would not ask for pardon or mercy. Some would say he should have killed himself to save his honor and that of the Army. A coward would have fled. An arrogant fool would have defended his actions as just and right simply because they succeeded. Glen felt that he must show that he was not above the laws and that he would not attempt to escape responsibility for his actions. It was the only way to preserve faith in the Army.

Colonel Mendoza returned a short while later to report the Grand

Debater was ready to receive him. Glen was slightly surprised when Mendoza took him not to her office but to her private library. The library was an intimate place, only a few square meters of floor space with two opposing walls of books, two comfortable chairs, a small table and a small stove heater in the front corner to the right of the door. One wall, made of expensive large-paned glass, looked into the inner courtyard of overflowing planters, elaborate fountains and stone benches. The Grand Debater stood with her back to him, long and thick gray hair covering her shoulders like a hood, hands clasped behind her back. Colonel Mendoza said nothing, simply closing the door behind him as he left.

Glen waited a few moments and when the Grand Debater continued to stare unmoving out the window, he pulled his folded resignation letter from the inner pocket of his best dress uniform jacket and laid it upon the table. Glen gave a brief ironic laugh when he realized he had laid the letter on top of a well-worn copy of his book, *The Web of Thought*.

She looked briefly and slightly back over her shoulder and said with a hint of sadness, "I suppose that is your resignation letter?"

"Yes, Jessie. It contains my full confession–"

"Hush..."

Glen said, "What?"

Jessie turned around, "I said 'hush'. I haven't accepted your resignation yet. You can still follow my orders can you not?"

Glen nodded and remained silent.

She wore flowing robes of purple and white that gave her an indistinct shape completely hiding her limbs and feet. Only her ancient, gnarled hands, wizened face and hair showed that a human occupied them. Her skin and hair showed her age, but her blue eyes twinkled with the enthusiasm of a child.

She literally billowed across the room and snatched up the resignation letter. She held it out before her, then flowed swiftly to her left, grabbed the stove mitt, opened the stove door, tossed the letter inside, and slammed the door shut. She shucked the mitt back to its place and stood warming her hands over the stove.

"These stove heaters are the greatest invention ever. Don't you think, Glen?"

Glen stood unmoving, blinking in disbelief.

Jessie looked sidelong at him and just continued to warm her hands for a few more moments. Then she said, "That was a simply marvelous campaign, Grand Marshal. Great Burning Blasted Golden Cloak marvelous."

Glen regained his mental footing, "You can't do that. I must take responsibility for my actions. I didn't have-"

"Hush."

Glen stammered to silence again.

She rubbed her jaw for a moment. Then, she reached into her robes and produced a sealed leather orders pouch. "I heard you lost your copy, so here's another."

Dumbly, Glen took the pouch.

She waved her hand, "Open it."

Glen broke the seals and extracted the sheaf of folded papers, setting the pouch aside. He stared at them. They were dated Summer 43, 3429. Almost 150 days ago, just a few days before his army began the move onto the Raffin leading up to this moment.

"Read them."

He unfolded them and scanned through the usual officialese of a Secret Finding of the National Council of War. Then, after reading the operative paragraph, he frowned in dismay and looked askance at the Grand Debater.

"I received no such orders...."

Jessie arched her eyebrows, "Nonsense. You would never do anything without proper authorization."

"My mistake, I should have killed myself."

"What?"

Glen calmly said, "I tried to be brave and take responsibility for my actions. My other good option was suicide."

Jessie snarled, "Oh sure. That would have helped you, but how does that help me? Quit being selfish. What do you think would happen if it became known that you acted without proper orders? My authority would be completely undermined. Faith in civilian control of the military would be shaken. Our institutional traditions would be gravely harmed."

Glen nodded sheepishly.

"Besides. We still need you. Our spies report that Murok has been furiously readying forces in Tangur. Harvey is demanding that the Imperium should be given all of Puck's domains above the Placid River, and we should withdraw our troops once his have arrived."

Glen shrugged, "Order withdrawal now. Then the Imperium will have to subdue the Cumar homelands by their lonesome. Feed the Cumar spies with quality intelligence on the Imperium force disposition and plans. The Imperium will have a total nightmare on its hands. Harvey will be very sorry and may even make a deal that gives us more than we would have gotten from a stare down."

Jessie rolled her eyes, "You and Chairman Rolf think alike. He suggested the same thing."

Glen chuckled, "Actually, that is Rolf's contingency plan not mine."

"Oh? What is your plan then?"

Glen shrugged, "I didn't have one. That is why I recommended his. Seems brilliant actually. His plans often are."

"Indeed. But I think Harvey is being deliberately provocative because he is planning for open war. If you were removed, he and the Imperium Council would be unrestrained. Once we consolidate our gains in Western Zetu, we will become a dominant force in the Bay of Lydaron and almost certainly a threat to the Zattan expansion plans there. They may even perceive us as a direct threat to the Imperium itself. And they would be right. Puck's former domains under more benevolent rule have the potential to double Jurasketu's wealth and power."

Glen nodded, "Jurasketu's might will be almost unmatched. But that will take a decade or more to realize."

"Precisely. Which is why I believe Harvey will move against us now while we are still weak by comparison and our best troops are scattered subduing the Western Zetu. Rolf did tell me that Murok's army won't be ready to move until midsummer. That's gives us more time. And with Rolf taking over Northern Command, I feel safer but both of you have always told me we cannot successfully resist a full blown Zattan invasion."

Glen merely nodded.

Jessie narrowed her eyes, "How exactly did you talk him into accepting that command?"

Glen frowned, "Didn't you talk to him before you gave official approval?"

"Yes. But I had other questions that pushed that question from my mind."

Glen smiled, "He made the request himself. Maybe the prospect of my pending removal motivated him."

Jessie shrugged.

"Did you tell Rolf about the Secret Finding?"

Jessie looked offended, "He didn't need to be told. He drafted the finding at the War Council's insistence. The National Council of War and I decided immediately what had to be done when we got the word. We surmised you had just seized the moment. Unacceptable politically of course, so we had no choice but to make it right. Naturally, I order both you and Rolf to pretend and swear you acted completely within policy."

Glen nodded again, "Of course. Success is genius. Failure is madness."

Jessie laughed, "Indeed. Speaking of madness, though, Rolf hinted that you have a plan to handle the Imperium threat both short and long term. But I'm curious, I don't see how resigning your post, killing yourself or being court-martialed and imprisoned would help facilitate implementation."

Glen laughed, "Well, my personal fate should not materially affect the plan at this point. Marshal Tang and Chairman Rolf should be able to execute their end with relative ease. The plan merely demands that Jurasketu apply a few resources to the right places at the right moments."

Jessie was nonplussed, "And how is this plan supposed to work exactly?"

Glen intoned, "The key is Murok. His maternal family is an important and popular political force in Tangur. He has long coveted the Governorship for that reason."

Jessie scoffed, "How does that help? That limits our ability to disrupt him by financing and inciting rebellions."

Glen continued, "Quite true. And so that limitation applies likewise to the Imperium should war breakout between Murok and the Council."

Jessie, looking very intrigued, "What? Were you hoping to induce a war between Murok and Council somehow?"

Glen shrugged, "Hardly. The Zatta Buruza is an expert conciliator. The destruction of Puck has presented opportunities and created risks that will keep the Council firmly united."

Jessie folded her hands at the waist and frowned in her signature pose of command unhappiness. She proceeded to stare at Glen until he couldn't help but smile. Jessie did not smile back.

"Grand Marshal, enough banter, what is the plan?"

Glen erased the smile and said, "I have it on good authority that Murok is planning to declare Tangur's independence during the Summer Festival. The apparent preparations for war against Jurasketu are really to prepare for war with the Imperium instead. Tangur has long resented Imperium dominance. He'll have plenty of internal support for secession especially given his family's extensive political influence."

"What?"

Glen nodded, "He has been planning this move for some time. With Jurasketu and the Imperium distracted in the West, this is the perfect time. Tangur is by far the richest and most populous province in the East. Of course, the Imperium will attack immediately with whatever they have available to test Murok's support. The attack will almost certainly be repulsed. And then we'll have a chaotic mess."

Jessie threw up her hands, "And then what?"

Glen nodded again, "Jurasketu will be faced with very challenging choices. Do we openly support either side? Do we secretly support either or both sides? Do we provide weak or strong support?"

Jessie, taken aback, "You would support Murok?"

Glen smiled, "If it achieves our strategic aims."

"How would helping a sworn enemy achieve our strategic aims?"

Glen shrugged, "A divided Imperium weighed down by years of civil war would be weaker than the stronger Jurasketu we expect to emerge over the next decades."

Jessie nodded, "We benefit significantly from trade with the Imperium. Civil war would diminish that. Depending on who and how much we provide in support, the factions could see an opportunity and turn against us. The Valruk may decide the time is ripe to attack with a significant fraction of our naval forces being diverted to the Bay of Lydaron."

"All true. Which is why we must choose carefully from the menu of options."

Jessie quirked an eyebrow, "I'm puzzled though..."

"About what?"

"How can you be so sure Murok is planning to just seek independence? Maybe his real goal is to overthrow the Council and seize the Zatta Buruza for himself. A bid for independence by the most powerful province in the Imperium where he fools us into helping him would be the perfect launch point for a campaign ending with his elevation to Zatta Buruza. And I know your spies are good - but why on earth would Murok reveal his plans for independence to anyone but his inner circle?"

Glen smiled, "He has told his closest confidant and no other person of his plans actually. And that was done in complete secrecy."

"That you even know that is impressive. So you don't actually know his plans then. You are just surmising?"

Glen kept smiling, "No. I know exactly what he said."

Jessie's jaw dropped and kept her voice to a harsh whisper despite the thick, almost completely soundproof walls and isolation of her private library, "This confidant is your spy? Great Burning Blast. No wonder everyone thinks you can read his mind."

Jessie then turned and stared at the table.

Glen glanced over and guessed she was staring at her copy of *The Web of Thought*. She must have been reading it. Entreska liked to read his book. He had always assumed because they wanted to better understand strategy. Maybe they were both trying to read his mind as well. A number of his senior officers and friends had always felt it unwise to have published a book that revealed his secrets in such detail. Or he should have at least limited the distribution list. His reply was always that the book merely contained musings on rational thinking and that should not be kept from anyone. Less violence followed from rational thinking - not more. They called him naive in return. He laughed.

Jessie looked back at him, "What is funny now?"

"Sorry. I was thinking about my book."

"Funny. So was I."

Glen smiled, "Indeed. What were you thinking about it?"

She continued to stare at the book and said, "I was thinking about your chapter on spying. How can you be certain this confidant is not gaming you somehow? You state quite plainly that highly placed spies can rarely if ever be trusted. And I would agree with you."

Glen feigned a frown, "True. In this case, however, I have strong reasons to completely trust the confidant in question. Admittedly, Entreska often accuses me of plotting against myself in my sleep."

Jessie nodded thoughtfully, then suddenly cocked her head and said, "I'm not surprised. How is it we trust you again? Technically, aren't you a highly placed spy for either the Imperium or Jurasketu or both? Who is your true master?"

"I am my own master. The Essence of Liberty is the belief that everyone is their own master and no others. Anyway, I openly serve Jurasketu and openly hold a seat on the Imperium Council. All members of the Council are assumed to be representing their self-interest and cannot be compelled or trusted to do anything else except that. If anything, I'm considered more trustworthy since I'm a sworn officer loyal to Jurasketu and must predictably respect Jurasketu law, tradition and duties. I cannot be called a spy in that context since my loyalties are known to everyone."

Jessie raised an eyebrow, "Trust? Hardly. They assume you would ignore Jurasketu law if you could keep it secret. And that would be true quite frankly. No. Don't deny it. Try fear. Remember I served as Jurasketu's Ambassador to the Imperium Council for nearly six years giving me the opportunity to study them in person. I think you sometimes forget the sheer terror you inspire in your enemies and wavering allies."

Glen feigned a frown, "Well. Yes. There is that."

"But why do you trust this confidant so completely?"

Glen smiled but said nothing waiting for Jessie to puzzle it out. Normally, he was very direct. But Jessie enjoyed puzzling out Glen's strategies and thought processes. So he always obliged her when time allowed.

He watched as she paced back and forth, hands clasped behind her back. He let his focus drift to the tile floor. The painted porcelain tiles were only twenty-centimeter square on each side and were laid out in a standard grid, but each tile was uniquely designed and expertly painted. The themes varied widely. Some were monochromatic abstract designs. Others contained entire scenes from myth and legend in full color. Still others held pastoral, littoral, or urban scenes. A number depicted ships and seascapes. The remainder consisted of natural settings, animals, trees, plants and sea creatures. It represented a fortune in artistic output, but he knew that all the tiles had been donated by the various artist guilds throughout Jurasketu. In fact, virtually all the art in the Aruskile Garden had been donated directly or indirectly.

Glen gave that a deep consideration while Jessie continued to ponder. While some certainly had donated their efforts for the name recognition, he knew and believed that most had done so out of hope and gratitude. The Jurasketu Army was comprised completely of volunteers. The Jurasketu people, despite their flaws, were always described as kind and generous. Their spirit carried forth in everything they did. That put a great burden on the leadership of Jurasketu. He knew that Jessie felt that burden of gratitude and support. Some days he did. Some days he did not. Sometimes the game of high strategy required a focus and detachment that did not allow for that burden. He needed to always return to that burden or he would be lost.

Jessie spoke but Glen failed to understand.

He asked, "I'm sorry. I was thinking distant thoughts. What did you say?"

Jessie smiled, "I have the answer. There can be only one explanation for your confidence."

"Indeed. And that is?"

"Murok's secret confidant is you."

Glen frowned, "Seriously? Where have you been? Murok hates me."

"You were known to be very close once."

"But we became bitter enemies when I entered the service of Jurasketu."

Jessie nodded, "Yes. Why didn't he set you up and have you killed then before showing his displeasure publicly?"

"We were kinsmen and close friends. He assumed I would come to my senses with a little time and his strong disapproval. When I did not, I was already forewarned and on my guard."

Jessie nodded, "When I sent word that Murok had been named Governor of Tangur, you ignored the problem and strongly pressed the attack against Puck. That seems crazy given the situation unless you knew somehow that Murok would not attack."

"Admittedly, that looks awkward, but I knew he didn't have the required near-unanimous support on the Council for a war declaration. And his forces are insufficient to achieve a quick victory that the Council could simply approve as a thing already done. If anything, I needed to change the long term strategic situation by defeating Puck."

Jessie smiled, "All very plausible, but I'm not buying it. You are the confidant. The whole bitter enemy thing was a sham that allowed you and Murok to manipulate the various factions of Zattan politics. That was a somewhat mature and high concept strategy for someone your age at the time and I'm suitably impressed. But I can't imagine your goal was simply some marginal balance of power strategy. What was your goal?"

Glen half-smiled, "It was the highest. Peace, prosperity, justice and liberty for all. But in the end, it is nothing more than a muddle."

"I know that feeling. Who else knows?"

"You. Rolf. Murok's son Jeruk. And they didn't know until

recently."

Jessie rocked her head side to side, "What is the strategy then? I assume the choices you outlined still apply."

"Correct. Although strongly supporting the Imperium against Murok would not be one. My personal choice is weakly openly supporting the Imperium while secretly strongly supporting Murok."

"Logical. How, when or ever do you reveal alliance with Murok?"

Glen shrugged, "Secret support for Murok would likely be revealed at some point, but we should deny it initially and avoid open war. I think we make it appear to be an alliance of convenience and blame Harvey's provocations for our actions. Eventually, when it becomes clear that the Imperium cannot defeat Tangur, we encourage peace talks and sign a series of treaties with Tangur that are designed to ensure its independence and our desire to promote peaceful trade and relationships amongst the various provinces. Should the Imperium move against Jurasketu, we will make open alliance with Tangur."

Jessie raised an eyebrow, "That is a good plan. I'm impressed. Your political instincts have usually been excellent."

Glen shrugged, "Sometimes. I've made mistakes."

"Welcome to my world."

They fell silent for a few moments.

Jessie spoke finally, "There is another matter."

Glen had a solid guess to the nature of that, "Yes?"

"Rolf told me a strange tale that he says should remain a state secret, but he also thinks it won't stay secret for long and so we need a cover story."

He had instructed Rolf to truthfully tell her about Colonel Owens and Entreska.

Glen shrugged, "The tale is so unbelievable that if we tell it with just the right dose of false sincerity it will be regarded as a completely ridiculous cover story that couldn't possibly be true."

Jessie nodded, "Yes. Unbelievable and completely ridiculous. So, you are going to tell me that what Rolf told me wasn't a cover story?"

"I'm not entirely sure what he told you exactly. But I told Rolf to tell you the truth as best we know it. We cannot trust Colonel Owens nor Entreska to tell us the complete truth."

"Why not?"

"Because they don't trust us."

Jessie frowned, "Why not? Did they say so directly? Are they a danger? Did you provoke them somehow?"

Glen felt slightly wounded by the last question, but he couldn't argue that it was undeserved. He laughed hard and long and then finished with a deep laughing sigh while Jessie waited with a slowly curling lip.

"I am convinced Entreska has the powers of the wizards from legend. But, as you know, she follows the Ultherian Ethic of non-violence. She is afraid that we will use her as a weapon in our games of high strategy. She won't want to be used that way and so she will keep the extent and source of her powers hidden. And she will limit our knowledge to prevent us from somehow gaining leverage against her. She may even limit our contact with her. She studies my book very carefully."

"But she used her powers directly against Puck."

"Yes. That was a great personal sacrifice. It will take some time before her spirit recovers from that. She is deeply wounded and on a totally unexpected path that neither we nor she knows where it will take her. This is not to say that she won't use her powers to help us, but it will have to be on her terms. We cannot force the issue. Also, I can safely predict that should Colonel Owens perceive that she was threatened in any way, he would not hesitate to interfere decisively."

Jessie nodded, "That sounds like a delicate situation. Are they lovers?"

Glen smiled, "They are friends and allies, but not lovers - yet. And may never be. He is a warrior and an assassin. I don't think they are compatible unless he can forswear violence."

"Assassin?"

Glen nodded, "A military assassin. Not a freelancer. But he has the skills should he desire to use them."

Jessie nodded, "He killed Puck did he not? Will he do other work for us?"

"No. He killed Puck for his own reasons - not ours. I think the threat would have to be something the equivalent of Puck for him to choose such a mission. Anyone that credibly threatens him or Entreska, however, should be certain their affairs are in order."

"He is that dangerous?"

"Even more than that."

Jessie sighed. "Is he a danger to Jurasketu?"

Glen sighed deeply, "Not directly unless we were to foolishly make him our enemy. Indirectly, however, there is serious threat."

"Rolf indicated that Colonel Owens has unusual weapons and tools beyond our ken."

Glen shook his head, "That is not the serious threat. The serious threat is that he possesses a library of knowledge that can be used to create many such things. Not just weapons. Medicine. Construction. Transportation. He has the power to completely remake our world in ways we cannot fathom. Once unleashed that knowledge will spread into friendly and unfriendly hands."

"Where is this library?"

"Colonel Owens carries it with him. And another copy resides at the Temple of Healing. Owens may already or will make more copies."

Jessie nodded, "I don't understand entirely, but Rolf vaguely explained that as well. And apparently the Black Scorpions are providing military protection to this Temple without official sanction?"

"Yes. I didn't know about it either. Colonel Tallrider took it upon herself."

"I thought she was a Captain."

"I promoted her."

"That seems to be a mighty high reward for violating orders and potentially creating an international incident."

Glen bobbled his head, "Well. It is a bit more complicated than that."

Jessie laughed, "I know. I'm teasing. When word leaks out, won't everyone, friend and foe converge on the Temple and go after Entreska and Colonel Owens?"

"Yes. That is a grave danger."

"Shouldn't we destroy it?"

Glen grimaced, "That would seem to be the prudent thing to do."

"But you wouldn't?"

"No. It violates my principles of liberty, justice and the rational quest for knowledge. But more importantly, unless we get his consent or forced cooperation, we'd have to kill or imprison Colonel Owens. Even if I was willing to kill or imprison him, which I'm not and I don't think you are either, we can't have anyone know or suspect it was us. Particularly Entreska. She might take it personally. Lovers or not. And success would not be assured. If we make him our enemy, we are lost."

Jessie grimaced, "You are correct. But do you think we can get his consent to destroy the Temple?"

"I don't think so."

"Why not?"

Glen laughed, "I already asked him as a hypothetical."

Jessie laughed.

"So how do we prevent others from capturing or destroying the Temple or Owens?"

Glen breathed out harshly.

"Well... Colonel Tallrider with the reconstituted and heavily reinforced Black Scorpions will stop the amateurs and those who would fear war with Jurasketu."

Jessie frowned, "I thought you said those troops were operating covertly."

"Yes. But the various Wokometu states have or will learn that the Temple Guardians are Jurasketu troops. We will continue to deny it officially, of course. But we think it will discourage anything rash. It would also be important to create the impression that we believe the Temple of Healing is merely that and has no military importance. And so no one will be denied admittance to encourage that view."

"Would it help for us to declare the Template of Healing under Jurasketu protection openly for humanitarian reasons?"

Glen nodded, "I think that would be helpful, especially if we continue the fiction that the Black Scorpions are really the Temple Guardians and independent of Jurasketu authority. That way, officially, none of our troops are operating in the Wokometu region. Obviously, some of the Wokometu states might welcome alliance with us once we establish firm control of Puck's former domains."

"I will pursue that path. But what about protecting Colonel Owens? And Entreska?"

"I don't know. They both stand out like chin warts. They have returned to the Temple of Healing where Owens needs to have a badly injured knee healed. They may stake themselves out there counting on their skills and the Black Scorpions to protect them, but with the steady stream of pilgrims coming to the Temple I would be very worried if I was in charge of their security."

Jessie laughed, "Aren't you? I mean she is your daughter and he's a valuable asset."

Glen breathed heavily, "At this point, they are beyond our control. They can do what they will and I can only reason with them. I would rather they escape to a hidden retreat under our protection where

Entreska can explore what she has become and Owens can begin transmitting the knowledge he possesses in a digestible manner to our best minds. If that were to occur, the ascendancy of Jurasketu and Liberty will be assured."

Jessie smiled, "So you are back to your grand plan instead of a muddle?"

Glen twitched and then smiled warmly, "Heh. I guess I am."

Glen looked out the window at the gardens and imagined a beautiful future. He ignored the purple Demon standing behind a sprawling bush with black blood spraying out of its eye sockets.

The Scenic Route

The low table held five cups of formerly hot tea and a small black box. The five glum faces stared down at the cold tea. Ursula tried a brief smile directed at Entreska, but she just ignored it. Buck scratched at his arm. Tamara just kept staring. The black box was silent.

Mallory shifted his weight and gently rubbed his newly repaired knees as he considered the gathering. The Chief Physician, Ursula Valcott, imparted the wisdom of a lifetime dedication to making others feel better. The Captain of the *Inky Darkness*, Buck Jules, supplied the practical experience of evading authorities, ruffians and nature depending on the hazard of the day. The recently promoted commander of Black Scorpions, Colonel Tamara Tallrider, provided the steady leadership and confidence all great endeavors needed. The transorganic computer, Vanessa, combined her healing abilities with an instinct for doing or saying what was right and good. And then there was Entreska and himself, the ones in need of a plan.

The major surgical repair of Mallory's left knee four weeks ago by Vanessa had been completely successful. All the ligaments and cartilage were fully regenerated and anatomically correct in all respects. It would take another four to six weeks of intensive rehabilitation to allow the repair to fully heal and reach reasonable strength. Vanessa had also cleaned up the wear and tear and was confident the knee would be better than ever. She had performed maintenance on the right knee as well claiming that the rehabilitation would be better balanced and he might want both knees in excellent condition should he be gone for another long while.

After a long silence, Vanessa's voice soothed out from the black box, "I'm sure you'll figure something out."

Mallory muttered, "Or not."

Ursula offered, "Why can't you just stay here?"

Entreska sighed, "We've been through that. It would be too tempting for our enemies and most of our friends. They would attempt to control us, capture us or kill us."

Tamara sneered, "And we would stop them."

Entreska snarled, "And many might die in the process. And a large enough force would turn this valley from one of healing to one of death."

Mallory shrugged, "I have deployed weapons that will allow Colonel Tallrider and the Black Scorpions to repulse any force regardless of size."

Entreska flustered, "Repulse. You mean slaughter?"

Mallory winced, "There is probably enough NK Gas to discourage large forces which should limit casualties. Admittedly, a determined force that managed to reach the perimeter would be slaughtered by the Black Scorpions using the heavy weapons I have provided them. Mind you, we don't want to reveal the existence of the powerful weapons at all if we can. We want to promote the Valley of Healing as just that with no fancy weapons or nothing desirable. And neutral. Welcome to anyone seeking healing."

Tamara nodded in agreement.

Buck raised an eyebrow towards Tamara, "What if you were ordered to detain them?"

Tamara shrugged, "I would ignore such orders. The Scorpions and I are legally under the command of the Temple of Healing. We are technically the Temple Guardians and not a unit of the Jurasketu Army. I have the written orders from the Grand Marshal."

Entreska sneered, "Orders can be rescinded. Would the Scorpions still follow your orders should that occur?"

Tamara bobbled her head, "I believe they would."

Entreska shrugged. "And what about assassins or suicidal saboteurs?"

Tamara looked irritated, "What about them?"

Entreska looked over at her, "They could harm a lot of innocent people before they could be detected and arrested."

Tamara sniffed in derision.

Buck rocked side to side and said, "I tend to agree with Tresh. If they stay here, others will come with plots from feeble to genius. Such plots will likely all fail for Colonel Owens and Wizard Entreska are mighty indeed. And Colonel Tallrider leads a most excellent and veteran force. But innocents will suffer and die. That seems unavoidable."

All five went back to staring glumly at the cold tea...

Ursula spoke a few minutes later, "I'll get a fresh pot."

Mallory nodded, "Good idea. Please do."

Buck, ever supportive, said, "Warm tea makes for warm minds. Warm minds make for creative minds."

Some time later five glum faces stared down at cold tea...

Mallory reflected on all that had happened and imagined his verbal report to General Lang covering the mission. She would be howling with laughter at his numerous blunders including several major violations of military code, practice, honor and policy. She would be literally in tears laughing at his current predicament stemming from having become literally world famous by taking down an entire fortress. Covert operatives were not exactly supposed to be famous.

Buck asked, "What's so funny?"

Mallory shook his head, "Sorry. I was just trying to imagine what I would report to my commanding officer."

Buck looked puzzled, "I thought you no longer had a commanding officer."

Mallory sighed, "I don't. But I was imagining that I still did and somehow still had to make a report. General Lang, my former commanding officer, always laughed at my reports. She has or I guess had a robust sense of humor - at least when it came to my mission reports."

Tamara smirked, "I wish my commander was as forgiving."

Entreska snickered, "My father is very forgiving. But I'll have to give him this; he takes life and death seriously."

Mallory shrugged, "He seemed to have a decent sense of humor to me."

Entreska nodded, "Oh. He does. A very sophisticated sense of humor at that. He's just serious about life and death. I give him full credit for that."

Mallory frowned, "Hmm... I always thought of General Lang as being very serious. She just thought I was funny because I always tried to do the right thing. But I always failed and instead used large doses of kinetic energy to complete the mission successfully anyway. She always gave me the impossible missions. I thought it was because she knew I would figure out a way. But now I'm beginning to wonder if she did it just because it was funny to watch me try to do the right thing and fail."

Mallory considered this line of thought darkly.

And then he reached a conclusion...

"Hey. I'm not cynical!"

Everyone looked at him.

Ursula said, "I don't think anyone accused you of being cynical."

Everyone nodded.

Mallory simply smiled, "No. You didn't. But I did. And I was wrong."

Buck rolled his eyes.

Ursula smiled.

Tamara shook her head in wonder.

Entreska looked sad.

Everyone went back to staring glumly at the cold tea...

Mallory considered Entreska. Vanessa had ascertained that she was infused with an unknown substance that she was still trying to isolate completely that was likely generating a coherent form of a special kind of field called a Quantum Interstitial Foam, commonly called a QI Foam. This was surprising and highly interesting since these fields were the fundamental basis for interstellar space travel. A special device, a Quantum Interstitial Foam Enervater, usually called simply a Foamer, generates a very specific kind of QI Foam that supposedly drastically alters the quantum density of the vacuum. Depending on the field's strength and tuning relative to unaltered space, light can travel hundreds of times faster than in nearby space and correspondingly a ship traveling at a comfortable pace at just one percent the speed of light can traverse many light-years in just a few months' time. Apparently, this planet held a substance that could naturally generate Quantum Interstitial Foams.

He had even read once about a theory that proposed a QI Foam could be used as a detector - particularly of thoughts. And here there was a natural substance that could seemingly allow a person to do just that. If he could build a small scale Foamer, he might be able to test the theory. Tuning it would be easy since he had a live example of what the proper field should look like. Unfortunately, the *Velvet Sea's* Foamer had been destroyed in the Accident.

A sudden thought occurred to Mallory. Maybe the substance was actually widespread on this planet and was generating a large Quantum Interstitial Foam field extending out into space that had interfered with the *Velvet Sea's* field inducing the Accident. Then he had another thought. Maybe the substance wasn't natural. He would share those thoughts with Vanessa. Maybe that would help her.

Unfortunately, while both Mallory and Vanessa had some training in biochemistry, materials science and physics, neither had the deep training, background nor likely enough talent to properly understand how QI Foams worked and what exactly was the substance that Entreska had consumed and how exactly it was generating her QI Foam field that Mallory presumed formed the basis for her wizard powers.

He laughed.

Everyone gave a sympathy chuckle.

Tamara asked, "What is funny now?"

Mallory replied, "Quantum Mechanics."

Tamara scowled, "And what is that?"

Mallory chuckled, "A complex and largely incomprehensible theory that explains the workings of the Universe."

Tamara scoffed, "Sounds like a number of religions and Ethics that I know."

Mallory shrugged.

Buck snickered, "It is ever so. Do you subscribe to the theory of mind that posits the Universe is merely what we think it is?"

Mallory gave Buck a thoughtful stare, but it was Entreska who spoke.

"Isn't the Iturrian Ethic an unusual one for a merchant sea captain? I would expect something less mystical and more practical."

Buck stone-faced said, "The Sea hammers the practical into one's bones. There is little reason to devote leisure thought to the practical. The mind hungers for the mystical. Besides, I think it suits a pirate quite well."

That brought excessive laughter.

When the laughter subsided, Ursula said, "Seriously? You follow the Iturrian Ethic?"

"Yes. Deeply. I learned from my mother who was a serious devotee."

Ursula and Entreska nodded sagely.

Mallory took a breath and said, "My apologies for lacking a proper education, what is the Iturrian Ethic?"

Buck shrugged, "A study devoted to finding the meaning and purpose of living - the source of life, if you will."

Mallory nodded, "And what would that be?"

"What?"

Mallory asked with a smile, "The meaning and purpose of life?"

Buck gave an amused smile, "Well, it is a lifelong pursuit. That is why it is an Ethic."

Mallory frowned, "Darn. I was hoping that someone who had spent years of study might be able to offer something useful to one such as myself who instead spent too much time planning and executing missions. Just some tidbit of insight that might help me along through my life if you will. Anything."

Buck spread his hands wide in apology, "Oh. You want a simple summation of my studies then?"

Mallory nodded, "Exactly that. From a theoretical and practical aspect."

Buck smiled, "Very well. First, you must answer my original question."

"The Universe is merely what we think it is?"

Buck nodded.

Mallory shrugged, "Not especially. Things are as they are regardless of what we believe them to be."

Buck nodded sagely and brushed his cheeks with the back of his hand.

Mallory titled his head, "And?"

"Sorry. Yes. I hesitate in that you have just revealed that you have come to the realization that you aren't cynical and I didn't want to damper your enthusiasm for life."

Mallory leaned forward, "Are you that fatalistic? I am not unfamiliar with that line of thinking."

"No. Not at all. I offer two summations of thought. One steeped in despair. The other infused with hope and endless possibilities."

Everyone leaned in to listen closely as Buck paused in apparent hesitation rather than for dramatic effect.

"The first is this: The hardest thing about life is having to pretend that any of it matters."

That brought a round of deep frowns.

"The second is this: Life only has the meaning we give it."

That brought nods of approval.

Mallory said, "I personally have always been fond of pretend."

That brought a chorus of laughter.

Ursula looked around, "More tea?"

"Please"

While Ursula went to prepare more tea, Tamara and Entreska excused themselves to visit the latrine. Buck relaxed back into a reverie.

Mallory reflected on the report Vanessa had compiled about life on his current and likely permanent home. Mallory had ordered her to create the report when he had first returned to the *Velvet Sea*. He had spent a significant portion of his rehabilitation time reading the summary.

Vanessa had collected DNA from everyone that had come seeking healing. In the end, she only proved what was already obvious that the inhabitants were clearly descendants of Old Earth. The original colonists had apparently been an indistinct blend of American and European Caucasians with the not unexpected smattering of other genomic groups.

Vanessa had also conducted an extensive language analysis of Jurasketu and several other languages that she had gathered sufficient information to warrant comparison. She and Mallory had been genuinely shocked. Jurasketu and several related dialects were almost certainly derived from 22nd century American English. Everyone on the planet spoke a version of Jurasketu as either a primary or second language. Wokometu supported several versions of morphed Español with Spanglish commonly used in Styphlee and Deliverance. The Cumar spoke a version of Español that retained the verbs, pronouns and grammar, but virtually all the nouns and adjectives had been replaced or shifted, and idioms dominated conversation. Even more curious, Zattan clearly had evolved from Euskara and supported a number of dialects. And finally the Valruk language was a bizarre version of English using fully inflected forms and with the articles dropped. The linguistic diversity and evolution supported a long planetary history spanning centuries. Vanessa's best guess was that some of the colonists had been from an American Basque refugee community. Mallory did not like that theory but had nothing to offer in its place.

The native living cellular structures superficially resembled Old Earth cells in an unsurprising case of convergent evolution given the constraints of cell efficiency. And like all known planets with multicellular lifeforms, the cellular mechanisms of the native life used DNA and RNA molecules. The set of amino acids were slightly different, but otherwise the basic functions were surprisingly similar. The disparity in amino acids meant that Old Earth life and the native life were mutually nutritionally insufficient and often toxic.

Except for a few nut, fruit, coffee and chocolate trees, native tree forms dominated the forests. The native trees had proved to be plentiful and superior sources of wood for all purposes. Old Earth grasses, food crops and flowers had rapidly replaced native savannas effectively exterminating a significant portion of the vertebrate and invertebrate fauna that had depended on native plant species. The food crops were all clearly descended from genetically modified cultivars designed for enhanced nutrition. Domestic and feral Old Earth animals quickly dominated the savannas. Native forms retained domination of the forests. The invertebrate population seemed to be entirely native although most species superficially resembled Old Earth species in form. The ocean fauna appeared to be entirely native. While otherwise inedible, sea creatures provided superior oils and surprisingly tough hides. The Old Earth animals and humans benefited greatly from the total lack of parasitic invertebrates and the associated diseases. Virtually all the aggressive native animals had been swept out from the human inhabited areas over time. Mallory always felt a twinge of sadness when given these reports, but that was invariably the way colonization played out.

At the microbial level, things seemed stable with a mixture of Old Earth and native species throughout the biosphere excepting the oceans where the native species maintained dominance. Fortunately, the innate and adaptive immune responses of the Old Earth life easily and effectively blocked the native microbes and vice-versa so no mass extinctions had been recorded from disease. Except for bread and beer yeasts and symbiotic fungi in the Old Earth plants, Old Earth fungi were largely absent.

Vanessa and Mallory had concluded that a supervolcano had destroyed and buried the Jurasketu civilization on the Raffin. The destruction of the forests and glaciers had seemingly accelerated or precipitated a climate shift that turned the Raffin into a desert. Oddly enough, an analysis of his planetary computer maps had revealed volcanoes were relatively rare on this planet. Indeed, no major eruptions other than the Great Burning Blast had been recorded in the last 4000 years.

But where did that leave him?

Like most Primitive Worlds, high level math, science and engineering had been deliberately excluded. Over the centuries, some math and engineering had been rediscovered, but basic calculus, chemistry and physics remained lost. Scientific methodology was completely unknown. Old Earth literature and music was completely absent as well despite a strong literary tradition kept in Jurasketu and Español. Sculpture and carving were highly advanced. Painting was imaginative but lacking in technical skill.

Unexpectedly, either the original colonists had lacked a strong religious tradition or their traditions had morphed into something entirely new without leaving a trace in the historical record. Entreska claimed that near universal literacy had existed on the planet for millennia, so Vanessa and Mallory favored the former explanation. Mallory had pondered that for a long while. The primary philosophical tradition was called the Body of Ethics and most Jurasketu and Wokometu belonged to one of the many dozen Ethic flavors. The Cumar, Zattan, Valruk had their own quite fascinating religious traditions. Entreska claimed the Body of Ethics stretched back millennia. Vanessa had speculated that the original colonists had probably been some kind of *Back to Nature* group that over the centuries had branched into shamanism and spirit worship.

Vanessa's report added more to the mystery. It seemed to place the origin of the colonization in the 22nd or early 23rd century. No colony from that or any era, primitive or not, successful or not, matched the geography of this planet. That makes it an undocumented or ultra-secret colony or Vanessa's analysis wrong. Colonizing a planet requires a huge logistical effort to have even a small chance of success. Doing so without anyone noticing seemed highly unlikely. Vanessa's analysis had to be wrong. Mallory threw up his hands in resignation. What did it matter anyway? He was stuck there, analysis be damned.

"What?"

Mallory noticed that Entreska, Tamara and Ursula had returned to the room and that they and Buck were all staring at him.

Entreska asked, "Who is wrong?"

Mallory stared agape for a moment before he said, "Me. No one. I was just talking to myself and verbalized it would seem."

Everyone knowingly shrugged.

Buck kept nodding and said, "I think I have a solution."

Everyone turned expectantly.

"Mallory and Tresh take up residence on the *Inky Darkness*."

Tamara frowned, "Wouldn't that just make you and your ship the target?"

Buck extended a finger, "Possibly. But it would be a moving one and possibly secret."

Tamara sniffed in derision, "Ships have to put into port. You'd be a sitting duck."

"We're pirates remember. We can get supplies on the sly if needed."

Ursula blurted out, "You mean steal them?"

Buck rolled his eyes, "We have funds. We would pay premium prices most likely for the extra trouble. Or steal them when we need some entertainment."

Entreska and Ursula frowned. Tamara and Mallory chuckled. Vanessa kept quiet.

Buck added, "Besides. We don't have to reveal that Mallory and Tresh are aboard. We could take port as we wished."

Tamara shook her head, "Seems risky. Are you saying your entire crew can be trusted not to reveal such unusual passengers either accidentally or deliberately? Even occasionally taking port would be dangerous."

Buck shrugged, "Transporting important persons secretly is one of our specialties."

Tamara took a deep breath, "It is one thing to keep a single voyage secret. Keeping the presence of Mallory and Tresh secret permanently seems a stretch. Your crew numbers over a hundred and fifty."

Buck frowned, "And sworn to secrecy under penalty of death. My crew is handpicked and completely reliable."

Mallory looked at him, "Seriously?"

"Well. I think they are completely reliable."

"No. I mean the offer of floating asylum."

Buck nodded, "Yes. I mean that with complete seriousness."

Tamara pursed her lips, "What if someone just guesses that Mallory and Tresh are aboard the *Inky Darkness*? When they disappear from here, it wouldn't take a great leap of reasoning to assume they might have stowed away aboard the *Inky Darkness* especially if the ship curtails its activities."

Buck nodded his head, "We don't have a regular pattern so that wouldn't be a dead giveaway. But that doesn't keep them from just outright guessing. It's logical to me for them to hide on my ship. It could be logical to someone else. We can avoid taking port entirely if necessary. But it would severely limit our commercial activities and recreation for the crew. My crew, while fiercely loyal, won't stay loyal for long if I can't pay them or allow them shore leave."

Mallory nodded and smiled, "The Grand Marshal gave me a

substantial share from Puck's Treasury as a reward. So, in a bit of reversal, I have more than adequate funds I can provide as payment for privately chartering the *Inky Darkness* for a few years at least."

Buck smiled and then frowned, "Indeed. But still... My crew would eventually chafe at the lack of shore leave."

Mallory twinkled his eyes thinking of Jules Verne, "We could create a remote secret base somewhere with a small support village complete with suitable entertainments. Since the *Inky Darkness* would be the only supply ship for the base, you would stay busy doing supply runs. We could even cook up a mission or two."

Ursula looked annoyed, "Suitable entertainments?"

Mallory shrugged, "Brothel. Gambling hall. Tavern. Entertainments."

Entreska jostled her shoulders, "I think it would turn into madness. Too many people required to make it work. Too many ways they could be maimed or killed. And way too much to ask of people to essentially join an underground army for an indefinite time for indefinite reasons. Instead, we need to find a hiding place that requires no keepers who could be harmed if we are discovered. That is to say, I would welcome and trust Buck's help in getting us there."

Buck nodded, "Despite my love of crazy plans, I think Tresh is right."

Mallory reluctantly set aside his grand Captain Nemo dreams and looked over at Entreska with a frown, "Yes. I would have to agree. Tresh is right. Well, Captain? You're the pirate. Is there such a place?"

Buck shrugged. "I don't know. I know many excellent places to hide in large cities. Like where you and I first met. But almost needless to say, between your ridiculous appearance and world-wide notoriety, you couldn't ever go out into the city which means you would require keepers to provide provender and other necessities. The risk of discovery and potential harm to your keepers would easily exceed that of hiding on the *Inky Darkness*."

Everyone nodded in resigned agreement.

Buck continued, "Obviously, there are hundreds of uninhabited remote isles. But there is no food. And it would take some time and physical effort to establish anything close to adequate. That means supply runs every few weeks. Again, hiding on the *Inky Darkness* trumps that."

Buck raised a hand dramatically and said, "On the other hand, there are a few abandoned settlements on small remote isles that have plentiful fresh water, mild weather, potatoes, onions, herbs, fruit and nut trees, grasses, feral animals and even decent shelter. I would rate several quite high on the paradise scale."

Tamara asked, "But Captain, if that is so, why were they abandoned?"

Buck shrugged, "The Great Burning Blast. They were established as remote resupply stations for the Jurasketu naval and exploration fleets. They were never meant to be self-sufficient. Tools and supplies were regularly provided by Jurasketu to maintain them. After the destruction of Duravon, exploring the remote reaches for exotic plants and animals was an unaffordable luxury and the inhabitants were withdrawn or simply perished."

Tamara frowned, "How do we know any would be inhabitable now? It's been more than a little bit since the Blast."

Buck smiled, "*The Inky Darkness* has visited several and spent more than a few weeks making repairs or gathering supplies at some."

Mallory cocked an eyebrow, "What were you doing in the remote regions?"

Buck smiled, "Exploring. Collecting exotic animals."

Mallory looked concerned, "Do others explore those regions?"

Buck shrugged, "Possibly. But I know of no others. And none of the islands showed evidence of visitation except by us. Supplies are a serious issue."

Mallory was puzzled and then had a revelation, "Oh. You have charts that others do not."

Buck smiled, "In fact, I have the only known surviving charts of those regions and stations."

Mallory smiled and made a mental note to examine his own charts, "Indeed. That would make it almost completely safe then from discovery."

Entreska sighed deeply and everyone looked at her.

"But that leaves us rather cut off from the world. And what would happen if something happens to the *Inky Darkness*?"

Buck spread his hands wide, "Yet, it meets your criteria. I can leave instructions and chart copies with someone trustworthy in the event the *Inky Darkness* finds an untimely end to its path. We can make semi-annual supply runs using a route that will be impossible to retrace and that I won't share with anyone but Karl. If you decide that you've had enough of loneliness, we can revert to the *Inky Darkness* plan. Or maybe you'll decide that civilization isn't so dangerous after all and decide to trust Jurasketu."

Ursula frowned, "Being so remote - you'll have no medical care."

Mallory demurred, "I can handle most of our needs. Certain risks are unavoidable. And I doubt we'll ever be able to trust anyone."

Entreska shook her head, "The future is very uncertain. My abilities may grow sufficiently that we can be less fearful."

Mallory shrugged. He thought otherwise but decided not to share just then. The more powerful Entreska became the less she would be trusted and the danger would grow exponentially for everyone. Their options were limited.

Entreska continued, "Our choices are limited. I fear that if we do not steal away, we invite death and destruction. While I would allow myself to be destroyed rather than cause death, Mallory, Buck and Tamara would not. And I cannot ask them to follow me down that path. I think remote exile gives us time for the situation to improve and gives everyone time to settle into a new pattern in the Web of Thought that allows Mallory and me to live openly in freedom. It won't be forever."

Ursula looked worried, "Will the Temple of Healing really be safe even if they have left?"

Tamara nodded, "I have let it known that the Healer can and will destroy itself and the Temple instead of being taken against her will. Also, Jurasketu is secretly sending additional troops and money under my command to defend it against minor aggression. Chairman Rolf says that he will recommend Jurasketu announce the intention to safeguard the neutrality of the Temple. That will keep larger forces from making a move. Admittedly, I am confident we would defeat them. But as Tresh pointed out, the loss of life would be high. So we will have to hope the twin threats of self-destruction and Jurasketu retaliation or intervention will suffice."

Ursula nodded firmly, "I think you should have a small contingent of others on the island to help you and do the hard work while you work your wills."

Buck nodded, "I agree. I think the right mix of a dozen helpers would be a good idea."

Tamara nodded in agreement.

Entreska and Mallory both frowned.

Mallory said, "We'll manage."

Entreska demurred, "I don't want to risk others."

Buck laughed, "C'mon. Don't be such an Ultherian. You're being selfish. You know you could use the help."

Tamara nodded, "Yes. Finding volunteers would be easy. And it can get pretty lonely."

Buck nodded, "Yes. If you decide it is not working or the volunteers change their mind, we'll withdraw them at the supply run."

Vanessa suddenly spoke causing everyone except Mallory and Ursula to jump, "Won't they be tempted to talk to their friends about the adventure?"

Buck laughed, "I don't think so. And what would they tell? That Mallory and Tresh are on some island somewhere? My crew has the same issue. I can assure you that finding the right island would take a miracle even if they knew the approximate location. I think everyone knows that this is a life and death situation and talking to anyone not connected would be extremely disloyal. It is a miniscule risk."

Tamara and Ursula voiced agreement.

Buck looked around, "Are we agreed? I will consult with Mallory and Tresh on the best choice from the several good candidates once we get to the *Inky Darkness*. I will provide a sealed packet to a trusted friend I will not name with our intended destination and coordinates."

Mallory considered for a long moment thinking he knew who that friend might be and wondered if that was unwise. Then again, if an unwanted ship appeared at their island exile, he could always just kill them or gas them and take their ship for his own. He decided that he should study sailing while in exile. Seafaring might be a good second career choice for him.

Mallory said firmly, "I agree. I think it is a good plan."

Entreska nodded and said with enthusiasm, "I agree. It is the best possible plan."

Tamara frowned, "I don't like it. But I agree that is probably best."

Ursula merely smiled.

Vanessa spoke suddenly again, "Why do we trust Captain Jules?"

Mallory laughed, "Because I do. I trust both his character and skill having witnessed both firsthand."

Vanessa replied, "Very well, Commander."

Buck muttered, "If you can't trust a pirate, who can you trust?"

Everyone laughed.

As the laughter died down, Ursula said, "Since we have a plan, I'm going to change my prescription from tea to ale. Anyone object?"

There was more laughter and hoots of agreement. Mallory caught

Entreska's eye. She smiled and nodded. He hoped that she would not despair during their self-imposed exile. He hoped that it would be relatively brief.

The next day, Buck, escorted by a contingent of Black Scorpions and his own bodyguard, set off for the *Inky Darkness* that had taken up a secret anchorage off the coast of Wokometu less than two days travel from the Temple of Healing. Buck would get the ship ready for their journey. Mallory's knees still required several weeks of rehabilitation before Vanessa would permit him to travel.

Over the next few days, Mallory gave Vanessa a long list of orders he hoped would cover most contingencies. He also pulled together supplies that he felt they would need including the spare solar powered Renderer that would allow him to create tools and other items using various industrial plastics he could brew up from his versatile yeast collection. The Renderer could make many practical items and a number of luxuries to make their time in paradise pleasant.

A few weeks later, after a tearful goodbye, Entreska and Mallory were sneaked out of the Temple using a supply cart that covertly brought them to the *Inky Darkness*. At Entreska's suggestion, Tamara and Ursula would keep their departure quiet for several days before allowing rumors to circulate that they had secretly gone into the Wokometu wilderness in search of a lost Wizard artifact called the Dream Maker.

Mallory and Entreska leaned against the ship railing. They periodically exchanged melancholy smiles while silently watching Wokometu slowly disappear over the horizon. He reflected on something that the Grand Marshal had said before they had departed the Citadel. *All paths lead to death. I strongly recommend taking one of the scenic routes.*